the
SCAMP

JENNIFER PASHLEY

Tin House Books
Portland, Oregon & Brooklyn, New York

Published by Tin House Books, Portland, Oregon and
Brooklyn, New York

Distributed by W. W. Norton and Company

Library of Congress Cataloging-in-Publication Data

Pashley, Jennifer.
 The scamp / Jennifer Pashley. -- First U.S. edition.
   pages ; cm
 ISBN 978-1-941040-11-9 (alk. paper)
 I. Title.
 PS3616.A83S33 2015
 813'.6--dc23

                    2015016032

First US edition 2015
Printed in the USA
Interior design by Diane Chonette
www.tinhouse.com

the
SCAMP

For GK—with all the madness in my soul.

A woman *is* her mother.
That's the main thing.

—ANNE SEXTON, "Housewife"

one

RAYELLE

One of the twins has his mouth sewn shut. He drinks gin from a rocks glass through a skinny cocktail straw. His brother, beer from the tap. There are only four people at the bar and three of them are related. That's everyone, except me and the bartender.

Behind the bar, a string of Christmas lights, multi-colored and blinking, still hanging in June, above the top shelf of bottles. I watch the pattern, waiting for the regularity of a heartbeat, an even space between on and off, but it's erratic. The door is open to the parking lot and a low evening sun, leaving a hot stripe on the black floor. I had driven out of the trailer park in a huff, windows down, radio blasting, fifty, sixty miles, almost to West Virginia. I stopped when I saw the rural Quonset hut bar,

two cars and a dust devil in the parking lot. Dead on a
Monday night.

A big woman at the opposite end of the bar who looks
under thirty tells me about the twins' accident. How they
slid in the rain and the car launched into a field. Out here,
the roads are slick with pebbles that rain down from the
mountain in a storm. It's like driving on marbles.

One twin had to kick out the windshield to save the
other. He'd written their names in blood on the inside
of the driver's side window, in case they couldn't get out.
Brady and Jamie Wilkes. Like a premature headstone.

They might have been identical, but they weren't anymore. Brady's jaw was wired. Jamie's wrist was broken.

You ever heard of such a thing? she asks me.

I have and I haven't. Freak accidents happen all the
time. A car off the road, a rockslide, a drowning. I ask the
bartender for a whiskey sour. Two cherries. No orange.

He's over fifty, looks ex-military with his haircut,
his straight spine and precise movements; his arms are
sleeved with dense, colored tattoos. He makes the drink
in a highball glass and sets it on a black napkin, then
goes back to buffing beer glasses.

I sip and hand it back to him. Stronger, I say.

I guess you do what you have to, the woman says,
for your siblings. She's wearing a tank top, her shoulders
padded and fleshy, her skin loose above the elbow.

I don't have any siblings, I say.

Or your kids, she adds.

Or kids, I say.

I left because it was my birthday, and my mother asked me if I wanted a pool party. I think she thought it was funny, thought maybe now was the time to laugh about it and get over it. But I was turning twenty-three by myself, without a husband or a baby when I'd been well on the way to having both. I wanted her to shut up.

When I show my license to the bartender, he says, Well, happy birthday to you, sweetheart.

I nearly put my head down to cry.

The one twin waves to the bartender for another gin. The TV plays a black-and-white movie with a lot of scenes with a man and a woman driving a car. The man, in a hat. The woman, blond, and polished. The scenery behind them, trees, a long road in the country.

Earlier, I'd thought about careening off the road. About my Escort, with its rotting floorboards and bald tires. I wouldn't have kicked my way out of a car that went flying. I wouldn't have kicked my way out of anything. Instead, I imagine lying there still, broken. The breathing of a cornfield around me.

The woman at the other end says, Don't drink till you puke, Brady, and laughs. That won't be fun.

He shakes his head, slow. I wonder how much it hurts.

She hoists herself off the stool and rubs each of the twins' shoulders as she goes past. I gotta get my kids, she says. Good night, Gil, she says to the bartender, and leans forward, pushing her boobs together, to kiss his cheek. On her legs, light capris that are tight around the knee, her calves blossoming out below.

You had dinner? Gil asks me.

I ask him to hold the sour and just give me a double bourbon. Two cherries.

No, I say. You got anything?

Not tonight, he says. He leans back on the register; a mirror behind shows his crew cut, thick all the way through, wiry and gray. Above the mirror, a pair of deer antlers with bright turquoise panties hanging on them. Where you from? he asks.

The twins play a miniature-sized game of checkers, the mute one stacking up his black king.

South Lake, I say.

That's quite a ways, he says. He takes a glass out of a steaming tub under the bar and works at it with two towels, one in, one out. You got family out here? he asks.

I think about my mother, in South Lake, sitting at the end of a bar called the Coop, waving on another gin and tonic. No one would be there either. Just the bartender and my mother, baseball on TV, but muted.

And Chuck, stomping through the trailer, picking up the mail, a newspaper, the empties we left behind.

No, I say.

At one, the twins leave. I ask for another drink, even though my head feels tight, like someone stuffed it with electricity and it's expanding. When I turn my head quickly, everything around me blurs, gold, red, green.

How you getting home? the bartender asks.

I'm not going home, I say.

I watch him wipe up, count out money, empty bottles into a bin in the back. He clicks the TV remote, and the screen goes off with a snap and a sparkle of color.

Well you know what they say, he offers.

I can't stay here? It comes out way more bitchy than I intend.

What's eating you? he says, his hands on my bare shoulders.

You are, I say.

Not a chance.

But he puts me in his car. I leave the Escort there, in the gravel lot, and he drives me about a mile away to a basement apartment where I fall asleep under a multicolored afghan on a brown velour couch. The room, low and spinning. My feet, sticking out from under the blanket.

I throw up in the kitchen sink. A clean, white enamel sink with no dirty dishes, no coffee stains, no slices of lime dumped out of a drink. It was gleaming. And now, filled with acidy bourbon laced with cherry juice. It looks like I'm dying. I imagine it to be guts, blood, bone, coming out.

Oh Jesus, I say, and lean my head on the tile counter.

You got someone I should call? Gil says.

No. I'd left my phone in my car. Couldn't find my way back to my car if I wanted to.

Sit down, he says, and hands me a glass of water he poured from the fridge. I'll make you breakfast.

He puts on music, some old-sounding soul, and fries up potatoes and eggs and makes a full pot of strong coffee. I eat it all. After, we lie on the living room floor, underneath the fan, which thank God is off. I couldn't take the spinning right now.

I look around the room. I'm sure he's got someone else. Some good woman his own age. The kind who grazes his shoulder as she walks past, and doesn't puke in his sink. One who kisses his neck, and hangs up his shirts. Who loves him, and doesn't take any bullshit from anyone.

What are you going to do? he asks me, his head propped up on his hand, his elbow in the carpet.

I think about the car, deep in a field with nothing but cornstalks around me. About the sound of the motor dying down, of everything settling. A crow. I don't answer him. Instead, I touch his wrist. There's a tattoo of a snake, coiled and hissing, and above it an American flag. On the underside, a sailor girl, dark-haired and pouting, her lips red, her tits busting out of her uniform.

You're going to die like this, he says.

I shrug. I don't believe it. I wrap my fingers around his wrist bone.

I could have killed you, he says. You could have killed yourself. People die from drinking, he says.

I pat my used-up, stretched-out belly. I'm too big to die from drinking, I say.

You could have killed someone else, he says.

Already have, I say.

That's when he kisses me. Even when you think a guy is the kind to take care of you, let you sleep off a hangover and make you breakfast, he still wants to fuck you. He mumbles, Oh sugar, and leans over, his mouth on mine, and then all of him on me, right there on the carpet.

My mother always says she could write her life story on one side of a piece of paper because nothing interesting has ever happened to her, but it's not true. It's not true for anyone, it's just the bullshit humility she puts out in the world. Poor me. Like she's never had her heart broken or fallen so far she can't stand up and walk again without help. Maybe it's just that she assumes that after all no one really cares what happens to you.

When Summer died, I fell into a well of sadness that no one could pull me out of. I got up in the night, sleepless and restless, because I thought I heard Summer crying, would shuffle to a dark empty room and stand in the doorway, stunned. I slept the rest of August, facedown in my old room in my mother's trailer. I couldn't stay in my own house anymore. My old room, hot and stale, the fan blowing dust around. I kept waiting for someone to come in, to sit with me, to stroke my hair. My mother, my stepdad, anyone. I was twenty-two, unwed, already the mother of a dead baby. I'd been investigated for nothing. *Not particularly guilty* is not a sentence anyone ever gets. I wanted someone to come pick me up.

Right before my birthday, my mother told me I'd better perk up.

I don't know what in the hell you're waiting for, she said.

But I felt leaden. Anchored to the bed. Weighed down, and sinking.

She stood in my bedroom doorway, her hair a flat and curly mess, up in a banana clip that was half falling out. Her shoulders looked small, her chest sallow and sunken. She's not a big person. Nothing like me. It's like I didn't even come from her.

She smoked a cigarette from a reservation pack, a long menthol light 100 not worth a damn thing, they burn up so quickly. Her eyes squinted when she looked in at me, on my back, half covered.

Nobody wants a girl as sad as you, she said.

You can't escape anything in a small town. The town knows everything, and not enough. All the guys you slept with, but not which ones you loved. People just make you up from pieces, glimpses of you seen around, at the firemen's field days, the bar, the drive-thru. They know I'm Rayelle Reed. That I had a baby out of wedlock with the Baptist pastor's son, and that the baby died. That my mother is Carleen Reed, and that they should stay off the roads when she's driving her Grand Prix home from the Coop at 3:00 AM, crooked, up the middle of Route 12.

If you've been in South Lake long enough, you know that my mother and her sister each married a Reed boy and so the cousins between those two families are extra-related, like siblings.

Chuck is a Reed boy too. He gives me money almost every day. Sometimes a crisp twenty from the ATM, or whatever he has in his pocket, a wrinkled ten and five. Go do something, he'll say, knowing my mother will be gone too. Most nights, guys buy my drinks for me. I keep a roll of unspent twenties saved up from all those nights of drinking for free, tucked in the top drawer of my dresser, underneath an old sweater from high school. I like to touch it sometimes, a soft roll of cash. To make sure it's still there, but also because it feels like possibility to me. It feels like a way out.

On a night like this, the sun hangs low and orange over the lake like a burning disc. The smell of the lake reaches all the way to town, hot, swampy, fishy. It's a good night for trout, the water still and the fish restless, and if you have the patience to sit at the shore at dusk, they'll jump right at you.

But I'm not looking to catch a fish.

I'm waiting for Chuck: my stepdad. My uncle. My dead dad's brother. My mother's live-in boyfriend. The man who raised me as his own when my real dad, Ray, dropped dead. Harsh, but he actually dropped into a recliner and died. I was just a baby, crawling around at a dead man's feet.

He smells like the day. Like a last cigarette in the car, a little like the french fries he had with lunch. His boots are dirty from the plant floor. He gives me forty dollars without asking, and I go.

Outside, the light is weird. Heavy and warm. And, lately, there's a feeling in my gut anytime I leave my room, or the trailer, or sometimes when I sit still in my car. It's like someone cut the last cord that tethered me to shore and I'm just out there, spiraling into the deepest water, and I don't mean in a boat, or even a canoe, something you could reasonably use to get somewhere. I mean it's like I'm in a goddamn inner tube, floating in circles away from anything solid. Arms and legs, useless. Dangling over the side. Good only for sunburns, and the occasional sip from the bottle I brought with me.

For a while after I moved back home, I crept, reaching for the walls of any room I walked into. I couldn't walk without bracing myself. But you can't even get to the walls in my mother's trailer. The baseboards are crowded with boxes full of papers and photos, laundry baskets of clean things that were never put away, cartons filled with beer bottles to take back, stacks of magazines and old newspapers. There's nothing stable to hold on to, and I end up like a kid in the center of a pool, treading water, with her neck stretched, her breath fast, anxious to grab on to the side.

Drowning.

My cousin Khaki used to know the ways that people would die, just by looking at them. She'd see someone and get a flash, a feeling, and without much speculation, she'd blurt it out: *Car accident. Pneumonia. Cancer.* She said it came to her in a full-frame picture in her head. It started when we were small, Khaki just a pudge-faced six-year-old. She slept at our house when Teddy's new baby was born. My mother always liked to see us girls together. We stayed out of her way, playing by ourselves, in the living room, in the backyard with the pines leaning over us, shushing.

In the morning, when the phone rang, Khaki said, The baby's dead, before my mother even said hello. My mother slapped her clean across the face.

Don't you ever say such a thing about your baby sister, she said. But Khaki was right. Dead of an infection, four days old.

My mother will tell you now, She was right. That little witch was right.

I wonder what Khaki would say if she saw me now.

I sit in the car. My head has a faint spinning feel to it, twingy at the temple. I can't stay home, and I don't want to go out. I follow the road out of the trailer park, to where it curves around the east end of the lake, the sunset coming off the water in blinding diamonds. I have all the cash with me. I go to find a motel.

I think of a motel as a happy place, a vacation spot where I stayed with Chuck in the summertime, sleeping in a strange bed and swimming in an in-ground pool, the room chilled with air conditioning, the bathroom stocked with tiny soaps. But the only place to stay in town is no longer a motel. It's been converted into shitty apartments and efficiencies rented mostly to drunks and felons, deadbeat daddies out on parole.

If I worked a little, I could swing a place of my own. But I can't even try. The only things I'm qualified to do, bartend and waitress. And every day now is a blur of recovery, for me and my mother both, a long hangover and a daytime nap, which is the only time I can sleep soundly, in the hot afternoon sun, legs stretched longer than my old twin bed, the rattle of a fan going.

Right down the line on Lakeshore Road, there's a sign in the window of a one-room omelet place that says HELP WANTED. A stainless-steel griddle, the air heavy with butter. They open at five, and close at one. Not my usual hours.

I park outside of Pine Bluff Estates, the sign with the silhouette of a running horse, mane free. The building is mustard yellow with painted black doors that burn your hands when you touch them. The whole thing sits sideways, perpendicular to the road and the lake, with the room closest to the water already taken. A man lounges out front of the last door, his feet splayed on the sidewalk, his chair tilted to look at the lake.

The woman at the desk wears a salmon-pink velour tracksuit. Next to her, a brass birdcage with a huge parrot who bobs around on his perch. The office is done up like Hawaii, with palm tree wallpaper, coconuts on the desk, the parrot. The manager's hair is dyed that sort of old-lady burgundy, even though she doesn't

seem that old. I ask if she can prorate me a room for
half a week.

She looks over her glasses, bright blue readers that
she wears on a chain.

You alone? she says.

At first, I take it to mean she can't believe that a
girl like me, young, blond, full of promise and bounce,
would walk in here without a guy, without a boyfriend
in a hot car, or on a motorcycle. And then I realize that
she wonders about the other tenants, the addicts, the
child molesters who aren't allowed to live closer to the
school. She doesn't know if it's safe for me to be alone.

But who would I have with me? I don't have a husband, or a boyfriend. My daughter is dead. I say, It's just
me.

Maybe it'll be the end of me. *Strangulation, strange
bed.* Maybe that'll be okay.

I fall asleep sitting up, with all the lights and the TV
on, and wake up like that, sweating, with my back
against a vinyl headboard that is screwed into the wall.
The chintz-covered bed sways low in the middle, and
I have to grab on to the nightstand to get up. I light a
cigarette and pour wine from a cheap box of Chablis
that sits on top of the air conditioner. The cup, flimsy
and white, was in the room. It says BEST WESTERN on
the side. The box is cold. The wine, room temperature
and sweet, coats my teeth. My heart, so loud in my
ears it takes a few swallows of wine and a few drags of

cigarette to get my breathing right again. I down the cup and refill.

This is why I go out. Because alone, I wake up in panic, shaking and racing inside. I'd rather wake up in someone else's bed, with the someone else still there. I turn my phone over to find the time. 3:00 AM. No messages.

I'll sleep when it's light.

There's always a guy. A guy who will buy my next drink, who'll have another of whatever I'm having. Who will offer to walk out back to the deck or the beach, or even to lock the door of the men's room while we're inside.

Sometimes, early in the day, I walk into a bar a complete mess, like an open wound, guts falling out and trailing. Not ready for the small talk of flirting, not even made up. My lips dry and my hair knotted and blown from driving with the windows down. Sometimes, I want to say to the guy next to me, Hey thanks, I'm having a double bourbon. Last summer, my daughter died because I wasn't paying attention.

It would stop him cold. A quick tangle in the car, in the men's room, on the beach, isn't as enticing when the girl he thought was all legs and sunny curls begins to self-destruct right in front of him. When she becomes more than the curvy blond veneer that drew him in. When her backstory is death and mourning, and more drinking. When he finds out that the only thing worse than a girl with a baby is a girl with a dead one.

He'd run. I would, if it were someone else's story.

But again, I meet a guy in a bar. He comes in just after I do, which is early, even on a Sunday. There's no football in June, and the working guys aren't in at five. No one is, except this one big guy, coming through the door with the light behind him. He sits right next to me, even though the whole bar is empty. He has a flip-top spiral notepad in his shirt pocket, and a pen next to it. He wears a button-down cargo shirt, soft and brown, with blue jeans and Converse sneakers. I wonder if he's taking measurements, or taking notes. The way he sits on the stool, our knees touch. He asks me what I'm drinking.

I'm not sure I'm in the mood. What are you drinking? I say.

He smirks and orders two shots of Cuervo, for himself. Then he orders beer and points at my wineglass and nods to the bartender to get me another. When the drinks come, he orders dinner, right there at the bar, burgers and fries for both of us, and we eat side by side, elbow to elbow, and no one else comes in.

He has a face like a Saint Bernard, big and handsome and sad at the same time, even when he smiles. His cheeks, bigger than my hands. His hair, going gray. He seems familiar and yet not like anyone I've ever met in town before. He's older than my usual delivery-truck-driving single daddy, and his eyes are different colors, different shapes. One is dark and muddy, the other steel blue. The blue one is near me. It's only when he turns to face me that I notice the other one. It's slightly lazy.

When the bartender, who wears a bolo tie like an Indian's, but is round and pink and bald like a baby, takes his plate, the guy leans over to eat the rest of my french fries. I swivel toward him, my knees against his thigh.

Tell me your name, I say. I can't remember if he already said it.

He swigs. Leans on his elbow. Couper, he says. Couper Gale.

I pull my hair around to one side, stretch out a curl, and let it spring back. I washed it with motel shampoo right before I left, and it's still wet underneath, the curls kinked up at my collarbone.

How do I know that for real? I say.

He slides out a credit card to pay and shows me the name on there: *Couper A. Gale. Chase Visa.*

You? he says.

I try quick to think of something fake, but all I come up with are stripper names: Candy, Crystal, Starla. I think, *Chase Visa.* He raises his eyebrows, waiting, moves his tongue around his teeth. His face breaks into a smile. Breaks. Not spreads, not eases. It cracks. Like it hurts him a little.

My name's Rayelle, I tell him.

He says it back to me. I've never heard that name, he says.

It's white trash, I say, the way you might say, *It's Polish*, to explain an ethnic name. He rolls into a laugh.

How'd you get that name? he says. He taps a fingertip on my forearm, but he's already got my full attention.

My dad's name was Ray, I say. And he loved his Chevelle.

You were named after a car?

I told you it was white trash.

Goddamn, he chuckles.

How'd you get your name? I ask. This is not a bar conversation I've ever had. By now, we ought to be talking about my legs, and how they'll look wrapped around his neck. When the bartender comes back, I watch Couper sign the receipt with big loopy writing, loose and upright.

It's my grandmother's maiden name, he says. Then he cups his hand on my knee and jiggles it. Come outside with me, Rayelle, he says, trying it. He drags it out a little. A little hard on the *yelle.*

My mother always warned us about dusk. You can never believe anything you see. Dusk is when you could hit a deer with your car, or a kid on a bike. Twilight makes things look one way that then turn out to be another. The way my mother made it sound, all cars were actually trains, barreling toward you. All men, actually wolves, waiting to devour you. What did we know? Dusk was magical, and scary like a fairy tale. You might slip through to someplace else. You might disappear forever.

My mother would stand on the step and call out to where kids stood in the street, on roller skates, on bikes. Gathered at the stop sign, sneaking a smoke, or a swig from a plastic bottle of booze.

Rayelle Christine, she would call. It is dusk. Get your ass inside.

But lost and never found is pretty appealing right now. I might go far to lose this shadow. To walk out of my dead skin.

I light a cigarette just outside the bar door. This place belongs to a motel, a different one, not mine. A happy one with kids and aqua-blue doors. The parking lot is full of yellow streetlamps, big like buckets, where bugs gather. They look like snow, like when you look out at the streetlight at night to see if it's still coming down. The bugs just hover there, like a haze of snow. Couper walks off through the parking lot. It curves in front of all the rooms, nothing but beach and sky behind the motel. He walks backward for a bit, waiting for me to catch up. Then he turns and steps up onto the grass around the swimming pool.

The parking lot is fresh with blacktop and paint. The curbs sharp and white. A few cars are parked around the outside of the pool, and each room has a gold number on the door and a pair of circular plastic chairs out front. No one's in the pool, or outside at all. At the other end of the grass, there's a white gate with a chained lock on it and a hand-painted wooden sign: POOL CLOSES AT DUSK. Couper lays both hands on the top rail of the fence.

I start to laugh. Really? I say.

Nine out of ten times, he says with a shrug, they don't catch you.

It takes only a minute for the sky to get dark. Just like that, it's over. The dangerous in-between of dusk. The pool is built into a mound of grass higher than the parking lot, but when you walk up the side, you can see it, a big kidney bean of water mirroring the sky, the moon, and the lights from all around. The low drone of a motor.

You've done this ten times? I say.

He hooks the toe of his sneaker on the chain link fence and, with more grace than I'd expect from a body that size, swings his leg over to the other side.

Not here, he says. Plus, it'd have to be more than ten times to be statistics. He unbuttons his shirt, his belly broad but taut, thatched with hair. Then he undoes his pants. He lays his clothes over a lounge chair while I finish my smoke with the fence still between us.

Come on, Rayelle, he says. He holds a hand out, still in his shorts.

I've never been good at resisting a dare.

two

KHAKI

What does it mean to be first? Like if you traced a line back through all the remembering, and found me, standing, still, at the very beginning. The first one. Everyone says, Well, who was your first?

I am the first. The first one to love you. The last one to see you alive.

When girls don't exist, they disappear. They become non-people, people's wives, and mothers. People's slaves. They sell their pussies out of the backs of vans like stolen goods. Nothing about themselves is their own. And no one looks them in the face, or tells them he loves them.

Sometimes, a girl dissipates like smoke rising up into the air. So thin, you can't see her anymore. She becomes a cloud. You breathe her in.

I am a safe house for women. I have a reputation for kindness.

When they learn who I am, where I live, they come to me, sometimes in the night, sometimes in the full light of day. Sometimes with only the clothes on their backs. And sometimes, even those are gone.

Who will love you at the end of everything? Who will take your face and hold your temples, wash you clean and kiss you to sleep?

I will.

I will love you harder than anything has ever loved you, even your mama. And it will be the last and best thing you'll ever know.

I had taken a new name and rented a small house on the edge of a field, with huge trees that lined the narrow road. The house had been for farmhands, on what was left of a farm that was no longer worked—just an outbuilding was left, a big square kitchen and a front room. One bedroom upstairs. A small, slanted porch. The owner, a woman in her eighties who had moved in with her son out in the suburbs. I rented cheap, and paid her in cash. I told her I was an artist and needed just a small space for myself, to paint and make sculptures.

A sculpture of bone. A painting in blood.

An installation only ever seen in pieces, never in its entirety. A bunch of clues too loose for the locals—too stupid, too lacking in vision and empathy—to really see.

There were near misses. A hitchhiking girl I picked up and drove to the bus station. I trailed her long hair on my finger as she got out, barely letting go. Or a woman who came to me for one night only, and never told me her name. I gave her my bed, ran her a bath, made her breakfast with eggs from the couple of brown hens who roamed the yard. She had skin like coffee, her hair, matted and dull. She stared at me with a desperation I knew I could soothe, but I never laid hands on her. I never read what ate her insides, what was looming, burgeoning beneath her skin, and threatening to kill her. She left, running. The same way she came.

There were others. An Oregon trail of girls, set adrift down a river, scattered in a ravine. Clean bones along the roadside, where anyone might mistake them for any other kill.

And then Montana came. Wild and free and big-hearted. Montana had eyes like the sky, and hair like corn silk. I loved her like no one had ever loved her. I gave her a new name, and a new soul. And let her die with that rapture in her heart, in her thighs. Because nothing but water and sky comes after that.

I just want to disappear, she whispered at my table, her hands outstretched to mine.

Disappear into me.

Montana had left behind a baby. She ran in the night, the baby asleep in his crib, his chapped face turned toward the light coming from the open door.

I'm the worst kind of woman, she said.

Her belly was scarred around the navel, a thin smile above her pubic hair, where the baby had slid his way out.

The worst kind.

I'd seen the worst kind of woman. It wasn't Montana.

Her husband wasn't even home when she left the baby alone in the house. Weeks before, she'd thought to kill them all. Might have set the house on fire. He don't wake up, she said. Then, I might have stayed. I could have gone that way. Sleeping, she said, breathing in the smoke. All of us just gone. In the end, she said, she was just running. Once her feet hit the pavement, she gained a momentum she hadn't known she had.

He's not mean to the baby, she told me.

He's not anything anymore, I said.

Her hands were hot with the fire she never started, the heat of anger and disappointment under her skin, waiting to burn its way free.

The baby was a boy. Blond and blue-eyed and big-boned like Montana. He was two, and wild. He threw things at her, toys, a bottle, rocks aimed at her head, because he'd seen his daddy do it. Knew to point at her crotch and say *beaver*, and would slap her breast when he was mad.

What will they say about me? she asked.

They'll say you got out alive, I told her. In her hands, I felt the fire that would have consumed her. Her own work. Her own escape. I gave her another.

It didn't matter. In my house, in my bed, under my care, she became something more than a mother, more than a wife. She was mine. Newly named, loved hard, and fed well. I put her together only to take her apart. I came just short of baptizing her, which I did, in a way, washing her in the river. She just wasn't there to know it.

At first, there were layers and layers for Montana to fall through. Lying on the bed and letting it happen, coming for the first time, after all the sex in cars and beds with boys and men. A teacher, she told me. Some girls are marked up with an invisible script over their bodies, inviting touch. I had to peel her down to a tight, tiny core. There was a long, languid week in between when she went slack. When no one said the baby's name. And no one threw a rock. I watched her open wet eyes after a bath, coming to the surface.

Montana, I said.

I made it a point not to remember their real names. To let the details of their previous lives fall off of them like dead snakeskin.

When I knew she had let it go, the baby's cry, the possessive hand on her cunt, the fear that breathed in and out of her skin, smelling like acrid oil and sweat, if only for a moment, a long day in the sun of my backyard, naked, and pink, and new—I set her free. In every direction. I loved her till she was empty, and I let her go with that.

I had set myself free, walking away from a deserted beach. The sky gray and the water green, and my heart a swirling wreck of loss. I pieced myself together after that. Dead, stitched. I was parts of everything I'd lost. A hollow shell, empty and white gold.

I tipped Montana back on the grass and did it quickly, with a garrote made from a silk scarf, and no resistance. Not for me. I'd given her nothing but a hot bath, a soft bed, the tip of my tongue along the tender inside of her thigh. Montana's eyes, so round and blue, bruised and popped. New freckles appeared under the flesh, like black stars. Her tongue, purple, protruding. I left no other marks on her. Not a cut, not a bruise. Not a hard hand on her face or her bottom, telling her what to do. Just the welts from mosquitoes in the woods, the scratch of low thorns on her ankles.

I used a long, curved boning knife and worked the joints. One hand, cut at the wrist, I washed in the water, the beautiful skin gleaming, and I let it go, rumbling through the rapids, sinking. Other parts I left out as bait. There were fox and coyotes in the woods, bears, and huge circling turkey vultures. By morning, everything was gone, carried off to dens and thickets, licked clean by animal tongues. A rib cage, a pelvis, the knuckles of spine.

I did the head last. I'd thought about snipping a long piece of that silver hair, but it wasn't Montana's hair I wanted. I washed her face and head in the river, my arms aching, dunking it under, the blood trailing downstream in ribbons, dissipating in the fast water, over rocks, feeding the fish and crawdads.

In the end, I didn't take anything.

I wasn't sentimental. And I wasn't looking for trophies.

Years ago, I stood at the tip of South Lake, where it comes together like the point of a heart. I had cast another body far out into the deepest parts. Small and weighted. The water so deep it couldn't be measured, the middle green like jade, or emerald. In the full sun, it didn't reflect, only absorbed, glowing from within like a jewel.

I crawled out of the lake naked, new. I padded through the pines on my hands and knees, up a rocky path and into the backyard of my own empty house. My childhood home, dark, without parents' voices, or a brother's. Not a soul left but a cousin too stupid to see the gifts laid out at her feet. She slept in my bed. Curly-headed and dumb.

Outside, I'd washed my feet, my knees and hands in gasoline, rubbing at the sap. I rinsed off the lake water, the dirt from the trail, with the garden hose, the water aching cold and metallic, running downhill to a public drain. Inside, over the toilet, I cut my nails so short my fingertips throbbed, beating with my heart. Any blood left behind, flushed away. I showered the heat back into my body in the downstairs bath, but by then, there was nothing left to wash away.

Upstairs off the hallway, the bedroom my mother died in.

In the kitchen, the floor where my father fell, so drunk he choked on his own blood and never woke up.

The backyard, where my only brother blew his face off with a cherry bomb.

Death surrounded me like a fog.

I wanted my own ending.

When I slipped into bed behind sweet, drowsy Rayelle, she pushed back into me, and I gave her what she wanted, what she expected between us. Her body slow and opening beneath my hands. She tried to talk, but I didn't want to hear her voice. I wanted the white silence of sleep.

I thought about the same upturned nose, the same look of dumb trust on the face of the kid in town.

I want to show you something, I had said to her.

You were gone a long time, Rayelle mumbled, but I hushed her with my own mouth.

Go to sleep, I said.

For Montana, I wore a dress, high-waisted and soft, something she might have worn herself, covered in blue cornflowers. When we went down to the water, I lifted it over my head. I was naked underneath, shining in the moonlight. She gasped, but I was so used to being naked, so used to my own hard body, that it felt like nothing to me. I hung the dress on a low branch where it blew in the breeze. I knew what she wanted. I would give it to her.

I burned the garrote in the backyard fire pit.

The dress, I put on again, my body clean from the rush of cold river water.

The knife, wiped down with bleach. I put it back in the drawer with the others. It was the only one with a white handle, plastic pearl, nonporous. A blade curved in a beautiful, shining arch.

What they found of Montana was a foot. There was no flesh left on it. Just the anklebone and some of the metatarsals, not all of them. They sent it to Alexandria for testing, but before that, there was a lot of speculation—a hunter, a missing woman from Knoxville. The foot was too large to be a child's. People hiked by the river all the time. There were banks where anyone could fall, could disappear, tumbling to an unknown death. But why only a foot? Why not the entire body? What animals could have carried off such large pieces? What kind of animal could take a whole body apart?

By then, I was long gone. A different name. Another town. Another state. Nevada. Georgia. Dakota. Tennessee.

Montana bore a scar on her wrist, twisted like a snake, where she'd caught her hand in a metal screen door, trying to escape. They all bore scars. Montana had broken a shoulder. Her eye had been beaten shut. When she came to me, barefoot and running, the deepest scars were on her heart.

Her heart I could heal.

Her heart, I could have kept, but I let it go.

I tried to keep their flowers, to name their birds. For Montana, bitterroot, a beautiful bright pink burst. I grew them from seeds in the sunny back windows, and cut them, kept them on the table in a glass bowl. Montana's bird, a meadowlark. Its belly bright yellow, and its throat open like a flute.

The day after, I took bitterroot by the handful and scattered it on the river. I looked, but nothing was left. Not a knuckle, not a joint. I went down at dusk, unafraid to be seen, the flowers tight in my hand. I lived here, a small woman carrying flowers through a field. I could be picking raspberries or wild strawberries. Not looking for bones. I stood on the shore with my feet warm on a big slanted rock, and let the flowers go, fluttering onto the water. They floated and moved south in a wavy line, like a row of ducks. One stuck. The broken branch of a tree lay across the rapids, making a triangle of water that pooled. One flower stayed there, its head open and pink. It looked up at the sky. I wondered how long it could live there, lodged, drinking in the river.

three

RAYELLE

When I was eight, Khaki, who was eleven, and fast, dared me to huff gasoline out of the lawn mower, pushing the back of my head down toward the hole, the fumes, heady and dense. After, I lay back on the grass, the whole world spinning at warp speed, until I threw up all the ice cream I'd eaten at the barbecue. I remember her watching me like I was a subject in an experiment. Her eyes squinted in observation. Huh, she said when I puked.

She was that kid. The one who could get you to do anything. I was the other kid, the one who would do it.

She ran away when I was twelve. When my body was going faster than my brain. When I needed her the most. She left with a boyfriend who had a car, was going to college. There was no one left at home for her.

She was just the first one of us trying to outrun her own dark shadow.

We swim without making noise, passing each other in the middle, with no splash. Couper goes in naked, me in my bra and panties, and I wish then that I'd put on black or lace ones, and not just plain white. I see him only from behind as he slips in, silent. The water, dark and opaque.

Music comes from one room, and the voice of a guy laughing. The thump of a back door that leads out to the beach.

Underwater, I feel like nothing, like a string uncoiling, arms and legs like electricity. I swim to the deep end, and bob up next to him where he hangs on to the side. The water feels like velvet.

What happens when they catch you? I say.

He smirks. The first time? he says. You can talk your way out of it. After that, they fine you. Trespassing.

I bob, but keep my eyes on him. What are you, some kind of pool-sneaking outlaw? I say.

I prefer to think of myself as an urban pioneer, he says, straight-faced, until I start laughing. It feels good, the laugh, the water, his foot underneath the surface, up against my skin.

What happens when they catch you? he says.

It kicks the air out of me.

There were no charges to be filed, I say, and I manage to smile, but it's hard, and if he looked close it would be grotesque, that smile, all teeth and stretch, the tendons in my neck hard and popped. I dip my head underwater then, smooth out my hair. Think about not breathing.

He grabs some kids' towels that were left on the fence, hanging out to dry. They're thin Disney towels, but better than nothing. Couper wraps one around his waist and then lays the other one over my shoulders, squeezing out my hair, rubbing down my arms.

He says, Well, Rayelle . . . You should probably know . . .

And I think, *Married.*

Or worse. This is when he tells me he has herpes, or a conviction. That he's staying at Pine Bluff Estates, an unemployed, drunken felon.

All women eventually fall in love with me, he says. His hands completely cover my shoulders.

I burst out a laugh. All women, I say. I mirror his smirk, his eyebrows, his cocked head.

No exceptions, he says.

None.

Well, very few, he says. When he laughs, I look at the odd shape of his mouth, at his lips that are full, but not pretty, and enough to swallow me right up. It feels like there's a trapdoor inside my gut that maybe he nudged open, just with his knee against mine, or his foot on my leg, his hands on my shoulders maybe. And I know it right then, what makes him different from anyone else I've ever picked up in a bar. This is a guy you could fall for, for all the wrong reasons. That's what makes him dangerous, naked in a pool after midnight, trespassing on private property. Hopping, like an outlaw, over the locked gate of my heart.

He keeps a little bottle of bourbon in his glove box. His car, a long, two-door avocado-green Gran Torino with white vinyl seats, the kind I've only ever seen at a car show. At first, I don't even believe it's his, the car is such a beauty, and I'm wet and stumbling through the parking lot, away from the pool. Until he opens the passenger door for me and ushers me in. He loosens the latch on the glove box and lets it fall open. I see the bottle in there on its side. Not a cheap jug of Early Times like Chuck keeps in the cupboard above the fridge. This is a square bottle of Knob Creek, the size of a paperback novel.

Go ahead, Couper says, settled in the driver's seat. I crack the seal and take a long drink. There's a new stereo, in the place where the old AM radio or eight-track went. It's amber, and out of place against the dials and chrome of the retro dash.

Amber, I think. I could have said my name was Amber. I smile at him with my mouth around the bottle. Summer's eyes were amber, when they finally changed from that slate baby-blue. I thought they'd be brown, like mine, but they never deepened past gold. Her father always said they were green, but they weren't. Eli and his mother, June Carol, both of them green-eyed, wanted to see themselves reflected in her face, not me, not a mix of me and Eli. You're always looking for yourself in your kids. Your eyes. Your mouth. Your curly hair.

I press my teeth into the bottle, bone against glass. Couper fiddles with the stereo, his big hand covering the light, and then letting it out when he moves away, like the moon coming in your window when you're trying to sleep.

Save some for me, he says, and I hand it over.

Something low and moody and twangy plays out, a slide guitar, a girl singer, but husky and deep, the way I'd want my own voice to sound. It sounds familiar to me, and when she gets going, I recognize part of it as "Blue Moon." *You saw me standing alone.* And there is a moon, low on the horizon, above the lake, hanging like a fingernail.

Couper takes a swig, then stashes the bottle back in the glove box, his hand against my knees. With his face that close, I put my fingertip on his arm where his sleeve is rolled up to the elbow. He's thick, his arms, his legs, not fat, but like there's more meat on him than on most guys. All it takes is my fingertip. He looks up, still leaned over. He smells like bourbon and pool water. His cheeks hot from the drink. His lips, like velvet, big and soft and all around mine.

He puts his hand on my belly. Under my shirt, like a big cushioned bear paw, above the top of my jeans, around my navel, his fingers warm and padded. Some guys won't touch you there at all, they go right for the tits, or the ass, but Couper swoops around there, on the extra flesh right in the middle, and of course, he can feel the corrugated stripes, the scars, the extra baggage I'm carrying around now, even though I'm young. Even though everybody says that when you have a baby so young you bounce right back.

I put my hands on his face, my fingers up along the sides of his cheeks, into his hair at the temples. His mouth is like an oven. I feel my spine give, and I make a low sound without expecting to, and he backs up.

Whew, he says. He sits back, behind the wheel. I guess we should drive, he says.

I sit sideways and watch him. He puts the car into gear with the wand on the wheel, past drive, and then back.

Whew, he says again. Then, I could steer with my dick, he says and laughs. And I laugh. And then we drive.

The bourbon hits me hard. That wine before liquor shit—which I've never believed—turns out to be no joke, even for a drinker. I remember laughing, driving fast on the way out of town, on that dark stretch of road where the pine trees sweep above on either side, making a tunnel of branches that whisper in the wind, where sand gathers on the sides of the road and in mounds between long stiff patches of grass. There's the run-down tackle shop and marina, and another parking lot, full of holes so deep the car rocks in and out of them. There's the lake again, and more trees, pines and willows along the water's edge, some picnic tables beside the parking lot. I remember a funny story about a teacher from my high school who got caught fucking the principal out here, and I tell it to Couper, with all the details that I don't even know, but that right now are so vivid in my head, that it's me with my legs in the air, and Couper is the principal, and I can feel the sliver from the wooden table in my back, and the mosquitoes at the bottom of my ass.

He parks. There's a small camper, rounded and white with orange lettering on the side. An *S* that makes a trail, like a comet.

This? I yelp. This is where you're taking me? I laugh, my throat still warm from the whiskey.

He gets out of the car and holds out his arm to lead me in. And I don't know, something about him said *money* to me. His shirt, or his Chase Visa card. The Knob Creek or the immaculate car. Not *shit-can trailer.*

He keys in and turns on some lights. He moves a stack of legal pads and a laptop, and then pulls the table right off its base and lays down a platform and mattress that make a bed. There are soft sheets, not new and glass white like I imagine in a fancy hotel, but real cotton and old, a flowered pattern from the eighties, like something my mother might have gotten for her wedding. To Ray. She never married Chuck. Chuck just kind of picked up where his brother left off, and no one argued with that. Least of all my mother.

Couper tells me to lie down. I'm ready for anything, tingling. The room feels close, like I'm inside a rolling soup can, or a big casket. I've got a rumble below my heart like a motor. I remember his lips under my ear, behind my neck, under my hair, on my shoulder. The press of his hand into the thin mattress, next to me. A knee behind mine. Pinned.

But that's all. And believe me, if you asked me I'd say I don't sleep through anything, not any night, not ever. But it's not true. I have a bad habit of sleeping through the most important stuff.

I wake up without pants. I think he must have slid them off me, to get me comfortable or—who knows?—to feel me up. I don't feel felt up. I feel twingy and restless, like I expect to have a killer headache but don't. I wake up all at once, thirsty, with the sun warm and pouring in behind my head. I know where I am. I remember his face and his laugh, the feel of his mouth on mine. His legs underwater. I feel fine. Sometimes, maintenance drinking has its payoffs.

He's not there. My mother always says you could throw a ball from one end of our trailer to the other, but sitting up on this bed, my head against the ceiling, I could spit and hit the other wall. There's a little counter and a tiny sink. A blue-speckled enamel coffeepot with a matching cup and a fresh-brewed smell. A little two-burner cooktop. A cube fridge. A screen door that is open to the smell of the lake and, from farther off, charcoal, the sounds of cars in the parking lot, seagulls, trucks going by on the road.

I hear my phone buzzing. It's in the back pocket of my jeans, on the floor, at the foot of the bed. I lean over to grab it, like swishing my hand in water from the side of a boat. There are two messages, both from my mother. One at 2:35 AM (when I was already sleeping) that says: *wtvr yr doing its not goood*, with the extra *o*, unless she meant gooed. And another at 9:05 AM that just says *Where* with no question mark. I picture her sending the first one from the end of the bar, her fingers clumsy. Squinting hard at the tiny keys. And the second one this morning at the table, before her coffee, her mouth dry, her typing not much improved from the night before. Her fingernails, long, yellowed, drumming while she waits for my response. Maybe thinking I found some place, someone, something that will take care of me. Me, on my way out of town, finally, burning up a trail of damage.

I delete them both without answering. There's no other activity. Who else would call? I haven't applied for any jobs. My old friends don't know how to talk to me and haven't in a year.

I imagine me and Eli, if Summer had lived. Me with Summer at my mom's, shuffling her back and forth between me and Eli. Seeing him less and less. Having a sticky-faced toddler to take everywhere. Registering for kindergarten. Explaining. And not. Alone.

No one else is calling.

When Couper steps into the trailer, the whole thing rocks a little.

Morning, he says. He hands me a bottle of water. I put the phone facedown on the bed.

I sit with one foot up and the other hanging, and his eyes are slow. The white cotton of my panties showing. It's a long way up my leg. I open the water and drink a long time, and he pours me a cup of coffee, black, just gives it to me and goes outside.

I pull my jeans on and walk way out to a dark wooden bathhouse to pee. It's cool and drafty under the stall doors, with spiders in the rafters, and webs over the windows. There's no paper, just an empty, rusted dispenser. After, I go to the sink and rinse my hands in water so cold it makes them ache. The mirror, clouded over. You can't see a reflection, just a general outline of color and shadow and black speckles coming through the other side, growing on the glass like frost. Which is good, because I'm pretty sure there's nothing in there I want to see.

I don't notice until I walk back where he is—in a blue padded camp chair under a willow tree by the water. He has a laptop and his little spiral pad at his elbow. He wears glasses, rectangular and low on his nose, like he needs them only to see the screen. When he looks up at me, he looks over them.

What are you doing? I say.

Writing, he says.

Why didn't you sleep in the camper? I ask. I don't actually know this. He might have for all I know, but I don't remember bumping into him, or feeling him against me while I slept, curled into him, or under him. I'm hedging.

He says, I didn't want to crowd you. He takes the glasses off, then lays them on the computer keyboard. Rubs his dark eye.

I cock an eyebrow. I want to touch him, put my hand on his shoulder, or his head, my cold fingers on the back of his neck. But I don't.

Crowd me, I say instead, and go inside.

He comes up from behind. Takes the hem of my shirt, which I slept in, and lifts it off. It peels away from the dip in my back where I'm sweaty from sleep and from the walk across the parking lot in the sun.

Couper, I say. I'm not asking. I'm trying it out, saying it aloud, feeling the shape of his name in my mouth. I slide up onto the bed. The sun is bright in stripes across the sheets, shining in my eyes when I lie back. I half expect the bed to buckle beneath us, but it's sturdy, and the movement is slow, deliberate, like he has all the time he needs. His hands, warm, make a slow sweep up the sides of me, over my hipbones, along my rippled middle like he's reading braille. It all feels extra real. Maybe it's the daylight. Coffee instead of whiskey. His age, or his weight. I feel small. I'm a tall girl, with substantial arms and legs, round tits, before and after the baby. After the baby, Eli felt small, like I was a gaping wound he couldn't fill. But with Couper, I feel small. He could pick me up, move me around to his liking. Has found a waist he can hold on to, wrap his fingers around.

Couper, I say again. I claw into him, pulling him closer, urging.

Shhh, he says, the way you would if someone was interrupting you, like you were trying to finish something, a sentence, or the rest of your story.

After, when he puts his shirt back on, the notebook is still there, stuffed into his pocket, its edges ratted from use.

What's this? I say, and run my fingers along the spiral. Are you a contractor? I ask. I'd seen it sometimes, a guy taking measurements for a project, a flat pencil in his pocket to sketch out the length of something.

Notes, he says.

I start to laugh. I didn't think I had anything to teach you, I say, and mean it. He seems to know what he's doing.

I'm sure you've got plenty, he says.

I watch the lines of his face in the sun. The gray at the edges of his hair. I think he must be over forty.

What do you do? I say.

I'm a consultant.

What does that mean, I say, but don't really ask it, just walk my fingers up the part of his belly where the shirt's not buttoned. I mean, what do you actually do? I say.

Pay attention, he says.

You get paid to pay attention, I say.

Yes ma'am, he says.

You can pay attention to me, I say, and he laughs.

I was about to . . .

I'm still naked, on my back, my belly flat and emptied, rippled.

What about you? he says, and I roll over, give him my bare back where he curves his fingers into the dip at the low part of my waist. What do you do?

I go soft. For all the times I've been tempted to tell my whole sad story to the next guy, the next townie I hope not to run into at the gas station or the beer store, the next guy who thinks he's found a willing lay, I can't. I can't spill it. Not yet.

Couper leans in, kissing, his lips inching up my spine. Home from college? he says. I feel his breath between my shoulder blades.

Ha, no, I say.

Are you married?

No.

Okay, then. He goes back to kissing, closer to my neck. Are you an outlaw, he mutters into my hair.

I was never very inside the law to begin with, I say.

Now, what does that mean? he says, but when I turn over in the triangle of space he's made with his arms, he's smiling, the dark eye with a heavier crinkle than the blue one.

I knock on the wall of the trailer. What is this? I ask.

A Scamp, Couper says, like it's a puppy, like he's describing himself, a tramp, on the rails, his belongings in a bundle tied to a stick.

Where you headed so fast? I ask, and add his word, the word that comes back to me from last night. Pioneer.

Looking, he says.
Looking for what?
Looking for you.

I spent my childhood summers on the road. I've been all over the country, riding in Chuck's clunker Malibu from state to state as far as Utah, from highway motel to highway motel. It didn't matter that we were poor, we had a working car. If all else failed, we'd sleep in it, parked at a rest stop under pines, or by a fishing hole, windows cracked open, listening to the rush of water. Some other families from home, even with kids, they never went anywhere. They just stayed in South Lake, like that was enough. But Chuck was restless.

Some men are, my mother said, like it was a condition of the soul.

Chuck wanted movement.

It feels good, he'd say, being someplace strange. Me in the front seat with a bag of chips and a Cherry Coke. It's nice to be somewhere where no one knows you.

I never questioned him. I didn't think he had anything to hide, just preferred not to explain. We'd check in and he'd call me his daughter, and no one knew any different. Not that I couldn't remember my real dad. Not that Chuck was actually my uncle. Or that my mother and her sister had married brothers from the same family. We wouldn't say who we were at all. Chuck would pay cash and use a different name. Mike Smith. John Miller. We could be whoever we wanted.

And then one June, everything changed. I was twelve, a metamorphosis in my own skin, busting out of the cocoon of childhood, wet, and bigger, and new. My uncle Doe had died. The eldest, Khaki's father, the last thing holding our rickety family together. Once he was gone, it was like we'd been dropped and scattered.

Then Khaki was tucking her leg into a red BMW, spinning out of town, another Reed gone.

One shitty month. I lost an uncle and a cousin who was also my best friend. Their house sat empty, the lawn uncut. When school let out, I left all my stuff—papers, mediocre report card, yearbook—just piled in the laundry alley in the trailer and took off with Chuck. He drove farther than he ever had, every day, a long rumble of driving. Past Kentucky. Into the red dirt of Oklahoma. South Lake was dead to him. At least for a few weeks.

I never saw him cry. But he'd get up in the night, pacing. The glow of his Camel lighting up with each inhale. He was the last Reed male. Technically unmarried, with no offspring of his own.

I asked him if we should look for Khaki. I thought of that car. I had watched that car all the way down Route 8 till I was staring at nothing. Wasn't anyone worried? I said.

Hell no, Chuck said. She left of her own accord, in a car, with a man. Even when that was how I'd imagined life went, that a man came along to take you somewhere, to make something of you, I hadn't expected it so soon. Henderson had come out of nowhere. Fast and smoky. Dark. On his way to a university down South.

The worst kind, my mother said.

I had expected us to be girls a little longer.

It was the last summer we traveled. Pretty soon, I was graduating by the skin of my teeth, waiting tables, tending bar. When I had Summer, I named her after my favorite thing. A long, hot, lazy day. An endless road. One more blond, chub-faced Reed.

It makes you wonder what's passed on through our blood. What kind of sentence you hand a baby, just by letting her be born.

I remember standing on the side of the road that last summer. It was just me and Chuck, who drove only as far as Oklahoma before he decided to turn around. There were Indians selling turquoise and plastic horses with real rabbit fur-manes, set up on tables along the roadside. The sun was hotter there, closer to the earth than it was at home. The dirt, like red blood, where at home, the driveway was filled with coal and slate. Chuck bought me a toy horse for five dollars. I'd liked them when I was little, but I was twelve. My body was racing toward adulthood. I knew things I shouldn't have, and no amount of driving across country was going to keep me from knowing more. Chuck tossed the horse into the backseat and turned the car around, right there. I don't think we talked to each other the whole way home, and I don't think he stopped except to gas up. We were too busy falling apart.

After Summer died, the last of the bare bones of my family felt gone. Maybe my spine. There was nothing left anymore to support me. Nothing to hold me upright. Maybe that's what makes falling into bed so easy.

Does anyone wonder where you are? Couper says.

We are a couple of days into this. A couple of days lazing around in bed. In between, he gets up and writes, or just reads. Sometimes, I'll watch him from the door of the Scamp, while he pauses, his glasses on top of his head, and he'll stretch his neck to look up at the trees, resting, or searching. I can't tell.

There are a million ways to answer him.

After Summer, I told my mother I'd rather die than go on.

Well, hop to it, she said, disgusted with me and my mourning. My sad face every day. You ain't getting much else done, she said.

I knew they wished I wouldn't come home. That it would be easier for everyone if I moved on, got my shit together, or even disappeared, whisked off the side of the highway, or into the trees. Picked up by someone who might take care of me finally, move me out to a strange city, or a suburb. Make a real woman out of me. A wife, and a mother again.

I tell him I don't always go home. I tell him that sometimes, in South Lake, girls disappear. The town is still haunted by the little girl they never found. Holly. Gone. I look out at the dark center of the lake and think, *God, it's been ten years.* She was walking home from a friend's house. Posters are still up in town, at the ice cream shop, the diner, the bulletin board at the library, yellowed, soft on the edges. Taking them down might mean we've given up. It was the same summer, ten years ago, when Khaki left.

I know, Couper says.

About Holly? I say.

He nods.

Are you from here? I say. I'm sure I've never seen him. Never seen anyone like him. Our men look different. Squirrely and rugged at the same time, with rough hands and harsh mouths. Something about Couper looks foreign to me.

No, he says. But I've done the research.

You're researching Holly Jasper, I say. I take a step back and cross my arms. For what? Then I blurt it out, Are you a cop? My stomach roils.

No, no, he says. He smiles, squinting in the sun. I'm a writer.

And you're writing about this? I say.

He puts his hands in his pockets, shrugs. It's what I do, he says. He turns in the gravel and heads back toward the Scamp and the car.

Maybe South Lake is no different from any other place, I think. Girls everywhere, expendable. Picked up like a twig and carted off.

After noon we leave the side of the lake and go to a pancake house that sits between motels. It's one of those breakfast-all-day places, and I eat like I've forgotten how. Good food is hard to come by at my mother's house.

She ignores the fridge except for tonic and limes that go moldy, the cupboards full of mismatched cups and plates. My mother spends the whole day at the kitchen table, smoking and drinking instant coffee, with a little TV going on some news that she's not even watching. Around lunchtime, she switches to gin. We eat a lot of chips and cookies, or cereal bars. Chuck makes peanut butter and mayonnaise sandwiches on white bread that he picks up at the bakery outlet. Milk goes bad. There's usually some beer, tall boys of Lite or Genesee in a box. That keeps. I buy a big new box of cheap white wine every couple of days.

The waitress at the pancake house is sixtyish and frosted and kind of jeweled up and sexy, like old pictures of Tammy Wynette, or even of my mother before she stopped giving a shit. She touches Couper's shoulder every time she comes over and never looks at me. When she fills his cup a third time, she asks, That your daughter?

No, ma'am, Couper says.

Well ain't you the shit, she says to him. She goes and comes back with a stack of pancakes for me, a plate of eggs for him. A little stainless-steel pitcher of hot syrup. When he eyes my stack with the ball of butter sliding off the top, he asks if he can have a bite. I let him have it.

When we go back, Couper walks to the edge of the water, where the lake curves out in a heart shape to the widest parts. The shoreline here a lighter, weedy green, the middle such a deep green it's almost black.

Is it really bottomless? Couper asks me. He watches me pull a Winston 100 out of a soft pack and light it. I can't tell if he disapproves. He hasn't said anything.

That's what they say, I say. When Holly disappeared, they dragged what they could, as far down in the middle as the equipment would go, the shoreline cordoned off all summer, the beach, empty and closed.

Even a weighted body will rise eventually, he says, and then stops looking at the lake. Instead, he eyes my face, my hair, the shape of my arms. Did you know her? he asks.

No, I say. I was older than she was, I add.

We didn't even know the family, but after, everyone did. And then they didn't stay. First the dad left, found work in Schuylkill and got out. Then the mom and the kid brother. It was clear Holly wasn't showing up, that the police weren't coming up with a thing. They were regular people. A couple with kids and a dog. Living in a small ranch on a neighborhood street. Holly was a good girl, her father said on TV. And not one thing, not a sneaker, not a hair tie, nothing was left behind.

Who do you write for? I say. Like, a newspaper?

Couper's face clouds over. I used to, he says. I'm on my own now.

Writing articles for no one? I say.

I can't imagine that he'll find anything, that there's anyone left who hasn't been asked, who doesn't have a dead-end theory, or hasn't searched themselves, turning over piles of leaves or stacks of wood, looking in vacant houses and storage units. In the years after, kids would joke about Holly's ghost, or her half-dead body, coming up out of the woods, covered in leaves, staggering toward us like a zombie. But the town stopped looking; the kids stopped telling tales. There were new things to talk about. A Walmart near the interstate, layoffs at the coal prep plant.

It's hard not to be suspicious. A stranger in our town, with a tricked-out car and a shitty trailer, swooping in to solve what we couldn't by our dumb selves. Like it was our fault all along, for not keeping a better eye on our girls, for not figuring out the danger that was right there among us.

It's freelance, he says finally. Investigation.

Investigation, I repeat. How often does your story change? I ask.

He smirks. About as often as yours does, he says.

Well, have you found anything? I ask him.

Not about Holly, he says, and looks at me with his cold eye.

I turn a bare shoulder toward him and shrug.

But, he says then, and he pulls the notepad from his shirt pocket, I think she may be part of a much bigger pattern.

four

KHAKI

I was the last one standing. My mother had four miscarriages and three abortions. One baby born dead. And my sister, Aubrey, who died of an infection at four days old. They brought her home, only to rush her back to the hospital. No one bothered with a car seat. My mother just held the dead bundle on her lap, screaming.

I didn't want any more babies. Babies had wrecked my mother from the inside out, and I was still too young to understand why she kept getting pregnant, or why she kept losing them. But by the time Aubrey died in her bassinet, which looked like a casket anyway, all pillowed and tufted in white, I thought I could will them to go away. I thought I was in charge of it all.

I leaned over her while she was sleeping. She looked like a doll. Like the ugly composition dolls in my grandmother's dining room. Aubrey was bald, which I thought meant she would be blond like me, like Rayelle, and not dark haired like my mother or my brother, Nudie. Aubrey's face was fat and smushed, her eyes squinted shut and crusty. One was pinkish, oozing. Her fists never opened.

You belong to me, I said to her. They don't want you.

Aubrey was what my mother called fussy. She'd been home only a day, restless, whiny. She was hot. Feverish. I remember my mother wrapping and unwrapping her, unsure of how to make her comfortable. She sent me to Rayelle's to play, to spend the night, the two of us in Disney nightgowns, watching TV on the floor in the living room and making a tent out of blankets and couch cushions. In the morning, Aubrey was dead.

My mother's body gave out on her. She weakened with every pregnancy, every miscarriage drained her a little more. She spoke less, smoked more, drank more. When she was thirty-five, they told her she had cancer and removed her voice box. She could speak through a robotic straw, but preferred just to whisper. If you weren't close enough to hear her, or weren't listening, she wasn't repeating it.

When her neck was uncovered, her throat had a red hole that moved with her breathing. If she went out, she wore a scarf. She had to cover the hole with a handkerchief to cough, or to smoke, which she kept doing. What the hell difference is it now? she'd whisper at me. When the opening wasn't covered, smoke trailed out of her neck, curling at her collarbone.

Nudie died before she did. She had to live through that.

She had the abortions after she got the cancer.

And still, he kept fucking her, even while she had cancer, while she lay in bed, sick from treatment. Her skin was sweaty all the time. Her once curvy body had shrunk down to a rack of bones, loose and empty. Her bed was her solace. Ivory satin sheets, an ivory peignoir I picked out for her at Macy's. I told her she looked like a movie star. She kept a glass of vodka neat on the bedside table. A row of painkillers. And a bucket to throw up in. And he kept coming in to fuck her.

Even while he was fucking me.

When she died, I was the one who found her. If nothing else was, that was how it should have been. I hate—and I mean I hate hard—to think of what would have happened if he had found her instead.

It was late. Past eight in the morning, and I needed a ride to school. The bus had come and gone, doing its slow creep at the edge of the driveway, waiting to see if I would come rushing out. Sometimes I'd open the door and run down the steps, and the bus driver, she'd wait. She'd also let us smoke at the very back of the bus with the windows down, if we were quiet about it.

You need women like that in the world. Women who are looking out for you. Women who turn a blind eye when necessary.

My mother wasn't what anyone would call well, but she'd been steady. She'd get up in the morning with me, sit at the glass kitchen table. We'd smoke together, have coffee. She'd begun to look breakable, frail under her peignoir. Her wrists seemed snappable, her fingernails, dried out. Sometimes she leaned her elbow on the glass and held her sweaty head. Her hair hadn't fallen out, but it was brittle, and its dark brown color had lost its red depths.

She'd whisper to me without her electronic voice box.

Good Christ, I hurt, she'd say. Sometimes she'd hold her arm, or her hips, like they were springing apart with pain. Mostly, she drank her coffee black in a shallow tea-cup, one that had come from her mother's house and had pink-and-black pagodas on the side, leafed with bits of gold. She smoked, and held the handkerchief to the hole in her throat.

But that morning, we both overslept.

My dad wasn't home. Even if he had been, he wouldn't have gotten me up for school. Though he'd woken me plenty of times. It was usually in the night, after I'd fallen asleep, when I was too drowsy in my limbs, my throat too dry with sleep to fight him very hard. When I rigged a makeshift lock for my door, he was so angry he took the whole door down, right off its hinges.

You put that door back, my mother whispered. A girl needs her privacy.

He roared at her that I was deceitful. That I was stealing from him, undermining him, sneaking boys in through the window.

She just pointed. Put it back, Doe.

The house was quiet. The living room, glitzed up like a nightclub, something my mother loved, a red-and-black carpet, red velvet furniture. Lamps that hung from gold chains. The kitchen had a black leather bar, a lit beer sign on the wall. Rows of bottles and shakers and my grandmother's ice bucket from the fifties, with a heavy weighted bottom and black and white polka dots on the sides.

He wasn't there. Not in the basement, or the garage. And the car was gone.

The back bedroom, where she spent more and more of her time, was different from the rest of the house. Instead of dark, it was all champagne and gold. She liked flowers, and I tried to keep fresh ones for her. Whatever I could get. Soon, the lilacs would be in bloom, and I could bring that smell inside to cover up the usual smell of stale smoke, spilled whiskey.

My father hated flowers. He said the room looked like a funeral waiting to happen.

The baby, Aubrey, had died in there. Tucked in satin. Burning with fever.

There was my mother, tucked into satin sheets. Sweating out Vicodin and vodka.

He wasn't wrong.

I couldn't miss another day of school. I'd been out so many times—up all night sick, morning sick, hungover sick, taking care of my mother sick, taking my mother to appointments sick—that they were about to fail me for the year on absences alone.

I missed that day anyway.

She lay facedown on her pillow, a dark, sticky stain next to her mouth. I moved her shoulder to rouse her, and then rolled her onto her back. All her life she'd been voluptuous, round shouldered and big breasted, with hips and fleshy arms. But in my hand, she felt bony. Underneath the nightgown, her chest was flat and sunken; her rib cage was puffy, like it was filled with water, and the skin showed through, purple, filled with blood.

It wasn't what I'd expected. I'd imagined sitting by her bed in a chilled hospital room, holding her hand, listening to her breath, to the beep of machines and the drip of IVs, the overhead calls to doctors in code. The soft pad of nurses in clogs in and out, checking charts, adjusting meds. Everything a cool blue light, like the inside of an aquarium.

My mother died alone. In her own bed.

Later, the doctor told us it was her heart, not the cancer, and not her lungs.

It happens, he said. Sometimes, it's just too much strain on the body.

She'd refused further treatment after her voice box was removed. What else? she'd whispered to me. What else can they do to me? What else can they take away?

I'd leaned over to light her cigarette for her. We sat that way, all morning. Quiet, smoking. The clink of her coffee cup on the glass tabletop.

When someone dies at home, you call 911, and they take them to the hospital, even when they know that the person is dead. Even when that person is your mother. They kept me on the line, and I was okay, I was numb, sitting there in her room on a padded oval-backed chair, watching her stillness.

911, what's your emergency?

My mother is dead.

When my father found me in the hospital waiting room, surrounded by other people waiting to be seen for emergencies and births, the bustle of deliveries, flowers, carts with lunches on them, orderlies and nurses and doctors walking together, he told me I was the woman of the house now.

I was holding a pen that a nurse had given to me, a click pen that said ENFAMIL FORMULA on the side. I kept opening and closing it, an undone word-search magazine on my lap. The nurse had given me that too, to keep my mind occupied, she said. She was an oncology nurse. Short and round. I wondered how many motherless girls she'd ushered through the last days.

And then Doe plunked down beside me on a vinyl chair that was connected to all the other chairs in a row.

Well, you're the woman of the house now, he said. It was eleven thirty in the morning and he smelled of whiskey, of sweat, and sex.

I jammed the pen into the back of his hand, deep enough to stick. I wished it had gone all the way through.

Because we were in public, he barely uttered a sound. He grimaced, and looked murder at me, and I could hear the stuttered click of his teeth clenching.

I walked out. I walked all the way down Route 8, without a jacket, to Rayelle's, where I didn't want her; I didn't know what I wanted. Something was different in me the instant I turned over my mother's body. The instant I realized I was alone, without her.

Why? I asked my aunt Carleen. Why would that happen? I hadn't seen it coming. Couldn't have known that was how it would be.

The heart has funny ways, Carleen said.

I knew it. Rabbits can stop their hearts out of fear, if in danger, or cornered. It saves them from the grisly death that was coming; like flicking a switch, they just turn themselves off and die on the spot. I thought about my mother lying in bed, about my father coming in anyway, smelling like booze and someone else's pussy, even though he said he hated the room, the light, the flowers, the pretty gold leaf in the wallpaper, the satin sheets. I'd hear it, the movement of their bed, the running water. Her dry, voiceless cough. He'd move to the couch after, and I'd hear him snoring.

What had decided for her? Her brain, or her heart? Which one threw up the white flag and gave up? Imploding. Cornered. Saved from something more grisly.

I wished I had been there. I should have been in that room with her. I should have held her hand, stroked her head, given her water, rubbed her feet, anything,

anything but left her alone in that room, trussed up like a dead body, where he came and went as he pleased. I hadn't heard her last breath. I hadn't seen her heart break. She'd been alone. Used up and broken. All of her shitty forty-four years, dead babies and miscarriages, Nudie with a goddamn bomb to his face, her unstoppable hound of a husband. All of it, too much strain for the body.

No one should have to die that way.

five

RAYELLE

Summer was born in the dead of winter. The house, a little clean-to-the-baseboards ranch that Eli's parents owned and rented to us, was so cold in January that I would undress Summer in front of the heat duct. I laid out her changing pad there, even the little blue plastic baby tub, with the dry forced air blowing on her, her skin crisscrossed white and pink, her lower lip shivering.

I felt like I made the house dirty, just being in it. The white walls, the sealed wood floors. The new windows. Like my dirty bare feet left tracks everywhere.

We moved in when I was eight and a half months. I hadn't told Eli until I was already six months. Not because I wanted to trap him. I didn't even want the baby. I'd just never been regular, and didn't know until I was pretty far along. It was nothing for me to miss a period.

Sometimes, they'd come every ten or twelve weeks. So when I saw him again, when he came into the bowling alley where I was still tending bar, not quite showing, but hiding underneath a billowing shirt, he took one look at me and said, I sure am glad you're here, because, he meant, I was fun, because he knew what it meant: a ride in the car, windows down, legs up, parked by the pines along the lake.

I'm glad you're here too, I said, and handed him a Coors Light. I'm pregnant.

Well, shit, he said. I remember him rubbing the back of his neck, not looking me in the eye for a long time after that. I said I hadn't known how to reach him. But his daddy was the pastor at South Lake Baptist. If I'd been crazier, or desperate, I might have rolled up in front of the brick building, and the Sunday morning congregation, looking for Eli, my belly big. His mother might have fainted. Elijah got the bartender pregnant.

June Carol did pitch a fit. I was the worst thing that had happened to them. At the very least, she wanted us married. But really, she didn't want me at all, a trailer park Reed, a bowling alley bartender, living in her house with her only son, raising a bastard child.

Just let us get settled, Mama, Eli said to her. It might have been the first time he'd stood up to her. I know you think it's that official paper that makes it real, he said, but right now, we need to take care of this baby.

That is not what makes it real, Elijah, and you know it. It's the sanctity of marriage.

I never saw her without mascara and lipstick both. Her outfits were meticulously matched. Her nails, tasteful and immaculate. She gardened. She cooked every meal to include each food group. She had perfect handwriting and always wrote thank-you notes.

I had never even felt very feminine. I thought about my own mother, in her jeans and ponytail, with her cigarettes and gin. The way she drove her Grand Prix like a motherfucker on the highway, speeding and listening to loud Springsteen. And there I was, in June Carol Jenkins's house, wearing a maternity dress from the Salvation Army and my grandmother's cardigan, the only things that would fit me, rocking in a chair with a baby I'd never intended to have, my hair piled in a bun on top of my head. I looked like a Mennonite.

Those eight months, the one before and the seven after she was born, were a disaster of me fumbling, me breaking dishes, me burning an entire lasagna so that the kitchen filled with smoke, me sneaking cigarettes out the bathroom window, me crying in the dark alone with the baby. I remember Easter—Jesus, Easter at the pastor's house—Summer laughing for the first time, the perfect square of a backyard coming back to grass and lilacs, camellias along the fence and the azalea bush in the sun like it was burning. And then she was gone.

I went back to the house once after I'd moved out. A few days before Christmas, when I'd been sitting in my mother's living room, trying to sort out ornaments, trying to put up some semblance of a tree, or any decoration, but just sitting with open boxes around me while the TV blared, and after no kind of supper, nothing that resembled a meal, just some Ritz crackers and some cheese that Chuck had picked up at Rite Aid, and a box of chocolate-covered cherries.

I left the boxes open, tissue paper scattered.

The house was closed up tight. Locks changed. Eli had gone back to his parents' home, just like I had gone to mine, both of us back to the opposite worlds we'd come from. I stood out there on the step like a fool, trying my key and trying again, while the lawn sparkled with frost under the streetlight. I felt cast out. Put to the curb. The house was never mine to have, only to borrow, only to shepherd a child through. June Carol always said you just borrow children from God. It's your job to take care of them for Him.

In the morning, by the lake, I come out of the Scamp, dressed, but sweaty, and I graze my hand over Couper's shoulders. I kiss his neck. He sits by the water in the camp chair, tapping away on his laptop. The water, rippled and bright.

What's the thing you remember most about Holly Jasper disappearing? he says. The one thing?

There wasn't anyone strange in town, I say.

He twists in the chair to face me, the metal legs stressed and bending. For days I've been wearing the same underwear, the same jeans, the same top. My hair, curlier and heavier at the same time.

What do you mean? he says.

It was a dead week, I tell him. In the summer, there's always something going on, a car show, a carnival, bikers. But not that week. There weren't extra people here. School wasn't out yet, I say. I mean, maybe a couple of fishermen, or retired people staying at the lake, but nothing big.

You think it was someone here, he says.

Yeah, I say, and shrug. I pick a stray thread off his sleeve. You know. The call's coming from inside the house. It was one of us.

Do you think she's still here? he says. Her body, I mean.

Maybe. But they sure as hell never found it.

Did anyone else disappear? he says.

Other girls? No.

I mean, leave town.

Her family, but . . . they had to, I say. They thought for a while, like, unofficially, people thought it was the dad. But it wasn't.

He starts to smile, the sun warm on his legs, but his face still in the shadow of trees. How do you know? he says.

I shake my head. I got a feeling. It just wasn't.

He pokes at the brass button on my jeans. How good's your feeling? he says.

Pretty good. I laugh then. For what that's worth.

That's worth a lot, he says. He closes the laptop and stretches, shoulders back, breastbone out.

What's in it for you? I say.

A contract, he says.

For murder? I say, only half-amused, and he laughs.

For a book, he says.

Oh.

He gets up, taller than I am, even when he's standing downhill of me. I'm only half as dangerous as you think I am, he says.

I need clean clothes, I tell him. I'm twice as dirty as you think I am.

I like that, he says.

When we pull into Pine Bluff Estates in the Gran To-rino, the contents of one room—not mine—are being thrown into a dumpster. There's a cop car parked to the side, dormant, lights off, with an officer inside, typing away on a laptop that's balanced on the center console.

Yikes, Couper says.

I scan the lot.

Um, I say, quickly, my car's not here.

Where did your car go? he says.

I don't know.

He parks next to the office, where we can see through the glass window that the manager is inside on the phone.

Couper gets out, he nods at the cop, why I don't know, and leans in the office door. Then the manager sees me sitting in the passenger seat with the window down.

Oh, honey, she says. Yeah, the cops came and got your car. That was a couple days ago, she says. Now, we got this going on. She and Couper both look down the line of doors to the room being emptied. Two guys come out with a mattress and hurl it into the dumpster.

Couper turns his head to her and before he asks, she says, Dead. She waves her hand. Happens, she says.

They come out with a cooler, and a suitcase. All his possessions, whoever he was, whatever he was in trouble for, once you die, they just throw out the mattress, your suitcase of belongings, maybe all you had in the world, and chuck them into a dumpster to drag away.

She comes to the side of the car. I don't want to get you in trouble, she says, but that car was reported stolen.

I huff out a nervous laugh. It's my dad's, I say. If I was going to steal a car, I say, it wouldn't be a goddamn '94 Escort.

Couper slides in beside me, and the manager goes inside the office, the black cordless phone in her hand. From the door, she says to me, You didn't have nothing in your room.

No. I didn't.

Well, Couper says. Where to?

I'd been planning to pick up my car and drive back home, take a shower, change my clothes, meet him somewhere out, or back at the Scamp, in my best jeans, a black shirt, my hair done and makeup on my face.

So I tell him how to get to the trailer park.

It's a road of trailer parks, one after another. Some are nicer than others. Some are senior parks, fifty-five plus. There are apartments back there, too, and next to the park my mother lives in, a huge cemetery with tall monuments, spires and angels, crosses. I point him into Cottonwood Park, on the left, and he goes over the speed bumps, down the five-miles-an-hour drive between tiny run-down trailers.

It's not the best park. We've been here since I was ten. Before that, we lived in a lone trailer on a rural route; before that, in a basement apartment; before that, in my grandmother's back room and back porch. My mom and Ray had their own trailer in another park when I was born, that I've only seen pictures of. It was yellow, a single, with a wavy edge that made it look modern, or old-fashioned, depending how old you were.

It looks like shit here. Jimmy the neighbor's trailer is up on cinder blocks because he needs to do plumbing and wire work below the floorboards. The one next door to his has a plywood window. There's a skinny dog in the street, just standing. Penny. She's a mutt and she's about sixteen years old. She always limps over to let me pet her soft head.

I don't want to watch Couper's face. I don't know where he's from, but it's not here. Even his tin-can trailer has some appeal to it, some ironic roughing-it bullshit that you can get away with when you have the money to get away with it. It's not ironic when it's your actual fucking life.

There are about twenty-five black trash bags on my mother's lawn, filled with soft material, bedding, curtains, towels, and some just half full, tipped over, with heavier things inside, books, old cheap brass picture frames. My mother's Grand Prix is parked on the gravel drive, but not the Escort.

Must be trash day, Couper says, before I even tell him that's the one.

Stop here, I say.

Here? he says, sort of forced and surprised.

Yes. I open the door before he has the car in park. I don't totally trust her to clean out her own shit, even when there's so much of it and I know almost all of it has to go.

She comes out of the sliding glass door, tiny and red-faced, heaving another bag. Here, she says, and thrusts it at me. It's soft, but heavy. I wonder if she took the burlap cushions off the couch.

Mom, I say.

Put it out, she says, and points. She goes back in and then reappears, sliding a twin mattress on its side. Blue satin flowers, old, flattened on the edges. Mine.

Mom.

She pushes it over the edge of the deck onto the grass, where it lands in a puddle.

She starts to fix her hair, taking it out of the ponytail and redoing it. She smoothes the wispies back from her forehead. And then she notices Couper.

Mom, I say, watching the water seep up the sides of the mattress. What are you doing with my stuff?

Who's that? she asks.

Couper gets out of the car. Can I help you with some of this? he asks.

No you cannot help her, I say.

Why don't you take this box spring, my mother says, and bust it up for me, and then we can bag it. They won't take it whole, she says. She goes inside and pushes the back of it toward the open glass door, and Couper has no choice but to grab it and pull. It comes out to the deck, just a rickety frame of cheap wood, and he pushes it off onto the mattress below.

Sledgehammer in the shed, my mother says.

Mom!

She comes out the sliding door, hunched over like a kid making a snowman, rolling another trash bag that has shoes—my shoes—spilling out of the open side.

Where am I supposed to sleep? I ask.

Where you been sleeping? she says.

I hear Couper open the metal doors of Chuck's shed. Who knows what's even in there. I know he has tools, but Jesus, I half expect Couper to find something embarrassing. A stack of dirty magazines. Or weird. Fucking moonshine. I watch Couper grab an axe. When he takes a swing at the box spring, the dull blade gets stuck and he has to wiggle it out.

My mother goes down the steps to him. You're kind of delicate for a big guy, she says. Then she points at the grid. You have to work the joints, she says, and takes the axe from him, swinging hard, way above her head so that he ducks, and when she hits, the frame springs apart, loose and broken. Like that, she says.

Yes ma'am.

I watch him break it apart, hitting it with the axe and then pulling with his foot on the frame, breaking off pieces that fit into a stretchy black trash bag, and then another. He gets it into two bags, sharp bits of wood jutting out. He wipes his forehead with the back of his wrist.

I need some clothes, Mom.

You should have thought of that when you disappeared and didn't answer my calls, she says.

I didn't answer the first ones. And then my phone died. I left the charger in the motel room. Which means it's probably in a dumpster now.

I hear Penny's tags jingling as she limps across the broken pavement, and her shoulder leans into my side. Whatever kind of dog she is, she has a head like an Irish setter, soft and silky and deep red on top. Around the muzzle, she's gray.

Hey, Penny girl, I say and her sore old tail swishes back and forth.

You can look, my mother says, pointing at the bags, her eyes small when she squints into the sun. Her arms, with loose skin. She's shrunk to nothing except a hard little body under her clothes. But, she says, it's mixed in with regular trash. I did some cleaning, she says. And when you didn't come back, I took it upon myself to move you out.

Does Chuck know? I say.

Does Chuck know what? she says.

That you did this? That you threw me out in trash bags, I say.

It was his idea, she says.

Bullshit it was, I say. You just said it was your idea.

She leans on the edge of the deck, against the rail where there's a partial awning, and she lights up a long, minty Salem. Look, she says, waving her cigarette fingers at me. If you want.

Couper comes up behind me. Don't worry about it, he says to me.

Who're you? my mother asks.

He does his thing where he leans out with his hand, striding up to meet her. Couper Gale, ma'am, he says.

Well, Mr. Fancy Pants, she says. Why don't you take her shopping.

There's a tallboy of Lite on the picnic table. I wonder how long she's been at it. I can't believe beer does anything for her anymore.

Come on, Couper says to me. He pats my shoulder. I'm standing stock-still, staring at my stuff in bags, at my mattress, facedown in a puddle, the sides muddied and soaking, and my broken bed frame. A bag that has books, probably my yearbook, books that were mine as a kid, maybe even photo albums, just thrown onto the grass. The bags take up most of the lawn, right up to the road.

Just don't get her pregnant, my mom says. She ain't no good at that.

I ball my hands into fists, and that's when Couper comes around the front of me. In the car, he says before I can charge her. Come on, he says. He has me by the arms, and he walks me backward until I'm sitting in the passenger seat again.

He bumps it out of there, five miles an hour, maybe ten, over every speed hump, through all the shitty-ass trailers, past poor Penny, whimpering as we pull away.

She is the meanest motherfucker I know, I say to him. When we're out on the main road again, he turns back the way we came, past all the other parks, Grovewood, King's Park, Long Acre. He stops at the four corners, where down the block there's another cemetery and, farther up, a corner store with penny candy and glass bottles of Boylan's, and turns to me.

How old are you? he says.

I see the fear in his eyes, but I laugh at him. I'm twenty-three, I say. I just moved back home, I say, and that's when I break up in front of him, all at once, my face crushed and wet and hot. Last summer, I choke out.

Hey, he says. He pets the back of my head, smoothing his hand over my dirty hair. Hey. It's okay.

I point for him to turn left down toward the corner store, where I can get a paper bag full of Goetze's caramels and a black cherry Boylan's. Inside, he strolls the aisles and buys fishing line, a ball of twine, a package of bungees. It's nowhere I can get clothes, or panties, or even a toothbrush, but all I want is that bag of candy, the sweet soda, like I could get when I was a kid, riding to the store on my bike with Khaki.

You ever get a feeling about someone, Couper says in the car. My mouth is wadded out with caramel. You know, like you did about the dad?

Yeah, I say, and I think he's going to say something about my mother.

I got a feeling about you, he says.

Yeah? I say. Is it a hard-on?

He laughs. Sometimes, he says. Come with me, he says.

Where you going? My face is scrubbed red and raw from crying, from pressing my hands into my eyes. My lips, where they're chapped at the edge, will stain black red from the soda.

I got a list of places, he says. Other crimes.

What kind of crimes? I say.

Missing girls.

I'm a missing girl, I say.

Not anymore, he says. I found you.

He shows me how to pack up the Scamp. How to hitch it to the Gran Torino, the two lined up and ready. He says, Make sure the coupler latch is open, and guides my hands over it, And then, he says, use the tongue latch to lower the coupler onto the ball.

I start laughing, bent over, and backed into him, and that's all it takes.

After, we make sure everything inside is closed up and put away. We put the bed back into the table, secure the dry goods in airtight bins, and bungee the cupboard doors closed. He keeps his computer and his bag of notebooks and pens in the car with us, with some water, some snacks and cigarettes. He asks me where the best place is to stop and get some clothes for me, underwear and a toothbrush.

In the next state, I say.

six

KHAKI

Depending on who you ask, I was either fourteen or seventeen, but the truth is, when I left with Henderson, I was sixteen. Just old enough to leave school, but young enough to get him arrested. Which I wasn't interested in doing since he was my ride out. So I told him, and everyone associated with him, that I was seventeen. Age of consent.

As if consent had anything to do with it, ever.

I might have hated him. But it was Henderson who got me on my feet. Who took me out of there, speeding down the highway in a diesel BMW, the backseat filled with paperback books, *No Exit* on the shelf by the back window.

He got me to Florida.

Not the actual state, hanging off the bottom of America. But to her. Her face, her legs. Until then I hadn't known what it was I wanted. Till then, I didn't know who I was.

With Henderson, I was trying to be something. I wore my hair long, past my shoulders. I went by Kat Henderson, like I was the little wife, but I was sixteen, and Henderson was twenty-two, a master's student. We lived together in tiny apartments rented to students for little money. He spent all his time on philosophy, all this stupid shit about God and Ps and Qs that in the end was just math, was just numbers, either adding up, or not. Mostly not. All of it, for nothing. The first two years our place was just a hallway with a kitchen and one bedroom and no common area. It was drafty and the water was weak and never hot enough. When he switched schools, he went into psychology, and would talk at me about sociopaths and narcissists.

We moved to Wilmington. Another small city. The university students occupied by their own little world of libraries and conferences. Labs and meetings. Classrooms like giant glass bowls. Outside was the real world. On the edge of town, down a rural route through some pine trees and into open flat expanses of land and miles of tobacco. A dirt road that led to a shack. People still had dirt floors, packed hard and swept clean. There were dogfights in basements and in barns. And cemeteries like mouths of crooked teeth, small as a front lawn, where everyone was related and no one was over forty.

Those were my people. That was my kind of family.

After a while, I started hustling. Henderson never made enough money, and he was always gone. Our cupboards were stocked with nothing but noodles, coffee, bourbon, and cigarettes. It doesn't take long to figure out who knows who, and who sells what. And it's easy to trust a little long-haired girl in a hippie skirt.

But it wasn't the students who wanted to buy. It was the locals. A man at the farmers' market who sold beeswax candles and scented oils told me about Tess.

Where would I go, I asked him, holding a rough-cut bar of lemongrass soap and pretending to read the label, if I wanted to buy weed?

I'd come to recognize his type. Sixty. Organic cotton or hemp T-shirt. Sandals. His candles and oil, hand-poured in his own workshop in the garage. Some of the soaps with bits of walnut in them to scrub with.

To smoke? he said.

I shrugged my shoulder, then put the soap down. If I was looking to sell, I said.

He wrote down an address for me on the back of a napkin.

Tess, he said.

Tess lived on a dirt road with no phone lines and no cell service. Her house sat between two hills, in a valley of clover and heather. It smelled like the Middle Ages back there, sweet and heavy with flowers and cow shit. I drove a truck that we'd bought for $200 after the BMW quit. It needed rods we couldn't afford yet, and I couldn't drive it over thirty-five. Which on that road was fine. Faster than that, and whole pieces might have fallen off.

Tess's husband had built their house from a kit. I thought I could picture it, living like that, even with Henderson if he wasn't so skittish, wasn't so unsettled in his thinking. He flitted from one thing to another, never finishing a task or, worse, a program. What's your psychological explanation for that, Henderson? What are you so nervous about? He would get hung up on which coffee cup to use. We would never end up like Tess and her husband.

Tess had goats to trim the grass, and free-range chickens that were often scattered in the road. Sometimes she had puppies to sell, terrier mixes from her own dog. There was an A-frame chicken coop, a garage, and a sunny greenhouse where Tess grew her plants. Row after row of tall stalks and beautiful buds, long and red-haired. She packed them into bales of triple-wrapped plastic, like loaves of bread. I'd pick them up and squeeze them, feel their weight in my hand, smell them. I carried them home in canvas grocery bags, back to our kitchen, where Henderson studied. There, we worked across from each other, him from a textbook, and me with tiny zippered bags. Like a woman doing crafts.

I sold them, mostly in one- or two-gram baggies, to vendors at the farmers' market, hippies running organic farms way out of town, to an artist who'd turned his whole yard into an installation of birdbaths and wind chimes. I'd walk up the path to his front door, and when the wind blew, my hair lifted, the chimes going. It felt like magic.

I was in the country when I saw Florida. Her mother tried to rob me with a kitchen knife, not knowing—how could she—that I carried a small, snub-nosed .38 in the back of my shorts.

I'd traded with the artist for it. I gave him half of one of Tess's bales; he handed over the gun. It was in good working order, small, concealable, and he took me out back to show me how to shoot it.

I know how to shoot a gun, I told him.

Have you ever shot this gun? he said.

I stood on his back porch, looking over an acre lot of lush mowed green, crab apples and cottonwoods to either side, and in the back, tall poplars and oaks. I held the gun steady with two hands and fired, the kick aching all the way up my right arm. I hit a wind chime, the metal clanging and the whole piped piece swaying from the crab apple, jingling away.

Well all right, he said.

When I was delivering, I always assessed the situation first, left the goods in the car, nested the gun in the small of my back. I liked the feel of it there, heavy, an anchor. The woman I would come to know as Florida's mother stood in the doorway with her shoulders squared in a terry tube top and gym shorts, smaller than I was, and when she stepped over the threshold, she pushed a paring knife to my collarbone.

I grabbed her wrist, pressing on the tendons of her thumbs so that she dropped the knife to the porch floor.

You have got to be fucking kidding me, I said.

Give me your cash, she said, twisting. She was itty-bitty, but strong, and I stepped on the knife, pushing her with one hand on her breastbone, back onto the dirt floor inside. I pulled the .38 from my shorts.

Sit down, I said to her, and she backed up onto a brown plaid couch. Behind her, the whisper of bare feet in the kitchen. A girl, young, with hips like a boy and breasts like a little mommy, skittered into the doorway, half hiding.

Here's how this works, I said to the woman. You give me the cash, then I deliver. The only cash I carry is what you're about to give me.

I don't have any cash, she said.

Then you wasted my time. I held the gun, not really pointed at her, but ready. How were you planning to pay me? I asked.

She pointed with a weak hand and the girl giggled.

I thought you were a man, the woman said. How'm I supposed to know.

The girl nibbled a fingernail and looked up from underneath a fringe of heavy bangs, her hair parted deep to one side, long, wavy, down her back. She smiled a little sideways, and then let go of the doorjamb, and disappeared through the kitchen. I heard a screen door slam.

I told her mother to meet me herself, at the gas station, and pay me with cash, not underage pussy.

Outside, I saw the girl, throwing a stick to a brown dog who bounded through the weeds and brought it back to her with such force he somersaulted at her feet. Her cutoffs were so short the pockets hung out. Her shoulders shone in the sun. I stood and watched as long as I could without her knowing. Without me knowing, either, that within a month's time, it would be her in the truck beside me. That once I started, I wouldn't stop touching her, that I would do anything, give up everything and everyone—stealing the truck in the night and rumbling out of town—just to have her with me.

We were two sides of the same coin. Me and Florida. Both of us beyond our years, damaged and outside of ourselves with mourning over what had been done to us.

No one wants a girl who's been touched. We all have ways of hiding it, but the truth is, once they know, they don't want you.

The first boys, boys in seventh grade, with their loping arms and smelly feet, they're grateful that you'll do anything. That you know anything at all about how they work, what they'll like. Your mouth is a goddamn blessing to them.

When the guys get older, they want to know how you got to be who you are. What hardened you down, like cold sweet cream. What whittled away at your soul. And that's when they're about done. When what they want is not you. They want a you that never existed.

In the car once with Henderson, he grabbed my hand and stopped me.

How do you know that? he said. Who taught you that? That's— He stopped himself.

That's what? I asked.

That's something a whore does, he said.

We were in South Lake, on a side street by the water, under the pines, where you could hear the loons. The word hung there between us. *Whore.* I laughed, because it was all I could think to do, the only answer that wasn't a roar, coming from deep in my belly.

Have you been with a whore? I asked him.

No, he said, his chin lowered, his face disgusted.

Then how would you know? I asked.

For girls like us, there's no first time, and there's no only time. There's nothing special, and there's no love. It just goes on forever, like a loop in your brain, one burning infinite fuck that rips you apart so your insides are one big scar.

I would stop Doe sometimes, if only for a moment, with my foot. When I think about that, try to remember any detail, sometimes my foot is small, a tiny kindergarten foot, round and pink and soft on his thigh. And sometimes, it's bigger, harder on the edges, with painted toes.

I'm sick, I'd say. Never enough of a deterrent.

This will make it feel better. Let me kiss it away.

Give me money, was a better one. Uh-uh, I'd say, pressing down like my foot was on the brakes.

You're kidding me, Doe would say.

Fifty dollars, I said.

I can break you in half, he said.

Try it.

I had nothing to lose. He'd broken me so hard it didn't matter what else he tried.

Sometimes, after, sweaty and wrecked, I'd crawl in behind Rayelle, knowing I shouldn't, that I was a contagion, a creeping germ getting into bed with her, going where I had no business going, my hand, a snake inside her shirt, her pants. It was all I knew: how to touch someone, how to make someone do what I wanted them to do, how to make someone want me. How to make them love me.

And then there was Florida, in the weeds behind a house that was shifting on its frame, careening to the left like it would fall over someday. Barefoot on a dirt floor. Sick in her own bed. Our matching wounds immune to each other. Broken and put back together.

By me.

seven

RAYELLE

For weeks after Holly Jasper disappeared, the girls in South Lake were on lockdown. No one walked alone. No one swam. The beach was barricaded and laced with police tape. Along the shoreline, the backhoes and boats they used for dragging. But the middle of the lake was so deep, the divers could go only so far, and the hooks, which were meant to scrape the bottom, just floated in the black depth, feeling blindly for anything.

Beyond the lake, the midway sat empty. None of the normal family activity, the kids running from bumper cars to the scrambler. The teenagers on skateboards or bikes. People with ice cream or cotton candy. At first, the workers would come and sit by the rides, and no one rode them. Every car that came through town was suspect, even the ones that belonged to people we knew.

Normally, June shimmered with sunshine and possibilities, long days at the beach with boys, bike rides, and booze snuck into backpacks. School was ending. It stayed light until nine o'clock. Kids were out, getting popcorn and ice cream, even on a school night, the rides lit up red and yellow, the street a din of motorcycles and loud car radios.

And then she was gone.

The longer it went on, the worse it felt. The first week, the town was a scramble of searching everywhere, in the woods, in the lake, behind buildings, in dumpsters. And as weeks went on, it got quieter, hotter, and nothing felt possible anymore. I was alone the whole summer, home after a doomed road trip with Chuck. Khaki was gone. I sat in the trailer by myself and sulked. Every day on the news they'd begin with search details, and no leads. They put dogs on it. They called the state for help. Volunteers came. No one found anything. And then summer was over. We went back to school, me, in seventh grade, taller than every boy in my class, and bustier than all the girls.

I almost failed that year. I spent most of it staying behind after school, until everyone had left and the building was empty, to drink stolen vodka and fuck Tim Kriczewski, an eighth-grader with a wide Polish back and a chipped front tooth, whose father owned the quarry on the other side of the lake and whose mother never checked her liquor cabinet.

They looked in the quarry. It was one of the first places they looked.

We didn't even really like each other. It just kept me from going home. It kept me from my room, alone on a school night, without even a phone call from Khaki. From biking past their old house, which sat empty and dark, and after a month or so had foreclosure papers posted on the window. The grass got long. In the fall, all the leaves fell and no one raked them up.

So Tim Kriczewski was your first? Couper asks me. He's amused by the story, by the vodka, the sex in the boys' bathroom, or the locker room, outside at the beach, with the spindly shadow of the rickety roller coaster over us. We go on like this, me telling stories full of color that he finds funny or sexy or sad. But what's missing is the hole she left in my heart when she took off. The loneliness of that summer, the years that followed. How I filled it with garbage, with sex and drinking and rough parties. That's what I leave out.

We are headed south. A small highway with a fifty-five limit, laid out in blocks of cement that bump with every second passing. The Scamp, listing behind us.

No, I say, ready, maybe, to tell him the truth about something, and not just a story good for the telling.

Who was? he says. He looks over, his hand at the top of the wheel, his eyes crinkled with a smile.

My cousin, I say.

I did have a boy cousin, Nudie, who was older than me by a lot, and who died when I was only eight. I remember and don't remember him dying. I remember some of the days after, a montage of staying with neighbors, of being left to play with kids I didn't know, to eat sandwiches in other kitchens, while the adults dealt with the loss, a quiet, closed-casket funeral, a private burial.

The accident happened in the backyard of their house. The lawn sloped down sharply toward the woods. Beyond that, the lake. You could sit on the hill, your legs pointed down, looking at the trees, dense elms and birches, low sumacs heavy with red flowers.

He put a quarter stick of dynamite in his mouth. As a dare, as a joke, I don't know. I remember what it looked like, the feel of it, as big around as a battery, red, waxy. The smell of the match. The smell of the barbecue behind us, charcoal smoke and charred chicken. The rest of it, black. Strange houses with different smells. Quiet. My ears, a fuzz of damage from the noise of the blast.

He wasn't my first. He might have been, if I'd been older, faster.

She was.

Khaki took my virginity, if you can call it that. There was as much taking as there was giving. I asked her to do it. I asked her for help. And she gave it.

I was eleven, and terrified of sex, of doing it for the first time. When I asked Khaki, she said she'd never been a virgin. I didn't know how that could be, but she said it again, I ain't never been. Then she told me she was born without a hymen.

What's a hymen? I asked her.

The ring inside you that keeps you whole, she said.

Sometimes, when she wasn't so hard, she'd curl against me in the early hours of morning, the room gray and cool. Before she'd get up to light a cigarette. She'd demand money or cigarettes or booze from Doe like he owed her. I tried that once with Chuck, when he'd asked me to take out the garbage.

Maybe you should pay me, I said, wriggling my fat kid shoulders, imitating her voice.

Maybe you had better shut your goddamn trap, Chuck answered and handed me a tied-up bag.

Khaki treated her father like he was a bad boyfriend. If he handed her a ten-dollar bill, she laughed and held her hand out for more. I don't think so, you pathetic piece of shit, she'd say, and he'd make it a twenty, or more. He bought her cigarettes, and booze.

She was everything I wanted to be.

I wanted to know what she knew.

You don't want to know what I know, she said to me.

No, I do. The boys at school were mean, snapping my bra, grabbing their balls. They didn't like me because I was tall. I was bigger than all of them, leggy and curvy, with a full C cup. They called me cow, or mama. I had too much body, too much hair, my teeth were big for my mouth. They wanted little, cute girls with small hands and tight pussies. Girls with straight shiny hair who came to school on Fridays in their cheerleader uniforms.

I wanted to have an advantage. At the least, I wanted to know what to do. Otherwise, I thought, some boy would agree to fuck me, and then spread it all over South Lake that he fucked the big Reed girl and she didn't know how.

Boys are assholes, Khaki said to me.

Will you help me? I said.

She tucked a curl behind my ear, sitting next to me on her bed. I will always do whatever I can to help you, she said.

She kept a dildo in a box under her bed. I don't know where she'd gotten it, or where it might have come from. I had never seen one, and there it was, between us, a big, flesh-colored, disembodied dick. Khaki took it out like it was nothing, holding it loose in her hand, and she poured clear gel on it and then started to use it. She went so slow, so gently, I didn't even bleed. She kissed my belly, below my navel. After a minute, it wasn't bad at all. She went in and out with a slight twist, and used her finger on me, so I came. Not bad for a first time. I wasn't even sure that's what it was, but when it happened—the rush of blood in my face, my limbs warm and buzzing—she said, There's my girl, like I was a dog learning a trick. Learning to sit up and beg.

I have always known what I wanted. I got that from her.

Light blinks in the windshield, bright, between leaves, and when I close my eyes, I fall asleep for a while. When

I wake up, we're someplace else, and the landscape is different, the trees lower to the ground, the grass a lighter, bluer green, rolling in the distance.

I watch it, silent for a few miles.

Where are we going? I ask.

Summersville, Couper says, like it's vacation.

Fuck you, I say.

He swerves a little. What?

Fuck you and whatever you think you know about me, I say. My brain races with what he might have found out, sitting around by the water in South Lake. *Mother Cleared of All Charges.*

Sweetheart, Couper says. He shakes his head like he's clearing his ears. The speed limit slows down to thirty, and we stop at a railroad crossing where a long CSX goes by, and he stares straight ahead.

Why? I ask him. Is that really where we're going?

That's my next case, he says. I see his jaw set, the muscles next to his ear working.

What do you want me to say?

You could not say *fuck you* to me, he says. For nothing. What are you even talking about?

Nothing, I say. But I think about her face, her squinted eyes when she laughed or smiled. The sun coming through the trees in the backyard. About how she looked, in a tiny white casket, in a white dress, her face like she was sleeping, and me thinking, *Now when I see her sleeping, I'm going to think of her as dead.* And then collapsing when it struck me that she would never be sleeping again.

We could get to Summersville in a day if we were driving a regular vehicle on an interstate. But with the Scamp in tow on a smaller highway, going fifty, fifty-five, it takes us two days. In between, we stop at a KOA and spend one night in a field next to a river on the fringe of a circle of campers with cases of beer and fire pits. The smell of char and hot dogs and pine trees and beer spilt into the grass.

It's hard for the two of us to stand inside the Scamp together. We get in each other's way. In the bed it's fine, but standing, trying to do anything, is crowded.

Look, I say.

Couper waits.

Look, I say again.

He leans his hand on the counter and watches me. Are you trying to apologize? he says.

I'm bad at it, I say.

I bet the cops loved that about you, he says.

Yeah? Fuck you, I say again, and it's my mother's voice I hear coming out of me, quiet and acidic.

When he smirks, I push past him and walk out. Where to, I don't know. I don't even know what state we're in. We may have crossed into Georgia by now.

The park goes nowhere. There's no lake, just a lazy river, and no mountains. It's a flat field of trailers and campers and tents. A bathhouse, a playground. I walk with hard purpose around the outer loop of campers, and through a gathering of tents, and end up at the playground, where some girls in dresses are pushing each other on the merry-go-round.

I sit on a swing. They're the flat kind, the plank-of-wood seats, and not the U-shaped rubber ones that squeeze your ass. You can stand on these, but I sit. I light a cigarette and watch the girls. One stands in the middle, one pushes, and one leans her head backward off the side, her hair dragging in the dirt. They laugh like high-pitched, giggling devils.

I always wanted a sister. Once, I had imagined myself, slightly older, with Summer as an adult, but all I could picture was the way I was with my own mother. I couldn't see it, us as adults together, friendly, doing things. Enjoying each other.

I hear Couper's feet behind me. The soft crunch of his Converse on the gravel path.

Look, he says to me, using my own word. He's out of breath. He holds on to the rail of the swing set at first, and then leans over with his hands on his knees. Shit, he says. It's tight, and whispery.

What's happening? I say.

I watch him purse his lips and breathe slowly. His breath makes a sound, a tight whizzing. I take a drag and blow it over my shoulder, away from him.

It's not going to help if you just run away, he says finally. His voice has lost its usual sexy rasp and has, instead, a flat coarseness, a breathlessness.

Couper, I say, I am literally running away right now. With you.

I mean continually, he says, from your . . .

Do you want me to go back? I say.

Stop running from your shit, he says.

Do you want me to go back?

No.

What happens when you get sick of me? I say, because I think everyone gets sick of me and my mouth, my defensiveness, my crying, my not getting out of bed, my driving down the road drunk. My not having a job. My asking for money. My smoking at the kitchen table. My drinking all your beer when I've run out of wine and I don't have my own money to get more. Everything.

But Couper starts to smile. If I get sick of you, I'll buy you a bus ticket, he says.

Funny.

I'm not sick of you, he says. We just started. He sits next to me on a flat swing. I swing slowly, and he just sits, his feet planted, pushing a little, like he's in a rocking chair. I notice that the girls have gotten quiet. That they're turning slowly, listening, and watching us. Above the trees, the sky is white, settling. Between the tops of the trees, the sun burns like fire.

What happened to your cousin? Couper says.

Khaki? I say.

Yes.

She left.

Moved away? he says.

I think about the shape of her leg, taut, tan, smooth as glass, pulling into Henderson's BMW. The car was loud, stunk with exhaust and cigarette smoke from inside. Go play, she said to me, something Teddy would say to us on a nice day, shooing us outside. Usually, she'd lock the door.

She left with her boyfriend after her dad died, I say.

Do you keep in touch? he says.

That sounds sweet, doesn't it? I say to him. No, we don't. A normal family might, I say, but no. I don't know where she is, I say.

I just wondered, he says. You don't have a sister.

Nope.

Another woman, he says.

I know where he's going. June Carol tried to get me to go to a mothers of preschoolers group at the church. I went twice when Summer was four months. They put the babies in the nursery, and the moms gathered in a big room and did crafts and drank coffee and talked about the Bible. I hated it. I spent the three hours wanting a cigarette, feeling underdressed and foul-mouthed, not wanting to glue glitter, or arrange flowers.

After Summer died, June Carol suggested another group, a mothers' Bible study. She was hell-bent on saving me.

I wouldn't go. What I did do was paw at Eli, to try to get him to want me, anything. I thought maybe we could make some sense of it, wordlessly. That maybe we could just pare down to our bodies, where it all began, and start over. He couldn't even look me in the eye.

I mean, Couper says, you have all these men to talk to.

What do you mean, all these men? I say. Who told you there were all these men? My mother? Did you talk to my mother?

No, he says, and shakes his head. Never mind. I just thought another woman might be beneficial to you. I just wondered, he says.

How do you know? I say. I look down at my feet in the dirt. The girls have gone, walking shoulder to shoulder across the field. Their mother, a thin woman in a pink shirt, with a low ponytail, stands at the edge of the playground, calling them to dinner.

I read the paper, he says.

When we walk back, we continue around the loop, through a tent city, past a sandy volleyball court and a kickball field. At first, we walk close, our shoulders bumping, and then he holds my hand.

I laugh.

Don't laugh, he says.

No one holds my hand, I say.

Not your husband? he says.

You didn't read very closely, I say. We weren't married.

We walk like that, though, my hand in his, his hand around mine, big and warm.

My cousin held my hand, I say, looking down at my feet on the gravel path. I remember the feel of her hands better than anything. More than the feel of my mother's hands.

He grips.

Tell me about Summersville, I say.

Summersville had two murders in the same week one spring. One, a seventeen-year-old girl, Alyssa Mitchell, was found naked with her throat cut in the abandoned part of a town cemetery. Couper shows me her picture. A cute girl, with dark hair swooped across her forehead, a black rock-band T-shirt on.

Borderline student, Couper says. Didn't have a boyfriend. Had moved recently to stay with her dad while her mom was in jail.

And this woman, he says, showing me a picture of a woman a little older than me, holding a baby. The picture cropped so that only the arm of a kid sitting next to her shows. She has reddish hair, long and pulled around her shoulders. Her face with that pale generic American pattern of freckles.

Jessa Loy, he says. Who was never found. They questioned her husband, but he had alibis.

How do they know she's dead? I say.

They don't, he says.

I mean, I start. Someone could think I'm dead. But I'm here, with you.

True, he says. We have the light on over the table in the Scamp. Couper with an open bottle of Blue Light, me with a cup of ice and chardonnay.

But you think she's dead, I say.

He moves his shoulder, looking down at the picture, but doesn't answer.

You don't think it was the husband, I say.

No, he says. I don't.

Couper asks me if I want to see the crime-scene photos. He has his hand in the envelope, ready to pull them out, before I say yes.

Her face was already bloated, the cut in her throat empty and dry. It looks unreal to me, her hair, in the leaves. The grain of the marble headstone behind her.

The unusual thing? Couper says. No signs of struggle. No fiber. No sexual assault. No semen.

Weird, I say. Are they always sexual assaults, though?

When you find a naked seventeen-year-old? he says. Most likely.

Was she killed elsewhere? I say.

No, he says. The ground was saturated with blood. Whatever she was doing there, he says, she wasn't struggling.

They brought in the mother's boyfriend for questioning, but had nothing to keep him. He'd been six hours away, at work, and said he hadn't spoken with Alyssa since she moved back in with her dad. Her phone records didn't indicate calls outside of town. She never went to visit her mother in jail.

What's your theory? I say to Couper on the road in the morning. We have four hours before we get to Summersville, had a hot night of light sleep in the Scamp. The pavement, already wavy from the sun beating down.

I don't have one yet, he says. And to my surprise, he gets on the interstate, cruising in the right lane till the next exit, where he pulls into a truck stop. The parking lot is filled with eighteen-wheelers, diesel pumps, guys in jeans and boots. There's a truck wash, a diner, and a drive-thru hut that sits high enough for a rig to pull up and order coffee and cigarettes.

Couper parks alongside the main building, near an air tank, and I can see the windows of the gift shop inside, where T-shirts and mugs are on display. He wags my knee. Let's take showers, he says.

eight

KHAKI

In Summersville, I went with a man called Carter. I told him my name was Jordan. Like the river. We met in the Summersville Baptist Church. Carter, a twenty-nine-year-old never-married carpenter and landscaper. Me, new to town. Henderson used to say there's only two stories in the world, someone new comes to town or somebody leaves. I had cut my hair myself, and darkened it to a light ash-brown and wore it just to my shoulders with trimmed bangs. I bought dresses. And a purse.

I needed a place to breathe. A place to sit down on a porch and think, simmering. In the heat of the little town, I was cold at the core. Henderson was two towns behind me. Florida was in the ocean. When her daddy turned up dead behind a Dollar General, no one knew to look for me. But it was better to be out of there.

I rented the back quarter of an old Victorian on a side street. It had a white-paneled kitchen, a back porch, a parlor with an old-fashioned chandelier and a small bedroom with a brass bed. I met Carter at a Wednesday-evening meeting. I had a paperback Bible I'd picked up at a thrift store. A pocketbook with a South Carolina license that read *Jordan McCollough* and a MasterCard I kept active in my mother's name.

On the back porch, on our second date, Carter asked me what my secret was.

To the sweet tea? I said, coy. Superfine sugar.

He held my hand over the table between us. I was barefoot, and goddamn it was hot, a hundred, a hundred and five. He rubbed his thumbs over my fingernails. No, he said. Your secret. What brought you here.

I told him a truth. I needed a fresh start, I said. I wanted to live quietly on my own. To clear my head. To think. To relearn what was important.

He nodded like what I'd said was a prayer.

I was burning up with anger and resentment and shame. I wanted time alone to cull that into something manageable. Something I could use. Hurl at someone.

I wanted to see what I could get away with. In a town like Summersville, where a woman like me gets noticed in the best ways. I made a quiet splash. Went to church. Dated the right man. Made the right acquaintances, but kept to myself.

By the time I left there, afraid of what was happening in a town so small and godly, and needing to care for my sick mother in Virginia, Summersville didn't know what hit it.

Nevada arrived as I was closing. I had shut down the machines, counted out the register. She was there on the sidewalk when I came out the front door with my key, locking up. It was a little coffee shop on the corner. Espressos and cookies and sweet tea. The owner was a fiftyish woman with daughters. I told her I had a mean ex, and needed to work for cash to stay under the radar.

You need to play on people's compassion.

She asked me if he knew where I was and I said no. I'm laying real low, I said. She rubbed my shoulder, said it was fine. That she would keep an eye out for me. I worked there for eight months.

Cash in my pocket, I was closing, and there she was. Nevada. With near-black hair and eyes that were green like a cat's. She wore white shorts and Vans sneakers. A T-shirt that said *As I Lay Dying*. She had a blue streak in her hair that came from under her ear and hung over her collarbone.

Oh, you're closed, she said to me.

What were you looking for? I said.

She looked at me a long time before she answered.

What she wanted was chai. I gave her my address and told her to meet me on the back porch in twenty minutes. I'd make her some tea. I wanted to change. I wanted to go home alone, and not be seen on the street with her.

I wanted to forget which direction she'd come from and see her manifested only on my porch, under the yellow light, a small patch of grass and a clothesline behind her.

For the record, when it happened, it was she who kissed me.

She was the only one I left like that. Where they could find her. Where everyone could wonder *Why?* And who.

It made the casual kissing, the minor petting that I did with Carter, more bearable. He was chaste. He made it clear that he desired me, but he kept it in check. It was unlike anything I'd seen.

I played with the buttons on his shirt. I said, I'm not a virgin.

And he laughed. I'm not either, he said.

I meant it as an apology to him. A warning. I said, In college, and he nodded.

When he fixed my kitchen sink, he found a small bottle of bourbon and the pack of cigarettes I kept in a junk drawer.

Jordan, he said.

I covered my mouth with my hand. Old habits, I mumbled.

He stopped the faucet from running a steady thin stream. I rubbed my hands down the length of his arms and laid my cheek on his shoulder blade.

Jessa, I met at church. She was shy, literally beat down by a second husband. She'd married at seventeen, had a baby, and then remarried at twenty-five and had another. We talked in the parking lot one Wednesday night, a long time. After ten o'clock. Standing under the streetlamp by her car. She told me about the new baby, about the older girl. She talked about books and about TV shows and nail polish. Her words had a warp speed to them, like she was thirsty, and I was water.

I touched her elbow. What's bothering you? I said.

We had done a study on Ephesians. *Be kind.* I carried my Bible tucked under my arm. Wore a rayon dress with a small flower print. Flat sandals.

Oh, she said. Sometimes I don't want to go home.

You want some tea? I said.

I would love some.

I took her home. And then I talked to her every day. Every day, until the end.

They'll never find Jessa.

I never met Nevada at my own house again. We met everywhere else. The cemetery. The quarry. The mill yard. Behind the fire station. On the baseball field.

I gave her the name Nevada that first night. She had an Indian look to me. She looked like a desert flower. One that blooms, full open and purple, at night.

I love it, she said. Is Jordan your real name? she asked me.

No.

Is it close to your real name?

Nope.

Her mouth was on fire. Her hands, small and square and strong. She had a tattoo on her hip, a blackbird, perched and watching me when I pressed my mouth on her. While I held her hips in my hands. Her spine, arched. Her mouth, open and singing.

With Jessa, I prayed. We sat at my kitchen table, which had come with the house, round and shell pink from the 1960s with pink vinyl chairs. We had coffee and a lemon cake she'd brought me. I held both her hands and she lowered her head, her eyes squeezed.

Lord, I said, deliver this woman from the evil that overpowers her life. Guide her with Your loving hand. Protect her and make her whole again.

Henderson used to talk about paradox. In his philosophy years. About how sometimes you couldn't be clean until you were dirtied. Couldn't be free until you were enslaved. Couldn't be whole until you'd been broken to pieces.

I kept that in mind.

Jessa's husband was mean in terribly usual, predictable ways. He called her stupid in public. He talked over her. He hushed her when she tried to assert an opinion. When no one looked, he pulled her hair and pinched the backs of her arms. He'd hit her on top of her head, which left her dazed, her brain ringing like a bell. She'd lost hearing in her right ear from him boxing it. It buzzed and if she plugged her left ear, everything was muffled, stuffed.

Why? I asked her. There was no reason why. But I wanted her to try to answer it. Why does he do this?

If I refuse, she said. She looked up at the ceiling, ashamed. Her body was soft and white. Her hair, reddish and long. She had freckles on her shoulders, on her eyelids. If I disagree. If I spend too much. She chewed the side of a thumbnail.

I wanted to yell at her. I'd seen my own mother, weakened from radiation, fall down the stairs to the basement when my father pushed her. She dislocated her shoulder, the blade sticking out at a frightening angle, my mother howling in pain, crumpled at the bottom of the stairs.

Oh, you got enough fat on you still to cushion a fall, Doe had said.

I pushed it back in for her, with a loud snap. I did it quick, afraid, acting without thinking. It was in the wrong spot; I put it back.

We sat there after, the two of us on the cellar floor. My mother, wiping at her face. Me, stunned. Thank you, she said to me.

It was the least I could do.

Carter wanted daughters. He never outright talked to me about marriage, but he'd hint sometimes. He wanted to know about my sisters, about my mother.

My mother lives in Virginia, I told him. In a little town, like this one, I said.

How come you didn't go there, he said, instead of here?

Well, you know how it is, I said. Everybody knows you.

You know all that's behind you, he said. Carter was a dedicated believer in forgiveness, ongoing. A clean slate. A state of grace.

About my sisters, I told him I had two: one in Texas, with four boys, and one in California, who was married but didn't have a baby yet.

And that's it? he said.

That's it.

Where's your daddy?

Oh, I said. I felt my throat tighten. My daddy passed, I said. When I went to college.

Carter nodded.

Broke my mama's heart, I said.

And yours too, Carter said.

Mine too.

I made sense to him. The way I talked about back home. My sisters, my mother. He knew that I spoke with Jessa, and thought I was doing right by her, to counsel her, to be a good friend to her. Nobody knew about Nevada. And I was the only one who ever called her that.

What I knew about Nevada was that she lived now with her daddy, who worked at the mill. That before, she'd lived with her mother and her mother's boyfriend, and that now, her mother was in jail. That her father was trying to undo some of the damage her mother had done, or let be done. I knew she was unsatisfied, living in this little town, that she had wanderlust in her soul.

That she liked to save kittens from the shelter, or baby rabbits when the mother died. She painted her toenails electric blue, and her fingernails green. She wouldn't go to church, and ate her meals fast and greedy, like a kid who had grown up the youngest in a house of men.

I left her in the old part of the cemetery. There was a front part, newer, close to the road, and another gathering of stones farther back in the trees. It was deep and wet back there, the grass long and moldy. The stones, hardly legible. The oldest graves were hidden by thick sumac and wild raspberries around the perimeter. If you were just driving by, you wouldn't know there was another part.

I made one clean hard cut to her throat, and only after took the blindfold from her eyes. It was loose around her temples, around the back of her hair. Not meant to bind. Meant only to cover her eyes. To shield her from the look on my face when rage took over. I took her clothes, and I burned them.

She was missing, and Jessa was gone. They found Nevada within two days. But over Jessa, there was just whispering.

Do you know, Carter asked me, where she went?

I shook my head.

There's a baby, he said.

I know.

And by then, my fictional mother was ill. My sisters were coming home, from Texas and California, to spend time with her in Virginia. I had never stayed so close to what was going on.

The officer who came to my back porch asked me when I'd talked to Jessa last.

We had coffee last Friday, I told him. And we prayed, I said. She was often distressed, I said.

They had found Nevada, naked, with her throat cut, he said, clear into the spinal cord. Her head was nearly detached. Dear God, the cop said to me, hesitant to suggest a connection, but it was there. People were talking. Who would do such a thing? he said.

I went to a prayer vigil, but couldn't stay. Carter put his coat around my shoulders and took me home. What was happening? How could it be so dangerous just to be a young woman?

I'm scared, I told him.

You should be, he said.

He walked me to my door and said he'd wait on the porch until I'd turned the deadbolt. A shame, he said. We don't lock our doors here.

And after that, I left. I called him once, to tell him I'd arrived safely, relieved to be away from what was going on in Summersville, and that I was in the company of my sisters, and my mother, that my California sister was expecting her first baby after all, that there was joy to be had, there among us, a family of women.

I called him on a prepaid cell phone that I smashed and threw out.

But first, from that same phone, I called home and told Chuck to wire me money.

Now why in the hell would I do that? he asked me. I could hear Rayelle chattering in the background. Rayelle, about to graduate from the high school we should have gone to together.

Why don't you put Rayelle on the phone and I'll tell her why, I said.

I could hear him move away from them, heard the click of a door, the hollow sound of his voice in a small, closed room.

I don't know why you are hell-bent on ruining things, he said. You could have stayed, he told me. We would have had you.

You can't rescue me, Chuck, I said. I ain't a kitten no more.

I asked him to wire a thousand dollars to a Western Union in Morristown.

I can't send you a thousand dollars, he said.

Yes you can, I assured him. You sure as hell can.

What kind of trouble are you in? he said. I imagined him sitting on the toilet, lid down, his head in his hands. His voice echoed like he was inside a cell.

You pay me, and you'll never find out, I said.

When I got to the counter inside a Kmart, it was there, all of it. I didn't ask him again for eight months.

At a Motel 6 in Kentucky, I shaved my head. I was in mourning. My head, cold and buzzed to just a shadow. The absence of hair, of the bangs I'd gotten used to, made my eyes look huge. My mouth, wide and soft. I flushed the light ash-brown locks down the toilet. In the morning, I pulled out in the truck that was still registered to Henderson, still insured by him. I kept it running, kept a jug of water inside for when it overheated. It was a mistake, the truck, its connection. But I knew he wouldn't report it stolen. Not with what I knew.

nine

RAYELLE

Wherever I went, those summers with Chuck, I sent postcards. I carried a bunch of colored Flair markers in my little-girl purse and bought cards I thought Khaki would like. Pictures of mountains or a main street in town. A waterfall, a river, a sunflower. Dakota, Carolina, Tennessee. I signed them with hearts. *Miss you. Love you. xoxo Rainy.*

Rainy was a phase. I sometimes signed them *Rainy Day Blues*, dotting the *i* with a heart. I thought if I ever got famous—for what I don't know, I can't sing for shit— that maybe I could use that name. When I got back, I'd find that Khaki had kept them, tacked up in her room, or stuck into the mirror frame on her dresser. All the places I'd been, the places she never went.

The shower stalls at the truck stop are tiny cells with only a plastic chair, a toilet and a shower, towels rolled on a rack, soap and shampoo in a pump dispenser on the wall. There's a mirror, and bright fluorescent lighting. Couper pays for two rooms and takes me down the hall.

It shuts off, he says at my door, and nods his head at the stall behind me. It's an eight-minute shower.

I lean my back against the doorjamb. I don't know if I can get my hair rinsed in eight minutes.

I can't believe you're going in alone, I say, even though I'm dying to get in by myself, aching for a hot soapy shower, to wash my hair.

Couper shrugs. I'm over fifty, he says. Shower sex is overrated. Plus, he says and points, these stalls are small.

Over fifty? I say, my mouth open. Over?

But he ignores it. Instead, he plants his hand on the open door beside me. You know what I like better than sex in a shower where truckers jerk off? he says.

Ugh, I say to an instant picture in my mind.

Don't think about it, he says. He raises his eyebrows. I like you, he says, in the Scamp. On our bed, he adds.

Over fifty.

He laughs. Is that going to be a sticking point for you? he says.

I guess not.

The shower is cleaner than I expected. In fact, it looks hosed down, everything white and gray and chrome. I wish I could wash my clothes, but I take them off and shake them out and hang them over the chair to steam up with the room. The water is hard and hot, and I stand under it, trying not to think about the floor or the drain, trying not to waste time, even though what I really want is just to stand still.

The shower in the maternity ward was the opposite. They work real hard at keeping it nonclinical, having it look like it might be the bathroom in your home instead of in a hospital. It wasn't even called a maternity ward; it was a birthing place. You were supposed to bring your whole family, and people did. There were women with all their sisters, their mother, and their mother-in-law surrounding the bed, a whole world of women, birthing. Everything was pink and blue and beige, with baskets of silk flowers and teddy bears, and in the bathroom, a bunch of shower gels that smelled like peach and melon and something called sweet pea or freesia.

Summer came in the middle of the night and by the next afternoon they finally let me shower. I stayed in so long, my head against the tile, the water pounding on my back, that I bled even harder, the blood trailing down the drain and then after too, sitting in my bed, wearing a huge hospital-provided pad and giant mesh underpants that they gave you one pair of and you had to wash out every day. Someone else was walking Summer around, feeding her, putting her down in a glass bassinet. I didn't nurse her. I bound my breasts up with a sports bra and an Ace bandage; inside, half a cut pantiliner over each nipple, to catch the milk.

I spent most of the first days and weeks handing her off. First to the nurses, and then, after I left the hospital, to June Carol. I don't know if Eli's father ever held her. I'd hand her to June Carol, and his dad would take Eli away.

Let the women do what they're best at, he'd say.

June Carol would come in the morning and stay all day. It was her house. She had a key. I'd find her in the kitchen, jouncing Summer, with a full pot of coffee for Eli, and scrambled eggs on the stove. I'd stumble out in a nightshirt that barely covered my ass, wanting a cigarette.

She came from a huge family of girls in Miss'ippi, as she pronounced it. When there was a new baby, they rallied together, joyful and excited. She told me all about Elijah as a baby. He burped sitting up. He preferred to sleep on his belly.

Of course now, she said, they tell you they should sleep on their backs. They'll change it again, she said, not to me, but to Summer, who stared into June Carol's face with wide eyes and a half smile.

I was in constant hesitation. Second-guessing. If I paused, June Carol didn't even ask, she just picked Summer up, fed her, changed her, and managed to do so while making breakfast for Eli, and wearing a twin sweater set.

All I wanted was a dark room to myself.

And a cigarette.

And a drink.

When my mother finally came to see Summer, it was nearly February. The cold hadn't broken. There was a thin layer of snow that was like hard, frozen dust. My mother parked her car out front. The driveway and sidewalk were clear, salted, swept. She came in smelling like her own house, like smoke and something fried, like maybe Chuck had made pork chops the night before. Her hair was up, in a ponytail she might have slept in.

Well, she said to me, let's see the little shit-ass.

June Carol's mouth made a small O. Why don't you wash your hands in the kitchen and then sit down, Carleen, she said, and I'll bring her out to you. Would you like some coffee? she asked.

Eli was gone. Working. It was me and June Carol, all day.

My mother declined the coffee. June Carol brought out a receiving blanket, fresh from the laundry she did separate in gentle detergent for the baby. She laid it over my mother's sweatshirt as a barrier.

For the smoke, June Carol said to me, looking back over her shoulder. She went into the little bedroom to get Summer, came back out carrying her upright, and said, The baby shouldn't be exposed to secondhand smoke.

I'm not smoking, my mother said.

But it's on your clothes, she said.

That's not secondhand, my mother said. It's secondhand if it's coming out of my mouth. If I'm blowing it in her face, she said, which I'm not.

Well, June Carol said. She stood while my mother sat on the couch with that receiving blanket over her chest. She didn't look like she was about to hand over the baby.

Let me see her, my mother said. She held her hands out and for a second I imagined them fighting over her, grabbing like two little girls with a doll.

I reached and took her from June Carol, my own baby, who'd been fed by her grandmother. She was awake, in that state of wonder babies that age have. Before they can hold their heads steady or focus on anything far away. I held her the way I knew how, in the crook of my arm so her face looked up at mine. I said, Hey, Summer girl, to her, and watched her eyes, wondered what was going on in her head.

I let my mother hold her, the way she did, out on her knees, with Summer's head in the palm of her hand. She inspected her, turned her head slightly, looked at her hands. I wanted her to say something, that she looked like me, that she remembered me that small, that she loved holding me or taking me for walks or anything that made a connection.

That's one tiny tyrant, my mother said.

June Carol stood at the kitchen sink, washing up the breakfast dishes.

After, my mother wouldn't come back to the house. She would see Summer only if I brought Summer over to her.

It's not your house, my mother said to me, but I think she meant *She's not even your baby.* I could have walked out then, run away, and Summer would have been fine. Someone would have watched over her the right way. She would have been clean and well fed, fat even, dressed in white dresses with tiny bows in her hair. Learning to walk, to say her prayers at night. To say *yes ma'am* and *no sir*, and to paint her fingernails a delicate ladylike shell pink. How to match a pocketbook with her shoes, and not walk like a whore who's digging in her purse for a cigarette.

I come out of the shower clean and not wanting to put the same clothes back on. The jeans and the white tank top I've been wearing smell like sweat and musk and everything we've eaten, pancakes and burgers and fried potatoes. The jeans have worn themselves too big for me, baggy in the ass and loose around the waist. I hate putting them on. I hate putting the bra and tank top on more.

I decide, right before I slide the jeans on, that I can no longer wear the underwear. I pull up the jeans with nothing between me and the denim.

My hair is wet and unconditioned. There's none of the stuff I use to make the curls smooth, to tame them. I squeeze them with a towel, and then make a fat braid that curves over my shoulder, a few curls springing out above my ear.

Couper's not in the hallway. Not waiting outside my door. I walk back out into the vast complex of fast food and stores. It's like a shopping mall, except I'm the only woman, slick and clean smelling and not wearing underwear. I see guys everywhere, with beards and baseball caps, jeans and boots. Guys on cell phones, on computers, getting coffee or chicken or magazines or cigarettes. But no Couper.

Anything I had, a little wallet on a wrist string with about forty dollars left, a cell phone without a charger, I left in the Scamp.

I think all I have to do is pick up the pay phone, dial zero, and say I need to call my mother collect. You can still do that, right? *I need to make a collect call.*

She'll never accept the charges.

I look down a hallway next to a line of vending machines, Coke, candy bars, ice cream. There's a bank of metal booths, the plugs empty, the wall with just a shadow where the phones used to be.

I think, *I'm going to have to hitchhike.*

I could get a ride with anyone here. What would happen? I might get home. I might end up in Florida. Or dead.

I walk slowly past the vending machines, out into the open court where the tables and computer counters are. I think, *The world is full of men over fifty.* Men who are losing their hair, and growing their bellies.

And then I see his square back, hunched slightly while he types on his laptop, which sits on a counter where you can plug in and charge, access the Internet.

Good God, I say, and lean my cheek on his shoulder.

There you are, he says, and turns, but he can't see me the way I stand behind him.

I didn't know where to find you, I say.

I look over his shoulder. He's got Facebook open.

What's your cousin's name? he says.

She's not on there, I say.

Are you? he says. I couldn't find you.

I'm not.

This amuses him. Why not? he says. You're young.

I squint at the profile picture of him, outside, leaning on the Gran Torino.

There's no Internet at my mom's, I say. And I'm not going to the library to get on just so I can find out that a girl I didn't even like in high school has put up seventeen new pictures of her cat.

Couper laughs. There are a lot of cats, he says, scrolling.

And I had been, but I don't tell him that. I had an account and took it down after Summer. Deactivated. There was nothing to say, no picture, nothing that I felt like sharing.

He has the cursor in the search bar. Humor me, he says. What's her real name?

Kathleen Reed, I say.

He returns over a hundred. South Central High School. St. Mary's School. Loyola University.

Ha, no, I say.

Not a college girl? he says.

She didn't finish tenth grade, I say.

They're all too old or too young. Too fat. Too brunette. Nothing clicks.

Tenth grade, he says. When did she leave?

He leaves the screen open on a list of Kathleen Reeds who aren't her.

That same summer, I say.

After Holly Jasper? he says.

Or right before? I say. When her dad died.

Is that weird? Couper says. I hadn't given the timing much thought.

She wasn't kidnapped, I say to him. I watched her leave. I wanted her to live with us, I say. She didn't have parents anymore. I wanted a sister.

He closes the window and then the computer. You've tried to find her, he says.

I have. I keep thinking that someday, she'll write to me, or something. I've always been in the same town. The same stupid trailer, even, except for those few months.

What few months? Couper says.

With the baby, I say. It's hard to keep my face from clouding over, from gathering tight at the brow, sinking into a hard frown, puckering toward crying.

He rubs my arm. I have some other resources, he says. We can try searching again, if you want.

I want it more than anything. But I don't tell him that. I nod. Because if I start talking, I'll start crying. I'd thought it, after Summer, before Summer. When I found out I was pregnant, the person I wanted to tell was Khaki. The person I would have had in the room with me when she was born, Khaki. When Summer died, I wanted to lay my head on Khaki's lap and let her stroke my hair and tell me it would be okay.

I'd missed her for so long.

Right now though, Couper says, I have to make an appointment with the chief of police in Summersville.

Summersville calls itself a city. On the outskirts, a textile mill, a huge looming complex of buildings billowing smoke. An entire system of machines cultivating, willowing, carding, spinning. The sight of it, so oversized and powerful, is threatening. It gives me a cold twinge in the pit of my stomach, the way a nuclear plant does.

The town itself has that slow creep that Southern towns do. There's nothing touristy, nothing to come visit except maybe family. It's not small and it's not big. It's hot and dusty, a grid of streets with plain houses, a couple of churches, a Laundromat, a coffee shop, a diner. Big enough to have its own school, its own grocery store, and a small newspaper. There's a creek that runs through the cemetery where they found the teenager. Alyssa.

The police department is not at all what I expect. The station back in South Lake, just a concrete building with a few cubicles, a secretary, one small holding cell they use mostly for drunks. Couper invites me to go with him into the Summersville precinct, a grid of half walls, desks, and phones. The chief of police has an office in the back, with glass walls and blinds. And she's a woman.

I'd been picturing a man. A middle-aged guy with a comb-over maybe. She's tall and has brown hair that's to her shoulders and unbound. She looks like a runner. Lean and strong. There are plants in the office, and pictures of kids and dogs. When Couper walks in, her face warms and she smiles and shakes his hand with both hands. She looks at me, the way I lag behind in hesitation, and then Couper introduces me as his intern.

Well, Mr. Gale, she says, I'm happy to have you take a look.

That's excellent, he says. I can't make any promises. But you never know when something might fall into place.

We haven't had a fresh pair of eyes in quite some time, she says. The nameplate on her desk says CHIEF OF POLICE, DAWN L. POWERS. Chief Powers.

How long ago did they happen? I ask. My voice sounds small in there, the room echoey.

It's been nearly five years, she says and walks around the side of her desk. Come with me, she says, I'll show you the file room.

It's a cold back room with beige metal shelves that are crushed together and wheel apart with a crank. Chief Powers has an office assistant come in with us, a young man in a short-sleeved dress shirt, with a trim waist and soft-soled shoes that don't make a sound.

Anything you need copies of, Chief Powers tells Couper, just hand to Kyle, and he'll make you a duplicate. And thank you, she says to him.

Thank you, he says.

She is almost out of the room before she says *Nice to meet you* to me.

His preliminary research takes forever. Couper sifts through boxes of interview transcripts, half reading, setting aside what he might need, putting others back. The room is like a refrigerator, and even Kyle doesn't stay. He works on his own filing for a bit, and then goes to a desk outside the room, where I think it must be warmer, and not lit like the inside of a morgue, and makes phone calls, and sits at a desktop computer.

Okay, Couper says. He has a stack that's an inch thick. I can read these at home, he says.

You haven't been reading them? I say. It feels like it's been hours.

Just making sure I have the right things, he says. He hands the stack to Kyle, who doesn't get to it right away. Couper lays out some photos.

More of the mother, Jessa, with her complete family, both children, the husband. Then some of her husband's car, the garage, their backyard, taken by police photographers, with numbered markers.

And the teenager, her face and her full body naked to the elements. Evidence of footsteps through the leaves in the back part of the cemetery, but nothing on the path in the main part, where the roads are paved instead of dirt or gravel.

How long before they found her? I ask.

Two days, Couper says.

Her face in the close-up is already puffed with bloat, her skin pale and marbled with blue markings.

She looks beaten, I say.

That's just the decay, Couper says. It's the beginning of the body breaking down, under the skin. There were no signs of trauma other than to the neck. He says this with his eyes on another document, not looking at me. I wonder if he remembers that he's talking to a mother. A mother whose daughter died.

I push the photo away and look up at the grid in the ceiling. If I'm not careful, all I see is Summer's face with the life gone out of it. Her sleeping baby face, lips like a rose, cheeks pale. If I don't stop, I think about her body, breaking down, marbling itself in decay. About what is left of her now, if it's just a small curve of bones, or only dust.

What's her mother in jail for? I say.

Larceny, Couper says. She was stealing from the company she worked for.

Is she still in?

Yes.

Jesus, how much did she steal?

Hundreds of thousands, Couper says.

For what?

What do you think? he says. What do you need that kind of money for?

Drugs, I say. I mean, unless you're buying up property. Or hookers.

Yeah, he says. He laughs a little, quietly though, and even then it echoes some in that metal room. When Kyle comes back with a packet of paper for Couper, Couper puts his hand on my goose-bumped arm and says, Let's get you out of here.

The closest campground is twelve miles outside of town, on a road called Dry Fork. The campground is full of fishermen, the sites dotted along a creek. When the guy shows us our site, he says he has a slot only because there was a cancellation. And when Couper sees it, between a willow tree and an elm, with the land sloping down to a wide and lazy creek, he says, It's perfect.

Now we're here, I say to him, in my own camp chair beside the water. Before, you were in South Lake, I say.

Yep, he says. He holds the papers that Kyle gave him, bound with a black metal binder clip.

What if you were supposed to meet someone in Summersville instead of South Lake? I say.

I already met you, Couper says without looking up.

But what if I'm the wrong person?

He lets the papers sag onto his chest and looks at me over his glasses.

You're not, he says.

Jessa's husband, Kevin, still lives in the same house, a brick Cape Cod on a side street on the edge of the village, where there are no sidewalks. The streets, curved and quiet. The yards, fenced and treed with flowering bushes, azaleas, camellias, and roses. The kind of street you can stand at the top of and see all the houses aligned in a perfect array, an arch of suburbia, like the curve of the world. The Loys' house has a white door, white shutters, and a white clapboard porch built off the back of it.

In the backyard, a wooden swing set with yellow plastic swings, a clubhouse, a blue plastic slide.

Before, Couper took me to Walmart. You need some better clothes, he told me. The police chief looked at you funny, he said.

My mother threw out my nicer clothes, I said.

But I didn't disagree. I also thought the police chief's aloofness toward me was because she didn't like my jeans, or didn't trust my face, or both.

Sometimes, I think people can see Summer's scar on me, that I light up with a neon aura that says DEAD BABY. One hundred and fifty pounds of damage coming your way.

We bought three summer dresses and a sweater to go over them. A pair of sandals, a package of underwear, a razor, and bras. It was hard to find one at Walmart that fit me, that wasn't ugly and sold in a box. But I found two in the right size. One of them was camo. Couper kind of smirked at that one.

And so, I show up at Kevin Loy's house in a deep-pink silky knit dress that has white hibiscus flowers, a scoop neck, and little cap sleeves. It falls to my knees. If nothing else, I look more like an assistant and less like a hitchhiker. Even if my insides say *runaway*.

Couper gives me a legal pad and tells me to take notes. I've never seen him take notes, but I think the two of us sitting there, waiting for details from a possibly still grieving husband is probably too much, so he gives me something to do. I write down the time, 1:15 PM, and the date, June 12.

Kevin's on his lunch break. The older daughter, in junior high. The baby, in kindergarten.

He won't look Couper in the eye.

I know that it's still very difficult, Couper says, and I appreciate your time. Chief Powers, Couper starts, and Kevin cuts him off.

Didn't do enough, he says. Did she hire you?

No, Couper says.

I look around the room. There are two loud clocks, out of sync with each other. Pictures of fruit in the kitchen, where we sit at an oak table. Grapes and apples and pears. Kitchen curtains with a pattern of wheat. A painting of a vineyard that says, *I am the Vine and You are the Branches.* Where we'd come in, the front door held a plaque that read, *As for me and my house, we shall serve the Lord.*

I'm just getting to the point, Kevin says, where I'm moving past it. Since there's no answer, he says, no lead, no nothing. What choice do I have?

He's pinkish, the way Jessa is in the pictures. Gingery, but hardhanded, muscled in a long, ropy way. He wears khakis and a denim shirt with the sleeves rolled to the elbow.

I understand, Couper says. Where do you think she is? he says.

Where do I think she is? Kevin says. Where do you think she is? I thought you were here to solve this.

Couper sits, quiet, and just watches him. He waits until Kevin repeats it.

Where do I think she is.

Yes, Couper says.

Kevin huffs and pushes his chair away from the table. Unbelievable, he says. There was no reason to suspect me, he says, and then he points one hard finger down at the table and thumps. They questioned the shit out of me, he says. And I was the victim. I was the one who . . .

That's not what I'm asking you, Couper says. He leans back in the chair, his chest broad and open. I scribble some equivalent of their conversation on the legal pad.

Kevin waits.

I'm asking you where you think she is, he says again, and then adds, in your heart, Kevin. What do you think happened to her? I'm not here to accuse you, Couper says. I'm trying to put together a life for Jessa, to trace some pattern, something that may point to where she is.

I think she left, Kevin says. And after that, I don't know.

Why? Couper says.

She was talking. Always talking. He stops, and pinches the bridge of his nose. To a woman, a friend from church who got it into Jessa's head that she didn't have to stand for this anymore. She pumped her full of ideas about what a woman didn't have to put up with is what happened, he says, and she left.

Who was the woman? Couper says.

What were the ideas? I say, because I don't believe him, and because *pumped with ideas* sounds like something paranoid my mother would come up with.

Ideas about me, he says to me. That I wasn't good enough for her. That she ought to have better than what we had, what I work for. That her life was bigger than caring for her own children, he says. No calling is bigger than motherhood, he says to me.

That's what I've heard, I say, and under the table, Couper pats the side of my leg. I can't tell if he's comforting me or telling me to shut up.

Who was she? Couper says.

Some girl, Kevin says and then laughs. Not even married. She didn't stay, he says.

Do you remember her name? Couper asks.

No, Kevin says.

I hear Couper sigh, and try to hide it. What do you mean she didn't stay?

She didn't stay in town. She wasn't from here, and she didn't stay here.

Did they leave together? Couper says.

No.

Are you sure? Couper says.

Yes, Kevin says. She was here after Jessa was gone. Ask Carter, he says then.

Carter?

Carter James, Kevin says. You can try him at his shop, on Elm.

I write this down.

He dated her, Kevin says. And they questioned her, too, he says. The problem, he says, is that when a woman wants to keep a secret from you, she can. And when a woman goes astray, you might as well let it go. There isn't much harder than saving a hardheaded woman, he says. And two of them together? He waves his hand.

What have you told your daughters? Couper says.

That she died in an accident, Kevin says.

Really, I say. I'm having a hard time keeping my mouth shut. I see Couper's face settle into something. Disbelief, or maybe resignation. He deflates a little.

What if she comes back? Couper says.

Then I'll let them believe in miracles, Kevin says.

Couper drives the car around the town. Elm Street is off Main Street, and the shop is at the end of Elm, past the houses and the school. It's a small metal warehouse with a covered lumberyard behind. The sign says THE CARPENTER'S SON. Couper drives past it.

Where are you going? I say.

I need coffee, he says, and rolls his head around the back of his shoulders, stretching his neck. With bourbon, he says. Then mutters, Self-righteous prick.

He goes through the drive-thru and I order something ridiculous, an iced coconut frappe latte, because it sounds cold and delicious when this town is hot and still. Couper orders his coffee black.

Is that what you think? I ask him.

He holds out his hand. Let me have some of that, he says. It's so cold and sweet I have a head rush. About what? he says after a sip.

About women, I say.

We are parked in the lot, the air on, the windows up, my hair blowing from the dashboard fan.

No, Couper says. Not at all. Then he adds, I been saved by plenty of women.

I bet you have, I say.

Inside the shop on Elm, Couper has to wave his arms to get Carter's attention. He's wearing earplugs and a mask and is running a circular saw. There's sawdust all over the floor, and that warm, sweet wood smell. Couper goes through his introduction, tells him that he's looking for information on a woman he believes Carter dated. A woman who was friends with Jessa Loy.

Jordan, Carter says. Jordan McCollough.

Is she still in town? Couper asks.

No sir, Carter says.

What were the circumstances of her leaving? Couper says. I hold the pad and scribble, but I'm barely taking legible notes at this point.

She moved back home, Carter says. Her mother was ill, and her sister was having a baby.

Back home? Couper prompts.

To Virginia.

When's the last time you spoke? Couper asks.

Not long after she left, he says. She called me once, and then not again. He looks down at the floor and pushes a pile of sawdust aside with the toe of his boot.

Did you try to call her? Couper says.

Once. It just rang.

And not again?

I'm not a chaser, Carter says. He stands with his back to a project, a ladder outline of shelves made from cherry, the wood raw and sanded, the grain pink, and deep rose in the darkest parts.

Didn't that strike you as odd? Couper says.

I watch Carter's eyes rise to the rafters in the shop. No sir, he says, it struck me as hard. Cold, maybe, but no, not odd. We weren't official.

Do you know if she convinced Jessa to leave?

No sir.

Do you know if she knew the teenager, Alyssa?

Do you know I have answered these questions a hundred times? Carter says.

I don't doubt that, Couper says. I'm sorry.

Carter looks at me. His face has a hollow sadness to it, a man in his thirties, alone in a woodshop all day, breathing in the scent of wood, of lacquer, the whir of the saw a constant in his ears. His eyes, though, are bright blue, in them a recognition that only some people have. People who have seen hope pass them by.

Was your father a carpenter? Couper says.

Carter clucks a laugh at him. That's a Bible verse, sir, he says. My father was a plumber.

Are you referring to yourself as Jesus? Couper says.

Sir, I have work to do, Carter says.

I'll take the phone number if you still have it, Couper says. For Jordan McCollough.

I write down the name. I have no idea how to spell it.

If you still have it, Couper says again.

Carter takes the phone off his belt and scrolls through. He reads me a number.

You want my advice? Carter says to Couper.

I watch Couper roll on the balls of his feet. Sure, he says.

Hold on to your girl, he says, nodding my way. And get out of town.

Couper smiles at the floor. Not a chaser, he says. Then, Are there other women who've disappeared?

No, Carter says. But you don't always know, when you just breeze in, what's already going on in a place.

That night, in a Dunkin' Donuts on the outskirts of town, Couper combs through file after file, scrolling a database. We drink coffee, and long after the coffee is gone, he's still searching.

That's not a Virginia or a Georgia number, he says. It's South Carolina.

When he calls, he gets a young man on the phone. No Jordan? Couper says.

No man, I don't know who you're talking about. You got the wrong number.

Hey, how long have you had this number? Couper asks.

I don't know man, a year?

What are you looking for? I say, when he hangs up. I sit across from him with my feet on his side of the booth.

Other missing women. Other unsolved cases. Oddities.

Do you think these guys are telling the truth? I ask.

Their version of it, he says.

Did you find Jordan McCollough? I ask.

Not a trace of her, he says.

I wonder if she's real. Carter described her to Couper, small with light brown hair, greenish eyes. Pretty, he said, dainty. When Couper asked if he had a picture of her, though, Carter said no.

No pictures? Couper said.

No. He shook his head like it was a silly thing to even ask.

We sit there with empty coffee cups until after dark, above us, a TV in the corner of the ceiling, with a Fox News interview show and a headline ticker across the bottom. I keep reading it for clues. Floods, hail in the Midwest. But all I can think about is a small dainty woman showing up in town alone, and then leaving alone, without so much as a ripple behind her.

ten

KHAKI

Florida was the one I took home. She was the beginning, and the end, of everything. She'd never been inside a house in a city, with an upstairs and a sidewalk out front. I learned she'd never been to school, ever, that her mother listed her as homeschooled, but she was really just unschooled. That she could read only a little, taught by her grandmother, but that her mama couldn't read at all. She'd spent all of her fourteen years on that dirt floor, in that back field, with different men in and out of the house, in and out of her.

I left her standing in the kitchen, her knees together, her toes turned in, her hair in her eyes, her hand near her mouth, almost giggling. She was nothing but a goddamn kid, and I was enthralled with her. She was the light of my world right then, in a pair of cutoff jean shorts. Henderson grabbed my arm above the elbow and pulled me down the hall.

Khaki, he whispered at me. What the fuck?

I wrenched my arm free. I don't care for manhandling.

She needs a safe place, I said.

She's like twelve, he said. He thrust his arm out, pointing back at the kitchen. Her safe place is with her mother.

Well, that's how much you know, I said.

I thought about what I might have been if it had just been me and my mother. With no father, no brother. No uncles, no cousins. Just me and Teddy, alone, in her big car, with me driving. Living anywhere. In an apartment, or a seaside motel, ordering takeout and feeding seagulls off the boardwalk. I imagined myself taking care of her. I imagined her well. Her body with the curves it was meant to have, not the gaunt boniness she was left with.

I thought about the things my mother taught me. How to fill in my eyebrows with a pencil and shape them to an arch. How to write in cursive. To sign a check. To drive. To leave a conversation before a man has the upper hand.

And Rayelle's mother. She would spout off things like, Keep your goddamn legs together, Rayelle, I can see clear up your twat. I could hardly believe my mother and her mother were sisters.

It wouldn't do any good. You could tell Rayelle the same thing twenty times and it wouldn't sink into her thick skull.

Florida was not Rayelle. She was my tiny hurt puppy that I picked up off the street, that I saved from being kicked again.

We cannot have a child living here, Henderson said.

I cocked my head. Why not? I asked. I was a child when I left with you.

You were not, he hissed.

The fuck I wasn't, I said.

He waited while I stared at him. The hallway, crooked, the floor slanting toward the stairs, toward the back of the house into the bathroom, which was the low spot. The floors, a slick dark brown, varnished too many times. The walls, white and dirty and hung with movie posters, unframed.

What else have you lied about? he said.

Wouldn't you like to know.

I could feel it ending, the thing between me and Henderson, which had never been more than a convenience. Love wasn't what put me in his car, wasn't what made me follow him into the South, from college town to college town, apartment to apartment.

That's desperation. That's gnawing your way out of your own cage.

He liked a companion. To have a girl to take to parties who could talk and drink with the guys. To talk to at night. To fuck.

If he'd been smarter, or half as good at lying as I was, we might have gone somewhere. We might have really made something. But right then, with a fucked-up, dirty-footed child in our apartment, it was pretty much done.

I'd told her to meet me at the gas station to pick up her mama's weed. I put twenty dollars of gas into the truck and waited, parked to the side, smoking a cigarette with the windows down, watching the light fall over the fields, and the clouds of mosquitos coming out, listening to the call of the killdeer, even as the dark came on.

When she leaned in the passenger window, her face was the moon to me. She had nothing with her but what she wore, a pair of shorts and a peasant top that fell off her shoulders, the twenty-dollar bill that would never be used to buy drugs.

What's your name? she said. She had a different drawl, not just Carolina, but something deeper, something backwoods.

Kit, I said.

Like Kit Kat, she said.

Like Kit Carson, I said.

She slid up onto the bench seat. I don't know who that is, she said.

Frontiersman. Robbed a bunch of Indians blind, I told her. The way the blouse fell off her shoulders, I could see her armpit, the round side of her breast against her arm. I had a tiny dime bag of weed to sell her mama. I had nicked some off the top because I didn't like her.

Do you have cash? I asked her.

No. Then, Well, I have my mama's twenty dollars.

I looked off down the road. A pickup, with its bed full of Mexican workers coming back from the fields, rumbled toward us with one headlight out. The road was peaked in the middle, and fell off to either side; it felt like you were falling off, into the ditch, off the side of the world.

What's your mama expect me to do with you? I asked.

That's when she put her hands on my face, bold. Her fingertips at the corners of my eyes, pulling them upward, slanting them. Her thumbs at the edges of my lips.

You got a face like a man, she said.

You got a face like a baby, I said.

I ain't a baby.

How old are you?

Fourteen.

Well, I said and laughed. Baby enough.

She sat sideways on the seat, her feet tucked under her bottom, and scratched her fingernails, ragged and unevenly long, on my bare arms. Then she leaned in and kissed me, full on. Her mouth like pepper and tobacco. Her skin, like velvet.

We drove into the dark, the heat coming off the road, the dashboard warm from sitting in the sun all day. The fields on either side were corn, high enough to dwarf you if you ran through them. The truck dipped through hills and ruts on the back highway. I'd seen her only three times, twice at her house, and then on that third time I tucked her away and kept her. I drove slow, looking over at her. We kept the windows open and the radio on. We picked up a bluegrass show and Florida rode beside me like she belonged. She asked for a cigarette, one arm wagging out the window, singing along with words that were mostly right.

I'm part Indian, she said when the song was up. She looked at the side of the cigarette I handed her, at the camel.

You are?

Uh-huh. Cherokee on my daddy's side.

Where's your daddy? I asked.

Dead, she said.

The road came to a T and I pulled off to the side by a stop sign. All the roads are the same back there, a cornfield in the dark, same as the ocean, ready to swallow you up.

Mine too, I said.

Drugs, Florida said. Dead in his own vomit. In his own bed.

I smiled. Drunk, I said. Dead on the kitchen floor.

The sound of the corn leaves was like paper chimes, like breathing.

Kiss me again, I said, and she turned and looked over her shoulder at me.

Why don't you do the kissing this time? she said. When I moved in closer, she said, How do I know you're not going to rob me blind?

I might fuck you blind, I said into her hair.

With what? she laughed.

Anything I got.

I wanted her so much I ached. I felt bones I didn't know I had, ringing like a bell, deep inside.

Well go ahead, she muttered, but then swung the truck door open, and went out into the corn, running until it closed up behind her. The moon was low and half full, yellowish, hanging over the field. I started calling, Florida, Florida, parting stalks that were taller than I was, their big leaves hanging out like tongues.

Her age didn't stop me. We lay in the long soft grass on the roadside and when I put my mouth to her she howled like something wild caught in a trap. I thought we were equal, her fourteen, me nineteen, but cut from the same damaged bolt of fabric. It was a leveler, what we'd seen. I meant to make it right for her, sucking on the wound like a witch doctor on a snakebite.

But it didn't stop Henderson either, not her age, or that I considered her mine. It never does.

When men decide they want something, when something tickles them in the darkest place, they will rationalize anything to get what they want.

She seduced me.

She looks older. Acts older. Dresses older. Knows things a kid wouldn't know.

She's emotionally mature.

Florida wouldn't have known the difference between good touch and bad touch if the bad touch electrocuted her.

When she'd been there a week, bathed in my tub, slept in our bed after I'd kicked Henderson to the back bedroom, a tiny half room with enough space for a twin bed, but not enough to close the door, I found him with his hands on her head. His knees open. Her face in his lap. Her shoulders, moving in rhythm.

And even then, the view of her from behind, her narrow waist and her tiny round ass sitting on her bare feet, was enough to prick me with desire.

I was the one who touched her. Who put my hands on her head, her hips, my mouth on her.

I slammed the door and heard the scramble of feet and knees and zippers in the back room.

Henderson said to me, It's not what you think.

I said, I ought to kill you with my own hands.

And Florida stood in the doorway like a goddamn vixen, her hair over one eye and one shoulder, her soles dusting the floor with just a whisper as she walked past me and Henderson in the hallway. I stood up to his shoulder, glaring at him. She grazed my arm as she went into the room we had claimed as ours.

Brush your teeth, I said to her.

She had a gash in the back of her calf, a wound that had never closed properly and left a divot you could sink your finger, or your tongue, into. Her mother had been chasing her with a knife. When Florida tripped and fell, running in the yard behind their dirt-floor house, her mother stabbed the knife into the back of her leg.

The whole blade sunk in, she told me. Just the handle was sticking out.

What did you do? I said.

I walked back into the house like that. I could feel it wobbling. My mother was screaming.

She pulled it out herself, and wrapped her leg in a kitchen towel till the wound closed slowly, leaving a dent behind.

We lay in bed with a full moon coming through the blinds. She told me her mother said a full moon in your eye makes you crazy. It shone in white stripes across us both.

But I like it, she said.

I ran my fingers down the center of her torso, between her breasts, down her belly. Why was your mother chasing you? I said. I knew these stories. They didn't need a reason. But I wanted more, of her words, her voice, her mouth moving in the dark.

She started to tremble. I could feel it in her belly, in her thighs, between. Then she snickered.

Do you have a knife? she said, sly.

Honey, you know I have a gun, I said. I tightened my hand on her mound and she squirmed beneath it.

I slept with her husband, she said.

I let go, loosened my fingers, but left the heel of my palm there, on the pubic bone.

When? I said.

She swallowed. The tremble came back.

I was twelve, she said.

Your mother's husband slept with her twelve-year-old daughter, I said, turning it around, taking Florida out of the action, trying to make her see. And she stabbed you, I said.

I took my hand away and slid both of my hands down her arms, out to either side. The moonlight had shifted, her face in darkness, but our bodies alight. I hovered over her.

I will never, ever hurt you, I said.

Henderson made us leave. Sitting at the kitchen table with his computer open and a cigarette going and a full pot of coffee, he said, You're going to have to get out.

And go where?

He shook his head. Doesn't matter to me.

I pay to live here, I said.

You can pay to live someplace else, Henderson said.

I made her shower with the door unlocked and partway open. I was afraid she would crawl out the window, would slip down the drain without me knowing. I feared opening the bathroom door to find only steam, an empty tub, an open window. That she would disappear from me forever.

I put it out there, that fear, into the stars. Into the moonlight above our bed. And it came back around, twice as hard.

When Henderson left for class and she came out of the bathroom clean and dripping and naked, I took every hidden stash of money there was. Any twenty-dollar bill I'd tucked somewhere for safekeeping. All the weed I had portioned out to sell. I took his grandfather's watch and pawned it. It was worth only its gold, and it wasn't all gold. They gave me seventy-five dollars for it. And I took the truck.

I figured maybe we were even after that.

For that little while, those few short months we were together, we lived in a room. One room, a block from the ocean. It was dark. It had one bed, an old heavy TV that brought in only a grainy shopping channel. The shower never drained well. The sink was out in the room, standing on spindly chrome legs. Florida ate a lot of potato chips and drank a lot of Pepsi and watched a lot of QVC. I would find her flipping through the Gideon Bible out of boredom. The verses she knew, she had memorized. If I pointed to a passage, she struggled through the words.

The manager cut me a deal. He sat in the office and I stood on the other side of the desk. I couldn't afford to stay long. Wasn't sure I wanted to, but I needed to bargain.

I won't fuck you, I said to him, figuring he made these deals all the time, depending on who moved through town and what he thought he could get away with. I was partially wrong.

I don't want you to touch me, he said. He had a constant sniffle. His throat, wet with nasal drip.

He had a boy to touch him. A kid. A guy who was maybe twenty, in a room like ours, with one bed, one vinyl chair, one lousy TV. He told me to stand behind him while the kid sucked him off.

I don't want to see you, he said to me. Or hear you. Or smell you, he said.

He gave me a scarf to tighten around his neck.

What if I accidentally kill you? I said.

He looked me up and down. You? he said.

I choked him to perfection. Liked the burn in my arms when I pulled. I could do it with my eyes closed. I wondered what he was paying the boy. If what the kid got was just a free shitty room.

The third time, I cinched the scarf harder. The ends of it wrapped tight around each fist, my arms hard with muscle, and my knee propped against the back of his chair. He tapped his foot, a warning to let up, and I leaned into his ear.

You're going to have to pay me cash, I said, in addition to the room.

I watched the boy's eyes widen. He was clean, with short hair, blond and old-fashioned looking, a look I expect the manager had handpicked. He looked like a Hardy Boy, in a striped tee. A pair of faded jeans.

Well aren't you smart? the boy said to me after. We stood outside on the sidewalk, where I lit a cigarette, and he held his hand out for one.

You can do better than him, I said. I never knew what his deal was, the kid. He had a brittle look to him. Like the old-fashioned veneer could splinter and fall away. I didn't even know his name.

There are men who want to fuck you. Who want to watch you. Who want to touch or be touched, who want a pretty little thing, in a skirt and knee-highs, or a filthy whore in heels.

What I learned to spot, and to deal with, were the others, the ones who require something more. The men who are empty or aching with some invisible damage they're working out on the surface of their skin. A belt around the neck. A spiked heel in the small of the back. A pillow so tight against their face it'd take their breath away. These were the ones I didn't have to touch, except with an apparatus, a yardstick, a brand. Who wanted to be blindfolded and bound. Tied to a chair like a hostage and pissed on.

That I could deal with.

When I left him, the motel manager, three months later at the end of summer, he was bereft.

He wasn't going to find another like me.

But it was time to go. When Florida learned that her stepfather was dead, shot in the head and his throat cut, so deep, she told me, so deep it nicked the spinal cord, she collapsed into me with weeping. She was racked, her torso spasming with sobs.

I had found him right where I thought I would. Where he didn't think he was doing anything wrong, not doing any real harm. The same man who didn't think anything of plucking a twelve-year-old daughter from his own wife.

I could have waited all night. Hot and still. Crouched against a wall with the words BONG WATER spray-painted on the yellow brick. The pavement, stained with oil, paint, sparkling with bits of broken glass. I boiled myself down to glass, invisible until the light catches it, until the shard is buried in your foot and you're bleeding. I didn't even smoke. My breathing slowed, my body barely moving.

He came after dark. The way I expected. Not behind the building, but near it. To meet another guy, a kid really, who could have been me as a boy, a shorts-wearing, shaggy-haired kid with a bag of dope small enough to fit in your palm. I watched them exchange. And when the kid left in a loud car, I stood up.

When you're five foot two and blond, with your legs hanging out of shorts, when you put your hands in the back pockets and push your chest out and say, Hey, to a guy in a parking lot, that guy never thinks, *This girl is going to kill me.*

Ever.

He thinks, *Hey,* right back at you.

He answered me, surprised.

Come here, I said, with my head cocked. I crossed my feet.

He thought I was a hooker, another druggie, looking for a quick fix with him. That maybe I'd offer my own exchange. Maybe he'd just get lucky.

I lured him with no resistance. Up close, I could see he wasn't even forty. His hair was shaved to a shadow, his face pocked deep. He smelled like cheap, skunky beer, his teeth and lips tobacco-stained. He was missing an eyetooth.

Hey.

I thought about his hands on her. His hands were dirty, the kind that doesn't come clean. Stained with resin and spray paint. Hard and unyielding. Hands that would hurt even when he tried to be gentle. Too rough for a baby or a dog, or a little girl.

I wanted him to know who I was. I tilted my head, a come-on. His hands were out at his sides, ready to grab. If I had to guess, his dick was already hard. I thought about cutting it off, and stuffing it in his own mouth.

But instead, I moved quick. I crooked my arm like I was going to put it around him, like I was leaning up for a kiss, to whisper something in his leathery ear. The only light back there was from above the store, shooting up into the trees, and leaving us in shadow. When I reached for him, he came right in, and I pushed his head back with the nose of the gun in his temple, before he could say anything, before I told him who I was. I held it so tight, I could feel my own pulse in my fingertips.

It wasn't enough. My head was clanging, deaf from the shot, my mouth tasted metal, and my teeth were vibrating against each other.

He lay there at my feet, empty, and I wanted to kill him again. Right then, I understood every gruesome hate-filled murder I'd ever read about. The woman who shot her husband not once, but fifty times, his gut like a sponge. Dead over dead over dead. I didn't feel bad. I wanted more.

But I couldn't risk another bullet. I pulled a folding knife out of my pocket instead, and slashed below his Adam's apple. In the dark, I couldn't tell how deep it went. I only knew how it made my arm feel: the pull of my own strength through his flesh. My arm ached into my shoulder socket. I tucked the gun in between my shorts and my underpants. I held the knife in my right hand. And walked.

It was nothing like Holly.

I killed Holly with my own hands, with effort that left me sore for days. My body raging with endorphins and then slack. I slept hard after Holly. I was hungry.

I left him on the pavement and walked up over a grassy hill behind the store, past dumpsters, and out onto a different street. I wore sneakers that I would discover the faintest spots of blood on. I'd been careful, but not careful enough. I cut down an alley between a barbershop and an apartment building, where I dropped the open knife, point down, through the hole on the top of a rain barrel. I heard it plunk in, sinking. I checked my hands. Clean. My shirt, black, and clean to my eye. I would burn it later with the sneakers.

On the sidewalk, out of the alley, I passed an older man taking garbage cans to the curb. He nodded at me in the yellow streetlight. I said hello, lowered my eyes, smiled. I saw a woman walking a small dog who sniffed my bare knee. I watched their mouths for talking. My ears, a fuzz of white noise.

I had left my truck a mile away. On a side street by a church whose yard was fenced with white pickets. I got in and drove, back to the water, but again, left it a mile or so away on a side street by a closed flower shop. In the window, arrays for a funeral, a wedding.

I walked to the ocean and sunk into the sand. I put my feet in, and then my hands, my arms. I went down to my knees and leaned my face in, the surf creeping up around me, salt burning my eyes and the insides of my nose. No one else was out there, not a couple making out, not a stray dog. Nothing but the sound of the water, muffled to me, with the static in my head.

I waited to tell her. And before I did, she heard.

Why? I said. Florida, I called out over her crying, in that dingy room, the TV just a crackle of noise, the single light missing one of its two bulbs.

I felt her kiss me when she left, but it wasn't enough to wake me, not enough to get me out of that swayback bed to follow her, to grab her, to save her.

When I left that motel, I left three bodies behind. One back home. One in a parking lot. And one in the ocean, where I never intended to lose her, my own mermaid, floating, singing, with her hair like a halo around her baby face.

By the time I left there, I could feel my own veneer splitting. I was becoming transparent, harder and harder to find.

eleven

RAYELLE

We leave Summersville in the morning, headed for the site of another girl found, this time on the banks of a river. They found only parts of her, Couper says. A femur, a mandible.

Just a mandible? I say.

Sometimes, that's all that's left, he says. Animals.

Who was she? I say.

Well, he says, there were a few possibilities at first, a woman, a child. A hunter missing from a few towns away. But the mandible points to the woman. Caitlin, he says. From dental records.

What if it's someone else's femur? I say.

He rubs his brow, squinting into the sun. It could be, he says.

We'd stayed out by the creek until almost dawn. The closest camper, to the right of us, had left while we were in town, and we came back to an empty spot of land in the trees, a fast-moving creek, sun in hot circles on the grass and bits of cool, damp shade underneath the pines. We lay on a blanket, listening to the creek, eating sandwiches, drinking beer from cans. I lay stretched out, my head and feet were off into the grass. Couper curled on his side next to me, leaning over, looking down.

What's under this dress? he said, his hand on my thigh.

Why don't you stick your hand under there and find out? I said.

It was a long time till we slept.

So I'm buzzing-in-the-limbs tired in the morning when we drive out. My head cottony, and my eyes hot. Couper gets huge Styrofoam cups of coffee and we rumble out of town.

Goodbye, Summersville, I say, watching it in the side mirror. It feels wrong, though, saying it. Saying even that version of her name.

Off those back roads, it's hard to tell sometimes, what corner of what state we're in. It's field after field out there. Red or bleached-white concrete, plantation houses and dirt roads. Couper comes to a four corners where there's a 76 gas station and an old shopping plaza with a jeweler, a bank, and a yoga studio with a Grand Opening sign. Across, there's a pink cabin that says MISS RUBY'S FORTUNES, with a phone number and a star and a moon.

Couper rolls into the parking lot, which is gravel and dusty, and deep with holes.

Really? I say, turning sideways on the bench seat. This is how you conduct your research? At roadside fortune-tellers? Come on, I say.

This is just his day job, Couper says.

What's his night job? I say. Carnival barker? Couper laughs, but I keep going. It's such bullshit, I say. You could put a quarter in an arcade game and get a fortune.

But while he's looking at me, I think about the way he was early this morning, the groan he made, deep in my neck, holding on to my hips something fierce, the way he curved beside me after, both of us naked with nothing over us, just under the sky like that.

I'm glad you're with me, he said.

In the car, though, he snickers. He reaches into the back for an expanding file folder. I've been in touch with this guy for a while, he says.

Well good, I say. Maybe I'll ask him a few things about you.

We get out and, in the parking lot, a cloud of dust hovers about our knees. I put on shorts this morning and one of Couper's soft dark blue T-shirts, a V-neck that hangs low over my cleavage. I was off duty, or so I thought. I could save the dresses for another day.

What about me? Couper says.

I don't know, I say. I keep sleeping with you, I say, standing right up beside him on the steps. But I don't know a thing about you.

Sure you do, he says. Pay attention.

There's a jangle of bells on the door, and inside, a living room with old-fashioned furniture. The room is filled with things, pictures, statues, candles, flowers, beads. Old photos on the walls of ladies from the 1900s, in hats and bustles, pictures of the Virgin Mary, pictures of Indian kids in a circle, holding hands. There are strings of beads off every doorknob and hook and light fixture. Wooden beads, glass beads, plastic colored beads. There's incense burning that smells like burning leaves or dry grass. The rug is plush and red, and there's a big green velvet couch against the back wall.

The psychic is expecting Couper. He's tall and fat, round in the wrist and shoulders in a real queer way. He walks kind of belly out, like a fat woman would, and is wearing shorts and a polo and flip-flops.

He is not expecting me.

The midway was always lousy. It was dinky, with rattly rides that were unsafe, and a few games. The bumper cars were no good. No one from town would go on the roller coaster, a metal contraption that went up into the trees next to the lake, because everyone knew that Randy Hinkel and his brothers had worked on putting it up and they couldn't build a goddamn thing. When the cars went over the top hump of the hill, the whole thing shifted, breathing with movement like it would fall apart.

There was a haunted house that was just a cart moving through the dark on a track where loud buzzers and screams startled us. As kids, we wanted monsters, weird green lighting, the touch of a creepy hand, or a bloody-mouthed vampire lurking in the corner. Probably, though, that lone cart on a path so dark you didn't know when it would turn, the loud buzz that seemed only to say you did it wrong, while you reeled through, blind—that was probably the scariest thing of all.

In the main building, painted to look like a circus big top, there was a bank of Skee-Ball lanes from the sixties, a few video games, and a counter where kids could trade tickets for things like bouncy balls or jelly bracelets.

And on the sidewalk between the big top and the haunted house, a purple shack that said PSYCHIC. They never committed to a name, like Miss Lydia, or a man named Vladimir. It just said PSYCHIC. I think they got whoever they could to sit in there. Probably, it was just someone's hippie aunt visiting from New York.

You had to pay five dollars for a reading, given to a guy who sat on a folding chair outside. Inside, there were two parts: an anteroom with jeweled mirrors and small bells hanging from the ceiling, and a back room, where the psychic sat at a table behind a velvet curtain. We went once. I was scared. I was terrified of her saying something awful and true, even though Khaki told me all they ever say is bullshit.

She's going to tell you something stupid, she said to me. Like, *You will see many places.* Or, *You will influence children.* She put on a fake European accent, deep and sexy, and I laughed.

She rolled her eyes. It was Memorial Day weekend, and the midway was busy with out-of-towners and their kids. We were off from school for four days; it was hot already. We padded down the pavement in flip-flops, her, almost sixteen, in white shorts that ended where her ass did. Me, twelve. I looked older in some ways, the worst ways, the kind that got extra looks from men. My body was enough to get leers on the midway. Guys who wanted you to go in the haunted house with them, or on the roller coaster, or who offered you a ride in their car to get you a pack of Four Loko at the gas station.

Khaki handed the guy outside the psychic's shack a ten-dollar bill. He sat on a metal chair in gray-blue mechanic pants and work boots, a white T-shirt. He slumped a little, with his arms folded over his belly. His hair, slicked back in ripples that were sandy gray.

Inside the door, I slipped my hand into hers. When the psychic moved the curtain aside, she said, What is this, a two-for-one deal? But she smiled at us. Come in, girls, she said.

She wore a long sleeveless dress and a band around her long red hair that went over her forehead like a crown. Strings of beads, a silver ring on every finger. She sat at a card table, on another folding chair. There was one chair on the customer side, and she had us sit one at a time.

I went first. She held my hand, palm up, traced her fingers over the skin like she was drawing off water.

Well, she said. She looked at my left hand and then my right. You have a long ways to go, she said. But it will be worth it.

I remember thinking, *Isn't that always the case? Like, isn't that just fucking life?*

She turned my hand over, looked at the side, and at the heel, where the lines disappeared into my wrist.

You'll meet a stranger, she said.

Everyone you meet for the first time is a stranger, Khaki said. She had her arms folded over her chest, stood looking at a hanging string of copper bells, tied with different colored ribbons.

Well, the psychic said slowly, this one is different. She winked at me. This one's a man.

Khaki snorted. Don't get into a car with a strange man, Rainy, she said.

Why don't you sit down, she said to Khaki.

My hands were slender and long. I wore a thin-banded opal ring on my middle finger. My nails weren't painted, just long and shaped, rounded on the edges.

Not Khaki. She never wore her nails long, and her hands were like hard squares. Her palms were broad and her fingers short and strong. She had hands that looked like they could take you apart. Often, she had them balled into fists.

The psychic held them, palm up, the way she had with mine, and she traced over them lightly, the same way.

You're a hard worker, she said to Khaki.

You think? she said. Then, I'm just a girl with big hands.

I watched over Khaki's shoulder while the psychic traced triangles on her palm.

Maybe you should read me, she said to Khaki.

Maybe. Khaki took her hands away.

You're going to break a lot of hearts, she said.

That's my fortune? Thanks, Khaki said.

Outside, in the sun, the barker in front of the games was calling to us. One shot, he said, holding a basketball. One basket and you win, he said.

Why did she say that? I asked. That you should read her?

Khaki snorted. She put her white sunglasses back on, lit a cigarette. She's just a dyke who wants my big hands up her twat, she said.

I tried to laugh. How do you know? I said.

How do I know she wants me? Khaki said. Oh Rayelle. No, I said, that she's . . .

A dyke? Oh Rayelle, she said again. I watched a clean straight line of smoke come out her nose. Her shoulders, square and brown in the sun. It takes one to know one, she said to me.

But she left with a man. She was the one who got in the car, not with a stranger, but with a man she knew, and left home.

And then, ten years later, I did the same.

Denis, Couper says, it's good to see you in person. Couper shakes hands with him, but Denis just looks at me.

This is my assistant, Couper says, Rayelle Reed.

Denis says hello, but doesn't shake my hand. He looks at me, looks away, looks at Couper, at the floor, anywhere he doesn't have to look dead on at me. Then finally he stands directly in front of Couper, his hand on Couper's elbow.

Likewise, he says to Couper. He flicks an eyebrow, flirty.

They sit on the couch with a glass coffee table in front of them and I watch while Couper lays out pictures and a blank sheet of paper, one at a time, like he's the one telling fortunes with cards.

I'm down to eight girls, Couper says. Holly. Alyssa. Jessa. Florida. Caitlin. Denise. Elizabeth. Haylee.

Plus this one, Couper says, and then glances at me before he lays down a picture of Khaki.

And there she is, her face, after all this time. She's a kid, maybe fifteen, probably the last school picture taken. The background, hot pink and striped. Her hair, with bangs that year, angled across her forehead, the tips of her hair to a point above her collarbone.

Where did you find that? I say.

On file at the school, he says.

Jesus, I think. Who knows what else he's found. She's not, I say, and Couper shushes me.

She's not dead, I think. She can't be. I could kick him for shushing me.

Haylee, Denis says, moving one picture out, has not been found yet?

Right, Couper says.

Haylee, a round-faced kid with pigtails, in a flowered tank top and a jean skirt. Like many of them, the picture is grainy, cropped, and zoomed in from some other shot, the features in the face lost in a bad reproduction.

Holly, from the posters in town, a picture in her own front yard in South Lake, holding the handlebars of her bike.

Alyssa, before and after.

Jessa, with the baby.

Florida, a sheet of paper with only the word typed in the middle.

Caitlin, a big-boned blonde, standing beside a pickup truck.

Denise, with a butch haircut and a leather jacket.

Elizabeth, from her college ID card. Small with light brown hair to her shoulders, wearing a smile that is shy, the kind of look that hides everything else.

The ruling for Florida, Couper says, is suicide. He rubs the back of his head. It was a stretch, he admits, including her. I thought it might fit the pattern of the others.

It's not the same, Denis says. He slides the piece of paper around to the front. The feeling I get from her, he says, isn't like the others. It's a different violence, a different sadness. Deeper, farther away. Neither does this one, he says, and takes out Khaki's photo. These, he says, moving Caitlin's picture forward, are immediate. Swift. Crushing. He pushes Haylee, still undiscovered, to the end of the line.

The others? Denis asks, That you took out?

Recently solved, Couper says, and isolated.

How many did you start with? I ask.

Twelve, Couper says.

Who is this? Denis says about Khaki.

Kathleen Reed, Couper answers. She left South Lake around the same time Holly disappeared, Couper says. Not exactly a runaway, but close.

Related? Denis says. He holds the picture up, peering into her face.

We're cousins, I say.

I look at Couper, who doesn't return my look, even though I'm boring into his head with my stare. I refuse to believe any of it. I don't believe Denis can possibly discern anything from just her picture.

They didn't find all of Florida, Couper says.

Are there pictures? Denis says.

You don't want to see the pictures. Her legs were gone, Couper says. The body, in the ocean for days. But there was no sign of trauma to the neck or the skull the way the others showed.

Haylee is still living, Denis says, pointing. He doesn't ask. He declares.

She's only fifteen, Couper says. Her sister made the call.

How do you know any of this is related? I say. Maybe she's just a runaway. Maybe she doesn't want to be found.

She is a runaway, Couper says. There's no evidence that she was taken. She ran from her sister's house.

Florida, he says, moving the paper, was also a runaway, according to her mother.

You think there's a man preying on runaway girls, I say.

Couper shrugs. It's not unlikely.

Holly Jasper wasn't a runaway, I say.

Nobody knows that.

She was nine years old, I say. And Jessa was twenty-six.

Are you saying grown women never run away? Couper says. He moves another picture. Caitlin was twenty-five, he says. Also with a baby.

Denis appears to labor with his breathing, out of breath like he's just come up the stairs, but he's sitting. I'm sorry to interrupt, Denis says. He holds his hands up, his eyes closed. He looks like he's giving a blessing.

What? Couper says.

Denis opens his eyes toward me. Could I talk with you? he says. Alone?

No, I say. The hairs on my arms tingle, all of them, like quills on a porcupine. I don't want to be read, I say. I stand up, ready to go out. I need a cigarette.

Just walk with me for a minute, Denis says. I'll show you the garden.

It's like the highway isn't even there. There's a tall fence, hiding it, but it's not even that. There are huge hollyhocks looming over your head and, looking down, roses, big bushes of something scrubby and purple, and paths of cut green grass that curve around with low flowers, pansies, snapdragons and marigolds and regular stuff and then all these other plants, tall and bright and waving in the breeze. There are bees and butterflies, the bees so big and heavy they barely take flight when they move from flower to flower. There's a pond and a little stone bench. Big goldfish circling in the water.

I can't smoke out here. It would be worse than smoking inside. All that fragrance and color. All that light. I stand still, and awkward, fidgeting.

Honey, Denis says, and when he touches my arm, it shocks me, not surprises, but like when you drag your feet on the carpet and then touch a doorknob. A crackle between us. In the dark, you would see the spark.

When he stands before me, he has to look up just a bit. I slouch out of habit, even with Couper. I've been compensating for everyone else's shortness my whole life.

Honey, he says again, gently, like he's afraid to startle me.

I remember, then, being in the front yard with Khaki when we were both little, maybe one of the first things I remember at all, at her house, not mine. Everything else blurs into one shitty kitchen.

Teddy and Doe lived out on Route 8 then, in an ugly little trailer that sat close to the road, and we played there in the grass, our hands and knees damp and stained, and Khaki wandered out, too close to the busy road. Teddy came up behind her, with that same gentle calling, not wanting to scare her, or startle her into running into traffic. She got down on her hands and knees too, crawling in the grass, creeping closer to Khaki, call-ing real soft, almost like she was trying to wake her up. She held a cookie out, crouched down beside the road while a truck went past, lifting up Khaki's hair like a fan blew under her chin. She was seconds, inches away from being dead, crushed by a tractor trailer.

Denis lays his fingers on my wrist bone. Beside him, a line of roses that are doubled, white and red, their heads so big and full of petals they don't even look like roses. I feel like I'm splitting open, like the shock he gave me is my skin breaking apart, that light is coming out of me, or bees, flying out of my mouth. He holds my hand.

You have, he says, slowly, closing his eyes. Quite a shadow. A sadness, he says, clinging to you.

No shit, I think.

I need you to work hard at moving away from that darkness, he says.

That's hard to do, I say. *Plus*, I think, *I'm here, I am moving. Moving is all I've been doing.*

He takes both my hands, and from far away, we probably look like we're getting married, standing in the garden, facing each other, saying our vows.

I'm worried, Denis says.

Don't be, I say. It's like I'm talking to Chuck. Like I'm being scolded for my lifestyle, my late-drinking, fucking-around lifestyle.

He seems to listen, his head cocked slightly, his eyes closing again. I'm afraid you're in danger, he says to me.

With Couper? I ask.

Oh, God no, Denis says. I've known Couper for years, he says. Couper Gale wouldn't hurt a fly. He might break your heart, he says, and laughs, but not before he tries to marry you. The way he laughs, warm and open, makes me wonder what else he knows about Couper. *Not before he tries to marry you.*

Then, It could be you, Denis says. In there, with those girls.

I shrug. I guess. What am I, but another woman running away, another woman taking up with someone who looks like he cares for her, looking for something else to hold on to, to move her away from what hurt her. I try to imagine the older ones, Jessa, Caitlin, hoping for something better than a baby and a man who hits you, and turning up in pieces on the bank of a river.

Summer, he says. Is Summer your sister?

Shut up, I say.

He smirks a little. Is she?

No. I yank my hands away.

Honey, he says, Rayelle, and reaches my arms before I back away from him to run.

Who is Summer?

That's it, I say. We stand there like a V, me pulling away from him, and him desperate to hold on. That's the dark cloud over my head, I tell him. The dangerous black hole I could fall into.

No, he says. No. Not at all. He lets go then and moves his hands round the side of my head, past my shoulders and down to my hips, like he's pulling something off, like you would pull someone out of netting, someone who has gotten caught in a web.

She's okay, he says to me.

Please stop talking.

Honey, no, he says. You're not hearing me.

She's not the darkness, I repeat, barely able to contain what wants to wail out of me. I'm ready to crumple onto the ground, next to the pond, to put my face underwater, and breathe.

Summer? No, he says. She's the light in your heart.

He leaves me out there, and goes back in to confer with Couper again. I stay in the garden. There are short Japanese maples along the fence, their leaves fanned out like hands, soft and feathery. I sit on the bench by the pond with the goldfish. There are mounds of gravel pebbles around the pool, banking it. Tiny gray balls, perfectly round, like what you would put at the bottom of your fish tank, but gray instead of electric blue or hot pink. I pick one up in my hand and let it roll around like a pea. Then I get down on my knees, heavy, all at once, sinking to the earth, and I pick up the stones, by the handful, sifting. I let them drop through my fingers, cold and smooth, and I dump them, as many as I can pick up, as many as I can sift from my hands into the water, filling up the pool, giving the goldfish nowhere to go, no water left to swim in.

Inside, Couper is scribbling from one page to another in his flip-top notepad and Denis is in a galley kitchen off the living room, making tea. The photos are put away, and when Couper finishes, pausing to look up at the ceiling, and adding a few more lines, he closes the notebook with a flap and slides it into the file he'd brought in.

Denis brings out teacups on a tray, each one old and delicate, the tea in a ball that opens into a spiky flower as the water darkens. Mine tastes like clover, grassy and sweet. Denis sits on the couch next to Couper and runs his hand over his shoulder. He traces his fingers in a circle.

What's this? Denis says.

Couper shrugs. Cotton? he says. He wears a military-style shirt, faded brown, soft.

No, Denis says, laughing. What happened here? I watch the movement of his wrist tendons, his fingertips circling. I picture his middle finger in a divot in Couper's back, but can't think of one, can't remember noticing anything there.

Couper's eyes go wide with wonder. He answers Denis like he can't believe the words are leaving his mouth.

That's where I got shot, he says.

What's left of the scar is just a wink. A tiny closed eyelid, or a dent from a fingernail, curved into the flesh of his shoulder blade. It's less of a divot than I'd imagined when I watched the way Denis probed it. I sit with my legs around Couper, his shirt off, my fingers, my lips, tracing his skin.

It's old, Couper says. Like the rest of me.

Does it hurt?

No. I forget about it most of the time.

I comb my fingers over the back of his head, by his ear. All the hairs at the edge gray, and the gray creeping into the darker hair on top. From the edges in, the way paper burns.

How'd you get yourself shot? I say, and lean, my lips meeting the smiling scar.

I was young and stupid, Couper says. And in over my head.

I hear his phone, its familiar burble of notes, and he turns it over, looks, and turns it back without answering.

A girl? I say.

Nope. He shakes his head and I feel the movement all the way down his big torso. The same way I always get myself into trouble, he says. Writing a story.

We park that night in a Walmart parking lot outside of Greenville. The lights stay on all night. The store is open all night, and the sound of cars, carts banging together, the downshift of tractor trailers pulling in, is constant. I want to ask him why he included Khaki, if he really thinks that she's connected, that she could be missing, in pieces in the woods or sunk into a lake, the ocean somewhere.

But it's late. Past midnight. Couper says, No more work tonight. Instead, he asks me about Summer.

You can say the unspeakable into the dark, even when that dark is interrupted by a streetlight, by head-lights circling the parking lot. In a daylit garden filled with sunshine and flowers, the truth is too bright.

He runs his fingers up and down the grooves in my belly, the lines, vertical, but connected at the tops and bottoms. He goes from one to the next without having to jump, a whole highway of scar tissue, all the places where my skin tried to bust open but didn't; it never broke at all, it only stretched.

It took days, I say. It wasn't, like, all at once and she was gone. They thought she would be okay, I say. But they couldn't get all the water out.

Like having pneumonia, he says.

I guess. They called it delayed, I say. Delayed drowning.

No one ever said it then. The doctor said it once, and then all the other people you have to talk to, the cops, a social worker, a funeral home director, neighbors, it's all just *sorry sorry sorry* until it means nothing. It's just people talking at you, words bouncing off you while you move like a robot and wish it were you, yourself, filled up with water and dying. Not a baby. Not your daughter.

The little metal fan rattles on the counter inside the Scamp. I wonder how long the batteries will last.

When? Couper says.

Last year, I say. Summer. I say it in my head. Last summer. The summer before. This is the summer after. There's next summer, and all the summers before that one.

It's pretty, he says. Summer.

I named her that because I loved it, I say. And she was born in a cold snap, in January.

Dead trees in the yard and gray frosted grass, and I was trying like hell to convince myself that the cold wouldn't last, trying to project myself forward, one summer at a time.

Couper dips his finger from one line to the next, this one a long one that hooks up around my belly button. It's deeper, and wider, than the rest. My knees shake.

Where were you? he says.

I was right there, I say. In the backyard.

I can feel the edge of the lawn chair in the backs of my knees. Smell the hose water and the cut grass. The azaleas along the back fence, hot, burning pink against white pickets.

Let's go, Couper says.

Right now? What time is it?

He looks at the phone. There are two missed calls. Almost four, he says. When he opens the curtains, the sky is still dark, still heavy, but lit by all the surrounding homes, the glow from the Walmart sign, the McDonald's, the tall, bright, boxed lights of the parking lot. I don't know how long I can keep this up, staying up all night, driving during the day, sleeping in the passenger seat beside him, interviewing, searching.

Couper says, There's a great barbecue joint about six hours from here, closer to where we're going. They open early.

You've driven this route before? I say.

Many times, he says.

twelve

KHAKI

I've seen reporters. Investigators. Cops. Some are better than others. In Sunbright, in the fall, I let a special investigator into my kitchen. I lived way out on a back road, a house that was mostly kitchen and porch with upstairs bedrooms and a cellar you could reach only from the outside. I was one of the few people short enough to stand upright in it. I'd grown my hair to my chin, dyed it a shining chestnut brown, and had gotten a dog. A big female German shepherd who had a purebred litter before I got her fixed. I sold them all for $1,500 apiece. Eight of them. The mother, mostly black, smaller than the big-footed tan male I mated her to. I named her Juneau.

The investigator said they'd found human remains. Most of a foot, he said, the long bones dug into the dirt, the round ball of an ankle.

A dog found them, he said, like this one, holding his hand out to Juneau, who rumbled a low growl at him. Near the riverbank, he said.

I kept Juneau tight at my side. She was smart and well trained, would sit still and wait, alert, until I told her to do otherwise. She didn't like men in or near the house, especially if they touched the property in any way. A mailman. A meter reader. An electrician. She could stare a man down.

I lived near enough the river. I had a reputation, if you asked the right people, for kindness.

You sometimes let strangers into your home, Miss . . . White? he asked me. He was a type. A balding, older guy who was tall and thin and had a bass voice. He wore regular clothes, plain-front tan pants and a button-down shirt with a vest, not a cop's uniform. But he carried a badge. And a gun, close on his hip. He probably had a wife he'd been married to a long time. A high school sweetheart even. Might have had a daughter he doted on. That guy.

When I didn't answer him quickly, Juneau growled louder. I stroked her soft head. Did someone tell you that? I asked him.

I heard you would not turn away someone in need, he said.

I let women in, I said. A woman who needs a place to stay, who's in trouble. Who needs shelter, I said. Sure.

Not men, he said.

I turned my body to face him, my hands out at my sides, emphasizing my stature. Me? I said. Alone? No.

I went to the stove and poured him coffee that I'd made in a percolator, which he drank with honey. A Southern thing I never caught on to. I liked my coffee strong, and black.

When did you start providing this service? he said.

I didn't set out to provide anything, I said. I just let a friend stay. And then another. That's not a service. I lowered my chin, raised my eyes, smiled gently at him. That's just how I was raised.

Lies, and not.

He had a picture of a missing Kentucky woman. Caitlin Rogers. She stood by a pickup truck with her hair in a long blond ponytail, her husband's hand on her forearm, guiding, holding her in place.

The same hand he would lay on her cunt and then tell her to hold still.

Montana.

She was thin in the picture. None of the weight of a baby in her hips, in her chest, yet. Her arms, long and slender.

I took the photo and held it, looked at her face, small with all that scenery around it. I remembered her face when she was in my arms, and again, looking up at the trees, blood leaking in the whites of her eyes as her windpipe crushed against bone under the garrote. Her face swollen and bruised when I held her by the temples and dipped her head in the river.

Have you ever seen this woman? he asked me.

No.

This woman did not stay here? he said.

No.

Who was the last woman to stay here?

Not Caitlin Rogers, I said. And not from Kentucky.

What was her name?

Do you need to know? I said.

He sipped the coffee, still cooling, in one of the handmade brown pottery mugs I'd gotten at a natural foods store miles away. They'd hung in the window of the shop, made by a local artist, each one different. Each one signed.

Her name was Jessica, I said. She was from Montana.

Her name felt cold on my lips. Montana. Cold, like river water.

Where was she headed? he asked me.

To see her mother, I said. In . . . I stumbled. Florida.

Her name cracked my voice.

Florida, he repeated. I hated to hear anyone else say it. I hated her name coming out of a man's mouth. I wanted to be the only one to say it. The only one to taste those letters, in that order. They tasted like honey and sweet corn when it bursts milk onto your tongue, buttered and hot in late summer.

Do you know if she got there? he said.

This is not her, I said. Jessica is small, like me, I said, and dark haired.

He shrugged. Do you know if Jessica made it to Florida? he said again.

No.

No she didn't?

No, I don't know.

He sipped, and then shuffled his feet in work boots under the table.

You cared enough to take her in, he said, but you don't know if she arrived there safely?

She wasn't my friend, I said. She was a friend's friend. So no. I leaned against the counter with the sink behind me, the faucet tapping a slow drip into the enamel. I crossed my arms. Sometimes, I said, a woman needs anonymity.

Sometimes we all do, he said. He slid the picture of Caitlin Rogers back into a manila envelope and thanked me for the coffee.

It's hard to find someone, he said, who makes a good-tasting cup of coffee. I'd put grounds and a bit of cinnamon, a dash of nutmeg on top to flavor it. He nodded at the percolator. But you sure do, he said.

Anytime, I said.

Well, I hope we are no longer strangers, he said.

But he never came again. I left there within weeks, and moved on to another river town, where I met Carolina, small as a mouse, underfed, misunderstood. I fed her down-home meals in a trailer kitchen, the kind of food they didn't feed her at college. She stayed the winter and I wrapped her in fur, her body blue with cold, crushed with ice.

thirteen

RAYELLE

The barbecue joint is called Hiram's. It's a lean-to shack with picnic tables outside, in the parking lot, under the trees, along a grassy edge of the road. People arrive at ten in the morning, and the smoke curls over the highway, sweet-smelling with hickory and spice. The air is heavy, hot and humid, with no breeze except what blows your skirt when a truck goes by. Couper ducks his head at the screened-in window, and a guy at the back with an apron and a spatula comes up when he sees him.

Man, you did come back, he says.

I told you, Couper says. Then, Give me a sweetheart deal, he says. He winks at me over his shoulder.

Uh-huh, the cook says. He scribbles it down on a pad. And how's your sweetheart doing? he asks. He cranes his head to where he can see me standing just behind Couper.

Oh, Couper says. Different sweetheart, he says.

I got you, man. The cook belly-laughs and heads to the back, repeating, Man, I got you.

Different sweetheart, I say, at a picnic table under a pine tree. It's sticky in spots and you have to be careful where you sit, or you'll end up with sap on your clothes.

I've been here before, Couper says.

I heard, I say.

A girl about twelve brings us a pitcher of sweet tea and tall glasses. She wears glasses and her legs, not far off the color of the tea, have that teenage wobble in the knee, a looseness in all her joints that will take her years to grow out of.

If she ever does.

I'm tired, and I feel a fight brewing. I'm about to rail on Couper for bringing me back to a haunt he's been to before with some other woman. Even though I have no claim on him. I'm just a blip in his fifty-something years of sweethearting around the country. Still. It burns me.

And then he says, Tell me. Were you drunk?

When? I say. There are so many yeses: the night we met, the day we left town. Last night.

When the baby died.

More cars come in behind us, crunching on the dirt and gravel parking lot, kicking up dust. I watch the teenage waitress bring a tray of ribs to another table.

Who gave you that idea? I say.

You did.

I never said that.

You didn't have to, he says.

No, I answer. I wasn't. When she died, I was in the hospital. It was nine in the goddamn morning. I wasn't drunk.

When she drowned, Couper says.

What, are you on to your next investigation? I say. It was settled, I say. There were no charges. And fuck you for asking, I add.

That doesn't make it settled, he says. You know that.

The girl comes to us next, carrying a tray with a full rack of ribs, a red-and-white paper carton of beans, and one of coleslaw. Between them, a hunk of corn bread. She lays down a stack of napkins and two square Wet-Naps.

Enjoy, she says in a tiny, tinny voice.

Couper eyes me over the food, waiting. Mouth watering, for ribs, for information.

I was drinking, I say. I wasn't drunk. I was sitting in the sun with her, I say. I just. I just put my head back, I say. And it all comes rumbling out of me. For a second. Just a second. I hold up my fingers like a little pinch. And in those couple of seconds, I say, she made her way over the side of the kiddie pool by herself. She fell in on her face. And I got her, I say. I got her out. In seconds.

You passed out, he says. He takes a knife and slices through the rack, pulling away pieces for himself, sucking on the sweet sauce.

I wasn't passed out, I say. I closed my eyes in the sun. While drinking, he says.

I could punch him right in the throat.

Or myself. When I moved into my mom's, that August, I went through a hair-pulling phase. I'd lie on my old bed, weave my hands into my hair, and pull as hard as I could, till my eyes teared, till my scalp burned. It was the only way I could manifest the pain. The only way I could give some shape to what was raging inside me, but it could have been anything. I could have clawed my own eyes out. Gashed my own wrists.

Summer was pissed. Her face full of water, the longest parts of her hair, on top, hanging down, dripping in her eyes. She coughed and spat and screamed. I pulled her out of the water by her arm, and jounced her around, her bottom full and heavy anyway. We went inside, into the cool back bedroom, and I changed her diaper, put her in a fresh cotton dress, and she was okay. She had a bottle, and then I put her down. She was sleepy from an afternoon outside, from a good cry.

I'd left the drink out there, on the arm of the lawn chair, sweating in the sun, the ice melted down so the whiskey was just a light, clear gold. I knew June Carol was on her way over before Eli came home. Coming with a pan of scalloped potatoes and ham. *Shit*, I thought. I looked in on Summer sleeping, flat on her back, her arms out, her legs fat and curved. *I'm going to quit*, I thought. I clenched my hands into fists. *Tonight.* When I noticed the glass, the evidence, sitting in the sun,

I rushed out and grabbed it, washed it out, and brushed my teeth.

Couper's phone, on the table, goes off, vibrating the wood. He looks, and ignores.

When did you take her to the doctor? he says.

In the morning. And then I give him the same rundown I'd memorized for the nurses, the doctor, for the cops, the social worker, everyone who asked.

I checked on her twice, I say, and both times, she was sleeping.

I pick at a corner of the corn bread, hungry, but disgusted by eating. The bread is sweet, though, like honey, and has whole kernels of corn in it.

You know what they say about sweet corn bread, Couper says.

No. What?

Made by a woman in love.

No one says that, I say.

He shrugs. What happened in the morning? he asks.

She usually got up early, five or six, I say, but for whatever reason, we both slept in. Eli got up, and went to work, and neither of us woke up until like nine. When I went in to get her, she was up on her knees, rocking and coughing. There was a strange sound coming from her chest, I say. Deep and rough, and she was spitting up this stuff that looked like foam. Like soap suds.

Did they admit her right away? Couper says.

They sedated her, I say, and kept her under for two days to see if they could clear the water from her lungs.

I went without June Carol, left before she came over, called my own mother and left a message, called Eli at work and left word that we were at the hospital.

We went in on a Tuesday. She was gone on Thursday. She was born on a Thursday. So was I. My mother always said Thursday's child has far to go. I sat out there in the hallway, outside her room, going nowhere at all, shaking from not sleeping, not drinking, while the nurses shuffled around me, waiting for my mother to come. Nine o'clock is pretty early for her.

What's it to you? I ask, sour. I watch him work all the meat and sauce off a long rib bone, lay it clean on the tray between us.

Sweetheart, he says. It's everything to me.

Don't lie to me, I say.

I'm not, he says. I never have.

Who were you here with? I say. Which sweetheart am I?

I was here with my wife, he says.

He has never said anything to me about anyone.

Are you still married? I ask. He doesn't wear a ring, but some guys don't. Eli's father thought rings were embellishments for ladies, were just a way that you secured your investment on the woman who would raise your babies for you, who would stand by your side through life.

It takes him a long time to answer. I pour more tea. I take a rib for myself. They are sweet and so tender the bone is pink and the meat comes right off.

No, he says.

Are you sure? I say. It sure took you a long time to answer.

I have a separation agreement, he says.

But you're not divorced.

His eyes watch the road behind me. The dark eye moves at its own pace, not quite in sync with the blue one. Not yet, he says.

Then he leans back, his tongue working bits of meat out of his teeth. He opens his chest, friendly, the way a dog rolls over and completely trusts you not to stab it, not to gut it open in the sun. His mouth is relaxed, not clenched, not turned in. He licks at the corner of his lip.

How did it end? I ask.

Which time? he says.

The teenage waitress comes back, replaces our pitcher of tea, and asks if she can get us anything else.

No, thanks, Couper says.

The cold of the new tea goes right to the center of my forehead like someone placed an icy quarter there.

How many times have you been married? I say. I press into my brow, rubbing away the cold. By now, a pile of clean white bones lies between us.

Four times, Couper says. Then, You're sweetheart number five.

We are in the car already, full, and sleepy in the hot sun of midday, before I think to ask him.

Wait, I say. Do you have kids? I think that if he does, they could be older than me.

No, he says. His lips fold in, his mouth closed and heavy. I watch him watch the road up ahead, not ready to pull out, not ready to drive. I let it go.

We're at a different KOA when he tells me about the pattern of twos. That that's the reason he pulled what information he could on Khaki and included her picture for Denis. That more than once, there have been two at a time. Alyssa, and then Jessa. Holly, and then Khaki. That Elizabeth, the college freshman, and Denise, a landscaper, went missing the same weekend. When they found Denise, he says, they found only her head.

Which is all they need, he says.

What about Elizabeth? I say.

She was hit by a car.

That's not murder, I say.

He looks at me a long time over the table in the Scamp. We're set up; it's early in the afternoon. Between us, an open bottle of Evan Williams, glasses of ice.

It could be? I say, grasping. That's a weird, ineffective way to kill someone, I say. Did they find the car? I say. A car with blood on it? Damage?

Nope, he says. Then, It was the middle of winter.

He takes one shot neat, and then fills a rocks glass for him and another for me.

What I wonder, he says, is if she was running.

Away? I ask.

No, he says, from the killer. When she got hit. Odd, he says, and the ice clinks in the glass when he puts it

down. She was wearing a fur coat. But naked underneath. Middle of the night.

That is odd, I say. Were they found close together?

Yep, he says. Mostly, I've only seen Couper drink beer,
but when he drinks whiskey, he drinks faster than I do,
and I can't keep up.

Near here? I say.

Thirty miles.

I hear his phone, and when he picks it up to check
the number, he stands, his head brushing the ceiling of
the Scamp.

I have to take this, he says to me. And then he goes
outside.

I should be paying attention, I think, to the phone
calls, to what he's saying. But with the whiskey warm
in my belly, all I want to do is lay my head down, close
my eyes.

When we drive to Sugarwood, I have a whiskey hangover,
my head sweet and cottony, my eyes red and my mouth
dry. Couper rallies on like a goddamn rock star though.

Early in the morning, a thunderstorm rolls through,
pelting the sides of the Scamp with pinecones, rocking
us with wind. But by the time we leave, the sky is clear,
the grass shining and wet, everything a lit, light gold.

Far off the highway, hills, looming and blue, heavy
in the hazy sunlight. Mostly, though, it's farms and run-
down houses, weathered and gray. I bet inside, a pot of
ramen noodles or mac and cheese, a thirty rack of cheap

beer and Indian cigarettes. Outside, porches slant toward front lawns of just dirt, where dogs lie in the shade, and rusted trucks or cars sit up on blocks. Cheap plastic furniture, a barbecue pit. A swing made from a tire. A kiddie pool.

We drive for an hour, even though I thought he said it was only thirty miles, me, sleepy, staring out the window, the air so heavy and warm it seems like time moves more slowly. I count porch dogs and flags, regular and Confederate, flower beds made out of truck tires, cemeteries, until we stop in a little town with a gas station called Fina. You can buy nightcrawlers out of a vending machine like cans of Coke, and the vending machine that does have soda is filled with shapely glass bottles of RC and Fanta.

Couper pumps eighty dollars of gas into the Gran Torino and then goes inside to pay with his credit card.

I wait, my body slumped, my head on my hand, my elbow out the open window.

He parks the car and the Scamp along the curb next to a village green where there's nothing but a sidewalk that cuts through, and what looks like a sundial or a birdbath in the middle. There's a tiny flag at the foot of it, the kind you buy at a dollar store and stick into someone's grave, your grandpa's or an uncle's, someone who served in a war, where sometimes there's a little metal medallion on a stake, marking the grave as belonging to someone who sacrificed something. For everyone else, all the regular people, you leave flowers and crosses.

Little lambs made of plaster. They fade in the sun and rain. Their fleece goes from white to gray. Their blue eyes washed away, only mounds left where the bright irises were.

We cross the street to a diner in the front room of an old house. There are four tables in there, blue-checkered curtains over the bottom halves of the windows, dark paneling and a counter with stools and a domed cake plate with sugared donuts on a doily. All said, you could fit about twenty-five people in there. My first job was in a place like this, in South Lake. We made sandwiches and soup. Had meatloaf on Wednesdays and meatloaf sandwiches on Thursdays.

We order sandwiches, ham and turkey, and Couper asks if the coffee is fresh.

Just made it, the waitress says.

I look at the pot behind the counter. I don't think she's lying. It's full, and not murky, and steaming. My mother went through a phase of always sending coffee back, no matter where we were. She'd order, and then send it back, and ask them to make a whole new pot for her. It made me want to crawl under the table and hide. Chuck too.

Couper looks sideways out the window. It's full of dust and cobwebs, the glass milky in the sunlight. I notice his eye has a streak of red that goes from the outer corner right up to the iris, fanning out when it hits the blue.

How far out is Sugarwood Mobile Park? Couper asks the waitress.

She turns our cups over on the paper place mats. They're lined with the names of local businesses. Rexall. McDougall Funeral Home. Jones Excavating.

It's not far out of town, she says, slow. She's about my age, maybe even younger, and real round in the hips like she's had some babies, even though her face is smooth and rosy, with teenage fat like she's still a baby herself. I wonder where her kids are.

This way? Couper thumbs behind him, the way the Scamp is headed.

Right down this way, she says. Her voice has an open yawl that is more rural than people had in Summersville. You don't even have to change roads, she says.

How long?

She shrugs a soft shoulder. Twenty, twenty-five minutes. Depends if the train is coming, she says.

Our sandwiches come on mismatched plates, mine heavy and white with a gold edge, and Couper's a finer white with blue flowers in the middle. I eat all my potato chips first, like a deer at a salt lick. It'll make me feel like shit later, waterlogged and thirsty. The waitress keeps busy behind the counter, filling saltshakers, wiping down the counter, even the tops of the stools. There's a cook in the back, a young guy in a baseball cap, and I wonder if they're a couple, if he's the owner, or the owner's son, and what that's like. How other people work. If her mother-in-law takes care of the babies for her. If she shames her for drinking or smoking, or not looking after the baby when she goes crawling toward the river out back.

Couper's halfway through his sandwich when he takes out his notepad and says, I'm going to say some names for you.

Okay, I say. And what?

Tell me if they seem familiar at all. Jackson McGraw, he says.

Never heard of him.

He was found dead behind a Dollar General in Carolina Beach.

A guy, I say.

Yes. He was shot, Couper says, but his throat had also been cut. Small-time drug dealer. Had a record. Nothing too crazy.

When? I say.

Six years ago.

Why is that significant?

He was married to a woman named Cora DeLaurentis, he says, who had a daughter, Florida.

I think of what I know. She was fourteen, which I imagine as small, a kid still. None of the strength required to kill a man, even one who has been mean to you. But I ask anyway, Do you think Florida killed her stepdad? And then killed herself?

I don't know, Couper says. I guess it's possible.

I thought Florida was out of this, I say.

I can't let her go, he says.

When the waitress comes back, she takes our empty plates and offers us dessert, something for the road, maybe? But then she just leaves the paper check, her handwriting big and round, like her eyes, her cheeks.

Couper leaves a twenty on the table, even though the bill is only about ten dollars.

Maybe it's me, slow in the limbs today from a night of drinking, a morning of driving, but Sugarwood is sleepy. Outside, there's no movement. There are no cars in and out of the Fina, no kids on bikes, no mail truck. We walk down to a Rexall on the corner. The door opens on the diagonal above a set of brick steps, the angle of the building lobbed off. There are things in the windows, a Styrofoam cooler, some suntan lotion, a tinfoil pinwheel, and a beach ball. They look like they've been there thirty years.

Couper says another name to me: Jessica Stark.

Nope.

Melissa White.

No.

Ashley Dunn?

No. Jesus, Couper, I say. Are there more girls?

No, he says.

Who are these women?

Jordan McCollough, he says.

Was Jessa's friend.

Yes. There's frequently a friend, he says. I'm having a hard time locating the friend. She seems to move on, out of town, take a different job, and then I can't find her.

Are they fake names? I say.

I don't know, he says.

Why would you pick such a normal, ugly name? Melissa White? I say. That could be anyone.

Exactly, he says.

We always played games with different names. We played house, and then we played school, and then we played club, which we would do only when Khaki's parents weren't around, in the kitchen, with the bar behind us, the beer light lit, the clock with its bubbles in the face, like champagne. Sometimes I'd be a cabaret singer, sitting on the bar with my legs crossed, lip-synching to Shania Twain, while Khaki, in a suit jacket, lit a cigarette and pretended to count money at the glass table.

I always picked a good name. Victoria Lee. Violet Paisley. Rainy Day Blues.

Khaki would go for the butch names, names that were hard and sexy. Shawn. Gray. Carson.

When the game was good, I was her girl, and she managed me with a hard hand. Sometimes, there were other customers, played by her, guys who came in to hit on me, guys who drank a lot. Guys who kissed sloppy and tasted like vodka.

Shawn wore her hair back in a newsboy cap. Black trousers with heels and a blazer, often without a shirt. She could save poor old Rainy Day Blues from the meanest of men. Whisk her out of that shitty honky-tonk bar to her own white bedroom, for a soft bed, and a sweet drink. A kiss on the neck, or lower. She took care of me good.

Couper says, You ever get a feeling about a place?

This town looks like a movie set to me, like there's nothing behind the buildings, and if you did look back there, you'd see the fronts held up with two-by-fours. There's not much beyond the main street anyway, a few backyards, most of them not even fenced, and then fields. Way back, the railroad track. A river.

Sure, I say.

Like, you want to stay? Couper says.

I wouldn't go that far, I think. It's too dead. What would you do here? They must drink a lot, or beat their wives. Who knows what goes on in those silent houses. White and gray. Like a town of old people. One front step is covered in bright green indoor-outdoor carpet. In one driveway, an old Edsel, immaculate and eggshell white. Maybe everyone is dead. Maybe they read. But there isn't even a library.

Or maybe, Couper says, like you shouldn't leave it? His voice has a funny tentativeness to it. A waver. In the sun, I can see the crow's-feet gathered at the corners of his eyes, wrinkled up as he squints at me. Nothing in the town moves. I close my eyes. Listen. There are birds. The birdy bird, close by in a tree, or on the village green, calling *birdy birdy birdy*, and some magpies, cackling, farther back, behind the diner, picking at the trash. Nothing else. Not the sound of a sprinkler, the bell on a bicycle, the bark of a dog following a boy down the street. Couper takes out his pad and reads me an address. The motor kicks on in the air conditioner that is propped in a window above the Rexall, and water drips down onto the sidewalk.

Who are we looking for there? I ask.

Ashley Dunn, he says. The friend.

fourteen

KHAKI

You ever watch a kid come? See her face light up with surprise and then flush with pleasure? Men think it's not possible. Think it happens only when you're grown, when it's their dick inside you that makes you moan. Not true. I've done it loads of times.

Rayelle would get herself up on the bar in the kitchen. Our parents out for the evening, and us girls home alone. The house was a fucking morgue mixed with a bar. All dark and red, the lamps in the living room dim and amber or smoke, the one in the corner with a naked lady in the center and cords of dripping oil around her. I'd turn on music and Rayelle would hold an old broken karaoke mic and pretend to sing.

Her hair was still short then. Still growing back from the explosion she barely remembered. The backyard.

Nudie. Afterward, Rayelle's hair was littered with ash and bits of skin. For years after it was cut off, it was just a curly round mess on her head, not long enough to pull up. I'd put glittering barrettes in, flowers behind her ear, drape her in a low-cut top that exposed a flat plain of fat down the middle of her chest, nothing there yet of breasts, just a padding of flesh.

And then I'd slip into character. Shawn, with her hair combed back under a hat. I wore a jacket, cheap menswear that I'd bought at Ames, with nothing underneath. I liked the feel of my nipples against the lining of the blazer when I walked across the shag carpet in heels.

Why is Shawn a woman? Rayelle asked. Why isn't Shawn a man?

Because that's cooler, I said. There's nothing cool about one man coming in to harass you and another man coming to save you. That's lame.

I lit a cigarette. I knew that when I leaned over, my hand cupped around the flame, she could see my tits.

Because that's the truth about life, I told her, straightening up. It's the guys who fuck you over, I said, and your girls who save you.

Shawn, she'd say to me in bed, wriggling. Shawn, fuck me.

I don't know where she heard it. It wasn't from me.

I was thirteen and hard across the belly, along the hips and ass, even though my face was still round like a kid's.

My brother was dead.

My mother was dying.

I'd been pregnant once already, by my own dad.

I wrecked little Rainy Day Blues in bed because I liked to watch her face squinched closed and then opening up with a gasp, a pant, her cheeks red and her hairline sweaty. She clawed her hands into my hair, into my shoulders, into the small of my back.

After Georgia, no one ever topped me again.

I went to a bar called Layla's. It was a thing out there, a dyke bar in the country outside of Sugarwood, something everyone knew about and understood and let go. It wasn't advertised, you just knew. It looked like a general store, with a front porch where a hundred years ago men hitched their horses while they went in for goods. Now, the parking lot was filled with pickups and Jeeps.

I felt cocky. I felt alone. So I went out.

Days before, I had smashed Carolina's skull and torso with the hunk end of an icicle that had come from the roof of the post office. The porch of the rural post office sat close to the county highway. I swung and hit. And when she staggered into the road and a truck came, it looked like a hit-and-run. The icicle melted away to nothing in the morning sun. People were looking for the truck.

I had dressed her up in a fur coat and nothing else. Took her for a ride in my truck. Promised her a surprise. The coat, real rabbit from a consignment shop as far away as Soddy-Daisy. In the road, at night, staggering, she looked like an animal, like a deer. Looming. The speed limit there was forty-five. There wasn't a split second to stop.

Jesus Christ, said a woman at the bar. She was big-assed, with a red ponytail. She repeated what the reporters, the police had said, that the dead girl looked like an animal, in that fur coat. So small. She was just an itty-bitty thing.

College girls, the bartender said. They ought to teach them how to cross the road.

I asked for a vodka, neat.

Yes, ma'am, she said. The bartender, a tall blonde with a sleek ponytail and muscled shoulders, a freckled décolletage in a leather vest.

She was the sleekest-looking thing out there. These aren't city dykes. Even the straight women are less than dainty. There's a toughness to them, from working a farm, from raising four kids. Everyone with a coat of sun on her shoulders. A wrinkle in her eye from the wind.

The music was good and loud. The food, lousy deep-fried frozen stuff. Chicken tenders, mozzarella sticks, and fried mushrooms. There was beer on tap, and a full wall of liquor. All I wanted was vodka. And maybe a casual fling.

And then Georgia walked in.

She was tall, and broad in the chest and shoulders, with meaty arms. She had nearly black hair that was styled like a bob if she wore it in front of her ears, but she tucked it, giving her a boyish cuteness. Her eyes were bright green. Her eyebrows, expertly shaped.

She sat a bit before she said anything. Cracked peanuts and threw the shells on the floor. Drank a double bourbon with two cherries, ice. When she looked over at me, I was already looking at her.

You look like sunshine to me, she said.

I'd be your sunshine, I said.

What do I look like to you? she said.

You look like a Georgia to me, I said.

I mimicked their sound, their peculiar inland drawl, my voice higher in that strain, sweet, like honey.

Georgia! she said, and laughed. Her teeth were straight and white. Her lips, glossed clear.

I shrugged a little, lowered my chin, looked up at her. I like a girl with a state name, I said. You don't look like a Virginia.

I ain't been a Virginia in a long time, she said.

We sat kitty-corner at the bar, her feet on the rungs of my stool, for another drink. I listened to her mumble along with a Toby Keith song. Then she asked if I smoked.

Sure do, I said.

She had a pack of orange American Spirits and a big silver Ford F-150. We sat in the cab with the motor running, smoking through a crack in the window, softer, moodier music on the radio. It was January. Everyone said it was colder than it had been in years. It would warm up for a day and then dip right back below freezing, everything that had thawed out slicked over with ice in the moonlight.

You want a ride? Georgia said. Her eyes looked lit under the sign that said LAYLA'S.

Sure do, I said.

We drove through town, around the village green, past the Fina and the diner and the drugstore. It was dead. Past one in the morning. Not a soul moved. Outside of town, we parked at an empty baseball field, the moon shining down on the diamond. She left the truck running under the trees, for the radio, the heat.

We kissed and writhed in the front seat. The extended cab of the truck, bigger than most. I buried my hand in her jeans, digging with my hard hands.

I don't know why I didn't see it coming.

She had my pants off me, my shirt undone. Her face in my pussy, my feet up on the dash. And then she turned me around, my arms over the passenger seat, my face against the heated leather, and before I could catch my breath, she was way up inside, pumping away, fucking me with a dildo.

I didn't want to think it was great. I didn't want to throw my head back and yowl, my hips backing into hers. But I did. She caught me off my guard. Off my game.

Someone else might have stayed. Another woman might have been swept away by Georgia and her swagger, her truck. The cigarettes and the country music.

After, I smoked two of her cigarettes while she leaned back in the driver's seat, pushed away from the steering wheel, her pants still undone, her hair mussed and over her ears like a blunt bob. Like a silent movie star. With those eyes. Those lined, lovely green eyes.

I stroked her face. You're something else, I said. Her head tipped back under my touch.

No one ever expects me to be as strong as I am. For there to be that much power in my hands, big, blunt, wrapped around your neck.

I can strike too.

I rummaged in the toolbox in the bed of the truck, wearing Georgia's own gloves, heavy leather gloves meant for hard gardening, in thorns or brambles. In the box there were typical tools, a hammer, a ratchet set, screwdrivers, and pliers. At the bottom, I found what I was looking for. A seven-piece deer-processing kit with knives of varying sizes, the biggest, curved with a black plastic handle.

I took the whole kit into the front seat. The truck was still running. I pushed the driver's seat back even farther and perched on the edge of the seat, my cunt still sore from her.

I drove a long ways. Out that far, it's trees and ravines and river. I parked the truck, buried in thick brush at the bottom of a dirt road that led to the riverbank. I left it running with the windows closed, but it wouldn't look like a suicide.

Not after I took the head.

The river never freezes. Back home, the creeks we had would come close, the ice creeping out from the shore, leaving a soft middle, the sides of the creek thick and gray with ice.

The water was bone-aching cold, fast-moving. The edges of the river defined by the jutting of flat red rock, places to stand and fish, to lie naked on a hot summer day and brown your skin on a warm rock.

The head lodged. The way the rocks lean out over the water like a dock, things get snagged in them. Branches, leaves. Ducks and beavers build nests in the crevices.

I don't know how long it sat there. Who reported her missing. When they found the truck, or where they looked for the head, or when they discovered it, licked clean by fish and animals and rapid river water.

I took the processing kit.

And the dildo. I couldn't risk leaving it behind.

The trailer wasn't worth keeping. I'd sublet it for six months from a guy who was working construction. I gave him the name Ashley Dunn. He liked the idea of a couple of girls living there to keep it up while he built houses out of town. But the trailer was run-down when I moved in; wind blew in where the door wouldn't shut. All around us, when people moved, they left the trailers behind, empty, sinking. Outside the park, a circle of new houses, the sounds of bulldozers and nail guns. But I'd housed Carolina in that trailer for weeks over the winter break that she didn't want to go home for. She wouldn't tell me why. She didn't need to.

I laid my hands on her small, mousy head. Her skin said *dead* to me. Dead already. For years. I saw the thumbprints of brothers and cousins on her. She was broken inside, unhinged and hemorrhaging.

She slept in my bed, small, quiet, while I stroked her spine, her limbs.

When they found her in the road, wrapped in a rabbit-fur coat, bleeding out on the icy pavement, she looked like a small deer. Hit and left to die. Under the coat, her skin was rubbed clean, shaved smooth.

Some winters are worse than others.

fifteen

RAYELLE

I try to imagine who any of them might have been, before. A kid, abused by her dad, or her mom, even, running as fast as she could from the home that hurt her, and failed to protect her. A woman with a baby, living out in rural Indiana, with a husband who was rough on her, and not enough money to pay the bills each month. A woman misunderstood. A woman alone. A woman looking for company. For love. For recognition. I get it. I might have run too. And nearly did, more than once, in the middle of a blue-black night, leaving a screaming, colicky Summer in her rocker seat on the living room floor. I might have gotten in my car and just driven, crying, down a dark rural road toward something, who knew, that might have killed me. Might have left me in pieces on a riverbank, my head miles away, lodged in the water. Rinsed.

I think about their pictures, posed with babies, or beside a car. Alyssa's teenage face, blue already, mottled in death.

And Florida. She might haunt me the most. Just the word, typed in the middle of the page. Not a picture left of her. Just the word. Florida.

She sounds to me like a dark-haired beauty, the kind of hula girl you put on the dash of your car, who swivels her hips and dances. Flowers in her hair. Nothing on her feet. Her belly curved like a little fairy's.

On the way to Sugarwood Park, we hit a blank spot of straight, flat road where nothing goes past except one old wood-paneled station wagon. There's no phone service, no radio stations. Just miles of hot white concrete.

How do you know when you're on the right track? I ask Couper. With anything, I think. The girls, the story. Me.

I don't, he says. I watch the sun come through the trees, dappling his face. I love so much the way his eyes crinkle in the light, the way his mouth curves up in a smile. The way his cheeks go slack when he's sleeping. Sometimes, when I think about Eli, the guy I was with the longest, and the only guy I lived with, I can't remember a thing about his face, his smile, the way he smelled.

Sometimes I have to just see when I get there, Couper says. It might be nothing.

I imagine an empty lot, a vacant field. And worse, no connections. Just a random scattering of dead girls.

What will we do then? I picture myself, dropped off at my mom's, with no room for me anymore. No job waiting, my car towed. Couper pulling away, headed to another state, another case.

When my lungs constrict, I try laughing. Doesn't that make you crazy? I say. It feels like we're driving in slow motion, but I know he's going sixty. On either side, ancient-looking trees, cows clustered in the shade, or near a low pond. Houses that are white turned gray, peeling to reveal raw but dried and brittle wood siding, with deep front porches piled with burlap couches and rocking horses, dirt yards.

We stop at the train track, like the waitress said we might have to, and wait ten minutes while a long CSX goes by, car after car, empty and see-through, or filled with barrels, cable, steel beams. It blinks, the space between cars a flash of light as each one chunks past.

No, Couper says, answering me finally. Then he smirks. Sweetheart, that's not what makes me crazy.

Sugarwood Mobile Park sits, low, flat, and awful, in the middle of a newly developing area. One deteriorating road through the last few rickety trailers and, all around it, land that has been bulldozed and dug out. The movement of cranes and backhoes, earthmovers and men in hard hats with trailers of their own that they disappear into to get coffee or have lunch, to run paperwork or print out invoices. Their work trailers, better than most of the trailer homes.

The foundations for new homes gape open like graves of cement, poured and left waiting for houses to be plopped on top of them, and beyond that, nothing but a row of trees they've left between the new houses and the little circular track of trailers. The guys look up, they tip their hard hats to see. We must look like we're moving in.

Maybe there's an open spot for us to park the Scamp and stay, instead of a KOA or a Walmart parking lot under bright lights. And maybe this is the kind of place I'll find Khaki finally, in a row of tin homes, where we can go back to being girls again, running in the grass, wandering down to the creek to catch snakes or frogs, a shoe box full of crickets. Sneak off into the trees to smoke a cigarette, or sip from a plastic bottle of vodka or bourbon.

The movement of the car is like a big-hipped woman's; I can feel it there, in my waist, swiveling as the car navigates potholes in the dirt road. My hips rise and fall, the weight of the car, of the Scamp in tow behind, like my own body.

Couper parks half on the grass at the top of the street and we walk to the first trailer. The road in a loop like a suburban cul-de-sac, but dusty and closer, with cars and kiddie pools and a cluster of mailboxes all together in one bank on the grass in the center. All at once it makes me long for home. Not my mother's trailer, with its broken appliances, its empty beer bottles and piles of old mail and newspapers. Something older, from longer ago. Something the color of an old photograph, pink and yellow. It smells like a sprinkler, and feels like summer dusk on your skin, warm, misty, sweaty.

Where I come from.

I ask Couper, Did you ever live in a trailer?

Ha, no, he says, which annoys me.

You do now, I say.

I do, he says. He pulls the notepad from his pocket while we walk up the side of the road.

You always lived in a full-fledged, free-standing house, I say.

No, he says. I lived in an apartment, in college. And after too.

Where? I say.

Seattle, he says.

Washington is a state we never made it to. It seems a world away, high in the mountains, all pine trees and ocean and weed.

How did you end up here? I say.

Here? he says, and points to the grass. Here is a long story. I ended up on the East Coast for work.

Detective work? I say.

No, he says.

What, then?

Newspaper work, he says. He tips his head and smiles at me. I was a reporter, he says.

Crime? I say.

Some. I did some beat writing. Some regular news, and then longer projects, investigative stuff. That's how I started doing book-length projects.

This is not your first, I say.

No.

I push his arm. Are you fucking famous? I say.

He laughs. Not so much, he says.

It's about ninety-five degrees in the sun. My feet cover over with red dust. When I take my shoes off later, it'll leave a pattern, like you see on Indian girls. I saw them one time, in Niagara Falls, with Chuck. All these girls with their long black braids and pink and red and gold silk, their hands and feet painted in a pattern just slightly darker than their skin. They giggled in the spray by the falls while a man took pictures of them. He had a white suit that buttoned higher than usual, and a fancy red turban.

Don't stare, Rayelle, Chuck said.

But I wondered about them, because they didn't look much older than me. Because the man took their picture together, and wasn't posing with them. Because I wondered what it was like to be married off to a man you maybe didn't know, wearing red instead of white, your body painted and your hair dressed with jewels.

At the first trailer, a little mommy—a girl with a ponytail high on her head and a couple of toddlers who wander in and out of the front door—slides a plastic baby pool into the sun and lays a running hose in it, leaving it to fill and warm up before she lets the kids get in. The hose makes its own whirlpool, moving in a swift circle around the plastic sides. It would pull you in, that vortex of moving water; you could never fight that. You would just get lost in the current, spinning around with your face against the imprint of blue plastic cartoon fishes.

I grab Couper's hand, cold and sweaty at the same time. My back, dripping, and my arms all goose bumps. He looks at the pool, the twisting water.

Do you want to wait in the car? he says, but he's distracted by the activity of the woman, another car pulling into the park. Couper shakes his head. No, you should come, he says. You can do this. He grips my hand and then lets go, walking ahead.

I watch the slope of his shoulders, the breadth of his back as he walks away. I have to fight not to let the image darken from the outside in, my eyesight fading and my head light enough to faint.

Couper sort of waves before he approaches her. She tries walking away, looking over her shoulder. She probably thinks he's summoning her, serving her papers, coming from the state or from child protective. He has to call out to make her stop.

Sorry to bother you, he says. Can you just tell me which one of these is number seventeen?

There's no number on her trailer, and no number on the one across the street. There's no mailbox on the house, only the metal bank of them in the middle green. In front of the trailer, the steps are warped, untreated pine. They look unstable, dry, splintery.

She walks back and bends down to swish her hand in the swirling pool water, her ponytail swaying to the side. There's more than enough water in the pool. When she stands upright, she's tiny in front of Couper, not even to his shoulder. She wears white sweatpants that come to her knee, and a stretchy white tank top with no bra, even though she needs one. She has so many freckles on her shoulders, chest, and arms, they seem to overlap in places. When I get closer, her face is the same.

Are you fucking kidding me? she says to Couper, and leans back on her heels, open and confrontational. She eyes the long-haired toddler on the grass, dressed in only a diaper, who picks up a stick, ready to run with it, and all she does is snap her fingers at him. He stops as soon as she snaps. Doesn't look back at her, doesn't even lift his head. He just drops the stick and moves to a pile of pebbles by the steps.

No ma'am, Couper says.

The kid grabs a handful of pebbles and peppers her leg with it.

Tyler! She snaps her fingers again. Go in the house and find Lexi, she says. Have your cereal. You can't get in the pool yet. When he doesn't move she lunges like she'll chase him and he toddles up the steps. Then she sizes us up, her head moving up and down, the pool filling right to the top.

You all the cops? she says, and kind of laughs. You don't look like cops.

No ma'am, Couper says. My name's Couper Gale. I'm an investigative reporter. This is my associate, Rayelle Reed.

He keeps saying my name to everyone, without asking me. Without consideration for my own anonymity. Why does she need to know who I am?

What are you looking for in seventeen? she says.

I was hoping to find the woman who lives there, Couper says.

She smoothes her hand from her forehead back to where the ponytail starts at the crown of her head. Then she clucks and shakes her head. Too late, she says.

She's not there? he says.

She waves her hand around. We're dropping like flies out here, she says. Nah, they don't live there no more.

He glances back at me before he goes on. There was more than one person? he says.

Yeah. I mean, the main one, she says, and then dangles her fingers down. And a few others.

A few other . . . women? Couper says.

She snorts. There weren't no men in that house, if you catch me, she says.

I don't know if I do, Couper says. How many women?

Just one, she says, impatient, but there were always others hanging around. I don't know who all lived there, off and on.

Did you know them?

She looks at me before she answers. No, I did not know them, she says.

Is there anyone left here who might have known them? Couper asks. He looks down the line of trailers. All of them on a tilt, facing the dirt drive, stacked like dominoes, ready for their own demise.

Darlene might, she says, slow. Then she holds up a finger and asks him to wait while she goes to turn the hose spigot. The pool is uneven. Water sloshes out one side. And why not? If a teaspoon is as dangerous as a gallon, why not give a baby a whole deep pool to drown in?

Darlene. Couper jots down.

Is the manager, she says, and points at the trailer across the way. But she don't have time to talk to you all, she says. We got a bit going on here, you know? She waves her hand around at the construction, the constant drone and pound of so many heavy machines. Dropping like flies, she says again.

I'm sorry to hear that, Couper says. He eyes the row of open basements in the hot field. Are they forcing you out? he says.

They don't give a rat's fucking ass what happens to us, she says.

Behind her, the little one comes back out the front door, leaving it wide open behind him, the sunlight shining in on a living room filled with toys on the rug, a big TV going loud against the wall. A shaft of bright light catches dust floating down. He comes down the front steps barefoot, undoes his own diaper and walks out of it, leaves it on the grass, his fat little legs working him toward the pool with purpose. He steps right in over the side, slips and lands hard on his bottom, the water up to his armpits.

It's too cold, Ty, she says. I told you.

He crawls, his butt up in the air and his nose skimming the water. It doesn't seem to faze him.

Anyone else? Couper says.

She looks down the street. Some are nicer than others, with birdbaths and hanging flowers. Some of them with just dirt lawns, a broken step, the aluminum sides of them rusty or dented. One has a window knocked out, and the curtain blows through from the inside.

Crystal, she says. She picks at a fingernail. The kid puts his face in the water and she stoops real quick, even though her back is to him.

Not your face, Ty, she says. Sit up.

These your little ones? Couper asks.

If I were the babysitter, she says, I'd get paid for this shit.

Where will I find Crystal? Couper says.

Oh, if she's down there, you all won't miss her, she says.

I stroll down the lawn then, back to the road, toward the next trailer and the next. Trying to slow my breathing. My heart, knocking against the top of my stomach, or maybe against the hard wall of my liver. It's a long ugly walk up the little street. I hear Couper thank her, and then he catches up with me. When I look back, she's still standing the same way, arms crossed, the kid wading in the pool now, the water to his knees.

You know, what they say ain't even true, she calls out. It's all a bunch of bullshit.

Couper stops dead and bounds back to her. What is? he says.

She ain't that special, she says. She's no goddamn savior.

Ashley? Couper asks, but I see her face, her eyes narrowed to a cold stare.

Ask Crystal, she says, and looks away, into the trailer, at the open door and another kid coming out, a little girl in a shiny metallic bikini and her mother's sunglasses slipping down her nose. It's all just smoke up your ass, if that's how you like it, she says. That ain't magic. That's just two lezzies and a dildo, she says.

The road has gone to weeds and potholes. At the end of the loop, there's a vacant trailer, dirty white and rusted in parts, that sits at an imprecise angle, like someone pushed it hard, shoving it back from the road. On the aluminum siding, a faded *17* written in marker. The windows are clouded over with filth or fog from the inside, steam from whatever is closed up and rotting in there.

The window of the laundry room at my mom's does the same thing. Opaque with smoky moisture.

There can't be anything living inside that's not wild. The door doesn't even quite close, and hangs off the top hinge enough to be diagonal, letting in light and flies and red dust. The wooden steps don't look like they'll hold any weight, much less Couper's, and the very bottom step has BAD spray-painted in orange. Someone has also keyed the word SLUTS into the metal door, and what was raw exposed steel is now rusted letters coming through the faded gray.

Couper walks around the perimeter, but the grass is so long, he has to wade through knee-high weeds. He can't get very close.

Because number seventeen sits at the very end of the loop, you can survey the rest of the trailers from there. People coming in and out. Which ones are empty, which ones are still occupied. A dust storm follows a little hatchback, and a woman gets out with plastic bags of groceries. An older couple stretches out their awning, the man up on a step stool, adjusting the corner. Theirs is nice, neat with plants and wind chimes. A younger guy with the side of his belly exposed from underneath a black T-shirt leans over the hood of a Monte Carlo. A woman with wide hips and big legs sits on the lowest step of a trailer and blows bubbles while her girls chase them over the lawn.

And one other girl, who pulls up in an old-style Ford pickup, and steps out in a pair of shorts that are cut so high you can see the rounds of her ass peeking out. She has long black hair and a yellow T-shirt with tiny sleeves that doesn't quite hit the top of the shorts, revealing a line of taut belly and lower back. Her sandals have a four-inch wooden heel.

Oh, Couper says when he sees her. Crystal. He sounds delighted. I'd like to kick him.

I remember Khaki in a pair of high wooden Candies she would wear as Shawn, the club owner, her chest bare under her blazer, her feet high and arched in those shoes.

Ho-ly shit, Couper says when Crystal turns around and bends to take something out of the front seat of the truck. You think? he says to me, checking.

I repeat: You all won't miss her.

Miss, he calls, and starts jogging. Miss!

She spins around, her feet planted in those shoes and her waist turning the way you can twist a Barbie doll's.

Did you just come from over there? she says, to me, though, not to Couper.

I lag on up behind him then, my steno pad loose in my hand, my pen tucked behind my ear and tangled into my hair. The assistant. The babyless mother, following the detective and letting him fuck her in the back of his tin-can camper.

I did, Couper says, pointing at his chest.

Did you go inside? she says.

She's a lot cuter from far away. Up close, her eyes crowd to the middle of her face, her shoulders and knees bony, her tits huge and fake, hard-looking with a deep wrinkly valley between them. Her hair is streaked white blond on the top, like a skunk.

That place is condemned, she says to me. You're going to have to burn that dress to get off all the cunt dust.

Crystal? Couper says, holding his pad and writing. I wish he would drop it. I'm Couper—

No, she says. I don't want your name, she says. And you don't know mine.

Crystal? he says.

Nope, she says.

She reaches into the backseat and comes out with a black instrument case, the kind that might hold a trumpet, but bigger. It has a decal in the corner like you'd see on a truck mud flap, a sitting, bent metal girl with big tits and flying hair.

Can I help you with that? Couper says.

She laughs, low and punctuated. No, she says, and eyes him, up and down, his rumpled shirt, his mussed hair. I might be able to help *you* with it, she says.

She cocks her head to the side, her ear tipped nearly to her shoulder, and holds the case with both hands, hanging down in front of her thighs. What are you looking for? she says to me.

And when Couper tries to answer for me, she hushes him, just as quick as the little mommy. Ah! she says, Shhh.

It takes me a minute to find my voice. Ashley, I say, clearing it. Ashley Dunn.

It's Ashland, she says, and she ain't here no more, and she never had anything you needed to begin with, she says to me.

Can you tell us where she went? Couper says, but Crystal's gaze is on me. It's like Couper has disappeared.

You got a ride out of here? she asks me. Even with this? she points to Couper.

Yes, I say.

Then go. Let me tell you something about Ashland Dunn, she says, coming closer, her heels tapping on what's left of the pavement. She looks nice, when she takes you in, when she washes your feet clean and holds your hand, and sings you to sleep. But she's meaner than fuck and you'll do better to stay away from her.

She looks down at the front of my dress.

You got a belly full of bones? she says.

What? No. And then I think about it, just as she said it, a belly, swelled up with a jangle of baby bones. No, I say again.

'Cause someone else can help you with that.

I don't need that kind of help, I say. My voice is dry, gone in the red dust.

She swings her hair before she goes inside with the black case. You don't need her kind of help at all, she says to me.

Any idea, Couper says, of where I might find Ashley Dunn?

That's not her name, Crystal says. Even Ashland's not her name, she says, and fake smiles at him. Then, Why don't you start at the river? she says, pointing to the trees beyond the trailer. And follow the trail of blood?

I expect Crystal to slam the door, but she closes it snug, and I hear the dead bolt slide into place. The windows are covered tight with blinds, not a movement again from inside, even though the whole thing is only about twelve feet wide, maybe thirty feet long.

I follow Couper back to number seventeen. Well, he says, and picks his shirt up, covering his nose with it. Here goes, he says.

He pushes on the door of number seventeen, and it opens until it can't. Until the angle makes the corner jut into the floor, dragging, ripping the carpet.

Inside, it's littered deep with dirty dishes that have sat so long they're fuzzed over with thick black, hardened to a shell. There's the low hum of flies and slow bees pinging against the windowpane. You can see everything from the doorway, the way you always can in a single-wide: the table, with its dishes and yellowed newspapers, a long green striped couch that's empty except for misshapen cushions, placed haphazardly so they don't fit together the way they should anymore. There's a counter across from the table with some small appliances, a toaster with a drawing of wheat on the side, a white coffeemaker stained brown around the edges. The pot has an inch of hardened sludge in it.

But the carpet is the worst. It's crusted flat with a dark rust-colored stain in the shape of a bean up the middle of the trailer.

I watch while Couper pushes aside a flowered curtain on a tension rod, revealing the back bedroom. He sticks his head in, but doesn't enter. There probably isn't room, just space for a bed, and some shelves, maybe, on the walls. It's hard to tell if there's anything worth the effort. There are no people here anymore, not even their important things. Just the shit left behind. It smells rotten. The kind of decay that grows.

I need to get out. I hop over the steps and stand in the tall grass to the side. There's a field behind that goes for miles, no farmland or crops, not even trees except for way back. Just wild. The houses going up off to the right of here, where another line of trees makes a sorry attempt at masking the development, the constant sound of tamping. That side of the trailer, solid, with no windows. Dingy white, dented in some places, with holes in others, like a variety of rocks had been sprayed at it. I run my finger over it, reading the pattern.

The moldy, closed-up smell in the trailer made me woozy, and outside, the air isn't much better. It's hot and stagnant, heavy with roofing tar and exhaust.

Honey, Couper says. He leans out the door and lets his shirt down.

Honey yourself, I say.

Rayelle, he says.

I look up at him leaning, and think if he comes out any farther, he's going to tip the whole garbage can on top of himself.

What? The sun burns the top of my head.

Can you come look at this? he says.

Is it a fucking body? I ask.

No, he says. He holds out his hand to me.

I try doing what he did, and pull the top of my dress up to cover my mouth and nose, but there's too much boob and not enough fabric. Pulling on it hurts my neck. So I let it drop, and try to breathe slowly, through my mouth.

He leads me to the bedroom, which is, like I expected, all bed with about a foot's width of floor to step around. There's a smushed-flat king-size mattress on top of a platform with drawers underneath, and moth-eaten red-velvet curtains over the window. A wire hangs on the side wall, with a string of postcards clipped to it. The pictures face out, mountains, a river, the ocean, daisies, and Couper picks them off one by one, handing them to me.

Tennessee. South Dakota. Nevada. Georgia. Virginia. Carolina.

Each one with the address carefully razored off so that side of the card is blank and worn soft like fabric.

The messages largely the same. *Miss you. Love you. Wish you were here with me.*

xoxo Rainy.

I feel my knees give, like, actually give underneath me so that Couper grabs my elbow and holds me up, walks me back out of the trailer with the cards in my hand. My cards.

Rainy? he asks outside, looking over my shoulder at the signature on each card.

It was a phase, I say.

For?

For me, I shout at him. It comes out as a roar, my throat dry and rattling. These are mine, I say.

I think he hasn't been listening to a damn thing I've said.

I hold them loose in my lap in the car. The names like a chant in my head. Montana, Nevada, Tennessee, Virginia. Caitlin, Jessa, Alyssa. Florida.

Think for a minute, he says to me, but I just look at my kid handwriting, curlicued and cute.

When did your cousin leave South Lake? he says.

June, I say. Right after her dad died.

How old was she?

Sixteen. Actually, not even, I say. She wasn't sixteen till August. But she left in June.

Right after, Couper says.

I know, I say. Yes. I don't know what he wants me to admit, what he's pointing at, or if I'm afraid of what he's suggesting. After Holly Jasper disappeared, I say. But Khaki didn't disappear, I say. I watched her leave.

With who?

I get a chill in that hot car, just like I did when I saw the kiddie pool in the sun, my arms go goose-bumpy and my head sweats along the hairline.

With her boyfriend. My voice is small, dry. He waits, and I say the name. Jeff Henderson.

Are you sure? he says.

I think. We only ever called him Henderson, I say, but yeah, I'm sure that was his name. I watch Couper grip his hands on the wheel, open, closed, knuckles pink and then white, until he's ready to turn the key and start the car.

I shuffle the cards in my hands. They're dusty, and they smell weird, like mildew, damp and rotten. Why? I say to Couper. I'm too dry for any kind of crying, but wind and red dust are rumbling around inside me. I'm too stunned, too filled up tight with fear to do anything but turn to him and ask him why, why we would find these here. Now.

I don't know, he says. He's unwilling to tell me what he's thinking. I hold the cards in my hands till the edges are soft from my sweat, deteriorating under my fingertips.

sixteen

KHAKI

The secrets under my skin have changed the shape of my face, which shifted from town to town, from girl to girl. I took on the shape of each place, the sound of their voices, the length of their hair, the color of their eyes. In Georgia, light ash-brown. In South Carolina, deep brunette. By the time I got to Tennessee, I was back to blond, going lighter all the time.

I cut my own hair. I shaved my head. I bought wigs. When the hair grew in, it was the color of pure light.

My eyes, like a cat's in the sun.

My mother told me about Rayelle after Aubrey. When she died, my mother went silent for a long time. She lay in bed alone, a habit I would know more and more as she got sick and died. But after Aubrey, I would some-times creep up beside her, slip my hand in hers.

The bassinette in which Aubrey died, still there in the room, sour smelling, the blankets with their sweet, oily, baby-milk scent, tucked into the sides, but with no baby to swaddle.

I had wanted a sister bad.

I was six years old, alone in the house except for a brother who was much older, a brother with hard hands and sharp breath.

I held Aubrey's soft squirmy body only once. Her face, smushed and red. Her eyes, squinted shut. Her nose like a candy button. And her lips, like a tiny flower, barely open.

They buried her in a casket the size of a shoe box.

Closed.

I was angry that the baby I had wanted so bad came and left so quickly.

I want a sister, I said to her. The sun came in the back bedroom windows, warm on the floor, lighting up the bedside table. It was midafternoon, the TV on the dresser on a soap opera I knew my mother didn't watch. She lay on her side with her back to me, but when I came in and said that, she rolled over.

You have a sister.

Not anymore, I said. I was disgusted. With everyone. I thought a sister could at least keep me company. Could sleep in my room, in my bed even, our fat kid legs mixed up together. I thought if I had a sister in my bed, no one else would come in at night. If my sister was there, I wouldn't wake up burning like I was being split in half, my legs wet and aching.

I watched my mother rub her eyebrows. When they weren't drawn in, they were just ash brown, just a shadow above her green eyes. Her hair, with its color washed out, was returning to its medium brown. She'd kept it darker for years.

I thought she was the most beautiful woman ever.

Rayelle is your sister, she said.

I slapped her hand, the way my aunt Carleen had slapped my face when I told her the baby was dead. The sound sharp like paper snapping.

She snatched her hand back from me.

Don't you say that, I said to her. It's not the same. It's not the same as having my own baby sister, I said. By then I was shouting.

Kathleen Suzanne, she said to me. Rayelle is your baby sister. She sat up before I could tell her to shut her damn mouth. Shhhhhht, she said, holding up her finger. Her face was thin, and sallow, yellow-looking to me. And don't you tell a goddamn soul I told you, she said.

Who knows that? I said.

The people who need to know, she said. Me, and you.

Does Dad know? I asked. I thought of the way he called me his girl. The way his breath smelled.

It's none of his goddamn business, she said to me, and then she dropped back. She told me to hand her a pill bottle that was on the dresser, and then get out of there. And shut the door, she said.

I thought she had every fucking thing in the world, an only child with her own room, with parents who were maybe better for her because none of them belonged to each other, not Carleen to Chuck, not Rayelle to Carleen. Three separate people. No one laid a hand on Rayelle except to smack her bottom when she needed it. Her trashy trailer that we could run through and kick our shoes against the wall without the booming voice of my dad. Her hand-me-down pink bike, rusted from her just leaving it on the lawn after riding. A stray cat bundled in her arms, and riddled with fleas. And summer after summer a road trip to some state I'd never even imagined, sitting up front in Chuck's car while Carleen slept in the back. Mountains, the ocean, fields where there was nothing but sunflowers as far as you could see. The desert. Every time she left in that car for the sweetest weeks of summer I felt part of me go along, like a long string stretched between us. I imagined her sleeping in a motel bed by herself, with the AC icy cold and her non-parents in the bed next to hers, ordering her hamburgers and Cherry Cokes. Watching cable TV. With no one's hands on her head, nothing in her mouth, or between her legs.

I hated her.

And loved her more than anything. Flesh of my flesh. My own girl.

Before my mother died she told me she didn't want to go to hell.

I had never heard her say such a thing. Didn't know either heaven or hell was any concern to her. I never imagined she would burn. For anything.

Mom, I said. I stroked her papery arm. Don't worry about that. There's nothing to worry about, I told her.

I didn't do enough, she said.

But I couldn't think of anyone who'd had more happen to her than my mother. When Nudie died, I thought I'd lose them both. He lingered for two long gray-lit days while my parents stayed at the hospital and I stayed with Rayelle.

They were two of the best days I had.

Mom, you did everything, I said.

I didn't do enough for you, she said. To protect you.

She closed her eyes then, the way she did in the last months, her hair sweaty and her lips dry. The Vicodin working hard in her blood. She slept like she was dead already.

I loved them all that way. The way I hated, hard in my gut, the things that had been thrust upon me, the things that cut hard and scarred.

I loved them so hard I crushed them.

Until I found Dakota. Dakota, who lay in the bushes like a dead deer, her body the same copper as the soil, her hair shining black like a vein of coal. She'd lost an eye. Her pants were wet with her own urine.

I crouched beside her like a fairy who'd found a giant. And when I put my hands on her head, I felt the throb of survival. Her skin spoke to me, singing like a vessel deep in the earth, alive.

I could never crush that.

seventeen

RAYELLE

Here's where I'm comfortable: at a bar, with strangers, drinking myself happy again. In a car, with a stranger, fucking someone who makes me feel, for an instant, like I'm happy again.

Right now I'm neither.

I'm not at a bar, and I'm in a camper smaller than the car that tows it. And Couper is less of a stranger all the time.

Was I happy with Summer? No. And people knew that, my mother, my friends, I just didn't think anyone would say it after she died. But that's when the people you thought were friends and neighbors, the people who lined up and said they were there for you, who brought you casseroles and said they were praying for you, that's when they say the shittiest things.

My very last friend from high school was a girl we all just called Sissy, but whose real name was Paula. It's no wonder she went by Sissy. Before Summer, we'd been going-out friends. Bars, parties. Her brother was a fireman. We went to the field days, played on a softball league. She had a boyfriend before I met Eli. And then I had Summer.

After, when by then we hadn't partied in months, Sissy said to me, Look Rayelle, I know you don't want to hear this, but all you ever said was that you felt trapped. Maybe now's your chance, she said. Maybe it's a sign. Get out and run, she said.

We were in the kitchen of my mother's trailer, the place I'd done all my homework, all my arguing with my mother, and where I didn't believe I would be staying again for very long. It was darker earlier every night. My mother stood at the counter, slicing up a lime, and I was waiting for her to slice off her finger. Her hands shake a little all the time.

You should go, I said to Sissy. She was wearing a baseball tee that said *Summer Fun*. She'd been working full-time since July at a Ponderosa off the interstate. I watched my mother nod her head.

Rayelle, Sissy said. I was afraid she was going to try to hug me. I shrank under every touch.

No, I said. I can't have this conversation.

Rayelle, my mother said. She sloshed a little gin onto her wrist as she turned with the glass. You know she's right.

Get out, I said to Sissy. And I'd tell you to get out, I said to my mother, but it's your house.

Goddamn right it is, she said.

I slammed my bedroom door so hard it knocked the cheap molding right off the tin wall.

Now, instead, I find myself halfway between Soddy-Daisy, Tennessee, and Wrightsville Beach, North Carolina, living in a trailer with a man whose stuff I'm rifling through.

We parked at a Walmart, even though Couper prefers to shop at Target. Target won't let you park there all night. There's nothing stopping anyone at a Walmart. Maybe because so many of them are open twenty-four hours. There's no telling if you're in the store shopping, or in your trailer sleeping. Walmart has better supplies for us, propane tanks and charcoal, but Target's stuff is prettier.

You're a little bit Target, I say to Couper, before he goes in to buy beer. And I'm a little bit Walmart, I say.

He smirks. I'm actually a little bit Nordstrom, he says.

Well, I say. I narrow my eyes at him. I've never been in a Nordstrom in all my shitty life, I say.

He shrugs. It's a West Coast store, he says. I'll take you sometime.

That's when I go through his stuff. When he's inside Walmart at 1:00 AM, buying beer and water bottles and barbecue potato chips, because that's what sounded good to me. I open the cabinets where he keeps his clothes, checking the pockets of the shirts and jeans. His

T-shirts feel like washed woven silk to me. His socks, too, thicker, but so soft. Not the pack of eight white pairs that Chuck buys.

When I look in the trunk that's inside the bench seats, I find an airtight bin with papers. Newspapers and legal pads. Some of them new and some of them filled with his scrawl. The size and slant vary from page to page. On some pages, he's doodled all the way down the side in tight crosshatching that looks like the weave of linen. The press of the pen making a dent in the paper that you can run your fingers on.

At the bottom of everything, there's a binder-clipped stack of legal-length documents, with places highlighted and marked by thin colored pieces of tape that flag off the edge of the papers. A pale yellow Post-it on the front page with the note *C, take care, K.*

Divorce papers, already signed by Amanda L. Kessler and dated June fucking fourth. All the lines with *Couper A. Gale* underneath, blank.

I hightail it diagonally across the parking lot, in the middle of the night, my dress blowing, my sandals flapping with each step. The papers rustle in my hand. I wait for him outside the automatic door, smoking a cigarette under the ugly light, and holding the papers behind my back.

He pushes a cart out, filled with a box of bottled beer and a case of water.

Who's K? I ask. He's startled to see me standing there, my cigarette making a cloud up around my head.

In what context? he asks. His face has this open surprise to it, his eyebrows high, but cinched.

C, take care, K, I say and I drop the papers in the cart
on top of the beer. He looks down at them and his face
changes from surprise to amusement.

Kaplan, he says. My brother.

What are you waiting for? I ask him.

Uh, he says, but I move in. I put the cigarette in my
mouth and put both hands on the cart, pushing back
toward the Scamp.

Go buy a mailing envelope, I say to him. The cigarette bobs on my lip.

We sleep for only a few hours. I can't get comfortable next
to him. It's hot and we're close to the highway, where the
trucks rumble down the off-ramp and their lights shine
in the windows, even with the curtains closed. In the
morning, Couper seems better rested than I expect him
to be, and he gives me a briefing on what he knows. That
Jeff Henderson is living in Wrightsville Beach. That he's
a special education teacher with a wife and a baby.

Was she beautiful? I say to Couper.

Who? he asks. I don't know what his wife looks like,
he says.

Amanda, I say.

He closes his computer. She still is, he says.

I want to ask him if she shops at Nordstrom, but I
bite my tongue. He's in work mode, straightening his
notes. He's already been over to the store, to use the

bathroom, wash up, and brush his teeth. He pours me a cup of coffee from the blue percolator pot. I've gotten quicker at putting the table back up from the bed, and I sit there at the table, drinking the coffee that I've gotten to like. Even black.

Do you think Khaki's dead? I ask him.

He pauses a long time. I don't know, sweetheart, he says. He stands, leaning against the counter with the sink behind him. Leaning is about the only way he can stand inside the Scamp. He says, I'll have a better idea after we talk to Henderson.

Do you think he killed her? I ask, and I don't wait for him to answer. I'll kill him, I say. I'll kill him with my own hands if he touched her, I say.

Let's just see, he says. He's a quieter type than I've known. What riles in me, settles in him. Sand sinking in water.

I ask Couper how he found Henderson, how he has found anyone. He tells me he has a subscription to a database that holds addresses and phone numbers and more background information than a regular person can find just searching the Internet.

I've had it, he says, since my newspaper days. But it wouldn't matter, he adds. Henderson's right out in the open, he says. I didn't even use the database. Anyone can find him. He's not hiding.

Is that good or bad? I ask.

I don't know, Couper says.

It's the first time, though, that I see him use a cover-up. A story to get in the door that's not about the girls. Every place we've been, it's been in the aftermath of a dead girl, a reporter doing a detective's work, asking the people left behind what they know, who they noticed, what was different. Waiting for the small detail that they overlooked, that will be the missing piece of his puzzle.

I listen to him make the phone call to Henderson. He says it's Couper Gale from the *Record*, and he asks Henderson if he's aware of a case involving a young developmentally disabled man who was tasered at a movie theater. If he can interview him.

He calls from the car. I watch Couper nod, the sleek, flat phone barely balanced between his ear and shoulder. He jots things in a small notebook.

Excellent, he says. It's a different voice, confident and in his professional element. It's just a few sly degrees different from the voice he uses on me.

Four times, I think. Four different women. Four different towns. A newspaper office where everyone leaves eventually, their things packed in boxes, and desks emptied, once the presses stop moving. Some people have one wife and four or five different jobs, but all Couper's had is this one thing, moving him along from city to city, from wife to wife. He could always write. It was the women who came and went. The houses, the cars. It all seems like interchangeable parts. The rest of it, just suburbs, just stuff. All your possessions in trash bags, tossed out on the lawn, put to the curb for someone else to come along and go through, to decide what's worth keeping.

We meet Henderson at a coffee shop that has about fourteen different types of coffee and a bunch of cookies that look grainy and healthy. My mother was never a baker. She would sometimes make brownies from a box, out of desperation, to stop me from asking her to bake something, and then I would eat the whole pan, even the dry edges, or the gooey middle where they hadn't baked all the way. She never had much of a sweet tooth.

There's a whole wall here of tea tins, green tea, oolong, jasmine, some shit I've never heard of. Matcha. Sencha. The walls are red, the room filled with brown leather couches and brown wooden tables. There's art on the wall that looks like a kid painted it, which probably means it's real, and expensive.

Henderson comes with his wife and their eight-month-old baby, who thank God doesn't look anything like Summer or I might have fainted on the spot. I haven't been around babies much. When your baby dies, people stop asking if you want to hold theirs.

Henderson looks different. Older, obviously, in his mid- or even late thirties, and clean-cut, not the scruffy stoner he used to be. His hair is just long enough to curl over his collar, but neat, combed back off his forehead. His eyes are bluer than I remember. His teeth, straight and white. His jeans, a dark-wash slim leg that he wears with gray tennis shoes. His shirt, a wrinkle that you pay for, not that you get by leaving it rumpled on the floor.

He shakes hands with Couper and grins. His whiskers, in his just slightly grown-in beard, have a hint of silver at the corners of his chin. He eyes me once, and Couper tells him I'm an intern. His wife's name is Vera. The baby, Kaia.

I flip open my steno pad and take a felt-tip pen out of my purse. I draw doodles. Circles, overlapping. Henderson looks, then looks away. The baby, sitting with Vera on a couch behind him, curves against her mother's breast and sleeps.

I've never even heard of the case Couper is talking about. I haven't seen a newspaper, or very much TV other than a ball game inside a bar, in weeks. Henderson begins by going along, nodding, and then when I look up from my scribbles—I'm not taking notes on this—I notice that he's just looking at me, and my pad, where all I've drawn are these circles, locked together.

Did you go to Roosevelt? he asks me.

Not for special ed, I say and snort.

No, of course not, Henderson says. I mean, in general.

No, I say. I feel like the sound of my voice betrays me, different from this drippy, coastal town. Pennsylvania girls have a different twang. We age faster, and wrinkle harder. It's in the water, in the coal, seeping up from the ground. We're our own fossil fuel, burning up at a different pace.

You seem so familiar, he says.

The baby begins to stir, and Vera, who is short, but looks strong like a fighter, olive-skinned with dark hair cropped short and choppy, gets up and walks outside with the baby low on her chest, rubbing her curved back in a circle.

Attachment, Henderson says to Couper. You got kids?

Me, no, Couper says. He folds his lips in, tucked over his teeth. I've never seen him do this. His mouth is open, is full and wet and pink and sensuous, the rest of the time. Even when he's sleeping.

Phew, Henderson says. It's wearing me out.

What does that mean? I ask. Attachment?

It's a philosophy of parenting, he says. She's always in physical contact with one of us.

Always? I say.

He chuckles. I'm so tired, he says.

He and Couper talk then specifically about rights and laws, and then more generally about challenges, about changing public perceptions and sensitivities. Empathy. I put the steno pad down, bored, and undo the braid I'd twisted together this morning, rake my fingers through my hair. It's straight in spots, from sleeping. The parts against my neck, kinked with sweat.

Henderson had been looking at me with a curious head tilt. After I take my hair down, he looks like he's seen a ghost.

Where did you come from? he asks me. He puts his coffee cup down and leans over when he asks it.

Um, I say. Where am I from? I try to ignore his weird question, like I appeared from another world. Just a little town, I say. Not around here. No one's ever heard of it.

He looks back over his shoulder at Vera, outside in the shade with the baby.

Try me, he says.

It's called South Lake, I say.

I watch his blue eyes lose their sparkle and darken to something grayer, something filled with lead.

You're her cousin, he says. The cousin-sister.

I have a cousin, I say. My heart knocks hard. I don't know what you're talking about, though. I don't have a sister.

Outside, Vera paces with the baby, bouncing her, rubbing. She takes a bench with her back to the ocean, and moves a wide, brightly colored scarf over her shoulder and most of the baby's body so she can nurse her.

I couldn't wait to detach from Summer.

Khaki, Henderson says to me.

She's my cousin, I say. My stomach fills with electricity. Couper scuffs his chair back and looks over at me.

You two know each other? he says.

Do you remember me? Henderson says.

I shrug, but my hands are shaking. I watch his mouth turn hard.

You knew that, coming here, he says. He looks at Couper. Who the fuck are you? he says.

I am exactly who I said I was, Couper says. He pulls out a press card, an ID from a paper called the *Record*.

Henderson looks at the card, at the photo that is clearly Couper, and pushes it back toward him.

Do you know where she is? he asks me.

How would I? I say. The last time I saw her, she was with you.

Pulling her leg into his car and slamming the door. Go home, Rayelle, she hissed at me. Go play.

Henderson picks up my note-less steno pad. You want to tell me what you're really here to talk about? he says. You're not even writing anything down. You're not a reporter, he says to Couper.

I am a reporter, he says.

You sure you're not retired? Henderson says.

No, I'm not retired, Couper says.

Well, what are you actually looking for? Henderson says.

I'm looking, I say. I need to find her.

No you don't, Henderson says. Jesus Christ, he says. He wings his elbows out, his hands in his hair. I don't have any information, he says. He gets up then, and goes to the door of the café.

Wait wait wait, Couper calls out. I'm just trying to make connections, he says. Please. Let me just ask you a couple of things, he says.

I'm not connected, Henderson says. He shakes his head, and he puts a hand into his jeans pocket. His body is tall, slim. Well cared for.

Please, Couper says.

Henderson sticks his head out the door. Honey, why don't you go, he says. This might be a little bit. You should put her down, he says, and rest. His voice, different, softer and higher pitched. Leaning out the door, he becomes a domesticated version of himself.

When he sits back down, Couper says, I'm not a cop.

That's good.

I'm a writer, Couper says.

Well, Henderson says with mock respect.

Couper takes a sheet that has all the girls listed, except for Khaki, from a folder. Tell me, he says to Henderson, if any of these names sound familiar to you. He reads them off, one by one, Holly Jasper, Jessa Loy, Florida DeLaurentis.

Florida's dead, Henderson says.

I know, Couper says. All these girls are dead. How did you know Florida?

I didn't, Henderson says. Khaki did.

Did you ever meet her?

What are you asking?

If you ever met her, Couper says.

I love to watch him work. I love the way he doesn't front-load his questions with bullshit. The way he leans back and shoots straight and gets to the heart of things without looking like he's trying. I like his body in the chair, the crinkle next to his eye. Even the dead eye. Even still.

Henderson fans his fingers out on the table and drums them. Yes, he says. I met her.

When? Couper asks.

A few months before, Henderson says.

Before?

Before she killed herself? Henderson asks. That's what they say happened to her.

Do you not believe that?

Henderson shrugs. I didn't see the body, he says.

Do you not believe it was suicide? Couper asks.

She wouldn't have hurt her, Henderson says.

But, Couper says.

Henderson shakes his head.

Did you see Khaki again after Florida died? Couper asks.

No. I didn't see her after she left my apartment. I just . . . heard things.

Like what?

Rumors, Henderson says, speculations. I don't care to repeat them, he says. I wasn't there. I don't have any information.

Florida's stepfather was murdered, Couper says.

Yes, he was, Henderson says.

Any speculation about that? Couper says.

Nope, Henderson says.

How well did you know Florida DeLaurentis? Couper asks.

It's Henderson's turn to fold his lips in. I didn't, he says. Khaki did.

And when Khaki left your apartment, Couper says.

They left together, he says. She left me, he says, for a girl.

They left together, because they were there together? In the apartment, Couper says.

I wouldn't let her stay, Henderson says.

Because she was fourteen, Couper says.

Yes, Henderson says. And because I didn't want them there. I didn't want her bringing random kids home. Random girls she just wanted.

How long did Khaki live with you?

Four years, Henderson says.

Were you in South Lake before that?

I worked there summers as a lifeguard, Henderson says. Yes.

Were you there when Holly Jasper disappeared?

Yes.

Do you know where Holly Jasper is?

No, Henderson says, and his face opens with disgust. I searched for her, he says, like everyone else. But no. And at the end of June, I moved. I was starting graduate school, he says.

Isn't June early for grad school? Couper asks.

I had another job, Henderson says. Do you know where Holly Jasper is? he shoots at Couper.

She's not the only girl I'm trying to find, Couper says, and it's weird, the way he says *girl*, like I could be included. Like he's trying to solve me.

Wait, Henderson says. Then, his face lighting up with a grim realization, Did you come here because you think I did it? He waits, while Couper doesn't answer. Am I your missing link? Henderson asks. You think I took Holly Jasper and left town, and then came here and took Florida too? Because the only person I had in my car when I left South Lake was Khaki, he says. And let me tell you something, I don't know what kind of a read you get off of me, or what you think, but one of us had a propensity for violence, he says. And it wasn't me.

Couper flips to another page. Did you live with Khaki in Tennessee? he asks.

No, Henderson says. Then, You know that, he says to me, his voice lowered. She told me what she did to you.

What she did to me? I say.

I found evidence of Khaki living in Tennessee, Couper says, possibly under a fake name. Ashley, or Ashland, Dunn, he says.

Henderson shrugs. She has as many names as she does credit cards, he says.

Do you remember any of them?

She used her mother's cards, he says.

Her—? Couper starts.

Her dead mother, Henderson says, nodding. She used her dead mother's credit cards. She dealt drugs, he says, she kept a gun. You came here, he says, looking at me, like I'm the end of the road, he says. And I'm not. I'm not even the beginning. He points at me. You're the beginning, he says. You don't know what you're getting into, he says to Couper. But unless you're getting paid good fucking money for this story, you might want to walk away from it.

I lean on the table toward Henderson. Melissa? I say. Jordan?

I don't know, he says. I don't know what she told other people. When she lived here, he says, she told people

· her name was Kat. Kat Henderson. But we weren't married. Beyond that, I don't know. I can't. I don't want to. And you shouldn't either, he says to me.

I appreciate your time, Couper says. He stacks the paper with the list of girls on it back into his folder. Let me ask you this, do you have anything that might help us place her beyond here? An address? A phone number? Did you know where she was going when she left here?

I didn't know, he says. But I do have, he begins, and stops to rub across his brow with his fingers pressing hard. I have one piece of mail from her, he says. It's not signed, he says. It doesn't have a return address. I don't know if you can do anything with it, he says. I don't know why I even saved it, he says. It's not sentimental. I just— He shakes his head. I kept it tucked away.

Can you find it now? Couper says.

Yeah, I know where it is. To me, he says, You cannot find her. His voice is soft, domesticated, like when he spoke to Vera. You don't have to, he says. You can choose that, he says.

No, I say, I do.

Henderson asks for time, to go home, to check on the baby, and so we wait, and have another cup of coffee, and a grainy raisin cookie that's actually pretty good, between us.

What did she do to you? Couper asks.

I don't know.

I mean, what do you think he means? The . . . He hesitates. The sex? he says.

I don't know, I say again, louder. Wouldn't I know that? I say. I flash back on all the times in her bed. With her, dressed as Shawn, with me, in a dress that was too big for me, falling off my shoulder. Her hands, her mouth. My own mouth, open wide and gasping.

Wouldn't I have some say in whether or not that was abuse? I say.

No, Couper says. Sometimes the kids are the last ones to know.

We walk from the café to Henderson's, just a few blocks from the ocean, upstairs with what Henderson calls a minor view. If you lean to the side on the screen porch, you can kind of see the ocean.

We stop on the wooden stairs that go up to the apartment. Couper stops first, behind me, and when I realize, I stop too, the skirt of my dress moving in the ocean breeze. He comes up and puts his hand just under the dress, above the back of my knee, his warm palm against my bare skin. If he didn't disarm me so, in interrogation mode, or driving mode, or fucking divorce mode, I'd ask him what he was doing. But he knows exactly what he's doing. That's how you get four wives.

No one lets us in. We wait while Henderson comes back to the door with an envelope. There's a note inside, like he said, handwritten in blue ballpoint pen on lined paper, unsigned.

This is the rest of it, it says. *Forget everything.*

The postmark, five years old. From Summersville.

eighteen

KHAKI

I tried to tell Henderson things, about me, about home, about anything, but it never did any good. It never made me put back together, or healed. And I couldn't tell him everything.

I told Florida.

We were driving in the truck at night, the windows down. I was smoking. I thought maybe she was asleep.

I killed someone.

You killed me, she said.

No, I said. Really.

You killed every man who ever looked at me, she said.

No, Florida, I said. We slowed till you could hear every pebble of gravel under the tires, and stopped at a four corners where nothing was open. A Gulf station, a coffee shop, a Baptist church.

Who? Florida said, her voice honey and slow.

A kid, I said. A girl.

A girl like me, she said.

No. Not at all like you.

I didn't know her name. I knew her movements. Where she was allowed on her own and for how long. Where she walked with her friends. I knew the way her knees knocked together, that she liked ice cream with sprinkles. That after eight thirty she walked home alone from a friend's house, across the bridge that went over the canal.

Henderson, working as a lifeguard since May, watching, but not the way I was. I'd spent the early summer either on the beach with him or shuffling the midway with Rayelle. I stayed with her, or I stayed with Henderson, and I tried not to go home. My father was alone in the house, without me, without my mother.

I didn't remember what she was wearing. I was surprised when I saw the poster and the picture. Last seen wearing a yellow T-shirt, denim shorts, white sneakers.

I remembered what she smelled like, heavy with the scent of caramel corn from the midway. A burnt buttery smell on her fingers and in the tips of her hair. The top of her head gave off that metallic outdoor smell that kids have. Sun and sweat and grass and water all mixed up in their skin.

She had a kid's mouth, with small lips and big front teeth that had a gap. Her hair felt like horsehair, long and dry and rippled with summer heat.

I had cut my own hair, sharp bob to my chin, and lightened it to a white blond. I looked different, suddenly older. After my mother died in March, I got thinner. My clavicle hollow, my hipbones sharp.

I saw her walking the bridge over the canal. I said, Hey, I want to show you something, and touched her hand.

We walked down the sidewalk, alongside the canal, and by the time we hit the sandy path through pine trees, she'd put her little hand in mine.

I had nothing to show her but white-hot rage.

The moon was over the lake, not a hazy summer moon, but a cold hard circle moon. I felt the cold creeping, the way it does, in crystalled fingers, through my blood.

You shouldn't walk by yourself, I said. You should have a girlfriend with you. I was barely taller than she was, and even though I was older, I was still another kid to her, not an adult. And not a man.

I told her all the things my mother had told me. Have your girlfriend walk you halfway home. Carry a flashlight. Don't look at the drivers when they slow down. Walk fast but not like you're scared. Put your shoulders back. Hold your chin up so you look confident, but not your nose in the air so you look stuck up. Sit with your legs together. Don't shave too high. You only kiss people you really really like with your mouth open. Sometimes you have to do things you don't want to. Change your underwear, you smell like a whore. Your pussy is your own business, so keep it clean. Why do you think dogs smell you there? That's how they identify you.

About halfway down the path she let go of my hand. She could have run. Her spindly nine-year-old legs booking back toward town, back to where cars were going by, where she could flag down help, another kid, an adult. Another girl, barely taller than she was, who told her not to walk alone.

But it was too late. Before she moved again, I broke her neck.

Don't be fooled. It's easy to break a kid's neck.

Her whole body was like a willow tree. Thin, wispy. She had little bird bones, in her neck, her wrists, her ankles. Her little ribs, still like a baby's. Her shoulder blades, unformed wings on her back. Her clavicle, a string you could pluck for the most beautiful tone.

I held her awhile. When I discovered how soft and green she was, I broke more bones, just to see if I could. Both wrists. A finger on each hand. I wanted to make something of her, an instrument I could play, strung with tendons. Her bones, hung in the trees for the wind to move through, the sound unlike anything anyone had ever heard.

But I needed to get rid of her. By that time, my fingerprints were all over her. I was sure I'd left stray hairs from my own head. I was less than a mile from home. It had gotten dark. I left her, in the shelter of a fallen tree in the forest, like she was a nymph, sleeping, like she might rise up in the dark, phosphorescent, dancing, her wings sprouting, her eyes on fire.

I crawled up the hill toward home and took things from the shed. Heavy pieces of cut pipe, duct tape, a kickboard we took to the beach sometimes. The pipes were wide enough that I could slide them over her arms and her ankles. I might not have needed to secure them, but I did, with duct tape. Wound and wound around her skin, around the pipes, her body, at first across my lap and then flat out in the leaves, the leaves in her hair. There was dirt on her lip. I wiped it off with my thumb.

And then I swam. I liked to swim naked in darker parts of the lake. There was a public beach, and many other entry points that we'd walk to through the trees and go in with just our bodies, or with a canoe, a tube even, floating out in circles on a hot summer day. I came out of the blue-tinted pines white and naked. The mark in the sand at the shore from her weighted-down body, like the line a canoe leaves when you drag it in.

I knew the moon shone on my head.

Someone could have seen that. My white head, the white light, the middle of the lake like a spotlight was on it. The middle of the lake, so deep no one had ever measured it. My arms ached from pulling her. From gripping the kickboard. My legs, on fire from kicking.

I got as close as I could.

On the way back to shore, I put the kickboard under my shoulders and let my feet drag at the surface of the water, my face turned up to the moonlight, my breasts above the water. Cold, clean.

I didn't want her to know the details. When I told Florida, I only said I did it, and she didn't ask, or didn't believe me. I didn't want to feel tempted to make her believe me. Her body was not a willow I could snap, was not something I wanted to take apart in that way. I had learned to make it sing, for me, but not apart. Not disembodied.

I didn't know she would go into the water too. I'd watched her on the sand, in the daylight, a gray day when the ocean looked green, stooped in the white sand and making a shape that was a mermaid. A woman's arms and hair, her small waist and, below it, a full-hipped fish tail.

I love mermaids the best, she said to me.

I want to be something else, she said.

The wind whipped us red-faced that day, even in the heat, the salt, the bits of sand. We left there scrubbed. I left there with her, and went back alone.

I went back to wait. The ocean, green with envy, seething, and holding on to her tighter than I ever could.

nineteen

RAYELLE

It's not a great time to ask him about a motel. We don't have a destination, and outside of Wilmington we hit a fantastic thunderstorm that wags the Scamp all over the small road. All I want is to sleep inside a real building, with hallways and doors. Maybe even with a storm cellar.

He drives for hours before he stops. The car nearly out of gas, the Scamp's connection to the car sketchy at best. We find an old Fina with nothing else around it. There's a farmhouse farther down, and on the other side, an abandoned diner, shaped like a train car.

Couper gets out to fill the car, and a paper sign wags on the pump. CASH ONLY. Shaky handwriting in magic marker.

Fuck, he says.

What's the matter? I say. I roll down my window.

He half laughs. I don't suppose you have any cash, he says. Never mind, he says. I have a little. I just have to get more. He scuffs his feet through the dust of the parking lot and pays inside before he pumps less than half a tank into the Gran Torino.

Where are we? I ask out the window. It's dry here, but storm windy, like it's following us from the shore. The sky, bits of bright bright blue and a dark steel-gray.

I don't know, Couper says.

What?

I don't know. He shouts it the second time, and when he puts the nozzle back, it goes on with a hard, heavy clunk.

I watch him use his inhaler, breathing in, waiting, blowing out through a thin space in his lips. It makes his cheeks flush, and his hands tremble. He holds the phone after, looking for service. I watch the phone wobble in his hand.

It's the inhaler, he says.

I know, I say, soft. I feel cowed.

I didn't want you to think I was so old I can't hold my hands still, he says.

Couper, I say.

I'm going to get on the interstate, he says.

Are you okay to drive?

Yes, I'm okay to drive, he says.

I'm trying to help, I say.

He pauses for a long time then, his hands at ten and two on the wheel, the car idling in park, the tremble in his fingers still apparent.

Are you? he says.

Yes, I say.

Are you the beginning of this? he says.

I don't know.

I need you to try harder, he says.

On the interstate, we go quickly through miles of flat farmland, past tractor trailers and rest stops, and the storm follows us, raining down hard and washing up red dirt on the sides of the road and the windshield. Where the farms thin out, we get to shopping plazas, housing developments. He pulls off at an exit for a boulevard with one of everything you can think of: a Walmart, a McDonald's, a Roy Rogers, and a Sizzler. And behind them, rising up out of the parking lots, a Hampton Inn, a Days Inn, a Red Roof Inn. Couper waits at a red light, weighing his options.

I cannot sleep in another Walmart parking lot, or wash up in a Walmart bathroom. I want a bed, and a shower.

The boulevard is packed with suburban vehicles, minivans and station wagons, SUVs with TV screens in the backseats and little kids watching cartoons and kicking the front seats. People are out buying groceries, filling up before vacation. The bigger SUVs make such a spray on the road it floods our windshield, blinding us for a few feet when we pull out.

Can we just stay? I ask. I should probably go about it differently, but I feel like a kid in the car with Chuck again: overtired, looking for a place to stop, to still the vibration in my core. Chuck would drive for twelve hours straight to make good time, rumbling along through all the daylight hours. I'd have to beg him at the end of a long, hot day to please stop. He'd always look at the room first, see if it looked clean, smelled nice. *What is the difference?* I always thought. *We're putting my mother in there. She doesn't look clean or smell nice. She smells like gin and she looks like hell.* I always wanted to stay at a place if it had a pool. At least there was that. Swimming at night with the lights underwater.

I think about Couper's leg against mine at the motel pool. Bobbing in the water at the deep end.

Please? I say and he swings into the first lot.

Goddammit, Rayelle, he says. I'm working on it.

I just thought it would be nice, I say, to sleep on a bed that is not also a table. Just tonight, I say.

He turns the car off under the overhang at La Quinta, where water pours in parallel lines off either end of the roof, drumming on the Scamp.

I thought you had a bed at home, Couper says.

You watched my mother throw it out, I say.

I didn't make you go with me, he says.

I didn't say you did.

Don't revise this someday into how I forced you to come along.

You don't even know where you're going, I shout. All I asked for was a room.

Well, he says. Shall I book the honeymoon suite?

At La Quinta? I say. Then, to make things worse, I add, I don't know. You probably have to file divorce papers first. Before you move in with wife number five.

He huffs a little, beginning to laugh. Wow, he says.

I don't need to be anybody's wife that goddamn bad, I say, but he covers me up.

Shhh, he says, and leans over.

Don't you dare kiss me, I say, but all he does is hold my face. He holds it still by the chin, with his thumb and forefinger, the way you'd inspect a kid.

Settle down, he says.

When he comes back from the office, he tosses me a room key, which would be more dramatic if it were an actual key, flopping on a chain, a big plastic key ring shaped like a diamond, but it's a card. It kind of flutters into my lap.

You're not coming? I say.

You wanted a room, he says. I got you a room.

I say it again. You're not coming.

He waits. I think he's going to wait for me to get out, but if I do, I don't know where he'll go. And I don't have a thing on me. Not a phone, not a dollar. Nothing. If he goes, I don't know if he'll come back, or where the fuck we even are. I'll sit in that room by myself for as long as he's paid for it, which is maybe only till tomorrow, and then I'll have to scrounge for quarters, or call home collect, to see if Chuck will drive to the middle of nowhere to get me.

The sun comes out from behind heavy, dark clouds. The sky, so much bigger here, the clouds like towers, the light, electric. It comes out like gold, and shines on the parking lot in one bright spot that blinds me. I have to lay my hand over my eyes. The water, still dripping from the roof like drops of light raining down.

Come with me, I say. Couper. I don't know what you want me to say.

I'm afraid of where we're going, he says.

I thought you didn't know where we're going.

I don't, he says. He starts the car up and takes it around the fronts of all the rooms, all of them with doors facing out to a sidewalk, and a fenced-in pool in the middle. It's a real problem, he adds.

I look at the pool. The fence is laced with plastic so you can't see through it, but no one is in it anyway, not in the storm.

Are you coming in? I say.

I have things to do, he says. He waits next to the car with the door open while I key in and then starts to get back in the car.

Like what? I say from the threshold.

Phone calls, he says.

To? I ask. It's dark and cool in the room, and the light in the parking lot is blinding, the sun coming from behind his head.

Rayelle, he says, but won't answer.

Fine, I say. Get yourself fucking divorced while you're at it.

Why do you care? he says.

That you're not divorced? I say.

Yeah, he says. What's it to you? Why do you care?

I laugh, annoyed, standing in the open doorway and letting in flies and letting out the cool air. What are you trying to get me to say? I ask.

I'm trying to get you to admit that you give a shit about something, he says.

You want me to say I give a shit about you? That's real romantic, Couper. Thanks for the swayback queen bed, too.

I do, he says, before he gets in the car. I give a shit about you, he says.

I'd like to know how he proposed to all those women.

The shower is weak, but hot. There's cheap and strong-smelling pink soap, and little plastic bottles of shampoo and conditioner that I have to use all of just to get through my hair. The soap dries my skin out, on my face, my elbows, even on my shins, where there's now a fine coat of blond hair. I rub my hands down the fronts of my legs. I don't mind it.

When he goes, Couper takes just the car. He leaves the Scamp unhitched, detached in the parking lot. It looks ridiculously small beside the building. When he returns, he's had his hair cut. He comes in with his own key, and goes right to the sink, where he gets out a shaving kit I've somehow never seen, a leather bag with a real razor, not a plastic disposable. I watch him lather with a brush, and pull the blade over his cheeks. When he's done, he doesn't talk to me, he just gets in the shower.

I leave the towel and wait, naked. The air in the room still drying out, the AC going full blast, cold and damp at the same time. I lie belly down on the bed, my legs bent at the knee and my feet up in the air. The bedspread, that slick chintz that water rolls off of. It has mauve flowers in a pattern that hides dirt, and who knows what else.

I kind of thought he would drop everything to fuck me. Instead, he doesn't even talk, just shaves, and gets in the shower for fifteen minutes, while I lie there thinking, *Why didn't he drop everything to fuck me?*

I've gone full speed from twenty-three to fifty-three.

I grab the remote. I'm not sure what day it is, and when I think to look on Couper's phone for the date, I realize he brought it into the bathroom with him, perched, I imagine, on the back of the toilet, or on the windowsill that looks out on the trees behind the motel. In case what? In case Amanda calls? Kaplan? I don't know if he's hiding me from them, or them from me.

I find the weather channel. Ninety-two degrees. Ninety percent humidity, which makes it feel like 105. I might have argued 150. It's oppressive. Scattered thunderstorms. Asheville. July 3.

They switch to some stock photos of fireworks, of families in the park, sitting on blankets. Fireworks over a river.

I have always hated them. I don't remember the time before, when I guess maybe I didn't hate them.

Last summer, the one time we did something as a family, me, Eli, Summer, she just bounced on her daddy's lap, unafraid. We had our camp chairs by the lake, waiting for the colors to boom over the horizon. Other families around us, other kids, running with glow necklaces. A barbecue going, the air like lighter fuel and smoke. We had a cooler of beers between us. I crossed my arms over my chest and leaned my head down on my lap, and shook.

What the hell is wrong with you? Eli asked. We were new at this, at the family outing. Out without his parents, without a safety net. No one to come whisk Summer away when we couldn't calm her down. He held her loose under her arms, her arms bare, and her tiny armpits silky soft. She was in that phase when all she wanted was to stand on your lap while you held her, and she jumped. Eli had a tallboy tucked in the cup holder of his chair. His face, sunburned from an afternoon at the lake, his brow, furrowed at me.

The sound of fireworks, the heavy boom and sparkle, makes an ashy taste in my mouth. Sometimes, you think you don't remember a thing that happened, a car accident, a bad fall on a bike, because it's just that thing in your head. Just the word, *accident*, without detail. But lying there, naked on a motel bed in the middle of a strange state, I see that old Fourth of July like it's happening right in front of me again. Nudie, sitting in the grass with a paper bag of firecrackers. He'd light a whole line of them, strung together, holding them in his hand while they went off one by one, and shaking them out like a match when it got too close to his fingers. All the men, Doe, Chuck, even, were stupid like that, pulling stunts in front of the girls, Look, watch how long I can hold this before it blows off my thumb. The crackle-sulfur smell of sparklers. The gun-barrel smell of snakes. The big red waxy barrel of a cherry bomb.

He held it so close to my face I could taste it. The paper, the singe of the lighter. But he laid it on his own lip like a cigarette. His hair, dirty brown and too long, limp on his neck.

Watch this, Ray, he said. His hands shook.

The blast lit up the inside of my eyelids like my brain was on fire.

It tasted like the flat chalk of ash and the salt of skin. I saw Chuck's mouth moving, open and wet, the look of his teeth, the front two yellowed from smoking cigarettes, his lips. There was a string of spit connecting his lips while he yelled. At me. I couldn't hear him though. I couldn't hear anything but the fuzz of the explosion. The trees, everything around me, silent and still. Chuck put me in the back of the car, deaf and stuck to the hot seat. I don't remember where we went from there. There was a hospital parking lot where I waited in the car, but that was later. Chuck in the front seat, smoking, waiting. That hospital is gone now, changed over to a medical center, just nurses and a clinic and offices. Not a place where anyone goes to die.

Couper comes out toweled off and undressed. I lie with my head on my arm, my face turned toward him, and the TV still going on the weather channel, the weekend outlook, the UV index, and firework safety. It's almost like I've never seen him naked, him standing there. I've never had a look from that far away. We're always so up close.

He's more athletic than I've given him credit for. Has less of a belly than I'd thought. If I had to describe him to someone, I'd say he was big in the middle, middle-aged, with two different colored eyes, but it doesn't do him justice at all. He's muscular in his arms and thighs, his calves, thin at the ankle, blooming with strength below the cup of his knee. His cock, just a few degrees off high noon, and completely out of sync with what he says.

I'm out of condoms.

You were out, I say, holding out my arm. Why didn't you get them?

He shrugs. Other things on my mind.

I've been having unprotected sex for years, I say.

Yeah? he says. How has that worked out for you?

Not great, I say.

Why aren't you on the pill? he says.

I've tried it, I say. I don't like it. It makes me feel fat and cranky and tired.

So does pregnancy, he says. He chuckles at his own joke.

What do you know about it? I say.

I said I didn't have kids, he says then. I didn't say I never had a pregnant wife.

When his face darkens, I feel a nervous flutter, high, in between my ribs, like a bird is trapped there. I prop up to my elbows.

Come here, I say, and it takes him a minute, but he does. He sits close and I sit up, and lay my hands on the sides of his face. Tell me.

That's when he decides he wants to fuck me. It takes me forever to get into it, because I can't stop thinking about what he means, and he keeps grabbing, not my ass, but my hands, he holds them above my head, and presses his face, his baby-smooth and sweet-smelling face, against my collarbone.

Even after, he doesn't say much.

What is there to say?

My first wife's name was Debra, he says. We were young. We lost a baby at five months, he says. A boy.

Five months old? I say.

Five months into the pregnancy, he says.

Jesus, I say, because I can picture it. A roughly formed baby with fingers and a heartbeat, so small you could hold him in your hand. Then, Do you know why?

No, he says. There wasn't the same technology back then. I mean, he says, and rolls his eyes to the ceiling, this kid would be older than you. Maybe it's better, he says then. That's what the doctor told us. It was for the best.

People say shitty things, I say. I try to sit up, but he holds me down, half underneath him. All kinds of things might be better, I say. It might be better if we died in a car crash tomorrow.

I know.

It might be better if you never met me.

No, he says. But I know.

What did you do? I say. With the baby? I'm afraid to ask, because I'm afraid the answer is, they just dispose of it, like it's waste. Human garbage.

After sex, he has an emptiness that makes me not want to look at him. The mask of confidence gone, his face, flushed but sunken. He kisses my forehead and moves off and we lie on our backs, in that cheap, clean room. The bed, softer than it should be in the middle, so your butt is lower than your shoulders.

It was born, he says. I mean, she had to deliver it, even though it was already dead. We had to bury him.

Did you name him? I say. I think of the graves in the cemetery in town, the old graves in the cemetery where Summer is buried with her whole name, Summer Rose Jenkins, that say only *Baby*.

Yeah, he says, but nothing further.

What? I say.

I named him Couper, he says.

Why? I blurt out. We left the heavy, light-blocking curtains open a crack and a strip of light wiggles across the bed when the curtains move above the air conditioner.

I felt like part of me died, he says.

What did she think of that? I say.

She divorced me.

We eat at the Sizzler. Beforehand, we go to Walmart and buy cheap bathing suits for the pool later, and Couper gets an atlas for when his phone doesn't work, and lays it on the table between us at the Sizzler. We've been eating fast food and gas station snacks for so long that this feels like Sunday dinner.

I can't remember the last time my mother cooked anything. She used to. Real stuff like pork chops and meatloaf. Cube steaks dredged in flour and deep-fried in a cast-iron skillet.

How long have you been on the road? I ask him. What I wonder is what Amanda cooked, or Debra, or the ones in between. I wonder how I will ever learn to cook anything in a borrowed house, in a camper.

All my life, he says. He smiles, still looking down at the map, but he reaches for my hand.

For real, I say. Before you came to South Lake.

He scratches his head. A few weeks, he says.

Where were you?

Down here.

The chill inside the Sizzler is too much contrast from the heat outside, and I shiver. When the waitress comes, I ask for hot tea.

Doing the same thing? I ask Couper.

Somewhat.

I watch his finger trace a line up roads on the map, toward the seam.

Are you just going in circles? I say and I'm kidding, and not, and I don't know how he'll take it.

I hope not, he says. He takes his finger off the road map. What happened, he says, with Summer?

After? I say. It just kind of fell apart.

I mean, is she buried?

Oh. Yeah. What else? I say.

I knew someone whose baby was cremated, he says. Human remains are small. Even an adult. When they give you back the urn, he says, most of what's in there is the wooden casket they use. The actual body, small. A baby, he says, even smaller. A Dixie cup.

No one has ever talked to me this way. With this frank, open clarity about what has happened. About the body disintegrating. I want to bust open. I want to hug him. I want to not be in the Sizzler anymore.

Eli's parents were really mad, I say.

At you? he says.

At all of it.

We stood on opposite sides of the gravesite, neither side talking to the other. Eli with his parents, the Reverend and Mrs. Charles Jenkins, and Eli's older sister, Naomi, who'd never even met me or Summer. Naomi was one of those rabid homeschooling fundamentalists, living in Virginia. Her husband worked for the government. She had all these boys, like a year apart, seven, six, five, four, all of them with her, but not the husband, and she kept crying into Eli's shoulder, and calling him Elijah, the way his mother did. June Carol was immaculate in deep purple. On our side, just me and Chuck, who held my elbow, and kept stepping away to cough, to clear his throat, from nerves, I didn't know.

My mother didn't come. She was going to, but they had the service early. It was supposed to be at nine, and they waited until nine thirty, nine forty-five even, the little boys still at first, but then bumping into each other and the littlest one started to cry so that Reverend had to shove him over to June Carol for sympathy. My mother didn't get up. Chuck had tried to get her going, but she wouldn't budge. She was coherent enough to swear at him though. Said she'd had bad dreams. Fucking spiders in my bed, she said, but that was all. So it was just me and Chuck, who's my uncle but not my dad, and not even my mother's husband. He wore his best shirt, which is striped and blue, and blue jeans that were clean, and boots. He rolled up the sleeves because it was August, and hot. I had a dress that was brown with flowers, sleeveless and long. Pretty. Not for a funeral. Not for the mother of a dead baby to wear.

Eli's father said the Lord's Prayer. He said the Lord giveth and the Lord taketh away. He said the Lord sees fit to gift us with children, and relies on us to shepherd them through life, to return them to Him, as faithful children of God, but that only the Lord knows when that return is coming. Stay awake, he said, and watch. For you know not the hour.

June Carol put a little paper picture of Jesus with the children and lambs on top of the casket, but then covered it with dirt.

The rest of us are buried in Huntington, a town away. All the Reeds in a row: RayJohn, my dad, Buddy, the youngest Reed brother, who was only twenty-six when he died four-wheeling. Newton, which was Nudie's real name. Theodora, Khaki's mother. Donald, who we called Doe. Aubrey, the baby who was only a few days old.

I don't know what they did with the miscarriages or the stillborn.

There are more of us dead than there are alive.

When Teddy died, they left the casket closed. We sat in the front row and my mother just folded in half, her face down on her knees. Khaki was late. When she did come, she showed up in her mother's own dress, a little big for her, but not by much. She filled it out better than anyone might have thought she would, looking at her in her regular clothes, her T-shirt and shorts. The dress was discoey and short, diagonal burgundy and gray stripes, off one shoulder, with an uneven hem, the side without a sleeve hanging lower than the other, and all the stripes slanting that way too. Khaki sashayed up to the front in stockings that were too big, sagging at the knee and ankle, and more opaque than sheer, and a pair of strappy sandals.

My mother pressed her face into her knees.

There was music playing, low organ music like you'd have in church, except that we weren't in church, we were in a generic-looking funeral home that used to be a restaurant and still kind of looked like one. It wasn't the type of stately home you see in some small towns, a big old Victorian with a front porch. There was no organ, just a CD playing. If you took out the churchy stuff, the flowers and the fake stained glass, it was just a room, like you'd have any meeting in. Khaki stood there in the middle of the aisle, with no one to greet her even, no one got up and went to her, and she just stood still, staring at the closed silver casket, the spray of white flowers laid over the lid. Doe came up from the back of the room then, and grabbed her shoulder so hard he left a red-and-white handprint on her bare skin. He turned her face to his and said something low in her ear, and when she answered him, he slapped her. That sound, the loudest thing in the room. They left, each of them walking down different sides of the room. We were the only ones there. Everyone else was dead.

twenty

KHAKI

Tennessee came to me with a monster in her belly. Her bare feet were bleeding, her little baby belly hard and beginning to show. She had run from an apartment in Venice Beach, after her mama had died from heroin, to her granddad's in Kentucky, to her sister's in Virginia, to me. She'd hitchhiked, she said, from California all the way to Kentucky, the last leg of it with a college boy who was driving to South Carolina.

He coulda taken me all the way, she said, her voice sunny and drippy sweet. Her granddad had a new wife, in her twenties, but he was still sweet on Tennessee, and now she'd got a belly the same way her mama had gotten one, from the same man, and at pret' near the same age, she said.

She rattled on a litany of women. Lila and Stephanie and April. April was fat like dough, she told me, and couldn't keep house or keep her kid from wetting the bed, and Stephanie, she said, tried to give me to Jesus.

She thought her baby might be deformed. When she ran from her aunt Stephanie's suburban home, from her well-groomed and well-fed cousins, she had walked and hitchhiked all the way, barefoot with nothing but the clothes on her body. She'd thrown up and walked off fifteen, even twenty pounds, so she was all arms and legs and little round bubble belly that you couldn't quite see, but you could feel.

They'd wanted her to have it. Her aunt and uncle.

Uncle Jason told me, Tennessee said, birth is a woman at her finest.

I smirked. He ain't never seen me, I said.

It was Dakota who found her, after I'd found Dakota. Dakota looked like a monster, with her blunt black hair and her eye sewn shut from where her own brother carved it from her head. She had a deep scar through both lips, making a C, forming an arrow with her mouth.

She found Tennessee asleep in the old part of the cemetery, where the grass grew long and soft. Where the trees made a bit of shelter.

You go ahead and kill me, Tennesee told her, but do it quick.

But Dakota is the sweetest, softest, strongest soul I've met. She picked up Tennessee like she was made of glass and brought her home to me.

It was Dakota who bathed her and put her in a white nightgown and laid her in my bed. When she woke, I was there with her, I held her hands, I asked her how old she was, if she knew she was pregnant.

I'm fifteen, Tennessee said. The baby's a monster.

All babies are monsters.

I told her I could relieve her of the monster. That I could give her a new name, a new life.

My name is Haylee, she said.

Not anymore it isn't, I said. I kissed her forehead. I ought to call you sugar, I said, but I think your name is Tennessee.

She said it back to me.

That's my girl, I said.

It took her three days to tell me her whole story, where she'd been and with who, and how many men and women had come and gone, had touched her or hit her or called her names. About how her mama was found dead and naked on a rooftop in Los Feliz. About a dust storm in the desert, where it got dark as night in the middle of the day and the truck she rode in had to pull over and wait for the red to clear from the sky. That they were afraid of opening windows, afraid of breathing it in.

She talked so much that at nighttime, I had to shush her, hold her by her little baby temples and tell her to please be quiet.

It only made her laugh at me. She was high on talking. She was high on kissing me, on being cared for, on living like a girl instead of an animal.

I blew my own breath into her to siphon out the baby. The pain after stopped her from talking for a bit.

I couldn't believe no one had killed her yet.

I'd gone with my mother. I'd done my own. I knew the basics and got better with time.

My own, in our yellow bathroom at home, the floor covered with yellow Valencia tiles shaped like the brackets Rayelle used to sign her postcards. *{Rainy Day} Love you. Miss you.*

The room looked like a garden on acid. My mother had a flair for design, but her taste was odd, garish or gaudy, too much gold, too many flowers. The sink was yellow and shaped like a lettuce leaf. Doe had gotten it from a guy at work, which meant it was stolen either off the back of a truck or directly out of a warehouse somewhere, that it was probably custom-made for some other woman designing a bathroom. My mother made the whole room out of it.

Above me, it rained, drumming on the skylight. After a long, soaking rain, the window would leak, a small drip finding its way to the middle of the floor.

I was afraid of making a mess. I rolled up the soft green rug and stashed it by the tub. The bare tiles hurt my knees.

I'd swiped an X-Acto knife from art class, covered it with a Bic pen cap, and carried it home. That alone was enough to get me suspended. I hunched over my knees in the bathroom, screwed it apart, and took the blade out of the handle and attached it to a crochet needle. I didn't have to steal the needle. I found it among my grandmother's things in the hall closet. A box that said *Nana.* There was a stiff black pocketbook inside that held a two-dollar bill and a tiny pillbox with a white cat on it and a mirror inside.

I took the rubber tubing from the shed at Rayelle's. There were all kinds of things in there, other than the usual motor oil, bicycle pump stuff. Air cans. Sticks of dynamite. Barbed wire.

I'd been with my mother last time. She found a private doctor in Harrisburg, a man she paid in cash. The cash, she got from my father. Probably the same way I got cash from him.

The doctor smoked in his office, not in the exam room, but in a wood-paneled office where we sat at a desk and the walls were lined with books that all looked the same. On his desk, a picture of daughters.

In the exam room in Harrisburg, I watched my mother hoist herself onto the papered table. I'd heard other doctors refer to her as Mrs. Reed. Her cancer doctor, my school nurse. This doctor called her Teddy. He had a low but singsongy voice, like he belonged in an old movie, or onstage.

Now, Teddy, he said to her, and felt the glands in her neck. He took her blood pressure and palpated her stomach. I sat on a vinyl stool, swiveling, holding a *Woman's Day* magazine. He lifted my mother's feet into the stirrups.

The metal was covered with knitted leg warmers. My mother's feet were knobby and dry. Her toenails, coral.

Teddy, he said.

Go ahead, she answered him. Yank it.

He glanced back at me on the butterscotch stool. Above the scale, a diagram of a pelvis, shaped like a butterfly of bone.

She don't know the difference, my mother said.

I watched him draw out tubing and a speculum. A long needle like they used at the dentist to numb your gums. I whispered through the pages in the magazine, pretending I was reading about lemon pie, hospital corners, sheer drapes, what your husband really wanted.

After, I let my mother lean on me all the way to the car. I lifted her legs into the passenger seat and she blew out a long, slow breath, tinged with pain. She handed me the keys. I'd been driving since I was twelve.

At thirteen, in the yellow bathroom, I siphoned. I let the shower run, the room hot and steamy. I heard footsteps in the hall, too heavy to be my mother's. I felt the pinch, way inside, and the lance, and I blew into the tubing and sucked. My hands filled with blood. I didn't see anything else, no tiny head, no feet. It was too early. The yellow room, with its jade-green counters, its hanging plants and the skylight where I imagined anyone could look in, looked like a murder scene. I bled for days, my belly cramped so hard I walked bent over. I wondered who would ever see me from above.

twenty-one

RAYELLE

In the morning, I walk outside the room, down the side-walk, into the parking lot, just to try to see what I can of the surrounding land, hills, or trees, or anything that seems natural, but it's all covered in signs that are high off the ground, visible on the highway for miles. At night, they light up the sky so you can't see the stars and it never gets dark. Instead of dark blue or black, the night sky, a neon pink glow.

Couper comes out and stands beside me.

Last night, we'd been in the pool, the lights in the sides on, the water heated and soft. Our bodies, quiet and moving so we became just that. Just arms and legs, scissoring.

What do we do now? I ask him.

Follow the trail of blood? he asks. He looks sidelong at me. His whiskers have come back, his face rough with silver points. I like him better this way.

Really, I say.

Wait, he says.

For what? I say. My eyes follow a hawk that comes out from behind a high Arby's sign, circles in front of the sun, and disappears.

I have to get my notes together, he says. I need to write. Some of it is waiting, he says. Sometimes, it's all you can do.

Sometimes, it's hard to take him seriously.

We pack up the Scamp. Inside, I make sure things are stowed properly. It's amazing how much they shift as we move. I lock all the cabinets, secure the table.

Something else will come to me, Couper says from the hitch. I'm sure of it. It has all along.

Do you actually believe that? I say. Isn't that a waste of time?

Do you have someplace to be? he asks. I can wait, he says. I have work to do. I just can't afford to do it at La Quinta.

He'll find another campground, something on a lake or a river, with kids and fishermen, canoes even, far away from a commercial boulevard, and in the woods. I make one last check inside, refastening the hinge on an overhead cupboard, and that's when something rushes past me like a swarm. It swoops above my head. I can't tell what it is, just that the movement and the darkness in front of my face make my hair stand on end. I tumble out, down the step, the screen slamming behind me. My heart, racing.

What's the matter? Couper says from the hitch. He straightens up, his hand on his lower back. You have to take it easy on that door, he says. This thing's an antique.

Something's in there, I say. You can see the shadows in the window. Dark movement.

An animal? Couper asks. I had a raccoon once. It was a pain in the ass to get out. Sometimes I worry about bears, he says, low and mumbly, because he's concentrating on getting the hitch right. You have to put everything away, he says. Bears will claw the door open if they have to.

I shake my head. Flying, I say.

He rubs his face, and lets out a long sigh that has voice. A moan. Are you sure? he says. Under his hands, his face is pale, his lips stretched white.

What? How is that worse than a raccoon? I say. A raccoon can bite you and give you rabies. Or a bear? I say. A bear can kill you.

He drops his hands and blurts out, I dreamed about teeth.

He'd been up early, shuffling in the room, packing. I didn't know why, just heard him, restless, before it was light even. When I asked him if something was bothering him, he only said he'd tell me later.

So what? I say.

Rayelle, he says, loud, but not at me. He sort of yells it at the Scamp. Look, I know, he says, you're all hard-boiled and you don't believe anything. But I'm superstitious, okay?

Hard-boiled? I say. I step away from the door to let him get a look inside. You're the detective, I say. But I know, I know exactly what he's afraid of.

When Teddy died my mother dreamed all her teeth came out, one by one, that she blew them out like you'd blow out birthday candles, but instead of just breath, teeth came out, spraying blood. Like spitting seeds from a watermelon. I thought it was just our family that believed that kind of stuff, bad dreams, broken mirrors, a hat on the bed. Khaki with her hands on someone, saying, *Car crash. House fire. Fireworks.*

I thought I had lost as much as I could stand. Baby-less non-mother. No one's wife. No one's sister. But I look at Couper, laboring under his own breath, his lungs constricting with the asthma that he tries to hide, afraid to face not one, but two bad omens.

He opens the door, pushes it with his arm and then stands back with it wide open, waiting. You can hear it batting around in there, against the metal walls, against the back window. Birds are stupid. They'll beat themselves to death trying to get out. He goes in finally, holding the atlas he bought yesterday and using it as a fan, to guide the bird out. A gray catbird comes shooting out, straight up into the empty white sky. There are no trees around the parking lot.

Couper stays in, still fanning the air. I inch closer, and another comes out, same thing, a round, gray bird. This one lights under a bush at the edge of the sidewalk, then disappears into the dark and mulch, making its weird call: *Keer. Keer.*

Couper? I call.

There's one more, he says. Then, What the hell kind of a bird is that?

It's a catbird.

Jesus Christ, he yells.

What?

What the hell is a catbird?

I don't know! I stand there while he fans the inside of the Scamp, moving things, pillows, opening and closing doors, trying to scare it out.

You know the only thing worse than birds? Couper says. Omen-wise? Fucking cats, he says.

It shoots out all at once, low and darting over the tops of the bushes around us.

After, he leans his head into the steering wheel. We wait in a Hardee's parking lot, pulled to the side next to a minivan with a thirtysomething mommy in a polo in the passenger seat, three kids in the back, and a bike rack in tow. They're so backed up with orders, the girl from the drive-thru window has to bring out our breakfast sandwiches and coffee. Couper just leans there, forehead denting in.

There are two spaces available at the campground when we finally stop, and we take the one farthest away from the facilities, farthest from a view, from a wide, meandering river with a waterfall, from the playground, the bathhouse, the cabins, and anything that might make it desirable. It's just a plot of grass and some trees. But it's nearing dusk already, so Couper takes it.

We tuck the Scamp under a canopy of four pines. During the day it stays dark, cool, the earth blanketed gold with needles and cushioned under your feet. There's no radio, no wireless, and you have to go stand in the middle of the parking lot to get any stitch of cell service. The portable TV picks up only snow with the sounds of local news all the time. I'm not sure how we're supposed to gather information here, but after a day of setting up, Couper develops a routine. He sits outside and writes. In the afternoon, he naps. Sometimes he walks way off into the woods, or out toward the parking lot with his phone. Then, when he comes back, he reaches into the Scamp for a beer, sits in a sling-back chair, writes some more.

The idleness of it makes me crazy. It's not relaxing. It feels like waiting, possibly for something terrible. And after a week of nothing, I stand at the corner of the Scamp and watch the back of Couper's head, watch him sitting out at the edge of the shade, writing away, completely happy with the little life he's made. What am I supposed to do? Homestead? Make dolls out of sticks? Sew my own clothing?

I decide to drive to town. He gives me the keys to the Gran Torino and I take it out to the closest four corners with a Laundromat and a market. I do all our laundry in one afternoon. The door propped wide open and all the windows open without screens. Unattended dryers running, tumbling blankets and sheets. It's humid. The air, thick with fabric softener and lint. There's a copy of *Parents* magazine on the counter with summer headlines. Water safety. I turn it over, facedown. I never see anyone come in to get the sheets.

After that, I make excuses to go into town every day. Beer, cigarettes, loaf of bread. Bag of charcoal for the cast-iron stationary grill at the campsite. Couper doesn't ask. He just hands me money, the way Chuck used to. I don't think he gets it. Doesn't know that this is how I found him, by taking twenty-dollar bills from a man in his fifties. It's a matter of time, I think, before I get in someone else's car.

I keep waiting for the moment. For Couper to get up out of his chair, put down his computer, and tell me he knows where we're going. That he found Khaki and that she's okay, that she's alive, and not washed along a river somewhere, with nothing left of her but a femur, or a mandible.

I had thought all along that if we found her, he could leave me there. Me and her, together again, wherever she is. That I could find work, that we'd make it, somehow, together.

But at night, we sleep under the whisper shush of pines, cool in our bed. And when I hold on to his arm, or put my hand on his belly, or his thigh, or press my nose into the back of his neck, listening to the storm inside him, I think I can never let that go.

The market is a little clapboard house with gas pumps out front and an apartment above the store. There's an attendant who pumps for you; he'll wash your windshield and check your oil. Inside, they sell milk and snacks, bundles of firewood and charcoal. The only imported beer they have is Heineken, which Couper says is skunky, but they do have Sam Adams, and big cheap bottles of chardonnay.

I buy a pint of hand-packed mint ice cream, open it at the store, and pick at it with a plastic spoon. It's my fourth time this week. The week drags on like it did when I was a kid, waiting for supper, waiting for Chuck to come home, kicking around the yard after Khaki had gone. When she was there, we spent every day together. Even when we did nothing, we did nothing side by side.

Earlier this week I bought barbecue potato chips, cheddar popcorn, canned peaches, which I ate whole with a fork and then drank the juice. They made me long for peach cobbler, something my grandmother made when we were small, and no one else did after she died. She always baked it in a red bowl. The whole house smelling like nutmeg.

Patty, the woman behind the counter, looks a little like a dark-haired version of my mother, not so much in the face as in her clothes and the tired wrinkle of her skin, her hair pulled up in a banana clip. She's a woman I know. I can't see them, but I'd guess that on her feet she wears canvas flats from Walmart. The kind you buy two pairs for five dollars. She scrapes her thumbnail along the glass cover that shows the variety of lottery tickets they have.

I used to crave, she says, watching me eat. I lean against the opposite counter. There's no AC in here, just the door open and a big fan, blowing my hair. Behind me, hot dogs roll on metal scaffolding, up and down in a sheet of grease. I used to crave hot peppers, Patty says, and laughs. Hell on you later if you get heartburn.

I put the ice cream down on the counter with the spoon stuck straight up in the middle. I fish a ten out of my pocket and ask her for a pack of Winston Lights.

That baby's twenty-seven now, she says.

Your baby? I say, taking her bait. She talks to me a little more every time. I've seen other people come in who stand and talk to her for a half hour, forty minutes. I try to listen, but I never hear anything important. Dogs and farming. Who's having a baby.

She nods and taps the pack on the counter, makes my change. You need matches, honey? she asks.

Yes ma'am, I say. Then, You don't look old enough to have a twenty-seven-year-old baby, I say, and laugh. That's older than me.

In the parking lot, a big old sedan pulls in, but doesn't stay, leaves in a red-clay cloud, spinning up tiny dirt devils above the potholed pavement. I watch out the door, long after the car is gone. Across the street, there's a house on the corner that looks vacant, the siding a hard weathered gray, the porch slanted and empty.

Patty says, What else you craving?

Oh, I'm not craving, I say. I'm just bored. It'll make me fat, I say.

She chuckles at me like an old aunt, not your mother, who might reasonably ask you what in the hell you're doing out in the middle of nowhere eating mint ice cream and living in a campground. An aunt sees through your bullshit and doesn't judge you. Teddy always took my face in her hands when I went to their house. She'd hold me still and say, Let me get a good look at you. I was afraid of the hole in her throat, and too shy to meet her eye. I'd stare at her forehead where her full dark hair met in a widow's peak. She looked like a movie star to me, but maybe one who had fallen down the stairs too many times.

Patty hands me a plain white book of matches, no writing, no advertising. See you tomorrow, she says.

Khaki told me I was too stupid not to get pregnant. She knew her way around her own body the way some guys know their cars, like she could take it apart and put it back together.

It stung. Partially because I didn't think I was stupid. I kind of knew I wanted a baby someday, but she made it sound like it was some little girl princess fantasy. Then she said, You're so stupid you'll probably get married too.

My mother asked me if I loved Eli. Because we seemed headed toward some kind of life together, with

Summer on the way. He'd already secured the house for us, Summer's room with blue-flowered wallpaper, a white crib and a rocker.

He's okay, I said.

And you're all right with that, my mother said.

Right now, I said.

You could still take care of it, she said.

Mom, I said. I thought about the baby, which I already knew was a girl, which I could feel moving inside my belly.

Out of state, she said. Or Teddy's doctor.

Mom, I warned.

You don't know half the shit my sister went through, she said. She got up from the table then, when nothing much got her to move, and she went outside, smoking. It was one of the last warm days, the leaves on fire, the sun bright, and we had been sitting inside, smoking, her drinking gin and me drinking tea. I watched her scuff her feet along the driveway, looking down.

The mint ice cream turns to soup in the car, but I slurp at it with a spoon anyway. I dig a straw out of one of the Scamp's drawers and drink some of it. I offer it to Couper, who's sitting in the shade with his glasses on.

It's like a shake, I say. You have to suck real hard to get the chocolate chips though.

He takes the Styrofoam container from me. It's melted ice cream, he says.

Try it. I watch him suck. I can see a black chip moving up the straw.

He shakes his head.

I got dinner, I say.

We take a blanket down to the water. It gets cool and cloudy, a welcome relief from the hot sun of the day, and we eat a rotisserie chicken with our fingers.

I think you're afraid of noncommitment, I tell him. You're the opposite of what women complain about. You'll commit to anybody. You don't know how not to commit, I say.

He pulls a long greasy piece off the side of the chicken, from underneath the wing, down toward the top of the thigh.

Where'd you get that from? he says.

Just thinking. All I have is time to think, I say.

So you're thinking about me, he says.

What else?

Your cousin, he says.

I'm not going to conjure her thinking about her, I say.

White pieces of pollen, the seeds of old dandelions, float down all around us like it's snowing. They stick to the chicken, in Couper's hair, in my hair. They make a coating along the riverbank.

You're overlapping, I say. You're overlapping your love interests.

I am not.

You're not divorced, I say.

I don't love Amanda anymore, he says.

Did you?

I did, he says. Or maybe an idea of her.

And now? I say.

Now I love you, he says.

No you don't, I say.

But he outright laughs at me, his eyes crinkled, a sheen of grease on his lips. Tell me you love me, he says.

No, I say.

It's okay, he says. I know you do.

When it gets dark we press together inside the Scamp. I curve against his back, sitting behind him, and lay my arm along the length of his arm, my hand ready to cradle his hand while he signs the divorce papers. And then he puts the pen in his left hand.

Over here, he says. I'm left-handed.

No you're not, I say. I shake my head, my hair loose and tickling his shoulders. I've seen you write, Couper. With your right hand. Why do you insist on fucking with me?

But he signs with his left hand.

I'm both, he says.

I put my lips on his ear. Why do you have to be so difficult, I whisper.

Because I'm old.

We flip through and find all the arrows and he signs away all the Couper A. Gales from all the Amanda L. Kesslers. He lets the papers fall to the floor after, and puts his hand behind my head, his lips in the hollow of collarbone, beneath my ear, his leg rough up the inside of my leg, the window behind my head, the screen, covered in pollen. He holds my wrist, my waist, my hipbone, my ass. We kiss, and I remember to watch his face, listen to the sound of his teeth, to the low howl that comes from inside his chest, swirling like wind against the corner of a barn. I put my hands at his temples, feel his pulse. Closed, his eyelids are purple and shot with fine vessels. Closed, I can't remember which eye is blue. On the floor at our feet, the papers refuse to scatter, held tightly by the clip that binds them.

twenty-two

KHAKI

I learned everything from my father. He was sharper than the rest of them. Faster, trickier. Smart as a whip and strong. I owe him everything.

I know. The easy answer is to point backward and place blame. To gather me up in pieces like a broken little doll, explain away the pain in my heart, in my thighs. Tell me it's not my fault.

Go ahead. Tell me it's not my fault.

The way I live now relies on the weakness of others. Their proclivities. Their darkness. I try to keep my own hands clean.

It's a role that Tennessee was born for. With her round face and her baby-soft limbs, her brown skin and pink lips. I don't have to guide her much. I let her practice on me. To a point. When I stop her, she pouts.

She straddles me where I lie on a leather chaise. Her waist cinched in, her tits pushed up high.

You won't let me whip you? she asks, chin down, eyes raised.

She's a natural.

Not a chance, I say.

I do, however, let her loose on Schweitzer.

You think a man is selling furniture, is working as the town clerk, or the postmaster, but behind a closed black door, he puts his face to the ground and begs you to piss on his back. He asks you to bind his hands in red satin rope until his fingers turn purple, to choke him till he comes seeing stars.

Ordinarily when he comes to me, Schweitzer goes right for the humiliation, his head bowed to the floor, my spiked heel in his back. I can spend a whole hour tickling him with one feather, and then five minutes blistering his ass.

He pays me in cash. They all do.

I tell him I have a new flavor.

I dress her in white. From far away, she looks sweet, a girl bride on her wedding night. Up close, the corset is stiff with metal boning. Around her wrist, a bracelet in the shape of a snake, its head pointed toward her thumb.

She does everything without touching, like I taught her. That first day, I stay, and watch. She leans in, her breath vanilla and spearmint from the garden. Her lips glossed hard and shiny. I lined her eyes to an elongated point, like a doe's or a cat's. Dusted her cheeks with copper.

Schweitzer kneels on the floor in his underpants, his hands bound behind his back, his head lowered. Tennessee pops a piece of gum into her mouth, a big square piece of bubble gum that she works with her mouth open and juicy. Her breasts are barely contained in their cups. Her legs, crisscrossed in ivory fishnet. She paces around him in five-inch heels.

I sure do wish I had a place to stay for the night, she twangs, exaggerating what is already slow and tinny about her accent. I watch her blow a bubble and then lift his head up with her toe under his chin. She puts her thumbs on her own nipples.

I know you got a place, she says.

Yes ma'am, he says. I do.

Who are you calling ma'am? she starts. How dare you answer me directly.

He tries to apologize, but she shushes him.

She might be a masterpiece. A dominant baby whore. It's hard to tell when a woman like that is playing you, all the time, some of the time. When she is ever telling the truth. If she is sweet to everyone, just to get what she needs from them. When she slips her hand inside your shirt or your pants, if that's for you alone, or if you're just next on her list.

I couldn't have made her better if I'd sewn her together from parts.

When it drives me crazy, the perfection of her, the silly sweetness of her voice, the constant performance, I step outside, where it's still light, the blue-green field behind our house shadowed by the building.

And I find Virginia. Crouched outside our place with her back against the brick wall. I've seen her in town. I know who she is. Worse, I know who her daddy is.

Please, she says to me.

Her skin looks like vanilla ice cream, her hair shiny like a crow feather.

Please what? I say to her.

Will you have me? she says.

I ask her what she's heard.

She describes a woman I never thought I'd hear of. Someone who will take you in. Who can suck the baby right from your belly, will polish you down to your feet and give you a good-paying job where you don't have to fuck anyone or suck any dicks.

My gosh, I say, and light a cigarette. That woman sounds like a dream come true.

She reaches for my hand. It's you, she says. Isn't it.

I should send her away, should tell her I have no idea what she's talking about. But the truth is, she's tongued my ego hard with that description. She plays me better than I might have played myself. And with her flawless skin and her dark hair, her small waist, she's too tempting to turn away.

Virginia is a disaster, a mistake. Virginia is my fault.

twenty-three

RAYELLE

It's predawn and Couper shuffles in the Scamp. We haven't even been sleeping that long. And it was one of those mornings when I could have slept clean through till noon, especially under the pines, the wind through them like the sound of your mother shushing you, telling you to go back to sleep.

Well, maybe not my mother.

When I hear him shut the screen door, holding it so it doesn't slam, I get up.

Couper, I say.

He doesn't answer me. He works the hitch over the ball, humming.

Can we sleep just a little while longer? Did something happen?

You sleep less when you're older, he says. He has a lantern on the trunk of the car, its light up on his face, on the back of the Scamp, but not so much where he needs it to shine on the connection. He feels his way over the joints with his hands. He can do it in the dark.

So, what? It's time to go?

Yeah, he says. It's time to go.

Right now?

He shrugs. Why wait?

We're an hour before the fishermen get up in the earliest light. We've heard them, sometimes, the bark of a dog, the crunch of gravel down by the creek, or smelled their cigarettes, their coffee brewing in nearby camps. Couper pulls the car and the Scamp out the long road through the campsite, only his parking lights on, five miles an hour over all the humps and holes in the gravel, while behind us, everything in the Scamp is shifting.

The road to the market is just that—FM12, farm-to-market route 12. Two-laned, forty-five-mile-per-hour zone. I've done seventy when I thought no one was watching. The windows down and the radio on. No one is ever watching. Right now, it's still dark, the sky just beginning to leak a purple-gray light through the farthest trees.

What did you find out? I ask Couper. I expect him to say there was another murder. Another girl.

Her last mailing address, he says.

Khaki's? I say.

He nods.

I would kill for a cigarette. And some coffee. I will try to steer him into Patty's market when we get closer.

How do you know? I ask. The last address took us back to where we'd already been, I say. I yawn. The seat is chilled and clammy, the air damp with fog low in the fields. The road, dew-speckled.

Couper says, I called your dad.

He doesn't know, I say.

This part of the road is flanked by tall, uncut grass on either side, high, up to your waist or higher if you stood in it. Driving through, in the first morning light, is like going through a parted sea. Like the earth has opened up for us right here, where it wasn't supposed to, and let us through. Like it'll close behind us.

He's not my dad, I say.

Who is your dad? Couper asks, and I laugh, but he's not joking. They're so fucking cagey about everything, he says.

Who? I say.

Your parents, he says.

I picture the way Chuck stands inside of the trailer, tall, caged. A little bit wild. An animal that might eat out of your hand, or might bite it to pieces. His knee wobbling with restlessness. His gaze fixed on the road, on some far-off point he'll never tell you about.

How did you find the number? I say.

Couper shrugs. It's listed. It's obvious to him, but it's not to me. I just thought I would try, he says. Out of curiosity. To see what they remembered or knew about where she went.

And? I say.

I got an earful, he says.

Who did you talk to?

I talked to both of them, he says. But I got the information from Chuck.

He has known where she was, I say, all this time.

No, Couper says. That's not the impression I got. What he told me is that she contacts him from time to time, and he . . .

He what? No one has even fucking tried to find me, I say, and Khaki and Chuck are talking?

But before I get any further into my rant, an animal darts in front of us and Couper slams on the brakes. The car lurches. I slide hard into the dash, and the Scamp bumps the hitch on the car and jackknifes to the side.

But it's not an animal. It's a girl, run out of the tall grass. She's wearing a torn shirt, and no pants, with a rag tied around one leg. Her hair, matted like it was wet from the river and dried with sticks and algae in it. Her arms and legs, scratched. Her feet, bare and bleeding.

She stands in front of the car and opens her mouth to scream, but nothing comes out. She shakes her head, looking through the windshield at Couper, but manages only a hoarse wheeze and then coughs.

Couper shifts the Gran Torino into park. I hold my arm where it hit the glove box. I wasn't buckled, just sitting sideways and sleepy, arguing with him. No one's ever watching.

He gets out in unreal light. The sky, purple and glowing. The landscape lit but indirectly, with nothing, like the light is coming up out of the ground instead of down from the sky. He tries to approach her, the way you would a wild animal or a trapped bird. She shakes her hands like they're wet, her body shivering.

Oh Jesus, she says.

Let me help you, Couper says. Rayelle, he calls to me, call 911.

No! she says. It's the clearest thing from her throat. She paces up the double yellow line and back, up and back.

I hold the phone in my hand, ready, and stand between the open door and my seat. I notice that it's the sleeve of her shirt, torn and wrapped around her leg, and that she's bleeding through the fabric.

No cops, she says. Please don't call the cops.

You need an ambulance, Couper says. What happened? He speaks soft, higher pitched. Where did you come from?

He looks off into the field, the grass tall, moving in the breeze.

Behind her, the grass rustles open, and she screams, an awful dry, bleeding throat rasp, and ducks her head into Couper's chest. A deer darts out. A big-bodied doe, leaping onto the pavement, startled by us, by the parked car. It freezes, as deer do when they notice people, and then launches the rest of the way across the road, into the field on the other side, the grass like paper, like pages, closing up behind it.

Couper holds the girl's shoulders. Is someone chasing you? he says.

I don't know, she says. Then, No. Not anymore. No, not at all, she says. She looks back in the direction she came from.

The sun comes gold down the center of the road, just above the horizon behind us. It shines in her face, over her cut knees, the dirty white T-shirt, wet and then dry again, stained greenish from river water and algae. She has nothing underneath it. From behind, the rounds of her ass peek out. In the front, you can see her brown nipples.

How far did you run? Couper says.

I don't know. She shakes her hands, her head. She shivers, and crosses her arms over her chest like she's holding herself together.

Let me give you a ride, Couper says.

No.

There's nothing out here, he says, sweeping his arm around, for miles.

She shakes her head again. Looks up and down the road, which is straight and flat to the horizon. There's nothing. But she seems to weigh which direction is better, as if she'll just keep running.

I won't take you anywhere you don't want to go, Couper says. But there's a market a little ways up. You can get some water. And bandages, he says. You need both of those things.

I flip through the phone in my hand, to look at his recent calls. Kaplan, twice. Amanda. Most recently, Carleen Reed. Three times.

She grunts, desperate. No cops, she says. It works into a whine that she repeats. I can't. There can't be cops.

I'm not a cop, Couper says.

Who is she? the girl asks, pointing.

Her? Couper says, looking back at me. That's my girlfriend, he says.

It's not a good time to laugh, but I snort, and toss the phone onto the seat.

He convinces her to let him walk with her. And convinces me to drive the car, five miles an hour, alongside them, with the window down, escorting them down the highway with the blinkers on, the Scamp careening slowly along behind. Less than half a mile in, she leans over, holding her thigh.

How far is it? she says.

It's still a little ways, Couper says. He stops with her, and is careful not to touch her, but holds his hand open and near her back like he would, if she'd let him. It's okay to get in the car, he says. I promise you.

I wonder how many times he's said those exact words, in different scenarios. I reach over into the glove box for my cigarettes, light one and hang it out the window in my hand. This car is old enough to have a push-in lighter, with the bright red coil inside, the kind you can press into the vinyl seat, or your hand, and leave a circular brand. Couper scowls at me. I blow out the window, but the smoke just comes back in.

The girl leans, and presses on her thigh.

It's okay, Couper says. Just let me get you to the market, he says. I don't even know where the nearest hospital is.

It's not till Delta, she says. It's a shitty hospital.

You need a better bandage, Couper says. Hospital or no.

She stops walking altogether. I'm not getting in with her, she says.

I put it in park in the middle of the road and get out. I walk around the hood of the car and cross over to the right-side shoulder, which there isn't much of. Not enough to park on. It's mostly gravel, and then a soft decline to a field. The grass blades, wide and sharp enough to cut you. A ditch that's dry now, but in the spring probably runs with a small creek, some lilies or cattails springing up from the green water.

Drive her, I say to Couper, walking ahead, my feet hard on the pavement.

Rayelle, Couper says.

I turn and face the sun, blinding me, the car facing west toward the market. He holds her elbow. I don't know what she has against me, I say, but you go ahead.

He folds her carefully, bare bottomed, onto the seat where I normally sit. And drives off, faster than I was going, leaving me trailing behind, on the side of the road.

I stand on the shoulder smoking and listen to the grass, moving, breathing.

I think about Khaki calling my parents. If I was there when it happened. If my mother answered, or didn't, or if Khaki waited until the middle of the night and called only Chuck.

I used to worry that something had happened to her. The worst things. A man, a knife. That she was working somewhere against her will. Had to turn tricks. Was in jail. Was homeless. I would lie awake sometimes, looking up at the seamed aluminum ceiling, wondering if she was sheltered, or if she slept outside, hungry, like an animal.

The farther I get from home, or the closer I get to her, I find it harder to imagine that she doesn't have exactly what she goddamn wants.

Couper could have dropped the girl at the market and circled back around to get me, but he doesn't. I must be too able-bodied, too protected, too clothed, to warrant picking up on the side of the road. Instead, I walk the last two miles to the market, the sun getting higher and hotter behind me as I go. I finish my cigarette and toss it into the field. I kind of hope the whole thing catches. I could burn the world down right now.

When I get there, she's still in my seat. Still with her naked twat on the vinyl.

Couper's inside.

Well, you're early, Patty says to me when I jingle the copper bells hanging on the door. I see Couper in an aisle with a big bottle of water, rolls of bandage and tape.

Not by choice, I say.

You by yourself? Patty says. She pours me a cup of coffee without asking and hands it over, black.

Nope, I say. I point.

He your fella? she says. She tips her nose toward Couper. He's not your age.

Nope, he's not, I say.

Outside, the air has that wet you-shouldn't-be-awake-yet feel to it. Still burning off the humidity of overnight. The grass and trees wet. The road, steaming in the sun. We come out with the water and bandages and the girl gets out of the car, and then Patty comes out too.

What in the hell is this? Patty says. She yells around the side of the building for Burt, the five-foot-tall wrinkled raisin of an attendant. Burt, she says, call the goddamn cops.

The girl waves her hands. No, she says. No calls. But Patty goes back inside without asking, and without listening to any pleas the girl might offer. Couper has her sit on a bench outside the door, her legs so thin that when she presses her knees together, none of the flesh meets in the middle.

He kneels down and pours the water over her feet.

What's your name? he says.

She huffs. Depends on who you ask, she says. Then, Virginia. Please don't call the cops, she adds.

When he pours the water out of the bottle and onto her feet, it makes a bloody puddle in the red mud. One at a time, he holds each foot up by the heel, the way you'd put shoes on a baby, washes it, dabs it with clean gauze, and then wraps it, bundling it thick and dry. He takes a pair of white plastic flip-flops, breaks the tag with his teeth, and slides them on, where her toes emerge from the gauze. Her toes have a perfect French pedicure.

I'm not a cop, Couper says. Who hurt you?

I won't tell you that, she says.

Why not?

She looks at me before she'll answer him. She'll kill me, she says.

I might, I say. If you don't back off of him.

Rayelle, Couper says. He looks back over his shoulder at me, standing there, holding my arm where it aches from hitting the dash.

I didn't even mean you, she says.

Couper opens a new bottle of water and hands it to her to drink.

You need medical attention, he says to her. For your leg, and whatever else happened to you.

There's no medical attention for that, she says.

Where did you come from? Couper asks. He holds her by the ankles now, his fingers working her Achilles tendon.

This time? she says. Or the time before that?

Either one, Couper says.

Delta, she says. Yellow Springs. Then, over his shoulder, to me, she says, You're going there.

I don't know where I'm going, I say.

I know your type, she says.

The hell you do, I say. I know your type, I shoot back.

Girls, Couper says.

You sound just like her, Virginia calls out to me. Except, she says.

Except what?

She's got a dead look, she says. A crazy dead look. You know who I mean, she says, don't you. Jesus, she wails. Jesus Christ.

Patty pokes her head out the door. On their way, she says to Couper.

No! Virginia cries. No, no, no. She gets up from the bench.

Couper follows close behind her, but she is running the best she can. She takes the flip-flops and chucks them, and runs on just her bare padded feet.

Virginia, he calls.

I watch her stop, right before the field behind the house, where the propane tanks sit, and a shed with the tools that Burt needs for changing a tire, fixing a belt. She turns and faces him.

You can't, she says. That's kidnapping.

I'm trying to help you, he says.

But she runs. I watch her disappear through the field, into the woods beyond.

I walk down to the entrance of the parking lot, where the trees are cleared around the market and the Laundromat next door, a bare space of road and horizon surrounded by dark pines. I don't see the cops or an ambulance coming yet. The house across the street, which always looks empty during the afternoon, the siding so dry and warped it looks like it would blow off in a storm, has a light on. An upstairs window with white curtains, the kind with little yarn balls on the edges, is lit up yellow gold against the gray exterior.

It can't be, I think, and look down to the lower windows, that I could have sworn were broken out with jagged pieces sticking up. The porch, slanted to the lawn, the front door, just a black slab. The curtains upstairs twitch.

I wonder where she came from. Out of the woods. Not from the direction of the campground. We would have seen her. Or if not us, someone else. Early risers. Her hair was matted and tangled in a way that looked like she slept on it wet, like it dried without being combed. Like she came up out of the river, and just kept walking. Up close, she smelled damp and green, like plant growth.

And I think about the hard sound of my voice out here. That there is someone else, dead-looking and crazy, with the same sound.

They send a lady cop, in her thirties, and a young guy, barely out of school. The guy comes to question us, where we saw her, where she appeared to be coming from. We've got almost nothing to tell him. She leapt in front of the car like a deer, Couper says. I almost hit her.

I try to describe her. Tall, thin. Dark hair down her back. She had scrapes and a gash on her thigh.

Did she say her name? the lady cop asks.

Virginia, Couper says.

No one has been reported missing, she tells us. I imagine it was some kind of domestic dispute. It happens, she explains. It's hard to help. Sometimes, by the time we get there, the woman won't say a thing against him.

I don't correct her.

It was a her.

We'll keep an eye out, she says.

They sit in the patrol car a long time, not looking for her. No one runs off into the woods to see where she went, if she's okay, if she's fallen down bleeding to death. She wasn't bleeding out, anyway. She was moving just fine on that leg, but still. You call the cops, you think the cops will go looking for the wild hurt girl you just described to them. The younger cop taps away on a laptop, the windows down, the police radio going. After a while, they pull out, in a cloud of dust, headed toward the campground.

You should probably ice your arm, Couper tells me.

I should probably ice you.

He tilts his head and gives me a stare then. How is that remotely funny? he says. After what we've just seen? After everything? he says.

I hold my arm, and it aches, deep, in the bone. I don't think it's broken, but it already feels hot and swollen under my fingertips.

What did Chuck tell you? I ask.

That he mailed her money, Couper says. In Delta.

He mailed her money, I say.

In Delta, Couper says. He kind of shouts it at me.

So what?

So, we just heard a girl who looked like someone tried to hack her to pieces say she was running from Delta, Couper says.

That was not hacked, I say.

Rayelle.

Why did he send her money? I say.

He rubs the back of his head. Another car pulls into the lot, already eight o'clock now, the regulars coming in for their coffee, their cigarettes.

He said he needed to do what he could to take care of those girls, Couper says.

Those girls, I say. Meaning who? Khaki and . . . ?

You, he says.

All I can do is shake my head at him.

Which one is your dad? Couper asks me.

Ray, I say. I told you that.

Which one is your mother? he says then.

What the fuck is that supposed to mean? I ask. My mother is my mother.

But I watch his brow come together like he's seen something, something you can't unsee.

Patty brings me a small bag of ice for my arm and tells Couper to take care of me.

I've been taking care of her, he says.

You took care of her all right, she says and laughs like a dirty aunt.

I remember my mother and Teddy sitting at the kitchen table while Khaki and I played on the living room floor. It was summer and I wore a sundress that was too short. Things were always too short for me. I grew fast.

Tuck the skirt in, my mother said. The whole world can see your puss.

I tried, but it didn't work. I went back to playing on the floor the way I was, my knees in the carpet. A pile of Barbies between us.

You can't tell that kid a goddamn thing, Teddy said. They lit their cigarettes. Poured coffee. I felt her watching me. Teddy, with her green eyes and arched eyebrows. This one wouldn't have survived Doe, she added.

Probably not, my mother said.

When Patty kisses my cheek and hugs me goodbye, I get a hard longing for home. It chokes me, her standing there, waving at us. And even though I had a big cup of coffee, when I get in the warm seat of the Gran Torino, I can't wait to close my eyes. I lean my head against the window, the sun hot enough to wilt you.

How far is Delta? I ask Couper with my eyes closed already, already half sleeping.

I think he says sixty miles.

I dream about my mother, that she's in the backyard at her house, on the back step with Summer, that

Summer is walking in the grass, big high baby steps, and laughing, and my mother, too. They both laugh, their mouths open in the same round shape.

Delta is an hour or more up the river, over a bridge that crosses at the widest point, where boats can go underneath, carrying fishermen, tourists. The road is dappled with light between trees that arc over and almost meet in the middle, like driving through a tunnel of elms or poplars. A tunnel with light at the end of it, like dying, or, probably, more like being born. It's maybe the most beautiful thing I've seen, even with my eyes closed.

twenty-four

KHAKI

Bury the hatchet.

They say that to make peace. To take a weapon of war, a sign of aggression, and put it away, to bury it in the ground as a means of stopping the argument, of ending the war.

There's no peace between us.

Virginia is the worst kind of girl. The local who comes snooping around because she thinks she knows something, because she thinks she heard something saucy, something to cure her of her pink-nail-polished girl boredom.

The sheriff's daughter.

With nothing better to do than plan her sister's baby shower, or get her hair done. She might as well play bridge and eat cucumber sandwiches with the blue-haired ladies at the Eastern Star.

She wore a cropped top and a gold belly chain, glinting on her taut skin. Her face looked airbrushed.

When she ran from me, her face was blotched with terror. The delicate gold chain, cinched around her neck. It left a burn, a permanent necklace.

If I see her again, I will chop her again. Completely. My only regret, not hitting her better before she got away.

I never meant to keep Virginia, to love her, or to take care of her in any way. Once she came, she wouldn't leave. She clung to me like oil. Make me your own, she'd say. Running from her sheriff daddy. Her body, unused, like undisturbed milk. She had no wounds, no damage. I showed her Dakota.

That's who runs to me, I said to her after. Is that you? Were you raped by your own brother? Did he cut your eye out?

She had gasped with a horror I wished Dakota had never heard. Pretty girls frightened of your face is not an alarm you get used to. Dakota, with her sewn-shut eye, her scarred mouth.

In Delta, I went by Parker Dealey. But Dakota knew my real name.

I offered it to Dakota in trust, in another town, another house, coaxing her to come along with me, to let me care for her the way she had never been cared for. My hands open, palms up, on top of hers. I can't tell you anything else about me, I said. But that's my real name.

She looked at me with her one eye, soft and dark brown, her lashes thick and black. Her skin, like copper velvet. I don't need to know anything else, she said.

Virginia, with her perfect manicure and pedicure, wanted to know everything. Eyeing the walls behind me while she stood in my doorway. Not a split end on her head. Not a chipped tooth.

I could be your best girl, she said.

I don't have a best girl, I said.

I made her sleep in the basement, on the velvet couch, where, during the day, I saw clients. At night, it was cool and dark, clean. It was safe, when safety was not what she needed or craved.

I never meant for her to stay.

I took her out after I caught them together. I told her to come with me for a ride. She kept saying, It's not what you think. Her eyes wide and her skin bare in an over-sized shirt that hung off her shoulders.

She's pissed, Tennessee clucked at her.

I stared hard at Tennessee's round baby face. You mind your own, I told her, and put Virginia in the truck.

It's not what you think, she said again. I lit a cigarette, let the smoke fill the cab.

A humid summer night, wet with dew. Fog in the low valleys.

Parker, she said. It's not anything. Me and her.

You'll have to show me, I said. I don't know what to think.

I'm not even, she started.

I drove to where the road dipped and rose, past the cemetery, between the canopy of poplars. At the treetops, in the twilight, bats, pinging out blind, circling back.

Not what? I said.

I'm not that way, she said. She squinched her tiny nose, her lip curled. I don't like girls in that way, she said.

Then what were you thinking, coming to my door? I said.

She huffed, her arms crossed over her chest, her delicate wrists tucked into her armpits. It wasn't cold. She was feeling exposed. I didn't think there was sex attached, she said. Not with you, she said. Or with her.

I stopped the car at a T. The bank in front of us, striped with layers of rock. The road curved down to the river one way, out into the flats the other.

With who? I asked.

Clients? she asked.

Who told you that?

Oh please, she said.

I had the hatchet tucked in the side of the driver's seat, its rubber handle where my fingers could reach around. I felt it, and kept driving.

Where are you taking me? she asked.

You know what they do, I said, when they catch pests? Rodents? And relocate them? They take them to the other side of the river, I said, so they can't smell their way back to town.

She gave a hard little clinking laugh.

Your father ought to be ashamed of you, I said.

He ought to be ashamed of himself, she said.

We pulled off, into an access point for fishermen, where there was a dirt parking circle beside willow trees, and a spot where the river was wide and slow. Kids went swimming there. People took their dogs to fetch sticks and tennis balls in the water. Some fallen trees had made a still spot. A pool you could swim in and not be swept away in the current. Beyond it, the river dipped down over rocks, a loud rushing, under a bridge, out, into thicker trees.

Past ten, it was empty. It was dark, except for the dashboard. You could hear the small waterfall around the bend, the water rushing over rocks and along the shoreline. There were frogs and crickets. An owl, high above.

What happened to you? I asked her. Something I would sometimes ask of the others, who came on their hands and knees, who came running, who still had wounds in their bellies, their backs, had black eyes, or no eye at all.

You happened to me, she said, coy.

It felt like frost moving in, down my limbs, over my face. If she could see it she didn't say. But she did back out of the truck.

I ain't happened to you yet, I said.

After, I buried the hatchet, literally, in my own yard. I washed it in a moving part of the river, wading in barefoot and ankle-deep to the waterfall and submerging the head of the axe in the water. I'd begun to tail her but she ran through the river and up the bank on the other side, scrambling.

I'd said, I'll show you what you're missing. By not being with me. By not being my best girl.

I can be, she said.

You're not that way, I said. Are you. I shimmied her out of her skinny jeans and her silk panties, threw them in the back of the truck. She was down to the shirt only, sloping off her shoulder, and I took a long, slow moment to run my fingertips on her skin, my lips near her ear. I wore a black tank dress, straight and simple, and nothing underneath. When I felt her tremble at my breath on her neck, I lifted the dress off.

I let her see me. Naked, the way I work best. Hard and shining. Strong like an animal. She was unmoved.

There was nothing there to be redeemed. Nothing to fix because nothing had ever been broken. She was a blank slate. I could lay my hands on Tennessee and read the damage on her skin, could hold Dakota's head and stroke her broken mouth, her punctured eye. But Virginia? No text at all. Just a brittle slate I could punch my fist through.

When she detected the cold hatred in my closed hand, moving up her thigh, she ran. She looked at my face, hard, closed, dead inside to whatever plea she might make to me, and she ran. She didn't scream, she just scrambled on her bare feet, slipping in the dust while she backed away.

I threw the hatchet, overhand, and it hit her in the thigh. I was aiming for her neck.

That's when she screamed, all along the riverbank, up toward nowhere civilized. I picked up the axe, slick with blood and caked with dirt, and stood listening to the sound of her voice getting smaller, farther away. I waded into the river naked under the moon, a small blond woman holding an axe covered in blood. I didn't know where she would end up, or who she might run into.

Risky. But I'm not a chaser.

I caught them, not tangled up in sex, not even kissing. They were fully clothed, in my kitchen, giggling, drinking, sharing secrets like long-lost sisters.

Tennessee behind the counter, pouring the drinks. Telling the stories. She put her hands in Virginia's long dark hair, twisted it around her hands.

Virginia, asking all the right questions about who liked what. How you tied up a man, or whipped his dick till it was swollen twice its size and throbbing.

Tennessee couldn't be trusted not to tell.

Virginia was disposable.

I'd been a lone wolf for years. Sunbright. Christiansburg. Lebanon. Sugarwood. Summersville. Wrightsville Beach.

Delta. A small house on a quiet road. A backyard with a fire pit, a slope down to the river. Deer in the early morning, picking at a row of berry bushes and eating up the flowers. Big wild turkeys nearly as tall as me, coming through to pick up the deer shit.

That's where I found Dakota, before I brought her here. When I was living as Melissa. Before I became Parker.

Dakota found Tennessee sleeping in the open, her belly stretched and distended.

Virginia found me.

I get harder with every girl. Every step away from the last, every new town, every new state, every little girl who runs to me in the middle of the night, running from a boyfriend, a father, a pastor, an uncle.

Women don't run from each other.

They find me with the radar of the heart, with the divining rod in their bones, they come to me. Carved hard and white in the middle of the woods, waiting for them. Calling out to their needs.

How come you don't get in trouble? Tennessee asks me. I watch while she pokes her ass out, leaning over the counter, playing with a ball that she rolls around the way a kitten would.

Because I got this town by the balls, I tell her.

Literally, she snorts.

Impudent little snot, I think.

I'd spank her if I didn't think she'd enjoy it so much.

Carey, the sheriff, patrols the kids out of the A&P parking lot. He pulls over drunks. He busts small-time weed dealers, checks in on domestic disputes, sometimes cuffs a rough husband and puts him in the back of his patrol car for a few minutes to cool off. He's got a square face and blond hair, a broad torso, two daughters who were high school cheer captains. The local wives like it when he tips his hat to them. He plays Santa in the Christmas parade, riding on the back of the fire truck, and he plays stand-up bass in a bluegrass trio that performs at the policemen's picnic, the firemen's field days, the VFW.

He works himself into a frenzy if I pee in his mouth. I have to let it dribble first, which takes a lot of control. The slow drip is what gets him, my feet on either side of his head, my bared crotch above his face. By the time I get to full stream, he's done, his face covered in piss, flushed in ecstasy.

That long line of restored Victorian houses on Main Street? You don't know what goes on behind their polished mahogany doors. What their daddies want. What their little girls go looking for in the dark of night.

The postmaster, painkillers. I send Dakota for them, to an unmarked house up north. No one fucks with Dakota.

There, she gets bottles of hydrocodone, Valium, Klonopin sometimes. The postmaster has me portion them out for him, folding a few into a paper packet every four days. He almost always comes back to me on the second day, sweaty and begging, full of excuses about what's difficult, the pressure of his job. Really? I say, with a sneer. You're the fucking postmaster. He likes me to shame him. The pain, he says, in his lower back, his legs.

When he carries on, I slap him. I bang on his hands with a flat, bamboo spoon, like a mother or a nun, reprimanding a schoolboy.

It's the other half of what he needs.

That's not what I mean, Tennessee says to me. Not them. The men are boring, she says. She mock yawns while she says it. Whip me, mistress, she mimics. I've been bad.

I wait while she pours me a tall glass of cold vodka, neat.

She wags a finger at me. I mean the girls, she says.

What girls?

How did you get away with that? she says.

The men looking for drugs, looking for punishment, for redemption in my basement follow the same invisible map the girls do. The ghostly road signs that point to need, the glowing snail trail of discarded invisible girls, dead or maimed, missing. All the way back to my own mother, my own sisters.

I don't know how far back Tennessee has traced. But it's a trail you should never follow.

twenty-five

RAYELLE

Delta is bigger than I expect; it sprawls. On the outskirts, houses with the paint worn off, dogs lying in dirt yards, porches with burlap couches on them. There are big working farms, farms up for auction, and smaller, organic farms with free-range chickens roaming, goats chewing down the grass. In town, the original general store, still operating, and an old clapboard church from the 1800s.

The address Couper has is a post office box.

You don't know that she actually lives here? I ask him.

No, he says. I only know that at one point, five months ago, she came into Delta to pick up her mail. Supposedly.

That's promising, I say.

He stops at a railroad crossing for a train that's nearly done going by. The lights flashing, the bell ringing. Freight cars rattling past.

You don't have to do this, he says.

Yes I do, I say. What do you mean? Are you trying to tell me not to? I say. Are you trying to get rid of me?

I think it scares you a little, he says.

I stare out the window at a red-winged blackbird, perched on a fence post. I don't answer him.

It scares me, he says.

It's an old, old town. The road in is a wide street with sidewalks and big houses with columns and front porches. Lilacs, past bloom, and red buds, with their flat bean leaves flapping, bending down to frame pathways, dotted with finches and catbirds. Camellias along sidewalks, azaleas that look like they're on fire. Some of the Victorian houses have cupolas on top, a widow's walk, my mother called them. She would know. But no one else recognized my mother as a widow. I don't remember anyone but Chuck in our house. How would anyone know what a family was made up of, if all they saw was a man, a woman, and a baby?

How would I know?

I think about Couper asking me, Who is your mother? And think of my mother, sitting at home at her kitchen table, the TV on loud, two cigarettes going, one that she forgot about in the ashtray, one in her hand.

And Khaki, behind me at night, her hand over my hair, stroking. You're my real sissy, she'd say. Don't you forget it.

You can drive through the downtown in one sweep. We do it, twice. In the center, a mix of storefronts, a bookstore, a coffee shop, a sandwich place. A bistro on one corner with outdoor seating. An old drugstore with a counter. A used-furniture store called Schweitzer's, the letters in orange plastic cursive. There's a wig shop where the window is filled with Styrofoam heads wearing black, blond, and red wigs, long straight hair, a flip, a cap of light-brown curls. All on faceless white molds.

In the middle of town, a fountain. The roads wind around it in a tiny traffic circle. In the fountain, statues that make a cluster of naked little girls, one bending to dip a hand in the water, another upright with a hand raised, like little girls playing in the sprinkler, the water splashing up on their bellies. Their torsos all even-toned like mannequins, no darker pink to make a nipple, not even a raised bump.

Behind the fountain, a green park with a gazebo and benches. On the day we arrive, the farmers' market is set up with tents and tables, Mennonite farmers selling eggs and bread and pies, their children in awkward shirts and heavy shoes, straw hats. Hippie farmers stand across from them, in dreadlocks and Indian prints, selling organic carrots and peppers that are purple and gold.

Couper goes to the end of town. We pass a new train and bus station, a glassed-in building of streamlined traffic, transfers, boarding docks. A line of flags at the top of the building, different colors, but all limp in the still heat, none of them waving. The tracks run behind the blue glass front. Couper circles around and heads back toward the green, but takes a side street, and drives west toward the river, past the school—all three, elementary, middle, and high school, together on one campus—with old high windows and a clock tower. There's another shopping plaza with a liquor store and a dry cleaner. The houses thin out after that, spaced farther apart. The sidewalks end at the village limits. Beyond them, another train station, this one the original brick building with a round clock, and a converted ticket window with brass bars. The train tracks dissect the town in two spots, one, right through the middle, just off the green.

Out front, a fat-wheeled cruiser bike with a basket on the handlebars. It leans against the ticket counter.

Back in town, Couper parks alongside a pizza shop. It smells heavy with garlic and frying oil, and the air is extra hot there, coming right out of the brick building. He turns the car off, the engine ticking as it cools.

Let's walk around, he says.

I expect to feel her in my bones, like a storm coming, a swell underneath the skin, and an ache inside. How could I not? Could I not know her after so many years?

But everyone here is someone else. A mom in capris, pushing a stroller with a mosquito net; a woman selling crafts, crocheted tea cozies and potholders; or a farmer with dark curly hair, deep-set eyes, and a purple sundress, who sells peas that Couper eats from a paper bag, pod and all. A street musician with pigtails and a

tank top who sings in front of the coffee shop on Center
Street. I look at her twice. She has a round face and thin
lips, rounded soft shoulders and a heavy chest above the
body of the guitar. Her brown legs tucked into cowboy
boots. I stop and listen to her while Couper makes small
talk with the vendors. She looks like someone I know
from home, someone I can't place. A little sister. I watch
her from across the narrow street, the buildings and the
mountains behind her. She sings a song that makes her
laugh, that cracks her clear voice with a giggle. She puts
her head down and stomps one foot. Then goes on to
the next one.

We walk the farmers' market arm in arm. Couper talks
to everyone. It's all babies and dogs out there. Everyone
friendly. At the fountain, he brings me a lemon ice, cool
on such a hot day, but acidy in my stomach.

The statues in the fountain capture girls at their
worst point, right around eleven, when your body is at
its most awkward, before you've grown into what's burgeoning, before you've stopped skipping, or playing in
the water.

I spent most of eleven playing nightclub with Khaki.
Dressing up in Teddy's sparkly tops and putting on lipstick that was too dark for me, sitting on a bar with a
fake microphone in my hand, sneaking sips of vodka
from Doe's bar, and getting felt up in Khaki's bed.

I would have done anything to stay with her.

I did do anything.

I was barely able to keep up with my body, and certainly not with hers.

And these fountain girls are just like that, fleshy, awkward, and, at first, I think it's all wrong, but the more I look at them—their faces open with glee, their bellies and thighs, the smooth Ys where their legs come together—I think whoever did it, whoever reclaimed that awful stage for them and depicted it with such unbridled joy, got it just right.

I leave Couper talking to a woodworker with a tent filled with beautiful rocking chairs and cross the street to the drugstore. Its aisles are cramped, taller than me and narrow, stocked tight with supplies. I stand for fifteen minutes in front of a shelf of pregnancy tests until a boy who is about sixteen, with dark, damp-looking hair and a pimpled forehead, asks if he can help me.

I kind of scowl. No, I say, and he walks away, straightening things as he goes. Obviously, he cannot help me, I think. There's a window at the back for a pharmacist, who is perhaps the person I should ask which test is least likely to fuck with me, or which test is most likely to tell me what I want to hear. Questions he cannot answer. To the side of the store, a counter where you can still buy soda, or lemonade from a plastic box that is always dripping.

I don't buy anything, but say thank you to the boy anyway and wander out, over to the bookstore.

I want to know my body better, to not always be surprised by what it does or needs. I ball my hand into a fist and kind of jam it into my gut. *Stop it*, I think at my belly. Or better yet, *Start it. Don't be late this time.* I remember Couper standing in the motel room. *I'm out of condoms.* And how many, many times since then.

I see Couper standing on the sidewalk, farther down the block, talking to a well-dressed man in front of the furniture store. They stand side by side, and he hands Couper a little cigar. They smoke facing the street, surveying the action of the market, the traffic. I look over a table of books outside, the girl singing by the coffee shop, Couper just a few yards away. I can smell the cigar smoke, sweet, like spices you could bake with, but I can't hear them talking. All I can hear is her.

I pick up a little paperback of Dashiell Hammett stories for a quarter. The original price on the cover says *10¢*. Behind it, I find an old paperback whose cover shows a busty blonde in the doorway to a tiny trailer. *The True Confessions of a Trailer Camp Tramp.* I decide to buy that too, delighted, to give to Couper.

Inside the bookstore, there's a big woman with salt-and-pepper hair in a big messy bun, and a cat lounging on the counter. When I come in the open door, the cat jumps and knocks a whole pile of postcards to the floor.

Oh, I'm sorry, I say to the woman. She waves her hand to me. She wears a ring on her thumb that looks like a spoon.

Honey, you didn't do it, she says. I put my books on the counter. Don't apologize, she says.

But I am sorry, I think, and I don't know how not to be sorry. I don't know how to get out of my own way. I pay her, and she gives me a bookmark with last month's calendar on it, the Sunday dates in June all in red ink.

I hear the pigtailed musician talking in between songs. Her voice high-pitched and drippy. A real rural Southern drawl. Like molasses and sunshine. Like bourbon with honey.

In front of Schweitzer's, I grab Couper's elbow, but he just nods at me, at his side, and doesn't interrupt their conversation. Mr. Schweitzer is thin, not as tall as Couper, and neat, his hair cut with a hard part, the way a barber does. He wears a short-sleeved shirt tucked into tailored pants, and a slender leather belt. The cigars are still going, pungent and strong up close. Schweitzer wears shiny shoes with tassels. He tells Couper the story of the fountain. From the sidewalk we can see only the backs of the girls. He says when he first came to Delta, in the sixties, the statues were plain stone, and a committee had them painted in the early seventies, to give the girls a fleshlike color. Part of Delta's first revival. But a group of church ladies—Presbyterians, he says—thought it was obscene, that the color on the girls made the flesh too real-looking. So the town voted to have them painted over. For a while, he says, they had blue sashes painted on. He motions with his hand, up over his shoulder, down around the pelvis. But they painted over them.

The poor fountain girls, Mr. Schweitzer says. They've been dressed and undressed. No one knows what to do

with them, he says. I can't place his accent. He doesn't
sound like the other people around here. No one really
wants them, he says. But no one will let them go, either.

He has a mustache that I didn't notice right away,
thin, right above his lip, and gray. He wears glasses with
black frames. A gold tie with tight checks.

I wait for Couper to introduce me with my full name,
my whole backstory, but all he says is, Mr. Schweitzer
has a place for us.

To stay?

Upstairs, Couper says, and nods. Above the store.

Couper, I say, wagging his arm, but before I can say
anything to him, about the books, about the musician,
he takes me upstairs.

The apartment is laid out like the set of an old televi-
sion show. Schweitzer has it furnished with items from
the store, a living room set from the sixties, square and
avocado, with an oval coffee table and two-tiered oval
end tables that are maple but look space-age. There's a
pole lamp in the corner, brass from floor to ceiling with
two yellow plastic globes hanging off it. The kitchen has
a table from the fifties, a white laminate top that looks
like cracked ice, and curved chrome legs, red vinyl chairs.
Everything is in good condition. Not perfect, but well
cared for. There's just the living room and the kitchen,
with a counter and pass-through between, one little
bedroom with a queen-size bed and a low cherry dresser
with an oval mirror, a bathroom with pink and black

tile. The medicine cabinet, arched like a church window with scrolls in the corners and, inside, a slot for a razor to drop into the wall.

Schweitzer stands in the open doorway while we look around, and then says he'll be downstairs.

It's extraordinarily neat, as though no one had lived here since the furniture was new. It's clean from not being touched, like a showroom, but fifty years old. Couper opens the heavy avocado-and-turquoise drapes on the windows that face the street. There's a record player on a low square table, and a milk crate of records tucked below. Three windows all together, touching. Outside, the sidewalk, the green.

I think I might cry if he doesn't take it. If we can't sleep in a real bed with a full-size open window, or fry an egg on a real stove in the morning.

What do you think? Couper says, and then slowly turns from where he was looking out at the green. When he sees me, standing with my face scrunched against crying, and my fingers, nervous and twisted together, he says, Sweetheart. I'll take it. It's ours, he says.

Couper, I say. It's her.

Who? he says.

Haylee, I say.

He looks out the window again. We can hear the faint strum of her guitar, but can't see her from here.

Are you sure? he says.

I put my hands on my gut. Yes, I say.

I don't know how other kids played. We were exclusive, our families intertwined; we spent our time with each other. Sometimes, at other kids' houses, I'd see their play kitchens and their Barbie houses and it seemed boring to me, babyish.

When we got tired of playing nightclub, she made me her pet. She'd put a belt around my neck like a leash and make me crawl down the hallway, into her room. I'd pick things up with my teeth. Sometimes she'd dress me as a man instead of herself, and she'd tie my hands, or spank me.

Men are stupid, she'd say to me, flattening the lapels on my jacket. Stupid like sheep or dogs, she said.

I thought about the men I knew. Maybe they were. Chuck. Stupid for staying. Uncle Buddy, too dumb not to get himself cut in half on a four-wheeler. Doe seemed smart. Crafty. I thought that was where she got it from.

One time, when I had my teeth in the pink carpet of her bedroom floor, trying to fetch a lighter for her, she pressed her high-heeled shoe into my back and pushed me down. I still remember the feeling, not a pain exactly, or not on my skin, anyway. It was a deeper pain, a humiliation that ran up my spine. I was older then. The game, getting old. After she put her foot down, she knelt behind me, her cheek on my back, and put her hand in my shorts. I remember that feeling, her squared-off nails, never very long, often painted dark red, working from behind, into my innermost parts. I jumped when she started, and she tugged hard on my hair to settle me. My cheek against the rug. I leaned my hips back into her while she sawed her hand back and forth. Neither one of us getting anywhere.

I look at Haylee's picture while Couper brings up our things. It's hard to tell from that shot, grainy and cropped in, that she's anyone at all. Her round cheeks, her baby-fine hair, seem so familiar. But it was her voice that pulled my gut strings. The tinny chime of her laugh, her syrupy singing out over the crowd. It was something in her voice, an emptiness, or a cagedness, that said, I am disappearing. I am this now. I am gone.

I know that sound like I know my own voice.

I ask Couper who we should call.

No one yet, he says.

But we should, right? I say. Her picture is probably up in a Walmart with an 800 number to call. You're supposed to call when you see those kids, right?

He shrugs, putting a few simple groceries away. Milk. Coffee. Bread. Eggs. Well, technically, he says. But that's not what we're going to do.

Why not?

For one, we don't know it's her. But once we turn her in, or return her to her sister—whom she was running from, remember—she's useless to us.

What do you think we should do? I say.

He pours me a glass of chardonnay from a cold bottle and puts it down on the table. A real glass. Sweating.

I think you should talk to her, he says. Befriend her.

twenty-six

KHAKI

I thought maybe my own brother was with me. We had lived through the same shit. But it turned out he was soft. Maybe Doe had broken him. All those times he'd hit him. I'd seen Doe break his arm. Crack a bottle on Nudie's head. Beat his back with a broomstick. Maybe it was too much. The pain to the flesh had broken the spirit.

He was fifteen when he died. It took two days. I'd never seen a death that was quick. My mother had been dying slowly for years. When the baby died, she was sick first and then dead. I wanted to see instant death. Death that happened while you watched it, like water down a drain. Gone.

When Nudie died, it was because they unplugged him. His face was gone. His brain, dead. They fed a tube through his mouth into his lungs to breathe for him. His heart kept beating. They told our parents to let him go.

The doctor said, It's amazing that it didn't kill him instantly. But he's not really alive.

I thought about his heart, still going.

That's one tough bastard, I thought.

Afterward, my mother wouldn't talk to my father, and I saw my father cry.

He was at the workbench in the garage. The overhead light buzzing. I lingered around the sides of the room. I liked the smell, the oil and rubber of a garage. Bits of wood shavings on the floor. Doe had nothing in front of him, just his hands on the counter.

What are you working on? I asked.

Goddammit, Khaki, he said and I noticed his face. Go play, he said.

I'm sure that he blamed himself, and should have. But they both misunderstood it. Only Nudie and I knew what was supposed to happen.

I meant that bomb for Rayelle.

You know that she's one of us, I said to him.

So what? Nudie said. We're all the same. We'd all be related anyhow. Why do you care?

I cared that she had an option I didn't. Because she was untouched, and had parents who wanted her. She was whole inside. And stupid to the world around her.

I wanted to know why it was her and not me.

The fireworks store was a warehouse off the highway. There was never anyone there, even the week before a holiday, even though they had fireworks, they claimed, for every holiday, Halloween, Christmas, Memorial Day, July Fourth.

Doe drove a black '92 Grand Prix. It was loud, like all Pontiacs. It had a moonroof. It smelled permanently of cigarettes. When we went inside the warehouse, my mother waited in the car.

Go on, she said, and waved my father away. She wore a fitted T-shirt and back then, when I was eleven years old, she was still filled out, her waist small and her boobs big. Even her arms were fleshy. She wore a small pink kerchief around her neck, to cover the hole. If you didn't know, you'd never suspect until you talked to her. Black cat's-eye sunglasses. Lipstick even.

She was the most beautiful woman I've ever known.

Here, Khaki, she said to me as I climbed out of the backseat around her. She handed me a ten-dollar bill. Get something for Rayelle, she said. I hate to see her left out.

I tucked the bill into my shorts pocket.

Inside, row after row of different explosives. There were ones that sat on the ground, spinning, throwing off different-colored arcs. Snakes that burned up on the driveway and smelled like gunpowder. Roman candles. Bottle rockets. And cherry bombs.

I filled up my paper bag like a kid getting penny candy. Nudie got strings of firecrackers, blacks and reds, and some screamers. I led him toward the M-80s.

Dude, he said, that's a quarter stick of dynamite.

Right? I said. I put a couple in his bag and a couple in mine.

All they are is loud, he said to me. They're not pretty.

I don't give a shit about pretty, I said.

I saw Doe along the back wall, looking at pinwheels.

Is it going to scare you? Nudie asked me.

I thought he smelled like the car, like smoke and gas and leather up close. I thought that was the way all men smelled, and that they started to smell that way at about fifteen.

Hell no, I said. I smiled. I don't know if he believed me or not.

Outside, my mother leaned on the car and smoked. She looked like a movie star to me, with her hair to her shoulders and flipped up, her cuffed jeans and platform sandals. Another car had pulled in, and I watched a man get out and nod at my mother, who held her throat and blew out the smoke in a straight line into the air. She didn't acknowledge him.

Nudie and I got into the back with our bags, and our father got in the driver's seat.

In or out, he said to my mother.

She started to walk away, I think just to put her cigarette in the can of sand at the edge of the lot, and not on the pavement, but he flew out of the car then, right up behind her, with his hand on her arm, hard, steering her toward the passenger door.

Get in the goddamn car, he said. I don't know why you insist on making such a spectacle of yourself, he said.

We know you need attention. We get it, he said. We're all watching.

He slammed it into gear.

But you're fucking thirty-nine years old, he said. No one gives a shit anymore.

We hadn't played together in years. Mostly, we stayed out of each other's way. But I lured Nudie through the kitchen, where my mother sat at the table, smoking and peeling potatoes for salad; out back it was sunny and early, the grass wet. The trees beyond, heavy with green.

He wanted to know why.

We sat on the steps of the deck, hot, red-painted wood, leading down to the backyard, which sloped down toward the woods, and farther to the lake. Our house, the top of the hill. The deck, the upper floor of the house.

He had ink and resin on his hands. Resin never comes off. It was caked right into his thumb from smoking weed. On his wrist, a deep scratch from helping Doe pull wire fencing out from under the deck. On his face, the slanted cut next to his eye from a left hook. On his back, faint scars from a belt buckle, over and over.

I pointed to his eye.

That's why, I said.

That's not her fault, he said.

It's not your fault, I said.

She's just a kid, he said.

I had the paper bag between us, and he took out the cherry bomb, turned it over in his hands, the barrel waxy and red. The wick, an inch and a half long.

Nudie, I said, she annoys the piss out of you.

He laughed.

I stood up to go down into the yard.

I want them to know, I said, that they gave the wrong one away.

It'll kill her, he said.

Nah, I said. Just some permanent damage.

I couldn't understand the bond between them. My mother, and her sister, Carleen, sitting out on the deck. Like two completely different creatures. My mother in a leopard-print tank top and white pants that stopped just below her knee. A pair of black heeled sandals. A black kerchief around her neck. And Carleen, in a gray American flag T-shirt and jean shorts. Her hair in a curly ponytail. Her arms skinny and long like a teenage boy's. She was half the size of my mother, like a half-drowned runt.

There were other people there. A couple of guys Doe knew from work, with their wives or girlfriends, or whoever they were. One of them had a baby she never put down, she just carried him everywhere.

Chuck was a full ten years younger than Doe. If I had to guess, he didn't have it any better than Nudie growing up. He always kind of ducked like a beat dog when Doe came near him. He was tall, and skinny, with big hands and feet. He looked like you could snap him in half.

We started small. I gave Rayelle a sparkler that she squealed over and lit and waved around in the air making circles that left a light trail. It was almost dusk, just getting toward twilight. The sun, behind the house. When the fireworks over the lake happened near ten, we could see them from the deck.

The adults sat around on the deck. When I passed through, going to the yard where Rayelle drew sparkler circles in the air, Doe grabbed my arm, patted my leg. His hand, up high on the back of my thigh, where the curve of my ass met my leg.

Get me another drink, sweetheart, he said.

I looked at the woman with the baby, who looked at his hand on my leg, looked into my face, and then looked away. I watched color creep into her face from her neck, up to her hair. She bounced the baby, and startled him, and he started to fuss. She stood then, and followed me when I went back into the kitchen.

There was a bowl of rum punch, a pitcher of margarita and one of whiskey sour. I knew he wanted whiskey sour. I poured it into a triangular plastic glass, sloshing onto my hand, and then lapping it up.

You okay? she asked me, staring over the table at me.

Why wouldn't I be okay? I said.

She kind of shrugged, shifted the baby, who had found his fist, jammed it into his mouth, and sucked away on his knuckles. I'd never seen a woman so weighed down with a kid. He never left her skin.

You okay? I shot back at her, but I smiled and took the drink out before she answered me.

From the stairs I could see him botching it. The cherry bomb, which was meant for her, to hold like a cigarette, for him to light it, a joke, a prank. Here you go, little lady, I got a light for you.

She took it and held it the way all the adults held their cigarettes. She took a pretend puff and blew pretend smoke into the air.

She knew what to do. I had already gotten her to take drags off a cigarette. I snuck as many as ten cigarettes a day out of my mother's pack of Salems.

He put his hand behind her knee. They sat on the hill like that, with their butts in the grass, and their knees crooked up. He tucked his hand right there, in the hot crease behind her knee.

Here, he said. You know how to work a lighter?

I watched her wriggle her round, bare shoulders, flirty. I ain't a baby, she said, and flicked. The bomb, on Nudie's own lip. The smell, ash and hair. The sound, a boom so deafening, it was a while before we could hear all the screaming.

They were worried about Rayelle. What she had seen, what had been done to her eyes, her ears, being so close to the blast.

When Carleen tried to clean out her hair, she had no choice but to cut it.

The clothes she had on, covered in bits of blood and skin. Around her in the grass, pieces of bone, and teeth.

They asked me not to talk to her about it. She seemed, for the weeks following, not to really remember what had happened. She understood he was dead, that there'd been an accident, but didn't recall the actual blast in her face. Not that she said, anyway. So they told me—all of them, one at a time, Carleen, Chuck, my own mother and father—not to talk to her about it.

Let it go, my mother said. If she doesn't remember, it's for the best.

When she had nightmares, sitting upright in bed and sweating, crying for no reason, I tried to comfort her. I would stroke her and tell her she didn't do anything wrong. And when we slept, she curved close to me, silent, drawing solace from our skin.

twenty-seven

RAYELLE

He's in the midst of giving me a new identity when he tells me about the truck.

Why do I have to pose as someone else, I say, just to talk to her?

Because you don't know what she knows, he says. Because I don't know what we're dealing with. But I do know, he says, that we're in the right place.

We sit at the kitchen table, where Couper puts his hands on my face, holding my hair back, my whole face exposed. Round, naked. He wants me to wear it up, the way I never do. Underneath, my hair is darker, kinkier, the curls in long ripples.

How do you know? I ask him.

I thought I saw her in a truck, he says. And then I saw another woman driving the same truck.

Was it her? I say. Was it Khaki?

I couldn't tell, he says. So I ran the plates. He takes his hands away from my face, and my temples are warm from his fingers. It's not her truck, he says.

I wind my hair into a bun, and clip my bangs back, away from my face. He gives me a pair of fake glasses to wear.

It's registered to and insured by Jeff Henderson, he says.

He looks at me. I feel different with the glasses on. Ugly. And liberated. I feel like I'm breathing for the first time, like I'm coming up for air from a depth I didn't think I could swim my way out of.

You should pick a new name for yourself, he says.

We decide on Rebecca. I can't come up with anything that's not white trash. Carly, Daisy, Sunny. Couper says it should be usual, but not too common.

Rebecca what? I say. We sit in the living room while he goes through the records. I expect him to find a name there. Davis. Monk.

Gale, he says.

Were you ever married to a Rebecca? I ask.

Not yet, he says.

I leave for the coffee shop armed with a book.

A book? I say to Couper.

You have to look like you're doing something, he says. He gives me an old paperback copy of Eudora Welty stories that I've never heard of, and don't intend to read.

Shouldn't I have protection? I ask. I hold the book over my chest like a shield.

He sighs and fidgets a little in a way that makes me nervous.

Just be careful, he says. He takes my shoulders, and when I want him to kiss my mouth, to tell me he loves me, he only says, Be careful, and kisses my forehead.

When we were kids, we collected crickets and kept them in shoe boxes. I don't know what kids do now, and I'm not getting misty-eyed over some bullshit nineties childhood, but we spent long days outside. When my mother still worked at the canning factory, putting up jars of sauerkraut on the assembly line, I spent my days at Khaki's. Teddy would send us outside at nine in the morning with a bag of potato chips and a two-liter bottle of orange soda.

Go play.

We went into the woods, we walked into town, or down to the lake. No one worried about drowning, and no one worried about strangers. We got harassed by boys at the playground, older, middle-school boys who'd say they wanted to bone us both. The worst things, though, happened right at home. Under your own roof, and in your own bed.

We upturned most of Teddy's garden to find the crickets. They lived under the big flat rocks she used for decoration between the petunias and marigolds. Crickets were big enough, and just slow enough, to catch in your hand. Some of them were plain, a solid dark brown, and some had thin, copper wings. We thought maybe that was the difference between males and females.

The males have wings, Khaki told me.

How do you know? We leaned over a box, our shoulders hunched, our heads together.

That's how it always is, she said. The best-looking birds are the boy birds.

I had never heard this.

Think about a cardinal, she said. Or a blue jay.

I did, a bright red bird with a pointed head. Or a tufted blue jay with black on his wings.

Those are the males, she said. No one even knows what the females look like. They're invisible.

Why? I said.

Behind us, boys were coming up on bikes, Nudie's friends. They rode BMX bikes and skateboards, and came crashing in when they arrived. We were on our hands and knees over the bed of flowers that ran under the front window, along the cement foundation of the house. When Nudie walked by, he slapped the back of my bare upper thigh with his open hand and I yelped.

Shut up, he said, and tugged on my hair. You're always yelling, he said. That's why it's part of your name.

When we found the crickets, Khaki always wanted the damaged one. She'd take the one with its leg missing, a cricket that hopped lopsided in a circle. We'd take a shoe box, poke holes in the lid with a ballpoint pen, and house ten of them in there, on a bed of grass and

dirt, a few small rocks. We fed them leaves, not knowing what else they might eat, and waited until some of
them turned white. We thought the white ones were
pregnant, but really, they were getting new skin, the old
copper-brown skin falling off and showing what was
underneath, white and fragile, brand-new selves that
were wet and shining. Khaki would wait, and watch,
because the white cricket was vulnerable, and the others would often attack it. We'd sit on our knees and
she'd make me wait with her, her arm across my chest
to hold me back, our big heads looming over the box
while a little damage was done: an antenna missing, a
front leg torn off or broken. She'd take it out, the white
one. Separate it until it turned back to the color of dirt.
Then she'd return it to the fold and wait for the next
one to turn.

I always thought she would save me. That she had
the power, like she did with the crickets, to reach in and
remove me while I was damaged, but not dead.

I went to her before I went to my mom. When I got
my period, at eleven, she showed me what to do. She
taught me how to shave my legs, with good cream and
a lady's razor, not a bar of soap and Chuck's razor, and
how to go all the way up, not stop at the knee. She would
brush my hair out straight till it shone like corn silk. She
taught me how to put on mascara, how to walk in high
heels, and how to hold a cigarette so I looked mysterious
and seductive and not like a trucker.

I never really got that one right.

Sometimes now, when I hold a cigarette, I put the lighter between my fingers and I can still feel it, the barrel of the cherry bomb, waxy and big, with the dent of my crooked teeth in it.

Sometimes, back then, I would just lie on her bed and let her pet me.

When it came time for Summer to be born, I was big as a house, and the only person I wanted around me was Khaki. They kept asking who was coming with me into the delivery room, and I kept answering, No one. I thought, *Unless you can find my cousin.* I didn't want Eli, and definitely not his mother. My body was bursting open, my belly so big and round it was abstract, unreal. I thought Khaki would know exactly what to do, could get me through it, howling in just the right way to work through the pain until it cleansed me, and there would be the miracle, the two of us, holding hands, and then cradling another one of us, another blond baby girl. Smooth, naked, and perfect. I thought we might people the planet with perfections of ourselves. Or at least our own little world.

When Summer died, all I wanted was to lay my head in Khaki's lap. To have her take the broken pieces of my heart and put them back together like a puzzle. To have my hair brushed to silk. To have her pet me and say, It's okay, you didn't do anything wrong.

I'm not sure which one of us is so good at it, at attracting each other, but we are drawn together, like magnets, instantly, at the coffee shop. The little pigtailed guitarist, the street musician who sings with her case open for tips, works here, making lattes and cappuccinos. Inside the shop, velvet chairs and purple walls. Shelves with books and music playing that she sings along to.

She has a nasal Kentucky drawl. Different from Deep South, like June Carol's and her sisters'. There's something else present in a Kentucky drawl, something hanging, like egg yolk at the back of your throat.

She talks pretty slow, high-pitched and tinny, like her singing voice and her guitar strings together. She wears a short triangle skirt that flares above her knees, red cowboy boots, and a white T-shirt with a red bikini top underneath, which you can see right through the thin fabric of the shirt. The red ties up around her neck. Her hair in tiny curled pigtails like a baby. A little girl, with hair mouse-brown and fine. I know exactly what that hair feels like, how to coax just the slip of a curl into a tie. Her long bangs sweep to one side, tucked behind her ear. She has squinty eyes, and full rosy cheeks, puffed like she's out of breath.

How you doing? she says. She asks me what I'm reading, what I'm drinking.

I order green tea—something I would never drink—and sit in a red velvet chair with the Eudora Welty book. The spine already cracked with use.

She rubs my shoulder before she sashays up to the counter to get my tea. She makes herself a frozen coffee drink swirled up with caramel, which she pronounces with all three syllables: *care-a-mell*. She brings me tea in a cup wide enough to be a soup bowl that sits in a saucer the size of a dessert plate.

I been watching you, she says, and winks when she sits across from me, a round table between us, with a board of Chinese checkers.

That so? I say.

She sips, but never takes her eyes away. Her lips, with a fine line of foam along the top. Since day one, she says. I watched you roll into town.

I want to call out to her, to say her name, Haylee. To call her sister, and tell her she's okay.

She says, My name's Tennessee, and holds out her hand, cold, from cupping the drink.

Rebecca, I say.

Tennessee's shift ends while I'm sitting there not drinking the green tea because I don't like the bitter planty taste of it.

I couldn't drink it neither, she says, nodding at the cup. I couldn't drink nothing, not even water, until after. She rubs her stomach down the front.

Oh, I say. I'm not, I say. *I can't be*, I think.

It's okay if you are, she says. Or if you don't know. I can help you. Her *can* sounds like *kin*.

Her bike is parked on the sidewalk out front. It's a white cruiser with a fat seat and upright handlebars and a wicker basket on the front, the one we'd seen at the train station. She hands me her guitar, to sling across my back, and then she pats the seat.

Come on, she says, I'll bike you.

Now? I say, thinking she's taking me for some back-alley abortion. I remember the feel of Khaki's hands on me. In me. My spine feels hot.

I just want to show you something, she says. Her face squinches with a smile.

I tuck the skirt of my dress between my legs and, just like Khaki used to, Tennessee stands up and pedals, her ass right in front of me. Her body small but strong, working the bike with both of us on it. I hold on to her waist, and she takes us out of town, past the green, riding into the lowering sun.

I still have the bike I got when I was eleven, at home, stashed behind the shed at my parents' house. I rarely rode it, because even then, at eleven, I was too tall for it. But I bought it with birthday money from an old Indian who lived out past the north shore of the lake, who always kept about seventy-five bikes for sale on his lawn. An orange ten-speed, a twenty-four inch.

Khaki's bike was white and silver and a twenty-seven inch, and about a hundred dollars more than mine, and from a store, not a lawn in front of an old Indian's trailer. It was too tall for her curvy little legs. No matter what, she had to stand to pedal.

We preferred to ride together. She was tough enough to stand and pedal while I rode, sitting back on the seat, my long legs hanging out and not dragging, her brown shoulders squared off and working. From her house to the corner store. From the corner store to the beach. Me, with two packs of wine coolers, one in each hand.

We go by the clapboard church and a field with hip-high daisies and Queen Anne's lace. The road dips and rises again, pocked with loose gravel. Lines of poplars rise up on either side of the street, and we ride through the tunnel, with the light flashing in between the leaves. Not very far out, there are no more buildings, it smells sweet like a cow barn and the velvet sweat of horses, and the only sounds are the low distant moan of the train, and the clink of the little circle leaves on the poplars, blowing in the breeze.

She bikes us to the cemetery gates, but then the road goes uphill, too steep for both of us on the bike. We get off, and I carry the guitar for her while she pushes the bike farther into the cemetery, away from the tunnel of trees. The heat of the sun is full even as it sets, hot and pink and clinging to everything.

She lays the bike down and takes the guitar from me and leans it against a headstone that says LOOK, in all caps, with no other names and no dates, the design just a curtain off to one side, like the show's about to end, the curtain about to close on the lousy one-act play of your life. LOOK.

Come look, Tennessee says, and takes my hand. We're both sweaty, and she doesn't go full-on palm to palm. Just our fingertips curl together. We walk uphill, and there are poplars and oaks all around the perimeter of the cemetery, with some low trees in the middle, spread out and knuckly with arms that nearly reach the ground. Rocks lie among the headstones, big boulders, too heavy to move. It's hot and still, despite the breeze, and it has been for days. The kind of heat that needs a huge storm to break it up. The kind of heat that causes a tornado.

Tennessee walks me down to the edge. The whole cemetery is built on a hill, the outer graves sloping toward the road, or to the side, where a stream cuts low beneath the grass. She puts her finger out, like a kid running a stick along a fence. The smaller stones all face out, and they're all children's. Whoever designed the graveyard lined them up that way, little bodies fanned out, protecting what's inside.

Do you ever think, she says, walking the narrow cement path around them, that maybe we're already dead? That this is it, the afterlife, this hell we're living? she says.

I have, I say. I have thought that.

The first grave I read just says BABY, not even named. I think about Couper's Couper, tiny and barely formed, but boxed up and named, buried. BABY has only one date. Less than one full day. Next to it, Samuel. Next to that, Harriet. Days, weeks, a few years. *Fever, measles, farm accidents, drowning.*

My mother told me kids die all the time.

Oh Jesus, Rayelle, she said to me where I sat at her table, smoking her cigarettes and drinking her wine. Children die all the time, she said. She wanted me to get up, to go out, to get out of her house, and leave her alone.

I was probably killing her buzz.

It's not the worst thing that could happen to you, she said.

What do you know about it? I asked her.

More than I'd ever tell your sorry ass, she said. Maybe we'll talk sometime when you're done being the center of the goddamn universe.

I kind of wanted to die right there in front of her, to prove her wrong, to make a point. She probably would have stepped right over me. And asked Chuck to clean it up.

There are so many of us, Tennessee says, making the circuit of all the child graves. We're an army! she says. Then she takes my hand again, and pulls me along. We walk a line of concrete, too narrow to be a sidewalk, like a border marking.

That's not what I wanted to show you, she says.

It's like walking a balance beam, our hands curled together, both of us in skirts.

She picks a spot in the open, and all around us, the sky settles to lavender, an eerie glow behind the black trees. We sit on some sharp, dry grass in the hollow in front of a stone that says BEAULIEAU. She sits cross-legged, and I try not to look under the taut lap of her skirt. The sun is like someone left a light on in the next room, shining in and warming the side of my face, burning one shoulder.

I sit with my legs straight out, and she takes that as an invitation to swing over, to straddle my lap. She puts her hands behind my head and undoes the clip, letting my hair down, and takes the fake glasses off my nose and lays them where the grass is long enough to swallow them up, invisible.

The weight of her is like nothing in my lap because she leans forward on her knees, with her hands on my shoulders, and kisses me. It's a long kiss. Not a joke or a dare, or a smack on the lips you might give your girl-friend after a night out drinking. It's deep and purpose-ful, like it might get us somewhere.

Then she says, Where you from?

Mm, I say, and wipe my lips with my hand. I'm afraid to lie about where I'm from, afraid I'll get the details and the sounds wrong, that my lying will be transparent. Not from here, I say.

You got an accent like someone I know, she says.

I chuckle. I don't have an accent, I say.

Everyone does, she says. You just don't know it. You would probably think she doesn't either, but she does. She sounds just like you, she says, and inches closer on her knees, her lips nearly touching mine. Right down to the way she moves her tongue, she says. She slips her tongue through the space between her teeth, and be-tween mine.

She takes my hands then and moves them around on her till I am holding up her tits. They feel like sandbags. I can't believe how heavy they are, and how small the rest of her is. She tips me over backward, my head in the grass, and leans over me. Except for her chest, she seems to weigh nothing, and it feels like nothing to me, her body, even her tits in my hands, the kissing. It's nothing at all like Couper flattening me out, the heft of his torso, the size of his hands, his legs, opening me up. Weeds are on either side of my eyes, tickly in my ears, and I can hear things scratching along under the brush, under the old, crooked trees, along the stones themselves.

There, Tennessee says, like she's accomplished something. But when I open my eyes and take my hands off her, she's pointing to a hole in the grave next to us. It's maybe eight inches across and goes down so far you can't see the bottom. Like you could stick your arm in there and shake hands with the dead. What do you suppose that is for? she asks.

She stands up, and in the twilight, I can barely see her. At dusk, you can see things that are far away, black silhouettes on the horizon, the lights from faraway buildings, but not what's in front of your face.

There! she says again. And there! And there! She spins, her white T-shirt ultraviolet in the weird evening light, and the more she points and turns, with the whole purple sky bearing down on us, the more I realize we're on perforated ground, like the holes Khaki and I poked in a shoe-box top. There are so many air holes here, for what underneath, I don't know, that I think for sure we will fall in before we can ever find our way out.

We follow a path back to the stone that says LOOK, where we left the bike and the guitar. She gets us back to the road before it's fully dark. Country dark is no joke. You can't see your own feet walking once it's nighttime.

There are no streetlights out here, but we crunch along the gravel on the side of the road until they start up again, just outside of town, and not far after, the sidewalks begin, the buildings appear. There's the sound of traffic, the train, trucks going through on the state route.

Parked out alongside the church, an old white Malibu like Chuck had. We must have seen thirty-eight states together, just driving and eating sandwiches, the windows down, the radio up. I spent whole summers in that car. I grew up there.

I peer down the alley between the church and the real-estate office, and a chunk of light comes through, blasting my eye. A headlight, or a train, coming right at us.

Around the corner, we go past an old, converted gas station that's now Yellow Dog Café, with tables outside and music coming from the open door. The old firehouse, which is now a community theater, with posters up for *Our Town* and *Seussical*. Beyond that, the old train station, quiet and stately. Redbrick with barrel planters on the sidewalk.

Come on up, Tennessee says. I'll make you a drink.

It doesn't look like anyone lives there. It's well cared for, like a public building would be, with pink petunias and a swept-clean and white sidewalk. There isn't a leaf out of place. Not a car out front. No sign of people. The front door opens to a hallway filled with more doors, painted satiny black with gold knobs, and no nameplates or numbers. Tennessee leaves her bike in the hallway and takes me through to a back stairwell that's all windows, looking out on the black field behind. What I imagine is nothing but flowers, and grass, and, somewhere, train tracks. There are stairs up, to a black door, and down, to another black door.

A sound from the basement like an industrial fan, whirring.

She takes me up.

There's another woman there, huge with black, bobbed hair and an eye sewn shut. She watches TV, sitting in a leather recliner with an open bottle of beer, but gets up when we come in.

Dakota, Tennessee says. This is Rebecca.

But she doesn't look at me. She nods at Tennessee and then goes up a set of metal suspension stairs to the room above, which has a mesh floor, like threads of wire, bouncing under her weight.

I think that I've never seen a woman so tall, so strong in her shoulders, and yet so wounded, and then remember that I have. That, probably, there are copies of all of us, somewhere. Another me, in another state, living another life.

A woman like Dakota ran a motel we stayed in once. I was nine, the summer after Nudie. We stayed in Colorado Springs for a full week, at the foot of Pikes Peak, the mountain always in view. The woman was tall, tough, and muscled with no chest to speak of, her hair dark like Dakota's but long, always pulled back into a severe ponytail. Her face, flat and unlined, from sun or smoking, and not made-up. She was alone there, running the motel, which felt strange to me. A woman without a man. Even though my mother worked, she wouldn't have made it without Chuck. They barely made it on two incomes. But I couldn't imagine her alone, without Chuck, without me. Who would she be, on her own? It was just the motel woman and her smoke-gray cat, hunting mice from the field. I remember sitting on her front step, a low cement slab covered with green outdoor carpet, waiting for the cat to come back with a mouse dangling from his jaw. He'd present it to her, and then crunch through it. That sound, the bone crunching, like nothing I'd ever heard before.

We usually spent most of a trip driving, not staying in one place for a week. The states I'd seen, a blur from the window as we drove through them, cornfield, sunflower field, mountain range, plains. I don't know what happened in Colorado Springs. The motel was nice, it was cheap, they liked the town. Maybe they thought they could see themselves there, someday, living a different life, with different names.

My mother spent most of that vacation by herself. She drank, she went down to the motel office to sit and smoke with the owner, she wandered off on her own. Chuck and I went into town; we drove up the mountain, the view outside the Malibu nothing but fog. We walked in the Garden of the Gods, all orange dust and weird needly sculptures that looked like they'd been dropped from the sky.

Of course I sent a postcard. *Love you. Miss you. xoxo Rainy.*

I caught my mother sitting with the woman. My mother, drunk as sin and uglier than it too, her eyes narrow with gin glaze. Her hair, loose, with its perm growing out so it was straight and flat, darker at the roots. They sat on a bench by the pool, leaned together, their foreheads and knees touching. She held my mother's hand and stroked it.

I wish I could remember her name.

Tennessee pours me a drink. There's a bar, against a brick wall, with top-shelf liquors and a wine rack built in. I'm used to Early Times and chardonnay, or maybe a little Knob Creek if Couper splurges, but she's got a tall bottle of Booker's, so I take that.

Neat? she says. Splash?

I take it with a splash of cool flat water.

Around us, on the walls, black-and-white nudes of women with old-fashioned bodies that no one has anymore, round heavy breasts, little potbellies, soft thighs, hair. There are no personal pictures. Everything has a low black sheen to it, everything is clean, put away, dusted, neat.

Even the fridge is empty of personality. On my mother's fridge, so many pictures of Summer, with sweet potatoes on her face, or curled like a fist and sleeping, slick and naked in the tub. Summer with me, Summer with Eli. Summer with suds in her hair and on her chin, a grim prediction no one saw coming.

What do you do here? I ask Tennessee. She pours herself a glass of vodka, neat. I hear Dakota upstairs, the *chang* of the mesh floor underneath her feet, the running of water in the bath.

We work, Tennessee says.

I mean, I say. You're so young. I think about what Couper said. Haylee is only fifteen. This place is so nice, I say.

It's not my place, she says. It's Parker's, she says.

Parker?

Parker Dealey, Tennessee says. My sister.

Parker. Shawn. Gray. Carson. These were her pretend names, androgynous and sharp. I think of her in the blazer, with nothing underneath, her small breasts loose against the fabric. Slim-legged pants and heels. A cigarette. Her hair combed back under a hat. The way she'd careen me into the bedroom, by the wrist, holding on to my knee when I hit the bed, the back of my neck.

This apartment is a long way from her house in South Lake, where I'd see Khaki come in and kick her dirty flip-flops against the wall and leave a scuff. And even farther from the vacant trailer where we found the postcards. There's no trace of me. Not a souvenir or a memento. I left the postcards inside the Scamp. But I think about bringing them in, stringing them up above the bar, where recessed lights shine directly on the rounded nudes framed on the walls.

Is it just you two? I ask.

Tennessee nods. We tried to let Virginia in, she says. But Ginny had to go.

The clock is loud here, in between sips. When the water stops running upstairs, the apartment settles to just that low hum, coming up from the basement.

We're all just dead girls, Tennessee says, finishing her drink. Waiting to rise, she says.

I feel the warmth of the bourbon on the top of my head, where, usually, it's shame and guilt creeping out of my skull. On a good night, a happy night, at a bar with a stranger, with a band, the bourbon hits my cheeks, my chest, it warms me with a healthy, sexy glow. Right now, it's coming out of the crown of my head like a halo.

I hear her tapping up the stairs before she comes in, all in white, her hair shining like white gold, short like a boy's and angled in the front to her chin. Tennessee skips out from behind the bar, across the room to her, and I watch Khaki—Parker—take Tennessee's baby face and kiss her lips, hold her temples.

I brought you something, Tennessee chimes to Khaki. She sweeps her arm around to where I stand by the bar. Rebecca, she says.

twenty-eight

KHAKI

They thought I didn't remember you being born, you, in the hospital with the mother we shared, but I did. It might be the first thing I remember. You changed the shape of her underneath me when I tried to sit with her. When her belly was big with you I couldn't climb into her lap anymore. When her breasts were swollen and sore from the milk she'd never give you, I couldn't lay my head there.

She would shoo me away. Khaki, go play. I'm tired.

She went into the hospital in the middle of the night, and dropped me and Nudie with Aunt Carleen and Uncle Ray. You don't remember Ray, but I do. He was tall, and handsome. Blond like Doe, like you and me, but prettier than his brothers. He had a mustache he would tickle my face with. He rode a motorcycle and had a deep sparkly purple Chevelle he would show at the fair in Bloomsburg.

When you came home, you came home with them. My mother came home empty. You had a new mother. A tiny shell of a mother who couldn't have you herself.

They thought I didn't remember all that. But I did.

I hated you like I hated my own skin.

All that time, you asked me for things. Khaki, show me how to shave my legs. How to light a cigarette. How to down a fifth of whiskey and not throw up. Where to put a tampon. How to kiss a boy. How to fuck and like it, or at least pretend to.

You didn't want it to hurt. You didn't want the boys to make fun of you.

I carried the stench of my own father between my legs. On the playground, at school. In the nurse's office, in gym class, at the beach. Sometimes it hurt to ride my bike.

Nothing would ever hurt you.

Except me.

And you'd never suspect it, because you asked for it.

You can theorize the shit out of what I've done. Out of every pretty little doe-eyed beaten-down mommy who took her last breath in my arms. Who felt the gasp of sex and the grip of death in the same blackout moment.

I can tell you it came from everywhere and nowhere at the same time.

I can tell you it made me feel alive and dead inside. On fire. And quenched.

It did nothing to make me feel whole.

Go ahead, Couper Gale. Write a whole fucking book about it.

twenty-nine

RAYELLE

Rebecca, she repeats back to me. Tennessee brings her a tall square bottle of vodka, and Khaki pours herself a drink.

She looks unreal to me. Like I know her with my innermost heart but wouldn't recognize her on the street. Because she's in heels, we're almost the same height. Her hair, lighter than ever, bright silvery platinum and sleek. Her clothes, a white backless vest and white pants. Shoes, white heels with a thin ankle strap. She's thinner than I've ever seen her, but taut with muscle and strong. The glass in her hands looks small. Her hands, with her arms so thin, even bigger. She could palm a basketball. Or strangle you one-handed.

Who gave you that name? she asks.

I did, I say, but she talks over me.

Couper Gale? she says.

My mouth goes dry and hot. She takes a cigarette out of a case that opens like a book and lights it. They're black, and strong smelling.

I don't know what you mean, I say.

Please, she says. I know when I'm being followed.

She motions for Tennessee to pour me another drink. She holds the book of cigarettes out for me to take one. My mind races back to Summersville, to Wrightsville, back home.

All you've ever had are names from men, she says.

That's not true, I say.

You are your father's junior, she says.

I watch Tennessee fade into the living room, listening, surprised.

Go get Dakota, Khaki says to her.

I didn't know, Tennessee says, her voice even higher, broken.

You don't know a goddamn thing, Khaki says to her.

When Dakota comes down, she's dressed in jeans and a black tank top, and her damp hair smells like vanilla and honey. Khaki rubs her arm, and walks her to the door. She hands her an envelope, then holds her face. Different from the way she held Tennessee's. She has to stretch up to reach Dakota. I see Dakota's eye nearly close, as she leans in. Her cheeks, like copper. Her lips, with their comma scar.

Sit down, Khaki says to me after Dakota goes down the back stairs. Let me look at you.

When I thought of myself in the future, I saw myself with her. I didn't know anything else. The two of us, always together. And then she was gone.

And then we sit, face to face on her leather couch. She pulls my hair around from the back and rakes her fingers through its tangles, smoothing it as she touches it. Her voice sounds flat to me, like a newscaster with no trace of origin. I remember that Tennessee said we sounded alike.

When did you start wearing glasses? she asks.

Yesterday, I think. After the baby, I say.

Tennessee tries to slip out, up the stairs, the way a kid who has pitted her parents against each other watches a fight ignite and then disappears.

Sit down, Khaki tells her, but I watch her stand still, her fingers bunched together. Why are you here? she asks me.

I wanted to see you— I say and stop.

Go ahead, she says. Say my real name in front of her. She doesn't know it. It doesn't mean anything to her.

I just wanted to see you, I say.

To see what?

I don't know, I say. Then, You haven't missed me? You haven't thought about me at all? All this time? I say.

I wouldn't say that, she says. How did you find me?

I shrug. Maybe I'm a cop now, I say, sarcastic. I keep waiting for her to bite, to break a little of the ceramic mask that covers her face.

She laughs. Her teeth, more perfect and white than I remember.

Oh Rayelle, she says. I know you're not a cop. I watch one bright yellow fish wave through an electric-blue aquarium behind her. Its body big and flat. I know what happened to you, she says.

How? I say.

I looked it up, she says, louder. I read the paper.

How could you know what happened to me, I say, and not reach out to me?

She stands up then, her face still and cold.

The same way you did, she says.

I watch Tennessee inch along the back wall, toward the door. I notice that there are large vases by the wall, four of them, bronze with black and red veins. When she bumps one, it gungs.

Tennessee! Khaki shouts at her, and Tennessee's brown shoulders hunch, rounded.

Khaki steps out of her shoes and stands barefoot, small, compact, but a powerhouse of strength in the middle of the room.

You all are like the stupid leading the stupid, she says.

Me? I say.

Tennessee leans on the ledge of the back window, the glass behind her bare, framing the dark.

Do you know why I killed everyone else? she asks Tennessee, who doesn't answer. Because I loved them, she says. Do you know why I'll kill you? she says.

No, Tennessee says.

Because you seem to think you know something, Khaki says. But you're wrong. About everything.

Tennessee folds her arms over her chest.

You know why you're here? Khaki says to me. She turns in the middle of the room. Her arms and back bare. In her hand, a small gun she must have had concealed in the waistband of her pants. It fits in her palm like it was made to nest there, barely visible.

I wanted to find you, I say.

You are live bait, she says to me.

I swallow hard, with nothing in my mouth. Not a drop of spit. My throat contracts and aches.

You can thank Prince Fucking Charming for that move, she says. He put you out here like a kitten in a pit-bull ring, she says.

What do you mean, I say, why you killed everyone else?

Please, she says to me. Do your homework, Rayelle.

I start to say their names. Alyssa. Caitlin. Jessa.

She holds her hand up. Those names mean nothing to me, she says. And there are more than you'll ever know.

Haylee, I say, and watch Tennessee's head snap up.

Tennessee whispers, Florida.

Khaki stretches her arm taut, the nose of the gun at Tennessee's forehead.

I didn't hurt her, Khaki says.

Why should I believe that? Tennessee says.

Because I said it, Khaki says. Because— her voice breaks.

You're nothing but a liar, Tennessee says.

At least that's something.

The sound of the small gun is so sudden I don't hear it until after I've tasted it. There's a metal tang in my mouth and a spray on the window. Tennessee's face, empty, gone, her body limp on the floor. The room, deafened to me. It smells like fireworks, like the snakes we set off in the driveway. My mouth, dry, metal, smoky. Like after a bomb.

One early morning, driving with Chuck, my mother asleep on the backseat of the Malibu, we hit a deer. A doe. Her big body fell in the middle of the road with her neck bent, her eyes open and blank. The thud on the car louder than if another car had hit us. She crumpled the hood. Left a crack in the windshield.

We got out and stood. From far away, deer are so beautiful, all gold and fawn with big white ears and giant dark eyes, so like a girl. Up close, they're crawling with fleas and ticks, and their fur is rough. There's nothing like the horror of all that blood, moving faster than you think it should, from the peak in the middle of the road where the yellow lines come together, and pouring off toward the shoulder, wide at the source, underneath the doe's head, and then narrow as it runs downhill. I'd never seen that much blood, or could have imagined it moving so fast and covering so much, pouring out of one body at that speed until you were just empty, just standing there, waiting for another car to pass, to catch someone's attention, to flag down someone who could CB the cops to come move the body out of the way.

I see Khaki's mouth moving, but can't hear her. Tennessee lies on the floor, slumped to the side like an unstuffed doll. What's on the window, more solid than liquid. And on the floor, a moving sheet of blood.

Khaki kicks over the vases along the wall. They spill a clear liquid across the floor, soaking into the throw rug, mixing in with the blood.

She waves at me with the nose of the gun, toward the back door. And lights a cigarette.

Outside, behind the building, the platform for the old train station. A wide cement sidewalk, potted flowers. Below, the tracks that aren't used anymore. Beyond, a field leading out to the river, the hills.

Inside, fire rushes and explodes. The building lit from within, and roaring with the rush of a chemical fire.

She kept the vases filled with kerosene, I think. *Just in case.*

She steps out of her pants, her feet still bare. She unbuttons the vest, and stands on the platform naked. Her shoulders angular and strong. Her breasts small. Her belly tight. She tosses the clothes inside the back door, the fire already rushing down the stairway.

Why? I mouth at her. My ears ringing. My mouth, still burning metal.

She touches my wrist. You're my sister, she says. Before she goes, she kisses me soft, on the mouth. Don't forget that, she says. Forget everything else.

I watch her for as long as I can see her. Across the tracks, into the field. White, naked.

I think for a moment about following. About lifting the dress from my own body, stepping off the platform into the dark, naked, clamoring along behind.

I catch one last glimpse of her white hair in the weeds. Head low, hackles up, rangy and hungry. Looking for the kill.

There's nothing for me to do but run into the street. My own lost soul, like Virginia's, but unharmed, stepping into traffic while the fire trucks and cops come barreling down toward the old train station. By then, the building is consumed. Fire shoots out the roof, it licks out the windows, the street is filled with black chemical smoke.

I sit in the back of an ambulance while EMTs check me over. There's not a scratch on me. Just a fuzz in my ears.

At the precinct, I sit at a desk while a woman cop asks me what I know.

How can I tell her what I know?

Where is Couper? I ask her.

He's with Detective Banks, she says. He'll be here shortly.

She asks me again to recount the order of events. The teenage girl. The shooting. The flammable liquid in the vases.

And the woman? she says. Is your relative. Is Kathleen Reed.

No, I say. I don't know who that was.

They send search parties, dogs, in the direction she ran off. In the days after the fire is out, they clear the remains of a teenage girl and, from the basement, an adult male.

I give a statement. I sign a release. I am given a full medical and mental examination. I spend a night in the small Delta hospital, quiet and blue inside, with just the padded soles of nurses, one doctor and then another, who examine me gently, with their hands, their words. And then I am free to go.

I don't see Couper until I come out of the public safety building. By the sidewalk, the Gran Torino and the Scamp, hitched and ready. It's dawn again, another day. The sun, hot behind the tail of the Scamp.

I don't ask him if he's waiting for me, or if he has to go back in for more questioning.

Did they find her? I ask.

No, he says. Not yet.

Give me the keys, I say.

My mother took me to the doctor after the cherry bomb. They tested my hearing, put large, tan, padded headphones on me and had me drop tongue depressors into a basket every time I heard a beep. I missed the highest and lowest tones, even after it was better, a few days later. But the damage, they said, was minimal.

We also went to a woman doctor I had never seen before, not my regular family doctor. She spoke to me in a quiet voice, in the room by myself, without my mother even. She rubbed my shoulders through the soft, thin hospital gown and asked me if I ever wet the bed. I said no, but she said she needed to check me down there, to make sure everything was intact. *Intact*, she said, like I'd been broken inside by the bomb, but all I remember of it was the look of the leaves on the trees, upside down, their silver underbellies turned up like a storm was coming, and the sound, rattling my teeth.

I remember her hands, in soft gloves, like nothing had ever gone before them.

She told my mother I was okay.

Then we went to a dermatologist who gave her a cream to rub around my mouth where my lips had broken out in a rough, pink rash.

He told my mother I was going to be okay.

My mother cut my hair herself, and then took me to a salon called Cut N Curl to have them do the rest. The hair, all around me on the kitchen floor, long ratted curls. She sealed them up in a Ziploc baggie before she put them in the trash. The beautician at Cut N Curl called me Bunny and cranked my chair up real high and cut as close as she could to my head without using a buzzer. When she washed my hair, leaning over me while my head dipped backward into the sink, I noticed she had soft, sparse black hairs under her arms. That she smelled like something warm and almost stinky, a kind of oil, or wax.

She told me I was a darling. And I looked at my new face in the mirror, my mouth covered in rash, my hair so short everything showed, all my freckles, my ears that stuck out, the nubs of my adult teeth, coming in large and crowded between two tiny baby teeth on either side. I had never seen anything so ugly.

I hated it.

I drive to a motel. I get blindly on the highway, ignoring the tractor trailers and the minivans and station wagons, and gun it. This car has power. I blow past them in the left lane, with Couper, slumped in the passenger seat, digging in the glove box for his inhaler. I don't think about what the speed does to the Scamp, or whether we will come unhinged.

My ears are still stuffed with constant buzzing. In my head, any time I close my eyes, the window, sprayed, the floor, moving with blood. Tennessee's empty doll body, crumpled. The smell of chemical burning in my nose, like it's been singed.

I pull off at a Days Inn where there's a Roy Rogers and an Arco on the opposite corners. There's no town. There's a sign for a town farther in.

Can you pay for this? I say to Couper. If I don't stop driving, I'll vibrate my way into a full scream. If I start screaming, I'm afraid I won't stop. The landscape around us, unreal, weirdly shaped and colored. The trees, like blue cotton balls. I don't know where we are.

He looks like I've taken a shot at him. I think I can handle a fifty-nine-dollar room, he says. But outside the car, he leans over, his hands on his knees, his body bent in half. Oh, Jesus, he says.

Inside, the guy at the front desk greets Couper by laying his hands—fat and dimpled like a little boy's—on the counter. Checking out? he says.

Checking in, Couper says.

I stand with my back to the high counter, looking at brochures for caverns and outlet malls. A pizza joint where a woman with a big blond beehive plays show tunes on a pipe organ that comes up out of the floor on a revolving platform. I can't believe anything at all goes on around here that's not a quilting bee or a tent revival.

Check-in's at three, the guy says. He has a thick drawl, drippy and slow.

You don't have anything? Couper says. I need something now.

The clerk hems, and shuffles, and when I turn, I see how heavy he is. His moving is slow and labored. He slides cards in and out of the pigeonholes in the counter. I'd have to charge you all twice, he says. Last night and tonight, too.

That's fine, Couper says.

Just you and your wife, sir? he says. He starts typing.

She's not my wife, Couper says, and I hear myself go *Huh*, hard, and not laughing. The sound, echoing in my stuffed head.

The clerk holds out a pen and registration card for Couper, but pauses right there, the pen on a ball chain connected to the counter. His still face is fat, but younger than its weight.

Couper sweats at the hairline, pale, like he might lean over to vomit.

I don't want any trouble, the clerk says.

I'm not giving you trouble, Couper says. He opens his wallet. I'm giving you cash.

Oh, he says, hesitant. You can't. You can't pay cash, sir.

There's music from above, old seventies country like we'd hear at our grandmother's house. The adults, as many as there were alive at that point, around the kitchen table. Me and Khaki and Nudie on the living room floor with old board games, Parcheesi and Sorry.

You won't accept my cash, Couper says.

Sir, I need to register the room with a credit card, and I need to run the card . . . for incidentals. The word comes out whispery and he wrinkles his nose when he says it. He looks past Couper at me, with my hair wild, my face glazed. I feel like I've been up for days. He won't look me in the eye, even though I stare right at him.

Couper lays out cash on the counter. Five new hundred-dollar bills.

Look, Couper says. I'm going to give you this money, and you're going to let me have a room just for tonight, and then we'll leave, okay?

I need your license.

I don't have my license, Couper says.

Sir, I can see your license right there, he says.

I watch Couper scoop up the five hundred-dollar bills like a dealer picking up cards.

Let's go, he says to me.

He drives down the country route instead, past a tiny town of just a Gulf station, a Baptist church, and a barbecue pit, with no stoplight even. A small wrought-iron fenced-in graveyard. Laundry stretching from the back stoop to a pole out back. Past the town, there's a motel with cabins, and another little roadside motel, brick, with a sign for color TV and a heated pool.

I wait while he goes in, and he comes out right away, with a real metal key on a plastic turquoise diamond-shaped key ring. It's for the last room on the left. It has one soft king-size bed, a counter with a sink outside the bathroom, and a TV mounted high up on the wall. It is indeed color, but out of register, the reds, blues, and greens all in separate stripes, making the people on the news—which I can't even bear to watch—seem alien and clownish.

I lie down, my body curved into the soft middle of the bed. But I can't sleep. Everything moves, burns up with flames behind my eyes.

I wait until he's sleeping and then I take his phone off the nightstand and sit outside on the curb to smoke a cigarette and call home. I prop the door with a brown fake-leather Gideon Bible, the night air almost as cool as the air conditioning inside the room.

It's near midnight. Couper and I both showered, and ate silently at the barbecue pit in the town we'd passed through. After, we lay on the bed and watched the out-of-whack TV. Neither one of us talking.

Outside, it smells waxy, like opened night flowers. In the trees, the sounds of a whippoorwill, up in the pines.

I think I've been here before. Where the Scamp is parked alongside the yellow brick wall of the building, you can see where the old name of the motel was, in scripted letters from the sixties. *Sunset.*

Alone, with Chuck. The summer that Doe died and Khaki left, and all hell came crawling after us. Me, alone with a man. Me, in a car with a man. In a motel. Running.

I light up his phone and dial my mother's cell.

At first, I don't recognize the voice. Couper, she says, urgent. We are just outside of Delta. Couper?

Who is this? I say.

Oh sweet Lord, it's her, she says, and then I recognize her. June Carol. I hear my mother say, Give me the phone.

But I hang up.

I wonder where we would be by now, naked and roaming the hills. Sleeping in a thicket like animals. Washing in the river. Kentucky. Deep in the Smoky Mountains. Tennessee.

For a long time, after I picked Summer up that morning, when she rocked on all fours, her mouth filled with foam, choking, drowning from the inside out, after that morning, at the emergency room, the two long blue nights in the hospital, waiting while they put her under, while they tried different antibiotics, different pumps, every time I closed my eyes, I was putting my head back in the sun, and the first thing I saw was her coughing up foam. The hot red behind my eyelids. Her face. Her eyes bloodshot from coughing, her mouth filling so much she could never clear it.

Now, it's Tennessee. Deflated. Everything inside, out the back of her skull, and spattered on the window.

I close my eyes and try to change the image.

I watch a white woman disappearing in a dark field. Her body, perfect. Her hair, like light. Like white fire. A torch, moving through the night.

How in the hell, I ask Couper in the morning, did you manage to get both my mother and June Carol here?

I didn't, he says, dryly. There's no coffeemaker in the room, and before I'd gotten up, Couper had gone down to the motel office, where they keep an old-style Bunn, and a pot ready every morning. He hands me a paper cup, hot to the touch, filled with black coffee.

I called your mother, he says, to let her know, and she said she was coming. I didn't know she was bringing anyone with her. Or that it wouldn't be your father.

He's not my father, I say.

Well, he says. Details.

She's also not my mother, I say.

I tried to ask you that, he says.

How was I supposed to know? I shout. But at the sound of my voice, he goes outside, and starts moving things around inside the Scamp.

I never would have traced the lines back to the same mother. Me and Khaki. Summer. I never would have left my own mother out of it. Carleen. Who was she if not my own?

I thought about riding in her car on the days before I went to school, going to the supermarket with her. Wanting a quarter to ride the horse out front. About sharing a bag of potato chips on the couch. Sitting on the bench seat of an old car, between her and Chuck, flying down the highway. About her face, before it gave in to booze. Her skin. I always thought it was velvet soft. Her cheeks under my fat little-kid hands.

I wanted Summer to hold my face like that.

I thought about the way Teddy would call me over to their kitchen table. In their black-and-red kitchen, the leather bar behind her. A clock that said *Seagrams* and had bubbles moving under the surface.

Come here, she'd say, whispering through the hole in her throat. She'd take my hands and hold out my arms, run her fingers through my hair, whether it was long, or short, after. After Nudie. She'd inspect me. Her eyes narrow. A cigarette on her lips. Let me look at you.

They pull up just after nine in the morning, in June Carol's cream-colored Buick with her Jesus fish on the back and her guardian angel on the dashboard. If they drove straight from South Lake, I'm guessing my mother hasn't had a cigarette in a good long while, and that she's had just about enough of June Carol. I watch June Carol bump the car against the cement barrier, and lean her head on the steering wheel. The car has barely stopped when my mother gets out of the passenger side.

I want to be mad at her. For throwing my stuff out. For telling me to get over it and get out of her house. For telling me that kids die all the time. For not telling me the truth.

But all I can think about is sitting up on the kitchen table while she cut my hair, her nose running because she was crying, silently, wiping at her cheeks with the backs of her hands, clipping me down to a close cap of blond curls, her hands holding my head. The scissor blades next to my ear. Telling me it was going to be all right.

I've never seen June Carol not dressed in her best. But now, she's in a pair of jean shorts and a pink T-shirt, white Keds on her feet and her hair in a ponytail, low at the nape of her neck. She's not wearing makeup, or jewelry. She looks like a forty-eight-year-old woman. Somebody's mom. Or grandma.

She hugs me hard. Sweet Lord, she mumbles into my shoulder.

It's just the two of you? I say.

Well who in the hell else, my mother says.

Chuck? I say. Where's Chuck? I look at June Carol. Where's Eli?

Oh, Rayelle, June Carol says. You know there are some things the women have to do alone.

My mother and June Carol get a room together, farther down the line, with two queen beds, and a better TV, and Couper sends me to help them settle, to rest with them. June Carol stretches her short body sideways across the bed, her feet barely touching the floor.

My mother sits outside their room in one of the two rounded-out plastic chairs, one orange and one brown, and smokes a Salem. The minty smell of it, like home to me.

They take naps, and showers, and in the evening, Couper brings us barbecue takeout, and we sit with their chairs and our chairs together on the sidewalk, me, my mother, June Carol. I watch June Carol drink a Miller right out of the can, and after supper, she asks for one of my mother's cigarettes.

I got a past, she says when she sees me watching her.

I laugh, but I can't stop shaking.

Why did you come? I ask her.

Because your mama asked me to, she says.

My mother crosses her arms over her thin chest, her arms, skinny and frail-looking, spotted with freckles and sun. The scoop of her T-shirt showing a cluster of sunburnt freckles.

You can never have too many mamas, June Carol says.

The only one missing is Summer.

That night I try to sleep with my mother. Her body small next to mine, curved away from me. She doesn't say she wants me there, or that she wants time alone. But when June Carol goes into the bathroom, she holds my hand, so tight it hurts me. All the bones colliding. I hold back. My fingernails stuck in the side of her palm.

But when she falls asleep, I go back to Couper's room. I think about keying in, slipping behind him into the bed, laying my cheek against his shoulder blade, near the bullet-wound scar, listening to his breathing. About snaking my hand around his waist, finding his hand to slip mine into.

He's awake.

What are you doing? I ask him. He sits at the round laminate table underneath the hanging lamp. His computer on, an open beer at his elbow.

Sending in my notes, he says.

To?

A national detective, he says.

I sit on the edge of the bed. Do you think they'll find her? I ask.

I don't know, he says.

Will you? I say.

I'm done looking, he says.

What about the book? I say.

Some things are better let go, he says.

I want to sleep.

I want to do it in a better bed, and not with my mother, or with June Carol in the bed next to me. When

I snuck out of their room, June Carol was in her night-gown, a pretty little white thing with lace edges and pink flowers. Buttons down the bodice. She prayed aloud before getting under the covers.

God our Father, she said, bless these women here with me and look after your daughters.

I watched my mother get into bed in the T-shirt and panties she'd worn all day. I lay for a moment in my clothes, my mother's hand wrapped around mine.

When we go to bed, we go out to the Scamp. Couper moves the table aside and puts the cushions on the floor, stacked vertical against the counter. He puts on the floral sheets, softer than any hotel's, covers the pillows, and leaves the top sheet for us to get under.

We get in naked, pressed together. Till morning.

thirty

KHAKI

Who would have me?

It's what I thought when I found Dakota. A six-foot-tall woman with a missing eye, pants soaked with her own urine and blood. Sleeping in a thicket like a bear.

I would.

I walk along the river in the moonlight, my feet on shelves of shale. They blacken with pine sap and soil. Even the rush of the river water won't take it off. I follow the shoreline until it's light, and then hide in the shelter of vines that pour down off a huge ash tree. They make a curtain of green, a lady's bowery where I can rest in the shade for an hour or two. My body cold and closing in on itself. I don't eat. My stomach tight with plain survival. I drink from the river.

At dusk, I move again.

It's days before I arrive.

When I do, I come up out of the weeds of the back-yard, rising like a sprite. Like a spirit. Like the image of a dead girl, coming up in vapors from the grave.

She stands on her back stoop, feeding chickens that scatter in the yard and come when she tosses out seed. Her hair in a bun. Ratty blue jeans cuffed at the ankle. Her yard, filled with wind chimes and stained glass. Coming from her kitchen, smells I haven't smelled in years. A woman who might bathe you, feed you, swaddle you like the baby you're going back to being.

My stomach rumbles.

Her arms are strong. Her shirtsleeves, soft and rolled to the elbow.

She watches me coming. Silver in the grass, a purple light above us. Naked and clean from the river, except for my feet. The chickens disperse when I walk through. One of them, a beautiful soft gold. Another, speckled deep brown.

She holds out the hand she used to scatter seed. To me.

What's your name? she asks me. My own voice, cracked and dry. She brings me flat clean water in a glass.

I tell her. Kathleen.

acknowledgments

I'm grateful to many writers and friends who held me upright during the long process of this book: Georgia Popoff, who gave me retreat and made me martinis; Lena Bertone, who read the earliest drafts and never doubted me; and Shanna Mahin, whose sassy daily texts and phone calls gave me a courage I never knew I had.

I could not have asked for this book to land in better hands than with Meg Storey and Christopher Rhodes. Both offered a fierce love and a keen eye to the details that shaped *The Scamp* for publication.

And for my closest dears: thank you for hearing my voice, for not expecting apology, for loving me hard.

JENNIFER PASHLEY is the author of two short story collections, *States* and *The Conjurer*. Her stories have appeared widely, in journals like *Mississippi Review*, *PANK*, and *SmokeLong Quarterly*, and she was awarded the Red Hen Prize for fiction, the Mississippi Review Prize for fiction, and the Carve Magazine Esoteric Award for LGBT Fiction. *The Scamp* is her first novel.